GOD

OF

NEVERLAND

*   *   *

ALSO BY GAMA RAY MARTINEZ

GOBLIN STAR

Nova Dragon

Runestone Fleet

Twinsun Sea

Starbound Soul

PHARIM WAR

Shadowguard

Veilspeaker

Beastwalker

Lightgiver

Darkmask

Lifebringer

Shadeslayer

GOD OF
NEVERLAND

A DEFENDERS OF LORE NOVEL

GAMA RAY MARTINEZ

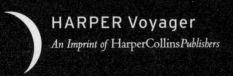

HARPER Voyager
An Imprint of HarperCollins Publishers

GOD OF NEVERLAND. Copyright © 2022 by Gamaliel Martinez. All rights reserved. Printed in Canada. No part of this book may be used or reproduced in any manner whatsoever without written permission except in the case of brief quotations embodied in critical articles and reviews. For information, address HarperCollins Publishers, 195 Broadway, New York, NY 10007.

HarperCollins books may be purchased for educational, business, or sales promotional use. For information, please email the Special Markets Department at SPsales@harpercollins.com.

Harper Voyager and design are trademarks of HarperCollins Publishers LLC.

FIRST EDITION

Designed by Paula Russell Szafranski
Illustrations © Shutterstock.com
Map by Nick Springer and Jessica Brams-Miller. Map copyright © 2021 Springer Cartographics LLC.

Library of Congress Cataloging-in-Publication Data has been applied for.

ISBN 978-0-06-301463-3

22 23 24 25 26   LSC   10 9 8 7 6 5 4 3 2 1

For my love, Melissa,

who makes me feel like I can fly

*   *   *

In Memory of David Wolverton,

I was already chasing my dreams when I met you,

but you taught me how to catch them.

This book would not exist without you,

and I am a better writer, and a better person

for having known you. Until we meet again.

Neverland

Never
Mountain

Indian
Village

Never Bay

*SKULL
ROCK*

*JOLLY
ROGER*

Lost
Boys'
Home

MERMAID ROCK

*Mermaid
Lagoon*

Dark
Swamp

GOD

OF

NEVERLAND

* * *

CHAPTER 1

LONDON, 1925

A shadow, looking very much like that of a boy, ghosted into the train's control cab through the front window. It came to a stop in front of Michael, which was strange, given how fast the train was moving. He stared at it for several seconds before looking up. There didn't seem to be anything that could cast such an odd shade, but after a few moments, he spotted a small cloud floating in front of the full moon. That had to be responsible. In fact, if he looked at the shadow, he decided that it didn't really look like a boy's at all—even when it seemed to wave at him. So he ignored it, telling himself it was only a trick of the light and a side effect of a long day. After a few seconds, the shadow's shoulders slumped, and it slipped out through the same window it had entered from—or, rather, the shadow did what shadows do when they're no longer visible. It certainly didn't shrug. Michael glanced back at the sky and found that the cloud had vanished into the night, and the doubt flooded in once again.

"A boy's shadow," he said to himself, under his breath. He shook his head to clear away the thought as the train pulled into Paddington, and he occupied himself with delicately bringing tons of steel to a stop.

He waited until the passengers had disembarked before

exiting his cab. The station was practically empty, as his train was one of the last to arrive for the night. People greeted their loved ones and headed sleepily for the exit. A few wandered the area with no apparent place to go, but none of them paid Michael any mind, so he ignored them in turn. It had been a long day, and he shambled toward the exit, looking forward to his bed.

As he approached the door, though, his eyes caught sight of the small shield and sword that had been chalked onto the ground, and the hairs on the back of his neck stood on end. For a moment, he considered walking past it, but duty had been ingrained in him during his years of service, and even now, he couldn't just ignore it, no matter how much he might want to. He scanned the area until he saw a cloaked figure not quite hidden in the shadows. The figure inclined its head. Michael eyed the exit and once again thought about taking it. They wouldn't follow. That wasn't their way. He could be done with this and go home.

He sighed.

It wasn't his way to ignore this sort of thing, and they knew that.

Finally, he let out a breath and walked over. The figure was a woman dressed in a long brown coat. Once he got a look at her sea-green eyes, he realized he knew her.

"Vanessa, what are you doing here? I told the order that I'm done with them."

It came out sounding more like a plea than a demand, but Vanessa smiled.

"It's good to see you, too, Michael."

Her eyes twinkled as she smiled in a way that reminded Michael of his sister, Wendy. Some of his uneasiness drained away, and he exhaled slowly.

"What do you want?"

"*They* want to see you." Her voice, barely above a whisper, was quickly swallowed by the ambient noise of the station. She raised her hand before Michael had even started his protest. "As an outsider. They've granted you a special dispensation."

Michael let out a low whistle. Outsiders had been permitted to see the ruling council of his old service, but it had happened only rarely. Michael could count the number of times it had been allowed in the past century on one hand, and he realized how powerful a request this was.

And how that *honor* didn't change anything.

"I'm done with them. I already told you."

Vanessa shook her head, a motion which barely disturbed her dark curls. "This is different. A god has gone missing."

Michael stiffened. Instinctively, he looked around to make sure no one was close, but of course Vanessa had made sure of that before she'd started speaking. They were purposefully out of the way enough to be private, while not appearing so clandestine that their conversation would seem conspicuous. Still, he thought he saw a shadow move on the other side of the station, but it had no apparent source. So, despite her well-chosen place, he moved in closer to her. His mouth had gone dry, and his heart raced.

A missing god. It was . . . unthinkable. Most of the pagan gods had withered as the world moved into the modern age, but a few were still active. Reality depended on them. They could fade, and probably would given enough time, but their abrupt removal could lead to chaos until the universe adapted to existence without them. He tried to sound like he didn't care, but he knew his reaction had already told his old companion otherwise.

"The Knights have better agents than me."

Vanessa shook her head. "Not for this."

"I've been out of the game for years, Vanessa. Surely—"

"The god is Maponos."

Ice ran through Michael's veins. Maponos was a god of the ancient Celts, the personification of youth. Unlike most deities, he had remained active in a world where few believed in him. He had even built a realm for himself, a place of imagination and adventure. Michael and his siblings had actually met Maponos long ago, when he was a child. It was before his parents had adopted six additional boys who had been brought from the god's realm. Aside from his sister, Wendy, all had forgotten where they'd come from, thinking it only a child's dream. The order Michael Darling had worked for—the one Vanessa belonged to now—knew that his adopted brothers had been called the Lost Boys, who had lived in the realm of Neverland, and that Michael had once known the god Maponos by another name.

Peter Pan.

"When do we leave?"

Vanessa motioned to the exit. "There's a car waiting for us."

Michael nodded and fell into step behind his former colleague. A part of him still wanted to believe that this wasn't happening. That part almost wept as Michael stepped into the car that would take him back to the life he had left more than a year before. Almost unbidden, the old phrase that he had heard so often before missions popped into his mind.

Half a league onward.

* * *

The car wound through the streets of London, traveling back roads and turning seemingly at random. More than once, they took a series of turns that brought them back to the spot they had been in only minutes before. The old ploy would've worked if Michael hadn't already known where they were going.

He gave Vanessa a level look. "It's late, and I'm tired."

She shrugged. "Procedures are procedures."

"Procedures are why I left."

"No they're not," she said softly.

Michael set his jaw and gazed out the window. They had entered one of the more unsavory parts of the city. Most of the lights were out, and the houses they passed ran together into a dark blur. Finally, they came to a stop before a broken-down building. It was the sort of place one would walk past quickly, and even hardened criminals didn't want to attract the attention of those living inside. Dim lights flickered in the windows of the three-story building. He had the unshakable sense that he was being watched. He shivered as he got out of the car, and he resisted the urge to leave. The feeling grew ever stronger as Vanessa led him to the door. It creaked open before she had a chance to lift her hand and knock.

The long hall stretching out before them was sparsely lit by flickering light bulbs and lined with hanging cobwebs for as far as Michael could see. A thick layer of dust covered a threadbare carpet. Michael had never been clear on whether the dust itself was an illusion or some other kind of magic at work. Regardless of how it was done, Vanessa left no footprints as she strode down the hall, nor did she disturb the cobwebs. The air held none of the mustiness Michael would have expected in a normal house that had been neglected as this place seemed to be. He took a deep breath, half expecting to be taken by a fit of coughing, but the air tasted perfectly normal, clean even. And yet he felt as if his chest was constricting and that every breath was a struggle. He always hated this.

He clenched his teeth and started after Vanessa.

The magic around the house parted like a curtain as he stepped inside, and the fear spell that had been placed on the building released him, only to be picked up by another spell. He could breathe, but now his head spun as they walked through the passages, and he felt nauseated if he looked at any one spot for too long. He knew that even though Vanessa was leading and was still an active member, she would be experiencing the same disorientation. Walking through these headquarters was done only with difficulty, and it was said the house itself determined where you would go.

Eventually, they came to a stop in front of a plain wooden door. Michael brought his hand to his forehead and looked over his shoulder. His vision swam, and he had a hard time focusing. He would've been hard-pressed to retrace his steps back through the twisting hallways. Still, the urge to run, to lose himself in the dusty labyrinth, almost overwhelmed him. He held on to one thought: the magic *made* him want to run, and he refused to let it. He turned back to the door. Vanessa pushed it open, and the solid wood swung on silent hinges. Michael nodded at his old friend before stepping inside to meet with the people he had left nearly three years ago.

The leaders of the Knights of the Round.

THE ROOM WAS DARK, WITH ITS CENTER DIMLY ILLUMI-nated by a single lantern hanging from the ceiling. The flame's light barely revealed a round table near the wall opposite the door. Five shadowy figures sat around one side, forming a half moon facing the entrance, their features hidden in the dim light. They were distinguished only by the golden pattern embroidered around the inside edges of their hoods.

Though their identities would be known among the upper ranks of the Knights, when speaking as the leaders, the nobles of the Court would be called only by their titles: the King, the Queen, the Lady, the Wizard, and the Knight Protector, representing Arthur, Guinevere, the Lady of the Lake, Merlin, and Lancelot.

"Who comes before the Court of Camelot?" the King asked in a booming voice that Michael felt as much as he heard.

He almost rolled his eyes. The King was always one for melodramatics.

"Camelot has been dead for over a thousand years, and you know very well who I am."

For a second, silence filled the room. He could practically feel them scowling at his disrespect. Stories said that their order had been founded by Merlin himself to protect humanity against supernatural threats, and that the true purpose of the original Round Table had been to stand against such forces. But these people fancied themselves the heirs to Camelot, and they had pulled Michael back into a life he had left after having given so much; he was in no mood to indulge them their arcane fantasies.

"Sir Michael—" the one on the far right said in a feminine voice.

"*Just* Michael," he interrupted the Knight Protector. "I left the Knights a long time ago, remember?"

The cloaked figures looked at each other before the Knight Protector continued. "Michael, then. The god Maponos is missing. He has not entered the world in over a year, and the link to his realm has grown tenuous."

Michael shrugged, and relief crept into him at the thought that they had overreacted. "A year isn't really that long for him. He gets distracted easily. He's probably off having some adventure."

"Do you think we would have summoned you if it were something that simple? His realm hangs on to this world by a thread. It could snap at any time, and Neverland would forever be lost to this world."

Michael looked away. It was several seconds before he could speak, and even then, it felt like the words were being dragged out of him. "Maybe it's time for that to happen."

Vanessa moved in close and spoke softly. "Would you destroy every wonderful thing in the world?"

"Peter isn't all wonder, Vanessa. He's chaos incarnate. That's not necessarily a good thing."

"Maponos holds the dreams of children all over the world," the Lady said, either ignoring or not hearing Vanessa's question. "Do you think it would be a small thing for that to die?"

"Not a small thing," Michael said, "but not necessarily a bad one."

"The land is wasting away, Michael," Vanessa said. "Creatures are disappearing and the sun barely shines. The waters are murky and I've heard rumors all the fairies have fled."

"How can you possibly know that?"

"Our agents around the world have been gathering reports of children's nightmares," the Wizard said.

Michael snorted. "Children have nightmares all the time."

"The same nightmare? One of a boy who is not a boy trapped by darkness?"

Michael hesitated. "A boy who is not a boy?"

The Wizard nodded. "When a three-year-old says those words, we listen."

Michael stared, having no response to that rather damning evidence.

"You may no longer see any value in it, Michael," the Knight Protector pressed on, "but Maponos . . ." The pause felt like it lasted for an eternity. "Peter is your friend, and I do not believe that you have changed so much that that no longer matters to you. More important, you have been to Neverland, where none of the Knights have. You have spoken to Peter face-to-face and have fought by his side. If there is another more capable than you to deal with this matter, we do not know him, but all of that is beside the point. You will accept this task."

Michael stiffened. "Will I? I seem to recall leaving you and everything you stood for."

"And yet you came when you learned why we wanted to see you. You had decided you would accept this task before you set foot in this house. Now stop playing these games."

"*Games?* Who is dressed up in robes, living in their little clubhouse with their special rules and secret codes? I left to get away from *your* games."

Michael seethed. A part of him wanted to just walk away at this point. The magic of the house would prevent him from leaving unless the Court allowed it, but he doubted they would stop him if he just turned and left. Still he hesitated. Because the Knight Protector was right. If Peter really was in some sort of trouble, he couldn't just abandon him. The Knights? They could have their dusty house and even dustier ceremonies. Michael had left the Knights because he had been tired of such mysteries, of things beyond the comprehension of most people. He wanted no more of a life in the shadows. No more adventure. No more *danger*. He just wanted to be part of the ordinary world, like everyone else.

But this was *Peter*.

He let out a long breath. One more mission. He shuddered at the thought but recovered before the Court could notice—although he could see Vanessa looking at him with a combination of curiosity and sympathy.

Okay, he thought. *I can do this much before I put the Knights, Neverland, and everything else behind me. For good.*

He searched his memory, not only for what he had learned of Peter when he was a child, but also for everything he had learned during his time with the Knights. He would need materials he no longer had access to—materials he'd rarely had access to during his own time as a Knight—and he doubted the Court would like the idea of giving those to an outsider.

Well, that puts the fate of Neverland in their hands, doesn't it?

"I'll help," he said, smiling at the thought of their reaction to his next request. "But before I do, I need access to the catacombs."

* * *

The eruption was everything Michael had expected. And hoped for. All five members of the Court shot to their feet. Each tried to shout over the others, which made understanding any of them all but impossible—not that he much cared what they were actually saying. On top of that, the magic of the house responded to the Court's reaction, and the air vibrated against Michael's skin, alive with power. A grin had crept onto Vanessa's face. No doubt she had been expecting this. She gave a barely perceptible shake of her head.

"What?" he said innocently, even as he gave her a half smile. "They had to have known I would ask for resources."

"Maybe for one or two pieces," Vanessa said. "Not to gain unrestricted access to the most extensive storehouse of magical items in the world."

Michael shrugged. "They're the ones who asked me to come."

"Yes, we did," the Wizard said, his voice cutting through the now-silent room. "You know only Knights may access the catacombs. Tell us what you want, and we will have it retrieved, or reswear your oaths and join us."

Michael shook his head and turned, heading for the door. "No," he said without turning around. "Let me do this my way or find someone else. Now, if you'll excuse me, I need to be up early tomorrow for work."

"What of your friend?"

Michael laughed. It sounded a little forced. "Peter has gotten out of a lot of dangerous situations. I'm sure he can make it out of this one, too."

"You don't believe that," the Wizard said.

Michael shrugged, idly wondering if the original Merlin had ever been so frustrated by one of the Knights. "Do *you*? Enough to let me just walk out of here?"

"But the nightmares, Michael," the Wizard said. "This isn't some child's game—"

"That's exactly what it is," Vanessa said before Michael could reassert his previous argument about this very thing. What she said next, though, surprised him. "This is Peter Pan, after all."

That made the Court exchange glances—it surprised them, as well. The King, Queen, and Knight Protector looked angry enough to just throw him out, but the Wizard and Lady entered into a hushed conversation. Michael waited in silence for their decision. All members of the Court had different responsibilities, and these two controlled access to the catacombs. Finally, the Wizard threw up his arms in frustration, but the Lady nodded.

"Very well—provided Sir Vanessa accompanies you."

Michael glanced at Vanessa, who grinned. He let out a long breath and nodded. The Lady uttered words in a language Michael didn't know. Michael's ears popped, as if the pressure had just changed. The Lady inclined her head.

"The distractor spell has been altered to allow you into the catacombs. I shouldn't have to tell you to be careful. There are things down there—"

Michael waved her off, and he could almost feel the noble's anger, but he had heard that lecture too many times to want to hear it again. He had left the Knights because he'd lived that danger for longer than he wanted to remember. He thought he should be admonishing them to be careful dealing with forces they didn't understand, but it felt petty at this point. Instead, he just motioned for Vanessa to lead the way. However, the Knight suddenly didn't seem so sure of herself as her eyes wandered from Michael to the Court and back again. The Knight Protector made a gesture that they should go on, and though the heavyset figure was the lowest ranked of the court, none of the others contradicted her, so Vanessa stepped out of the room.

Once again, there was that peculiar twisting of the mind as they walked through the halls. They passed through even more corridors this time until Michael was sure they had walked through more passages than the building could possibly contain. Finally, they stopped in front of an old door that was barely hanging on its hinges. It scraped against the dusty carpet as Vanessa pulled it open, revealing a wooden staircase that looked more than a century old. Several of the steps had rotted through, and most appeared as if they couldn't support human weight. When a fly buzzed past him, he was afraid that if it landed on the stairs, the whole thing would collapse.

Vanessa looked over her shoulder at him and grinned. "Half a league onward."

He stiffened and tried to keep the pain he felt at that off of his face.

Her vanishing smile said he hadn't succeeded. "Are you sure about this? One wrong step down there, and we could end up as pigs or something. Once was enough for me."

Michael snorted at the memory as they started down. "You knew we were in a witch's lair. What possessed you to drink a potion?"

She stiffened but didn't turn around. "I didn't know it was

Circe's. Anyway . . . never mind. Look, don't pretend you know what's down here. You left a long time ago." The wooden wall gave way to a natural-looking cave wall, and the illusion hiding the stairs faded, revealing steps of worn stone. "We've had additions since you were last here."

"Like what?" Michael asked, his curiosity piqued.

There was a sound like waves crashing against the shore. Vanessa kept walking down. "An empty genie's lamp. We found Faust's lair late last year and brought his copy of the Necronomicon. We used that to capture a wraith haunting the Tower of London. The Lady sealed that in a wraith cage. There's also a rogue water elemental. It sank a few ships in the channel last week."

"Mashikoon?" Michael asked. At the surprised expression on Vanessa's face, he elaborated. "I always suspected it was somewhere in the channel."

Vanessa nodded. "We didn't even have its name to help fight it, but we managed."

She glared at him, but he just shook his head. "It was in my report."

She rolled her eyes. "It was only a couple of days ago that the Wizard learned it was Mashikoon. Nothing like Comshemar, but still a nasty one."

Michael shivered. The water elemental Comshemar had been one of his last missions. Far more dangerous than anything Neverland had ever birthed, it was the only such creature anyone had ever heard of with teeth. And while it had escaped Michael's pursuit into the ocean, the Knights had apparently caught another one, if not quite as vicious. Still, any water elemental was no insignificant threat, and that would be one of the least dangerous things down here. The Knights had spent more than a thousand years gathering objects and creatures that could become a threat to humanity. Many were kept in the catacombs, while others had been hidden away at safe houses around the globe. Michael suspected that given a chance, there were some who would even imprison Peter here, but just as there were things too dangerous to be allowed back into the world, there were others too dangerous to be removed.

Which was why they were all so concerned about his absence. If Michael was being honest with himself, the thought worried him, too.

"What are we looking for?" Vanessa asked.

"Fairy dust, first of all."

Vanessa stopped and glanced over her shoulder and scowled. "Pixie?"

Michael nodded.

"You could've just asked for it, you know. They would've given that to you without question. We've all heard the story of how you got to Neverland the first time."

She started down again, and it was a few seconds before Michael responded.

"Would they have given me a dragon's-blood potion?"

Vanessa missed a step but caught herself before she fell. She turned and stared at Michael for several seconds before shaking her head. Her eyes were wide, though he could just make out the edges of her mouth turned up in the beginnings of a smile. "Probably not. There are only six of those left. They're this way, but why stop there? We found the Spear of Destiny last year."

Michael almost tripped over his own feet. He put a hand on her shoulder and she turned around with a wicked look on her face.

"Won't that destroy anyone who tries to use it?"

"Except the worthy."

He shook his head.

"What? You're not worthy?"

"Let's just stick with the potion and dust."

She sighed—or laughed, he couldn't quite be sure—and turned down a side passage. Michael could barely hear the current of the underground river that ran through the cavern. Aside from that and their footsteps, the only sound was a faint dripping that echoed through the passage. For some reason, it made the hairs on the back of Michael's neck stand on end. The sound was faintly metallic and felt familiar, but he couldn't place his finger on where he had heard it. It was probably just something he had heard the last time he was in these catacombs. At least that was what he told himself as he forced thoughts of the sound from his mind.

Vanessa led him to a small enclosed chamber. Like many of the other rooms in the catacombs, it seemed like any natural cavern with rough stone walls. What made it so different was what was inside. Several glass vials, as well as platters, cups, goblets, and other containers, sat in cavities carved into the rock. Some of them seemed to glow from their own internal light; some were glowing from whatever was inside them. The light was both warm and menacing, which fit exactly with Michael's previous run-ins with magic. He quickly scanned them before picking out a golden bottle no taller than his hand. He pulled a handkerchief from his pocket and wrapped the potion.

"Why do you need to talk to animals in the first place?" Vanessa asked as he deposited the vial in his pocket. It felt heavy, even for a container made of gold.

"Because there are sources of information that the Court obviously didn't consider."

Vanessa narrowed her eyes. "You know, you're annoying when you're being mysterious."

Michael snorted. "If you don't want mystery, you're in the wrong organization."

"Is that why you think you left?" Vanessa asked as she led Michael deeper into the catacombs.

They had gone half a dozen steps down before Michael answered. "I left because I realized how much it would cost if I didn't grow up."

"Strange to hear one of Maponos's companions say that."

"Didn't you have imaginary friends when you were a child? Ones that you don't talk to anymore?"

"None that were gods, if that's what you mean." She pursed her lips. "I always wondered if it was because of Dmitri."

He clenched his teeth at the name but didn't answer. The babble of the river and the odd dripping became louder as they turned a corner and came into a wide cavern. A portion of the river flowed through the far end of the room, and Michael could just make out the water. The metallic dripping was louder here, but he tried to ignore it. Vanessa led him to an opening on the other side of the chamber, moving with a practiced grace. Michael, on the other hand, stumbled as he moved across the rough stone. They entered a small room and froze.

The wooden shelves that had held containers of fairy dust had been reduced to splinters. Dusts of all kinds of fairies, not only pixies like Tinker Bell, but also that of nixies, brownies, will-o'-the-wisps, and a dozen others Michael didn't know, lay scattered across the floor, intermingling with each other.

"What happened here?" Vanessa asked.

"It looks like someone got here first." He knelt and reached for the dust.

Vanessa hissed, "What are you *doing*?"

He waved off her concern and ran his finger through the dust. Mixing magics was dangerous business. A person could generally handle a couple of effects at once, but they had to be placed on the person directly, not combined beforehand. This was all unstable, and dangerously so. Yet a single finger's worth wouldn't be enough to have any significant effect. Instead, it told him something important. "It's wet."

"Wet? How would that happen?" Vanessa asked, glancing around the cave.

Michael looked to the shore. "The water elemental?"

Even as the words left his lips, he knew he was wrong. Vanessa shook her head.

"It's imprisoned in the river, and it can't go more than a few feet from the shore. Even if it somehow broke through the wards, the Court would know instantly."

The dripping grew louder, and Michael suppressed a shiver. It was moving closer. He kept his eyes on the river, not quite willing to admit to himself what it was. "We need to get out of here. I think something came in through the river."

"That's impossible. We're protected."

"Then how do you explain this?"

She shook her head, and then she cocked it, listening. Her eyes widened as if noticing the dripping for the first time. "What is that?"

"It's not something you have imprisoned down here?"

"Not that I know of."

Something screamed in Michael's mind, and goose bumps appeared on his arms as a wave of cold washed over him. The next thing he knew, he was on the ground, shivering. A shadow stood over him, and it took him a second to realize it was Vanessa.

"Michael? Michael, what's wrong?"

A thing that looked like darkness in human form materialized behind her. His eyes went wide, and he tried to say something, but his tongue froze in his mouth. Something in his expression must have warned her because she spun, and gasped.

"Wraith!"

She pulled out a pistol and fired, though the creature didn't so much as flinch as it glided forward. It extended a spectral claw. It sank into Michael's face, and he felt his strength draining away. He pulled free and struggled to his feet just as Vanessa turned. She took his hand and pulled him toward the entrance.

"Come on. We can't fight it—we need to get out of here!"

It was an effort for him to nod, but by then, she was practically dragging him down the hall. Slowly, his wits returned.

"Where did that come from?" he asked between heavy breaths.

"Run now. Questions later. We're not out of danger yet."

The cold washed over him again. He stumbled but didn't fall this time. They kept running, starting up the stairs. He looked up and would have gasped if he'd had the breath to do so. Silhouetted in the light of the door was another shadowed figure.

It practically leaped downstairs. Both he and Vanessa threw their hands up, but the figure jumped *over* them. There was the distinctive sound of metal on leather as the shadow drew a sword. Its tip glowed blue as it stabbed into the wraith. The creature hissed, and Michael's nostrils flared at the smell of rotting fish.

"Go!"

Michael recognized the voice of the Knight Protector. He and Vanessa did as she suggested, running up the stairs. As soon as they were in the hall, Vanessa punched him in the side.

"What was that for?"

"You just had to run your finger through the dust, didn't you?"

"You're not serious, are you?" Michael blinked and wiped sweat from his brow. "That shouldn't have been enough to call a wraith."

"There was wisp dust in there," a strong, feminine voice came from the doorway. The Knight Protector came up into the hall. "Brownie as well. It might not have been enough to summon a wraith, but to draw one that was already nearby . . ." She let out a breath. "Still, I am surprised that drove it into enough of a frenzy to break out of the Lady's prison."

"Did you destroy it?" Vanessa asked.

The Knight Protector nodded, and Michael thought he saw the faint hint of her face in the shadows of her hood. "I tried to drive it back into the wraith cage we had it in, but the wraith had shattered it when it escaped. It's a shame."

"A shame?" Michael shook his head. "Why would you even keep an undead thing like that down there in the first place?"

"Wraiths aren't undead," Vanessa said. "They're not dead, either. Not exactly, anyway."

"How can something be not exactly dead?"

"Did you forget everything from your time as a Knight?"

"I didn't encounter wraiths, thankfully. I was usually after bigger game."

It wasn't a boast, and Vanessa didn't take it as such. She said, in answer to his question, "Wraiths are the spirits of the forgotten, or maybe the abandoned. We don't really know how they're made, but they could be dead. Or they could just as easily be something like the ghosts of a forgotten childhood."

Her words hit a nerve. "I shouldn't have asked," he muttered. "Okay, never mind that. Why do you *have* one of those, dead or not?"

The Knight Protector chuckled. "You've been gone too long. There is much we still don't understand about wraiths. The catacombs are the safest place to keep one for study."

"It *was*," Michael said. "Until it breaks out."

"If it breaks out, we would know. Why do you think I came down to help? You're just lucky it didn't touch you for long. They can drain the life right out of you." Michael blanched, but the noble went on. "Did you find what you needed?"

"Everything but the pixie dust." Michael bit his lower lip and thought back to the dripping, only now he realized it hadn't been dripping. It was too metallic, too regular, more like . . . a clock. "Knight Protector . . . there was something else down there."

He proceeded to explain about the ticking. The Knight Protector listened without saying a word. After he was done, she stared down the stairs for several seconds.

"Do you have any idea what it is? You said there was ticking. Could it be—"

"I don't know," Michael said, cutting her off. Because the thing was, he thought he *might* know. But it couldn't be that. He didn't even want to admit the possibility. "We didn't want to stay long enough to find out."

The Knight Protector nodded. "I'll inform the Wizard and the Lady. Are you able to proceed without the pixie dust?"

"What other choice do we have?" Michael said. "We'll just have to improvise, I guess."

"That sounds ominous," the Knight Protector said.

"You've just described every mission Michael has ever been on," Vanessa said.

He threw her a dirty look, but she just looked back, as if waiting for him to challenge her.

He couldn't.

"I'll get you to Neverland, and then I'm done."

"Very well," the Knight Protector said after a beat. "Go with honor."

Vanessa inclined her head to her, but Michael gave the noble only a slight nod. The magic of the house still befuddled them as they moved through the halls, but it seemed to be lessening, as if the house was happy to see them go. The feeling was mutual. The car that had brought them here was waiting for them, and they got inside.

"You're lucky she was so distracted by what happened that

she didn't ask what you *had* taken." When Michael didn't respond, Vanessa snorted but went on. "Okay—so where exactly are we going?"

"First, I need to get some rest. Take me home, and then meet me at the train station tomorrow."

"What then?" Vanessa asked.

Michael pulled the potion out of his pocket, its golden container shimmering in the moonlight. "Then, we find a fish."

* * *

CHAPTER 4

First thing in the morning, Michael went to the train station. He spoke to the foreman and arranged for a few days' leave. As he left the foreman's office, a part of him hoped Vanessa wouldn't be there to meet him, but she greeted him as soon as he got on the platform with their tickets in hand. They sat in a private car, but neither said anything as the train horn sounded and the vehicle began its lumbering journey.

"Why exactly are we heading to Gloucester?" Vanessa asked after several minutes of silence.

"Because once, long ago, Maponos was imprisoned there."

Vanessa said, "Maponos was really there? I never heard that. When?"

Michael glanced out the window as they passed out of the city and into the countryside. "Some fifteen hundred years ago."

Vanessa didn't respond for nearly a minute. Finally, Michael looked back at her. She was staring at him. "Fifteen *hundred*? Before the founding of the Knights?"

Michael nodded once. "Or just after, depending on who's telling the story. The legends aren't really clear on who held him, but they do say how he got out."

When he didn't say anything more, Vanessa glared at him. "Are you going to make me drag this story out of you?"

Michael smiled. "In order to win his bride, King Arthur's cousin had to free Maponos. They called him Mabon at the time, but it's the same being. No one knew where he was, so they asked all the oldest and wisest animals. None could help them until they found the Salmon of Llyn Llyw."

Vanessa raised an eyebrow. "You mean you were serious about finding a fish?"

"After all the things you've seen—we just fought a wraith, for god's sake!—*this* is what surprises you?"

"I guess I just wasn't sure if you'd gone completely mad."

"Oh, I think I have." Michael pulled out the dragon's-blood potion and held it up to the light. The gold vial glimmered in the morning sun. The potion, once taken, would grant the drinker the ability to learn the language of animals. "Completely."

She rolled her eyes, but there was a faint smile on her lips as she turned away.

They arrived at Gloucester after a few hours of companionable silence. The hustle and bustle of the city was already well underway, and it more than made up for their lack of talk. Most of the men wore seemingly identical business suits, though some, both men and women, wore the garb of factory workers or the like. A nearby fat man with a pudgy nose complained when a woman bumped into him. Michael caught something about how women shouldn't do jobs meant for men, but of course many men had been conscripted to fight in the Great War, and the factories had to keep running. Once Germany had been defeated and the war had ended, many of those women had kept going to work, and he thought men like the one complaining needed to get over it. The world was changing, growing up, one might say. Michael found himself chuckling at what Peter would think of that.

Michael and Vanessa's final destination wasn't actually in the city, and they hired a car to take them to a house the Knights maintained on the outskirts of town. The old house had the same ominous feel as the headquarters in London. Like many such buildings around the country, it served as a safe house and rest area for any Knight in need. It was unoccupied at the time, though the pantry was well stocked. They ate a quick meal before packing additional supplies and heading into the wilderness outside of Gloucester.

Llyn Llyw, where the salmon was supposed to be, wasn't really a place, at least not in the traditional sense of the word. It no more existed than Atlantis, or Tartarus, or El Dorado. Or Neverland, for that matter. The unwary could stumble into such places by chance, or a person could be brought to them by some cosmic fate or divine will, but deliberately reaching one was difficult unless one knew exactly what they were doing. Michael was hoping he fell into the latter category. He had never been to Llyn Llyw, but he knew of it. The stories said that the home of the salmon was upstream from the place Maponos had been imprisoned. That had been somewhere in the city itself. The River Severn was the only river of note running through the city, and Michael guessed that must be the river in the story, so they followed it north.

The sun was already high in the sky when they started, and it crept steadily nearer to the western horizon as they searched. Michael doubted that Llyn Llyw would be along the Severn itself. The river was too large and too well traveled to house a place like Llyn Llyw. It did have a number of tributaries, however, and Michael suspected one of those would lead them to the mythological place.

He pulled a map out of his pocket. A place like Llyn Llyw wouldn't be on it, of course. He needed to find a tributary that wasn't on the map. But with so many offshoots, they could be looking for weeks.

I should have grabbed a luck charm down in the catacombs. Would help us find the right tributary.

Then again, he shouldn't be here at all, so maybe it wouldn't be the worst thing in the world if they *didn't* find Llyn Llyw. He kept a close eye on the map as they walked downriver. Whenever he found a fork that wasn't depicted, they took it. Most of those were simply branches that were too small for a mapmaker to bother with and which dribbled off after a few miles. A few times, however, the tributaries were larger, and he found himself getting excited. They always ended up having to turn back, though.

As the sky darkened with the approach of twilight, the pair stopped to have a quick meal of bread and cheese. Owls hooted, and insect song filled the evening air. They made camp just as a fog bank rolled into the woods, blanketing the area so thickly that Michael couldn't see more than a few feet ahead of him. Their small fire set odd shadows dancing in the trees. Once, Michael saw a shadow that almost looked like a person, but it had no source, so he decided he had just been up too long and doused the fire. He was about to retire to his tent when a wolf howled.

Michael flicked on an electric flashlight and looked around but saw nothing. He couldn't shake the feeling that unseen eyes were watching him. The air itself seemed alive with energy, and he felt his heart racing. He moved to the bank of the river and noticed that its current had slowed significantly. The water looked different, too, but he couldn't tell exactly why.

"I think we're here," Vanessa said as she came up next to him.

Michael nodded and spoke under his breath. "I didn't expect it to come to us."

Didn't need a luck charm after all. Or maybe I needed one to keep it from us.

It was too late now, though. The temperature had risen, banishing the chill of the night. The songs of birds who rarely called this late after sunset filled the air. The wide river disappeared into the fog. Shadows swayed from tree to tree in a way that made a shiver run down Michael's spine. He tensed and had to force himself to relax. This was why he had come.

He took off his shoes and stepped into the river. Vanessa cleared her throat, and he looked at her as the cold waters washed over his feet and mud rose between his toes. The fog had changed things. The whole place had an ethereal quality to it, and even the trees seemed different, more alive somehow, or maybe more aware.

"This is definitely the place," he said.

"Are you sure about this plan, though? I mean, you said this all happened fifteen hundred years ago. How do you know the salmon is even alive?"

Michael shrugged. "From what I could tell, it's an oracle spirit. Those tend to stick around."

"And you're assuming it'll know where Maponos is right now?"

"Maybe. Maybe not. But it's a place to start, and if this salmon really is as wise as the stories say, it should at least be able to point us in the right direction. More to the point: Do you have a better idea?"

"No."

"Then be quiet—you're scaring away the fish."

Michael withdrew the potion from his pocket. Long before the Knights had been founded, a Viking hero had killed a dragon and drank its blood, which had given him the ability to speak with animals. Since then, others had duplicated the effect, though the scarcity of dragons made the substance incredibly rare. Fortunately for him, the Knights had managed to get hold of a few samples over the centuries, though a Knight had been granted permission to drink one only rarely. The stopper came free easily, and he brought the vial to his mouth and drank it all down. It was warmer than he'd expected, given the coolness of the night. The thick liquid had a bitter tang to it, and he felt it oozing down his throat. Immediately, warmth spread through his body, but a heartbeat later a chill washed over him. He shivered, but after a few seconds more, the sensation passed as the magic took hold of him.

He took a deep breath and called out, "Salmon?" He felt more than a little silly, standing barefoot in a river, calling to a fish who might not even be close enough to hear him—again, this was often his experience with magic. "Salmon, are you there?"

The waters continued to flow past him. The birds chirped in a way that he could almost understand, and when he focused, he realized he could indeed catch a few words. No voice came from the river, though, and after a few minutes, he sighed and stepped out of the water. He was about to walk away when a deep voice called after him.

"It has been a long time since anyone has sought me out."

Michael spun and scanned the water. The surface was undisturbed, but there, no more than ten feet from the shore, a shadowed figure as big as a horse floated just beneath the surface. It was hard to tell its exact shape, but it might've been a fish.

"Salmon?"

The shape in the water quivered. "Yes, I am here. What is it you wish of me?"

Michael eyed Vanessa, but she just looked at him blankly before saying, "Can I assume those bubbles are from the fish?"

For a second, Michael was confused, but then he understood. Vanessa hadn't drunk the dragon's-blood potion. She probably hadn't even heard the fish, much less understood it.

"Yes," Michael said. He turned back to the water. "Once, you helped Culhwch find Mabon. We need that service as well."

The water rippled out from the shadow as it swam in a circle.

"It has been over a thousand years since I last laid eyes on the divine child. Why would you think I know where he is?"

Michael took a deep breath. "Because we don't have anywhere else to go."

It was several seconds before the shadow responded. "I am sorry. You have made this trip for nothing."

"Can't you tell us anything?"

A ticking sound echoed from downstream. Michael and Vanessa exchanged glances.

"Is that the same ticking you heard in the catacombs?" Vanessa said. "What is it?"

"It is my death if I do not leave here," the salmon said, apparently understanding her. It turned and started swimming upstream.

"Wait," Michael called out. "Mabon is missing. We have to find him. You have to know something!"

The shadow was already out of sight, and for a moment there was only the sound of rushing water. Then, the salmon's voice drifted to him, barely audible over the current. It grew softer as the salmon spoke, and its last word was hardly more than a whisper. "Seek one who has seen him before. One who was his enemy, though who does not hate him personally. Such a one may be able to take you where you need to go. Failing that, find the one who took your place."

"One who was his enemy? One who took my place? What does any of that mean?"

The ticking grew louder, and the salmon did not answer. Michael backed out of the river and looked around, but he found no source of the strange sound. He met Vanessa's gaze.

"We should go, before whatever that is comes any closer."

Vanessa nodded. "My sentiments exactly."

However, they had moved only about a dozen yards from the riverbank when something exploded out of the water. It landed on the ground with a heavy thud, throwing a spray that very nearly reached Michael. For a second, he could only stare, not willing to believe what he was seeing. He had left the Knights, left all of this, behind. And while a part of him had known what the source of the ticking had been the moment he'd first heard it in the catacombs, he had hoped upon hope that he was mistaken. Apparently he wasn't.

He had started this quest by looking for a way to Neverland, but he had never expected Neverland to come hunting him.

Before him was a crocodile that was far larger than any such creature had a right to be—and that was saying something after he'd spent the previous few minutes speaking to a giant salmon. It had to be at least twenty feet long, and Michael couldn't imagine how it had leaped into the air.

The creature opened its mouth slightly. There was a bone lodged between two of its razor-sharp teeth, and Michael didn't want to guess what it had come from. The creature closed its mouth, and he heard a sickening crunch. Its slitted eyes focused on Michael, and a low rumble escaped its body that didn't quite drown out the ticking sound, which came from the clock it had swallowed so long ago.

"Is that . . ." Vanessa's voice trailed off, but Michael nodded, guessing what she had been about to ask.

"It's the crocodile that killed Hook."

*　*　*

CHAPTER 5

The creature lunged forward before he could give more explanation. Michael cried out and fell back, the crocodile's jaws missing him by inches. There was a loud bang as Vanessa pulled out a pistol and fired, but the bullet bounced off the crocodile's thick hide. The creature spun faster than an animal that size should have been able to, and it snapped at Vanessa. For a second it seemed like it had latched on to her foot, but as Vanessa pulled away, there was a rip as the hem of her dress tore free.

Michael used the distraction to pick up a heavy branch and swing it, slamming it into the monster's head so hard that it sent a jolt up his arm. There was a loud crack as the branch snapped. The crocodile regarded him as Michael might look at a fly. Its growl mingled with the ticking sound of the clock in its belly. It was so close Michael could smell its rotten breath.

"What do you want?" Michael asked, but either the dragon's-blood potion didn't work on crocodiles or the animal was simply ignoring him. He took several steps back, but it lumbered after him, its slowness mocking him now, a wicked intelligence in its eyes. Michael had the sense that it was toying with him. He eyed Vanessa. "I don't suppose you have any ideas."

She fired again, but the second shot had no more effect than the first.

"I guess not. How did Peter Pan beat this thing?"

Michael continued to back up, and the crocodile followed him step for step. "He didn't. He just fed Hook to it and let it go on its way."

He hurled the remnant of the branch as if it were a spear, but it just bounced off the creature, doing no more damage than Vanessa's bullets. His back brushed up against a tree. He tried to go around it, but he tripped on a raised root and tumbled to the ground. The animal's green eyes made his blood turn to ice. Time slowed down as it opened its jaws to take a bite out of him, and Michael was overcome with the certainty he should have just walked out of Paddington Station last night. The shadows of his life passed before his eyes.

No, that wasn't it. An *actual* shadow fell on the creature's head. Then, it seemed to fold in on itself until it rested on the crocodile's eyes like a blindfold. The animal thrashed about, its tail crashing through small trees and sending splinters flying. Michael scrambled on the ground, trying to stay out of the way of the flailing appendage. Vanessa grabbed Michael's arm and almost pulled it out of its socket as she forced him to his feet. She practically dragged him away from the riverbank, though after a few seconds he found his stride. It was all he could do to resist the urge to run. Doing so in the forest at night was a sure way to break your neck, but they moved as quickly as they could, despite his lack of shoes.

"What was that thing that covered its eyes?"

"No idea," Michael said between heavy breaths. He hadn't kept up his exercise routine since leaving the Knights, and his lungs were burning as he and Vanessa forced their way through the forest.

I grew up, but when did I get this old?

"You knew about the crocodile in the catacombs, didn't you?"

Michael ignored her question. "Look, in Neverland, everyone was afraid of the crocodile. Even Hook. Even *Peter*. If there's a way to beat that thing, I have no idea what it is. We just have to hope we can get away."

It continued to thrash behind them, and they kept pushing through the woods until sounds of the struggle had faded into nothingness. They stopped for a few minutes while Michael caught his breath, though Vanessa had no such trouble, which she made a very pointed remark about.

"Hey—I've still got it!" he replied, and she laughed.

"Prove it. Let's go."

Finding their way back to town was slow going. They had left the river and had to navigate by starlight. Michael's feet were sore and frozen, and he regretted having to leave his shoes on the riverbank. He was practically shuffling along like a zombie—which he *had* encountered before—as he shambled after Vanessa. It was close to midnight before they finally made their way into Gloucester, utterly exhausted. They stumbled in the direction of the safe house.

The city streets were darker than the hour could account for. The moon and the stars seemed muted, and none of the lampposts shed any light. Given what he had just seen a shadow do, Michael was wary of the darkness. He thought he saw movement at the edges of his vision, but that was only his imagination. Probably. But then Michael and Vanessa exchanged glances, and without need for speech, they quickened their pace until they were very nearly running.

"I didn't know that thing ever left Neverland," Michael said between heavy breaths.

"It shouldn't be able to," Vanessa said. "I doubt it accidentally crossed over. With the link between here and Neverland so weak . . ." She shook her head.

"You think it came after me deliberately?"

"What else could it be? Unless you really think one of Neverland's most feared inhabitants just happened to show up both in the catacombs and here."

Michael sighed. "I suppose that does seem a little unlikely, doesn't it?"

"And that's saying something, given what we do."

"What *you* do."

"I'm sorry—were you not about to be eaten by a giant, magical crocodile, too? And speaking of magical animals, did you learn anything from the fish?"

Michael started to shake his head, but paused to stare into the shadows. A chill ran over him, and he motioned her to silence. She stiffened and her eyes hardened, but she nodded. They passed through the streets like burglars, hardly making a sound, but Michael hadn't had to move like that in years. A couple of times, he kicked a pebble or stepped awkwardly. Vanessa turned to glare at him, but she never said a word. They walked for another half an hour through the streets of the city before reaching the Knights' safe house.

They slipped in the door. As soon as they shut it, Vanessa looked as if she was about to criticize him about, well, everything, but Michael shook his head. "The wards."

"I don't think those would keep out the crocodile, but . . ."

She laid her hand on the door and mumbled a few words, being careful to keep him from hearing. It was protocol, and even though Michael knew the words, only she could say them now. The incantation wouldn't respond to anyone who wasn't a Knight. He felt a gentle hum of power.

Vanessa gave him a level look and motioned for him to sit. "The wards are fine. Now, why don't you tell me what that fish said?"

Michael nodded and fell onto the couch, adjusting himself

into a position that was a little more comfortable. "Nothing useful. Just a riddle about finding someone who had been to Neverland before."

"Which is you."

Michael shook his head. "It said this person was Peter's enemy."

Vanessa looked back into the woods and paled a little. "You don't think it meant the crocodile, do you?"

Michael thought for a second. With the power of the dragon's-blood potion, he should have been able to communicate with the creature, but it hadn't seemed very willing to do so. He doubted a future encounter would change that. After a few seconds, he shook his head. "It doesn't fit. They weren't really enemies. It's more like they weren't friends. The only ones who were really his enemies were the pirates, and most of them died in Neverland. Unless you happen to know where one is, I'm at a loss."

"Most?" Vanessa pursed her lips. "Pirates. I think I've heard something. Let me get in touch with my sources."

Michael nodded, then got up to look through the supplies in the safe house. Aside from the food, the house hadn't been restocked in a while, but he did find shoes that fit, as well as a bit of D'Artagnan's healing salve, which he used on his feet, feeling immediately relieved. Although he was full of nervous energy, he decided to try getting some rest. There were half a dozen sleeping quarters, each little more than a bed in a small room. The bed he chose was spartan, but the mattress was soft. As soon as his head hit the pillow, the weight of the day caught up with him and he drifted off to sleep.

AN ODD BLUE LIGHT FILLED THE AREA, SHIFTING AND RIP-pling against a ceiling covered in stalactites. The smell of mold

and salt hung heavy in the air, and the wet wall reflected torchlight, filling the cavern with an eerie illumination. On a worn
stone floor lay a boy in chains. He wore green clothes and an
odd hat, though many of his garments sported rips and tears.
Michael walked around him, feeling nothing but contempt until he could look down on the boy's face. Peter's eyes were as
blue as the summer sky.

"Where did you send it?" a voice that sounded like Michael,
yet was not, asked.

Peter blinked at him and smirked, looking as confident as if
he had been free and his captor in chains. "Nowhere. It just got
away from me. It does that sometimes."

"Come now. We used to be friends. You can tell me."

"I don't know where it went." He gave a boyish smile. "Why
don't you send yours to find it?"

Michael lifted his hand to strike the boy, though he had a
feeling it would pass right through him, as if his hand lacked
the solidity to land the blow. Still, that would cause harm, too.
Who was this boy that he should so insult him, this child who
would never be anything more?

Peter met his gaze and continued to smile. "I know you're
there."

He felt himself scowl. "I've been here for days."

"I wasn't talking to you. I guess it worked then. I was worried you'd grown up too much."

"What worked? Who are you talking to?"

"You should hurry up and get here. I don't think any of the
others will come, not even her, but you can find people to help
you here."

Peter's head whipped back as Michael's hand passed through
his face. Ecstasy pulsed through Michael as a little more of
Peter's life force was drained away. He felt himself grow stronger, more solid. Peter recovered from the blow almost instantly,

seeming completely unaffected, though he was undoubtedly weaker.

Michael growled, "Answer me when I talk to you."

"I still don't know why he's doing this. Be careful. It could be a trap. I wish I could send you more help, but I've done all I can. The rest will have to come from you."

Michael loomed over Peter, casting an ominous shadow. Blue lights danced across Peter's face, and it was only then that Michael realized Peter lacked a shadow of his own. Things began to come together in his mind, and once again, Peter smiled. If the boy had been able to, Michael was sure he would've been jumping up and down with joy and crowing a cry of triumph.

"Yes! Yes, now you understand! You see? You have all the help you need."

"What are you talking about, boy? Where have you sent it? *Who are you talking to?*"

The world started going dark. Michael tried to hang on to the dream or vision or whatever it was. He managed to grab something, but it felt like water, and it slipped through his fingers. Sight faded, though Peter's final words came through as barely a squeak.

"Help me."

* * *

CHAPTER 6

Michael woke gasping. His mind reeled, and for a moment, he didn't know where he was. He tried to roll out of bed, but it was narrower than he was used to. He tumbled to the wooden floor, banging his arm and tangling himself in his blankets. As he scrambled to his feet, he knocked over a nightstand. There was a loud *crack* as it hit the ground, and Michael uttered a curse. The next thing he knew, light shone through the door. He blinked and looked up at Vanessa as she stood in the doorway, the light bulb flickering above her. She had changed out of her torn dress, though the one she wore now seemed almost identical. She didn't look tired at all. For a moment, he was filled with an irrational hatred of her, but the emotion faded after a second as the grogginess of sleep wore off.

"Michael, what happened? Are you all right?"

Michael took a few seconds to catch his breath before nodding. "I'm fine. It was just a dream." He blinked several times. It had been so vivid, and it felt nothing like any dream he'd ever had. "I think it was a dream, anyway. It's not important." He looked out the window where the full moon shone down. For a second, something dark flew in front of it, and Michael suppressed a shiver. He told himself it was only a cloud. *And*

I'll keep telling myself that, he thought stubbornly. He closed his eyes and let out a deep breath. If he tried, he could almost believe that.

They went into the living room. He examined his feet, but D'Artagnan's healing salve had worked as well as it ever had for the Musketeer. They sat on the couch, though he couldn't quite get comfortable on the lumpy piece of furniture. He thought he caught the faint odor of mold, though he couldn't tell if that was from the house or a lingering memory of his dream. It had just seemed so real. He looked up. Through the windows, Michael saw only the glittering starlight.

"What time is it?" he asked.

"A few hours after midnight. I've been talking with the Lady since you fell asleep."

Michael rubbed at his eyes, wishing the dream would fade, but it remained vivid in his mind. Finally, he looked up at Vanessa. "Is there anything I should know?"

"Most of it was making plans. She and the Wizard detected a hole in reality in the catacombs. She said something big came into this world. She couldn't tell its origin, but I think it's safe to say that was Neverland."

Michael nodded. "The crocodile. It wanted to keep the Knights out of Neverland."

Vanessa rolled her eyes. "To keep a Knight who was a personal friend to Maponos and who's been to Neverland already out of it, you mean. I'm not sure you can go there deliberately unless you've already been."

Michael started to shake his head but paused. He considered for a few seconds before allowing himself just the tiniest hint of a nod. Rather than pursue that line of questioning, he grabbed for whatever distraction he could think of. "Have you decided what we're going to do today?"

Vanessa nodded and gave him a curious smile. "That I can

help you with. The fates are on your side, it seems. He's in town—not far from here, in fact. Put on your shoes."

"Now?"

"No time like the present."

"Won't whoever you're talking about be asleep?"

"Maybe," she said with an air of smug mystery, but left it at that.

As soon as he was set, she led him out of the house. She walked down the street, her stride so casual Michael might have thought it was the middle of the day if the sky hadn't told him otherwise.

He moved in close to her and spoke softly. "I'm still confused. Who is in town?"

She grinned and pitched her voice low. "You said you needed a pirate. I found one, one who claims to be the only man James Hook ever feared."

"Unless we're going to talk to the crocodile—"

"Just because he claims it doesn't mean it was true. Anyway, I know Hook wasn't a native to Neverland, so it could be someone who knew him before . . ."

Michael was already shaking his head. A mix of excitement and dread had started to form in the pit of his stomach. "No one ages in Neverland, not even those who went there as adults. Hook was Blackbeard's bo'sun before he went, and that was over two hundred years ago. Anyone who knew him before he left is long dead. If this person actually knew Hook, he had to have known him in Neverland. That means he crossed over at some point, and as far as I know, none of the pirates used fairy dust. So who is he? And where has he been hiding?"

THE "WHERE" TURNED OUT TO BE A PUB THAT VANESSA LED him to, a sleepy little place, the kind that one would walk by without even noticing. Michael didn't even see the name as he entered. The wooden floor creaked under his weight. The place smelled of old beer and stale bread. The door didn't quite manage to keep out the chill of the night air. In spite of the law requiring that places like this be closed at such a late hour, the pub bristled with business. It also seemed to cater to a rougher sort. As soon as he and Vanessa entered, they drew half a dozen pairs of eyes. The men examined them and just as quickly dismissed them, though a few leered at Vanessa. For her part, she carried a calmness about her and stood with the confidence of one who was truly dangerous in her own right.

Michael doubted these men would see that. Which would mean it was on them if they decided to find out.

"I've faced trolls that weren't this unpleasant."

"Me too," he said in all seriousness. "Vanessa—who is this pirate?"

Vanessa scanned the room. "He gives a different name every time, but it's always the same person. He'll tell tales to anyone who will buy him a drink or a bite to eat. He has a face like leather and a pot belly."

Michael sniffed. He couldn't help but look down on those around him. "That sounds like every man here."

They approached the bar. The bartender looked up from the conversation he was having with a pair of rough-faced men, which was saying something in this place. He eyed them for a second, his gaze lingering longer on Vanessa, before returning to his conversation. Michael stiffened, but Vanessa put a hand on his shoulder. She pitched her voice low so only he could hear.

"For a train conductor, you're not very well acquainted with the average working man."

"Blame it on my father. He never approved of 'average.'"

"Don't worry about the barkeeper. I doubt he would answer

any questions anyway. What we're looking for shouldn't be hard to find."

"What if we wanted a drink?"

"Do you?" she asked, incredulous.

He looked at the filthy mugs the men were drinking out of, and the equally dirty rag the barman was using to "clean" another glass. "Not really."

She nodded, and they started walking through the establishment. It wasn't large, and in under a minute they had reached the other end, finding nothing. They were about to give up when a man who was alone at a table, asleep or drunk, snorted, and the words *Jolly Roger* escaped his lips. Michael froze and stared at him. He was a portly fellow, and the past two decades had not been kind to him. What little remained of his hair was stark white, and his leathery face, dominated by a too-large nose, had obviously seen too many days at sea and even more days at gin or ale. Michael motioned to Vanessa, and the pair sat down across from the old pirate. As soon as they settled in, the man stirred and looked up at them. His eyes were red, and he blinked several times to clear his vision, even as he adjusted his spectacles. There was no mistaking those eyes, though a part of Michael refused to believe it. He cleared his throat, and was torn between wanting to be wrong and hoping Vanessa was right.

"Do I know you, lad?" the man asked.

The sound of his voice washed away all of Michael's doubts. He knew this man, or at least he had known him, though he'd only been four at the time.

"I need to talk to you, Mister Smee."

CHAPTER 7

* * *

Color drained from the man's face, and his words tumbled over each other. "Smee? I know no Smee." Yet everything about the way he said it betrayed him. He looked around, his eyes darting from one end of the room to another, and his voice rose in pitch as he spoke. "I'm sorry. I seem to have fallen asleep. Oh look, it's nearly morning. I need to go. Things to do, you know."

He stood up so fast his chair fell over. Smee squeaked and looked at it for a second before taking a step toward the door. He was shaking, though whether that was from fear or from too much drink, Michael had no idea. He didn't much care, either. Vanessa moved behind Smee and put a hand on his shoulder. He looked up at her and seemed to take comfort in her calm expression.

"Sit down, Smee," Michael said, pouring every ounce of authority he could into his voice.

If the old pirate hadn't been befuddled, it might not have worked, but Smee paled even more. He gulped and slowly picked up his chair. He sank into it with a look of surrender on his face.

"You've been telling stories," Michael said.

"Don't know what you're talking about," he muttered.

"Sure you do," he said, pointing to Smee's cup. "It's how you've kept yourself liquid, so to speak."

He looked up at Vanessa once more and again seemed to calm a little before turning to Michael. The contrast in their looks shook Smee, and almost immediately he paled and started stammering.

"Those are only stories, young master. They're not real. I'm just a poor old man trying to find his way in the world. All I have is my stories. They don't mean anything." He let out a nervous laugh. "Truth be told, they didn't even happen to me. One of my shipmates told me about them. They're only stories, though."

Michael thought he heard Smee's teeth chattering. "You and I both know that's not the case, Smee."

"I don't know why you keep calling me—"

Michael glared at him. "Because it's who you are. Smee, bo'sun to James Hook, who was bo'sun to Blackbeard himself."

Smee shook his head so hard that for a moment, Michael wondered if it would roll right off of his shoulders. "No. No, I don't know what you're talking about."

He started to rise, but Vanessa pushed him back down with a stony look. He tried to pull free, but it was like the strength had been drained out of him. Also, Vanessa was clearly stronger than Smee expected.

Michael shook his head. "If you didn't want to be found out, you should have at least changed people's names when you told these stories. But of course you couldn't, could you? No one would buy a meal for someone who was feared by some unknown pirate, would they? It had to be Hook."

Smee shook his head. "No, I . . ." He let out a long breath and his shoulders sagged. "What do you want?"

Michael leaned in and spoke softly. "We need to know how you crossed over from Neverland."

Smee looked around, but the closest couple of tables were empty. There was no one in the smoky pub who was close enough to hear. He let out a breath and fear was replaced by resignation. He nodded once. "Truth be told, I don't know. After the army attacked our ship—"

"The army?" Michael didn't bother to hide his smirk. "You mean Peter and the rest of the children."

Smee started and adjusted his spectacles. He stared at Michael more closely. "Who are you?"

Michael glared at him. "I'm the one asking the questions. What happened then? How did you get here?"

He glanced at Vanessa for a second before responding. "As I said, I don't know. I was thrown overboard. I remember floating at sea for a long time, holding on to a piece of driftwood. Eventually, I washed up on the shore of England."

"You have to know something else."

Smee shook his head and spoke softly. "I left Neverland a long time ago, lad. I don't care how I got here—I'm just glad to be home. I have no desire to return there. Not ever."

I could say the same thing, Michael thought. "How did you get there in the first place?" he said instead. "Somehow, I don't think you used fairy dust."

"Fairy dust? What do you know about it?" Smee looked at him a little closer. "You look familiar. Have we met before?"

This time it was Michael who shook his head. "No, I would remember."

"Are you sure?" Smee squinted. "There's something familiar about you."

Michael shook his head more vigorously. "No, you must be imagining it."

"But I'm not imagining that you know things you couldn't possibly—"

"Tell me about how you got to Neverland in the first place," Michael said, cutting him off. "How did you do that?"

Smee gave him a long hard look, staring into Michael's eyes so intensely that Michael had to look away. Finally, Smee let out a long breath. "Truth be told, it was much the same as how I got back here. I was on . . ." His eyes seemed far away for a second before shrugging. "I'm sorry. It's been well over a century. I don't remember what it was called, but I was on a ship very much like *Jolly Roger*. There was a storm. I got washed overboard, and the next thing I knew, I was waking up on the shores of Neverland." He chuckled. "I guess it's a good thing the mermaids didn't get me on my way in." Then, as if realizing what exactly he was laughing about, his face turned a little green. "Turn away from this path. Only a fool tries to get to Neverland without Pan's permission, and no one but a child has ever gotten that permission."

"Peter's gone missing." The words were out of Michael's mouth before he realized he'd spoken. Vanessa glared at him sharply, even as Smee squinted and adjusted his spectacles. Then, his jaw dropped, and his eyes went wide. He started shaking again.

"I do know you!" The cry brought silence over the pub. Those few who hadn't been staring at them before had their gazes locked on the trio now. Smee didn't seem to notice, but Vanessa's hand went to her weapon. She met Michael's eyes and sighed. That would draw too much attention. She left the gun alone, but angled her chair slightly so she could get up smoothly. She was obviously ready for a fight.

"You were one of them, weren't you?" Smee continued. "One of the Lost Boys."

After a second, Michael nodded. "I guess I was."

"Did you come for your revenge, then?" The old pirate's voice was barely above a whisper.

Michael stared at him for several seconds, struck silent not only by Smee's fear of him but also by the old man's resignation to his fate. Finally, he shook his head. "That was a long time ago, Smee, and it was more a story than real life. You were the villain. I was the hero." He let out a bark of laughter. "Okay, Hook was the villain and Peter was the hero. We were little more than side characters."

Smee shook his head. "I don't want to be the villain again. I want nothing to do with that place."

"This isn't a story, and I'm not asking you to go back. All I want is information. Do you know where Peter is? Do you know how to get back to Neverland?"

Smee stared down into an empty cup. "The last day I saw Peter Pan was the day I was thrown from the deck of the *Jolly Roger*. If you had a ship, maybe I could guide you there. Hook knew how to do it, and I think I picked up the trick of it."

Vanessa smiled. "A ship? We can get one of those."

Smee paled and shook his head. "No. Just because I *can* doesn't mean I *will*. I told you I want nothing to do with that place."

He looked up, and his eyes went wide. Relief washed over his face. Michael and Vanessa exchanged confused glances just as a deep, rumbling voice spoke.

"These people bothering you, Reggie?"

For a moment, Michael wasn't sure who the newcomer, a burly man with arms like tree trunks, was talking to, but then Smee stood up, wiping sweat from his brow. All trace of fear was gone. "Not at all, Lance. Actually, I was just leaving."

Michael grabbed his arm. "We're not done yet."

"Oh, I think you are," Lance said.

Michael looked around. As before, every eye was on them

now, but this time every patron seemed poised for violence. Even as a pirate, Smee had always been a genial man. Michael had almost liked him. All of the Lost Boys had, but apparently, that part of his personality had changed. Smee gave Michael a wicked grin, no doubt having finally realized that he, not they, had the advantage here.

Vanessa got Michael's attention and shook her head. "Let him go."

"But—"

"Let him go," Vanessa said again. "There's nothing else we can accomplish here."

Lance cracked his knuckles. "Listen to your lady friend. Trust me, you don't want to bother Old Reggie."

Michael's muscles tensed, but he relaxed after a second and let out a long breath. Vanessa was right. They couldn't exactly make Smee help them, at least not like this. "Fine. We should go, too."

"No!" Smee cried out. He took a deep breath. "No, they said if I didn't do what they say, they'd find me outside and teach me a lesson."

"What?" Vanessa asked, seemingly incredulous that the old pirate would lie. "We said nothing of the kind."

Some of the men actually seemed to growl.

"So you're calling Reggie a liar," Lance said. "We don't take it kindly when an outsider attacks one of our own."

"Why are you doing this?" Michael asked.

Smee started to walk away but looked over his shoulder before he opened the door. There was anger and hatred in his eyes. "Because we are not friends. I don't know what made you think we were." He snorted. "Pan was not my friend. I did have friends, though, back when I encountered you and the rest of the Lost Boys. But you and yours killed them and would have killed me, and you came here, trying to force me to help you. You even threatened me if I didn't. What else did you expect?

"Did you think I'd forget that, *Michael*?"

And without another word, he slammed the door as he left, and the rest of the men closed in on Michael and Vanessa.

*   *   *

CHAPTER 8

L ance swung a meaty fist, but Michael twisted out of the way and delivered a sharp jab to the man's stomach. He had been a field operative when he'd been with the Knights, and a part of his training had been the ability to defend himself in combat. Still, he had been out of practice for a long time, and hitting this man was like punching a brick wall. Pain shot up his arm. Michael pulled back just as another fist crashed into the side of his head. He tasted blood, and the next thing he knew, he was on the ground and the room was spinning.

Vanessa seemed to be faring better than him, her opponents obviously having underestimated her. The Knight had already knocked down one assailant and was holding off two others with a stout cudgel, though Michael had no idea where she'd gotten it. As blurry as his vision was, he could still see her skills hadn't atrophied like his had. Even so, they were too badly outnumbered. In under a minute, she was on the floor next to him, though she had taken down at least three of her attackers. Someone kicked Michael's stomach then, but before they could do anything worse, the door burst open.

A trio of large men—equal to that of Lance and the rest— rushed into the pub, their faces hidden by deep hoods. Moving with the liquid grace of those used to combat far more dangerous than barroom brawls, they glided through the room, quickly incapacitating any who got in their way. A few of the patrons tried to resist, but the trio moved like a single organism, easily defending themselves against the unruly mob that came against them, and then lashing out when the opportunities presented themselves. One tore off the man that was on Michael while another helped Vanessa up. The newcomers radiated a sense of danger that even the men of the pub could detect, at least those who were still standing. Their glares parted the crowd, and the five of them strode out of the pub without looking back.

The city had just started to come alive in the light of the rising sun. Michael had to lean against a wall to remain standing, and they were attracting more than a little attention. There was nothing to do about that now, though.

"Gawains?" he asked.

One of their rescuers, a tall man with the blond hair and beard that made him look almost exactly like a Viking, nodded. "Captain Glover, of the Order of Gawain, at your service."

Michael eyed Vanessa. "You called for reinforcements?"

"We just ran from a magical crocodile only to come after a former pirate to figure out how to get to the realm of a lost god. Of course I called for reinforcements. Are you upset that I did?"

"*I'm* upset you went by yourselves," the captain said before Michael could answer. "You should've waited for us before you went in."

"We were trying to remain inconspicuous." And the Gawains, the combat arm of the Knights, were anything but that.

Glover looked to the pub door. It hadn't closed all the way, and many of the people inside were staring at them. He gave Vanessa a pointed look. "Good job."

Vanessa ignored the jibe. "I don't suppose you saw the man who left just before that whole thing started."

Glover eyed his companions. One of them, a silver-haired man whose scars spoke of a lifetime of fighting, waved down the street. "That way."

Michael struggled to rise, but pain held him down. He winced. "We have to go after him."

Glover shook his head. "You're in no condition to go after anyone." He motioned to the silver-haired man. "Bradford, go after him. Seize him if you can do it without being noticed."

The big man nodded and ghosted down the street, making no more noise than a shadow. Michael stared after him for a second, feeling an unreasonable jealousy that Bradford would be the one to catch Smee. Almost immediately, he suppressed the emotion. He hadn't wanted to be a part of this in the first place. Maybe if the Gawain found him, Michael could return to his life. His current condition should be reason enough for that.

He chuckled and looked at Vanessa. "I guess I'm off the assignment."

Captain Glover snorted. "Last I checked, Mister Darling, you had left the Knights of the Round. You were never officially *on* assignment." Michael nodded, but the Gawain went on: "Nothing has changed about your situation. Besides, from what I've heard about you, you've never been one to let a few wounds stop you from doing what needed to be done. I have some of D'Artagnan's healing salve. That should make you good as new."

Michael clenched his teeth and refused the proffered container. "Not anymore. I'm done with that."

"With healing lotion?" Vanessa asked. "You took some last night."

"With being a Knight."

"People don't change that much, Michael," Vanessa said as she took the salve from Glover.

Michael didn't look at her. "Sometimes they change. Sometimes life changes them."

"Then grow up and realize you're in this," she snapped. They glowered at each other before Glover politely coughed.

"Where do you want to go?" the Gawain asked, waving at a car parked nearby. "We can take you home, if you desire. Let you regroup."

Michael nodded, but Vanessa pursed her lips. "Are you sure that's the best idea?"

"Can you think of a better one?"

"I just think we've been going about this the wrong way."

"What do you mean?"

She shrugged. "Well, anyone could talk to a fish or track down Smee. If that was all the Court wanted, they would have asked you a few questions and then sent you on your way. That's not why they summoned you."

"Then what do you think I should do?"

"They wanted you because you've been to Neverland, and you knew Peter Pan. Maybe we should pursue that line of reasoning."

"How exactly should we do that? We have no fairy dust and—"

Vanessa gave him a level look that stole his words. Michael suppressed a shiver and was shaking his head before he realized what he was doing. "No. I'm not dragging her into this."

"Do you really think you should keep this from her? She was closer to him than anyone."

"She was also never a Knight."

"Only because she turned us down."

Michael stiffened. "She made her choice, and she was wiser than I was."

"Who are you two talking about?" Glover asked.

For a moment, Michael refused to answer, but the hard look in Vanessa's eyes said that if Michael didn't speak, she would.

In spite of all they had been through, Vanessa was a Knight first and a friend second. Michael sighed. He wasn't sure if Vanessa would approach her without him, but she *would* tell the Knights. Then they would send someone. He should spare her that if he could.

"I need to speak to my sister, Wendy."

The Gawain nodded. "I can have you at her home in a few hours."

Michael started to nod, not really surprised that the Knight knew where Wendy lived. He paused, remembering the date and realizing what time they would be arriving.

"She won't be at home," he said. "At least not at first. Today is April fifth. Do you know where her husband is?"

The big man nodded without a moment's hesitation. He offered Michael an arm and helped him to the car. "Ah yes. Of course. I should have considered that." He opened the door for Michael and helped him in. Vanessa sat in the seat beside him, and the Gawain got in. "I will have you at the graveyard in a few hours."

CHAPTER 9

*   *   *

Vanessa applied the salve to Michael's wounds as the Gawain captain pulled away, and they began the long drive back to London. Her own wounds were much less extensive, and she didn't require nearly as much care as he did. Michael mumbled a thanks and stared into the night, wondering if he had made a mistake agreeing to this mission.

The moon gave the fog an eerie glow. As they drove past barely visible buildings, he thought he could see figures in the mist, which he imagined as shadows from his own past. When he'd been a full member of the Knights, he had kept his everyday life separate from his missions and adventures, but now they were going to see Wendy, and the barriers he'd erected between his lives were about to come crashing down.

He hadn't gotten much sleep the night before, and the weight of the past couple of hours settled down on him. He drifted off before they had gone a few miles.

Swirls of black smoke surrounded him. He wasn't sure how he distinguished them from actual darkness, but he knew there was a difference, and a terrible one. Someone, a boy who was not a boy, cried out. Michael thought he should recognize the voice, but the identity escaped him. It cried out again, and the sound was like a knife in his heart.

He woke, gasping, as the car rolled into London. His neck was cramped from having slept in such an awkward position, but he still felt worlds better, or at least his body did. His mind couldn't help but focus on the dream.

Vanessa saw the look in his eyes. "Another nightmare?" she asked.

Michael almost denied it before thinking better of it. "A boy who was not a boy consumed by darkness."

Neither said what both were thinking. If adults, even adults who had been close to Peter, were having the dream, then things had to be worse than the Court expected. He tried not to think about that as he looked out the window. The morning mist had practically burned away by the time they arrived at the graveyard, but enough of it remained to give the place an eerie look. Only a few people were there, gliding through the rows like ghosts. Michael took a moment to make sure they weren't *actual* ghosts before dismissing Captain Glover. The Gawain tried to argue, but relented when Vanessa nodded. They were close enough to Wendy's house that they would be able to walk, and he doubted she would want the company of strangers after a morning spent here.

Besides, what he was about to tell her was strange enough.

Once the captain was gone, Michael entered the cemetery, leaving Vanessa to wait for him. He stopped by a pair of tombs to pay his respects to his parents. The grave markers were well kept, and each bore fresh flowers—signs Wendy had probably stopped here first. The mist seemed to curl around them. He stood in silence for several seconds. Though they had adopted the Lost Boys when Michael, Wendy, and John had returned from Neverland, they had never really been able to accept where they had come from. At least, Michael didn't think they had. He had never been sure just how much they knew, not that any of that mattered anymore. What had mattered was that they were good parents, both to their own children and to the children who'd become his new brothers. And now they were gone.

"I miss you." His voice was so soft a breeze could've swallowed it up. He wiped away a tear before continuing on.

It took him a while to find the proper spot. Though he had gone to William Harden's funeral, he hadn't been back to this cemetery since. Wendy stood over her husband's grave like a specter. He approached her silently, not wanting to disturb her, but as he neared she looked up at him with tears in her eyes and a sad smile on her lips. That sent a pang of pain through Michael. It had been seven years since William had been killed. In the final days of the Great War, his ship had gone down with all hands. There hadn't even been a body, and they'd buried an empty casket. Wendy obviously still felt the loss just as keenly as she had the day a naval officer had brought her the news, and Michael regretted that he hadn't been there for her more often. He had been selfish with his own haunted memories, and right now he realized how bad a brother he truly was.

He stood next to her for a long time, neither saying anything.

"A few more months, Michael. If he had only lived a few more months, he could have come home."

"I know," he said as he drew her into an embrace. "I'm sorry." And suddenly everything between them was right again.

Just because I've been a bad brother, it doesn't mean Wendy was ever anything but the best sister.

She sniffed and looked him up and down, her eyes widening slightly at the sight of his bandages. "You've obviously had a rough day."

He grinned. "Actually, today has been rather mild. Yesterday, on the other hand, was one for the history books. Have you seen Mother and Father yet?"

She nodded. "I went to see them before I spoke to Will. It never seemed right to do it the other way around."

Michael smiled and held her tight. "Ever the proper lady, Wendy."

She let out a musical laugh that sounded out of place amidst all the gloom, and they held each other for several seconds before she pulled back and wiped away her tears.

"You always did find clever ways of diverting questions," she said.

"You didn't ask a question," he said as he glanced around. The fog was thinner now, but it could still be concealing danger. Even with Vanessa out there, he didn't want to take any chances. "Anyway, this isn't really the best place to be talking about things like that."

She gave him a slow nod. "Will you walk me back home?"

"Of course, dear sister."

She gave him a gentle shove. "I've asked you not to call me that."

He laughed and took her arm but then paused. He could just make out Vanessa's outline in the fading mist. Wendy followed his gaze, and her expression darkened.

"Michael, I've already told them no. My answer hasn't changed."

"How did you—" He shook his head. "No, never mind. That's not why she's here. But really, we shouldn't talk about it out in the open."

She opened her mouth to speak but closed it as Vanessa approached. She inclined her head toward Wendy.

"Miss Darling."

Wendy stiffed. "Harden. Not Darling."

Vanessa smiled. "It's Wendy Darling whom we came to see."

"Then, you, Miss, are out of luck," Wendy replied, not smiling at all.

Before this could devolve even further, something caught Michael's attention out of the corner of his eye. He thought it was some kind of figure darting from shadow to shadow, but when he looked, there was nothing.

"We need to leave."

Vanessa followed his gaze. She stared into the darkness for nearly a full minute before glancing at Michael and nodding. After all they had been through, neither of them were eager to take chances. She motioned for them to go first, and she fell into step behind them.

Wendy walked faster than she normally did—at least, faster than Michael remembered. She wasn't panicked, though. She had never been trained as a Knight, but she had seen more than most at an age when those who would grow up to be Knights still hadn't mastered their multiplication tables—being friends with Peter and the Lost Boys will do that to a girl. Still, when they arrived at her home, the same home Michael had grown up in, she was visibly relieved. She fumbled with her key for a second before opening the door. She dismissed the woman who'd been watching her daughter and directed Michael to sit on the couch. Vanessa tried to speak up, but Wendy shushed her. The incredulous look on Vanessa's face almost made Michael laugh. Vanessa might have an iron will, but that was nothing compared to Wendy.

The couch Michael sat on was a hard and lumpy piece of furniture, but it had belonged to their parents, and Wendy didn't have the heart to get rid of it. Without saying a word, she disappeared down the hall, then returned with rags and clean bandages. She hummed as she began unwrapping his wounds.

"They don't really need to be changed," he said. "They're still fairly new, and we used—"

"Hush," she said as she peeled back a bandage on his arm. "Indulge an old navy nurse."

"With respect," Vanessa said, stepping forward, "we really do have things we need to discuss."

"And I have bandages to change," Wendy said without looking up. There was a moment of hesitation. "Or maybe I don't."

He looked down at his arm, but it was completely healed. Wendy looked like she was about to say something but she looked from Michael to Vanessa. Her shoulders sagged in resignation as she removed the rest of the bandages. By the time she was finished, unshed tears had welled in her eyes.

"Wendy . . ."

"I'm sorry," she said. "I always get like this when I go see Will." She sniffed. "Are you going to tell me what happened to you, or shall I guess?" She glanced over her shoulder at Vanessa before returning her attention to him. He opened his mouth to speak, but she cut him off. "You went out drinking with the men from the train yard, didn't you? And you got in a fight."

He drew back. "What? No, of course not."

She gave him a small smile. "Michael, you don't really have to hide that from me. You're more than old enough to do as you wish."

Vanessa chuckled, and Michael felt his face heat up. "Wendy, it's nothing like that."

His sister shook her head, and for a moment Michael thought she didn't believe him. After a few seconds, though, she sighed. "I was just hoping it was something mundane—but if it was, she wouldn't be here, would she? The Knights of the Round, then?"

Michael nodded. "I'm afraid so."

"Not as afraid as I am, for you." She gave him a level look. "Michael, they were your whole life until you decided to leave them. But since then, it's like you have nothing left to live for. Is the thrill worth it?"

"It's not about the thrill. They asked—"

"—and you couldn't say no, Michael. Because you're so wrapped up in duty. When was the last time you had any fun?"

"Wendy, life is about more than fun, at least life as an adult is."

She nodded. "But it's not good to neglect it entirely. You don't have to be so grown up all the time. You used to understand that. So did the others, but you never forgot our little adventure. Why did you change so much?"

He stiffened, knowing what she was asking, but not wanting to go into it. It had been one of the reasons he had avoided her so much in the past few years. Eventually, he realized he could use her question as an opening. "That's actually part of why I'm here. The Knights . . ." He floundered, unsure of how to begin.

Vanessa broke in. "Peter Pan has gone missing."

Wendy gave him a placating smile before turning to Vanessa with a raised eyebrow. "Peter took my daughter to Neverland just last summer. He hasn't been gone long enough for anyone to know if he's missing. He could be gone for the next twenty years, and it still wouldn't be long enough."

Almost on cue, "Uncle Michael!" rang out in a squealing, high-pitched voice as a girl, only eight years old, leaped onto him.

He winced at her weight, so much more than the last time he'd seen her. Of course, it had been a long time. Still, he ignored the sensation as the little girl hugged him tightly, her soft brown hair feeling like silk against his skin. She smelled like flowers.

Wendy was trying and failing to hide a smile. "Jane, get off of him. Give him a chance to breathe."

"It's fine," Michael said as he hugged the girl tighter. "She's so ugly that probably no one ever hugs her. I'm just trying to be nice."

Jane giggled. "You're the ugly one."

Wendy laughed. "Someone obviously missed you."

"I missed you so much," Jane said in a whisper.

"I missed you, too," he said, briefly wondering if Wendy was right about him being too grown up. He had to be, of course. When he hadn't been, others paid the price, but he still envied the little girl's simple joy. He cleared his throat and once again wondered what danger he was putting them in. He glanced at Vanessa, who was standing against a wall, visibly uncomfortable. She could face down an entire crypt of wraiths, but this simple domestic scene unsettled her. She was part of another world, a dangerous one. He'd been part of it once, and he wouldn't bring it into Wendy's house. "This was a bad idea. I should go."

Yet Jane hugged him tighter, and Wendy shook her head, though she looked at Vanessa before she responded. "Don't be ridiculous. You've only just arrived, and I'm sure Jane would enjoy spending time with her favorite uncle."

"Nibs is my favorite," Jane said, "but you're the second."

Wendy had a slightly horrified look on her face, but Michael laughed. Even Vanessa cracked a smile. "I understand that. Nibs is my favorite, too." He winked at Wendy, who glared at him, but her expression softened after a while.

"Why don't you stay for lunch?" She hesitated. "Both of you."

He looked down at the pale-faced little girl. Her brown eyes had gone wide and she was nodding vigorously. He smiled. "Well, with such an offer, how could we refuse?"

*   *   *

CHAPTER 10

L unch consisted of a bowl of soup and a plate of chilled fruit. The soup had been spiced just right, and Michael enjoyed both the peppery taste and the feel of it going down his throat. He had eaten precious little the day before, and the meal filled him with a warmth that he hadn't realized he was missing. Vanessa ate in silence. Jane had initially been intimidated by the stranger but now seemed to have forgotten her and was practically bouncing in her chair across from Michael as she popped pieces of fruit into her mouth. Wendy scolded her and told her to use her fork, but the little girl was too distracted by the presence of her uncle. Eventually, Wendy surrendered with a sigh of gentle resignation.

"Can you tell me about the time you went with Peter?" Jane asked through a mouth full of fruit.

"I don't think that's a story for children," Vanessa said.

"I don't think it's a story for anyone else," Wendy said wryly. "My daughter has been to Neverland, Vanessa, and more than once."

Vanessa sat up straight. "I'm not accustomed to speaking about these things, especially not with children." She let out a long breath. "I suppose I should expect as much from a veiled family."

"A what?" Wendy asked.

"Veiled," Michael said. "Those who came to the mystical when they were children and never forgot that it was there. Those who never had to pierce the veil of the ordinary world to learn that it exists."

"Uncle Michael . . ." Jane drew out his name, and he looked from the little girl to his sister.

Wendy only shrugged. "You may as well. You're the only one who will talk to her about it."

Jane nodded. "Mom says the others got too grown up. They don't remember anymore, not even Nibs."

"Well, I'm sure you've heard that story more than once. Your mother was there the whole time I was, and more besides."

"But I haven't heard *you* tell it."

It was sound child logic, and Wendy sighed. "Just tell her. She won't stop pestering you—and us—until you do."

Still, Michael hesitated, but when he saw the look on Jane's face, his resistance melted away. "Well, it started when Peter came into our room."

"Actually, it started before that," Wendy said. "Peter's shadow came in, and he followed it. I had to sew it back onto him."

Michael shivered. "Yes, that's right."

Jane rolled her eyes. "Mother, I've already heard you tell the story. I want to hear Uncle Michael."

Wendy smiled. "All right. I'm sorry. Go ahead, Michael."

Michael inclined his head and went on with the story. "After your mother sewed his shadow back on, he took us to Neverland. Do you know where Neverland actually is?"

Without hesitation, Jane pointed out a window to the sky beyond. Both Michael and Wendy laughed. "How well can you read a map, Jane?"

"They haven't taught us that in school," Jane said, frowning.

"Right. Now remember that Peter never *went* to school. He

never learned how to read a map, either. So even though he told us that Neverland was the second star to the right and straight on until morning, that wasn't really true—such directions didn't make any sense. Besides, there's no way to fly there on your own, even if you know the way. We couldn't have found it if we didn't have a guide, and even then, it took days or weeks."

"Which one?" Jane asked. "Days or weeks?"

Michael and Wendy exchanged glances and smiled, remembering that night, when they had been children and everything seemed possible. It felt like it had happened to another person. "It's hard to say," he said. "I don't think time works the same way when you're flying."

He went on to tell the story of their journey to Neverland. He spoke of their many encounters with Tiger Lily and her tribe of natives who lived on the island, as well as the final battle with Hook and his pirates aboard the *Jolly Roger*. Strangely enough, Vanessa seemed as enthralled as Jane was.

Though Wendy's daughter must've heard that story a hundred times, she now looked at Michael and Wendy with something very close to awe. Michael reached across the table and ruffled her hair.

"What about you?" Michael said. "Your mother tells me you've been to Neverland a few times. Surely, you're not going to tell me that you've been there and not had a single adventure."

She started to speak but paused after a second. She glanced at Wendy before sighing. "I'm not supposed to talk about that."

Wendy laughed. "That's all right, dear. Uncle Michael is an exception to that rule. You can talk to him all you want."

She opened her mouth but looked at Vanessa. Michael smiled. "It's okay. You can tell her, too. She's never been, though, and she's really jealous that you have."

Jane giggled and went on, heedless of the darkening expression on Vanessa's face. She told them about her adventures in parts of Neverland he and Wendy had never been to. There was apparently even a dark version of the magical island that one could get to only by going underground, where ghosts and gremlins lived.

"I had no idea Neverland had an Underworld," Michael said. He gave Wendy a look of mock reproach. "And you let Peter take her there?"

Wendy brought her hand to her chest and looked away, pretending to be offended. "Well, I need to give that boy a stern talking-to." She turned back to them and laughed. "Of course, if I did, he would forget about it five minutes after the talk was completed and then take her anyway. I don't think anything could hurt her while Peter was with her—and to be fair, I didn't know about it until well after it had already happened."

Michael grinned. "I suspect you're right."

Vanessa cleared her throat, and gave him a look that said all that was needed, the reason they were here: Peter Pan was missing, and no amount of reminiscing was going to help find him.

The joviality drained out of Wendy's expression when she saw the look on Vanessa's face. "Oh, I see. Jane, why don't you go upstairs and play with your dolls?"

"But Uncle Michael is here."

"I promise I won't leave until I say goodbye, but I need to talk to your mother."

The hurt expression on the little girl's face said that she hadn't understood what he meant at all. She sulked as she walked up the stairs, looking as if every step were a monumental struggle. After a few seconds, Michael started to speak, but Wendy lifted a hand.

"Young lady, I had better not find you listening at the top of the stairs," she said in a loud voice.

A few seconds later there was the sound of a door closing, and Wendy smiled. "I swear, she's gotten up to so much mischief since Peter came into her life. She seems a lot happier, though, so I can't really complain. Besides, how many people have seen what she has?"

"Not many," Michael said.

"Now, why don't you tell me what has you looking like death?"

* * *

CHAPTER 11

W"e already told you," Michael said. "Peter's missing."

Wendy shook her head. "And I already told you, Michael, that you're overreacting. When he came here two years ago, he came for me. He hadn't noticed the passing of two entire decades. He came back for Jane last year. A single year isn't long enough for anyone to know for certain."

"The Knights are sure," Vanessa said. "We watch for things like this. The link from this world to Neverland is weak, and it could break at any moment. Peter Pan is nowhere to be found."

"Has Jane spoken to you of nightmares?" Michael asked.

Wendy hesitated for a second. "A few, but children have nightmares."

Vanessa glared at him, but he continued: "Nightmares about a boy who is not a boy consumed by darkness?"

"A boy who is not a boy? She . . . she used that exact phrase."

"So have children all over the world," Michael said. "Have *you* had the dream?"

Wendy nodded after a second. "Last night. I thought it was only because of what Jane had told me."

"You know who he is, don't you? The boy who is not a boy?"

Again, Wendy hesitated. Then, "Peter." The name was barely above a whisper, as if it had been dragged out of her.

Michael glanced to the stairs Jane had gone up. There was the barest hint of movement. He raised an eyebrow and turned back to Wendy and Vanessa. The Knight had the faint hint of a smile on her face.

"Wendy," Vanessa said, "you said Jane seemed happier since she met him. What if she lost that? What if every child all over the world stopped dreaming of adventure, stopped imagining what could be? What if they all became . . ."

Wendy met Vanessa's eyes before turning to Michael. "Like him?"

Michael drew back, his amusement vanishing. His voice quavered a little but steadied quickly. "Wendy, that's hardly fair. We all have to grow up sometime. You did."

"I did," she said, "but I never pretended that I wasn't a child first. That I didn't have the adventures I had. For you, it might as well have been someone else that went to Neverland. It's been years since I've seen you laugh as much as you did a little while ago, but you've already closed up again." She looked at Vanessa and gave a smile that somehow conveyed a tinge of remorse. "You're not much better."

Vanessa sat up straight. "Excuse me?"

Wendy shrugged. "You. The Knights. However you came to this life, you've all rediscovered what it meant to be a child. That's all well and good." She glanced at Michael. "A lot of people could benefit from that, but you're hoarding it, trying to keep it even from children."

"That's not—"

"She has a point." Michael's voice was soft. "I left the Knights for a reason. I wanted to get away from all the mystery. From . . ."

From losing a friend and not even being able to mourn because his whole life was a secret.

"But you can't, can you? It's a part of you, no matter how much you wish it weren't. That little boy is still a part of you."

"I'm not him anymore, Wendy. I haven't been him for a long time. But I couldn't turn down this mission. I wasn't as close to Peter as you were, but he was still my friend."

"So you want to go to Neverland to help him."

Michael stood up and walked toward a window. A crow perched on a nearby lamppost. It seemed to look at Michael before cawing and flying to the east. He sighed. Somewhere in that direction lay the way to Neverland.

"It's not a matter of wanting. I *need* to get there," Michael said, "or at least find a way to get one of the Knights there."

"Why do you need to, then?"

But he couldn't answer that. Not yet, not without lying. And he wouldn't lie to Wendy.

Wendy looked into his eyes for a second, expectant—then disappointed. She shook her head. "No, it would never work."

Michael was about to argue, but the look on Wendy's face stopped him. She spoke with a certainty that he lacked. "What do you mean?"

"You want to save Peter, but you're still trying to hide from the magic of what it means to be a child. You can't do that. You can't be grown-up and go to a place that isn't for grown-ups."

"Hook did," Michael said. "So did the pirates."

"Is that how you want to go there? Like the pirates?"

"Wendy, I'll go there any way I can. We even found Smee drunk in a pub and tried to get him to help."

"I take it that didn't work out too well."

He motioned to the bandages that Wendy had unwrapped. "Those weren't just for decorations. I had cuts and bruises all over."

Her hand went to his face, and though it didn't hurt anymore, he shied away from her touch. She looked to Vanessa and pursed her lips before shaking her head. "I'm not sure you can go to Neverland like that and be a hero."

"I'm not trying to be a hero."

"No, you're just trying to save Peter, who from what you've told me is a god, from whatever force has imprisoned him in his own realm." She looked around with exaggerated motions. "You know, I believe I have Father's dictionary around here. Perhaps you can look up the definition of the word 'hero' for me."

Michael gave her a level stare. "That's not the point, and you know it."

Vanessa looked at him intently. "Actually, she may be right. The Lady taught me a little about the crossing between worlds. And belief has always been a major part of it."

"But I do believe—I've been there before, so I know it's real."

"I don't think that's what the Lady meant."

"It doesn't matter what she meant—she's never been there!"

"And the last time you were," Wendy said, "you were a boy. And a *hero*."

"Look, I can deal with that if I have to."

"How do you just 'deal' with becoming a hero?"

"I . . ." He stopped himself, exasperated. *Why is this word so important to them? It's just a word. I'll go to Neverland and find Peter. Who cares what my mindset is when I do it?* "Listen, do you have a way to get there or not?"

Wendy looked into his eyes for a long time before turning away. "I'm sorry. The only times I ever went to Neverland, Peter took me. Even if you had fairy dust . . ." She looked up. "You don't, do you?"

Michael shook his head. "The Knights had some, but Hook's crocodile ruined their supplies."

Wendy perked up. "Hook's crocodile?"

Vanessa shrugged. "It's been an eventful couple of days."

"Apparently," Wendy said.

He let out a long breath. "I have to do this, don't I? I can't hide from this anymore?"

"I don't think so. I'm sorry, Michael. I wish I could be more help."

He glanced at the stairs. "What about . . ."

"What do you imagine she knows that you don't?"

"You made a good point when you said it wasn't a land for grown-ups. Maybe I need someone who isn't."

Wendy sighed. "I suppose it's worth a try. I'll go get her."

Michael chuckled. "I don't think you need to do that." He raised his voice. "Isn't that right, Jane?"

Wendy scowled and shouted up the stairs. "Jane, are you up there?"

There was a squeak, and Jane poked her head out from behind a door at the top of the stairs. She looked like she was pretending to feel guilty, but the effect was spoiled by the grin on her face. "Sorry. I couldn't help myself."

Wendy glared at Michael and Vanessa. "You both knew she was there?"

Michael nodded. "Yes."

"How?"

"I'm a member of a secret society," Vanessa said, "and Michael had the same training as me. They taught us a few things about hiding. Your little mouse is very skilled, but she does have a few things to learn." She looked at Jane. "You stepped a little too heavily when you came back from opening and closing that door, and you need to work on not fidgeting when you're trying to eavesdrop."

Wendy narrowed her eyes but looked up at her daughter after a second. "You may as well come down and join us, but we're going to have a talk about this after Miss Vanessa and Uncle Michael leave."

Jane looked like she wished she could be anywhere else, but Wendy cleared her throat, and Jane meekly walked down the stairs.

Wendy glared at her. "How much did you hear?"

Jane looked to Michael, pleading for help with her soft brown eyes, but he shook his head. "I knew you were there, but it was still your choice. You have to live with the consequences." Jane opened her mouth to speak, but Michael went on. "Keep in mind, I know the answer to your mother's question, so don't try to lie about it."

Jane closed her mouth and looked like she was going to be sick. "All of it." She glanced at Michael, who nodded. She sighed. "Sorry."

Wendy turned her anger on Michael. "If you knew she was there, why didn't you tell me?"

"Maybe I want her to like me better than Nibs. Or maybe I thought this was something she needed to hear."

"And don't you think that, as her mother, I should've been the one to decide that?"

Michael raised an eyebrow. "You let her go into Neverland's Underworld with a boy who has the tendency to forget entire decades."

"And you're not Peter."

Vanessa snorted. Jane stared at her for a few seconds, a mix of nervousness and wonder in her eyes, before turning to Michael.

"Is he really a prisoner?"

"I think so, but I need to go to Neverland to find out. Do you know how I can get there?"

Jane nodded. "You need fairy dust."

"We don't have any of that. Hook's crocodile broke into our base and mixed all our dust from different kinds of fairies together. After that, the magic wasn't any good anymore."

Jane bit her lower lip and thought for a second, unperturbed by the casual discussion of magic no longer working, as if it were an everyday occurrence for her. "Well, if you don't have any fairy dust, you need to find a fairy."

Vanessa pursed her lips. "Can't argue with that logic."

"Me neither. Except I haven't seen a fairy in a long time," Michael said. "Have you?"

Vanessa shook her head, and he turned back to Jane. "Do you know where I can find one?"

Jane also shook her head, but did so violently, her braids whipping around. "They come to see me sometimes, but I never know when they'll come."

"They do?" Wendy asked. "Why have you never told me that?"

Jane shrugged. "You always told me not to talk about things like that."

Wendy's jaw dropped. Vanessa let out a curt laugh. Wendy abruptly turned to her, but the young woman seemed unperturbed. With little choice, her expression softened as she turned back to her daughter.

"Dear, you can tell *me*."

"Never mind that for now," Michael said. "Jane, do you have any fairy dust I could use?"

Again, Jane shook her head. "They don't like just giving it out, and I didn't have anywhere to go without Peter, so I never asked for any."

Wendy raised an eyebrow. "Not even to Neverland?" Michael had to admit his sister had a point—this little girl seemed like someone who wouldn't hesitate to go back to Pan's country.

"I thought about it, but it takes a long time to get to Neverland, just like you said. I didn't want to get lost."

"Smart girl," Vanessa murmured.

"Well, there's that, at least," Wendy said.

"How often do they come see you?" Michael asked.

Jane shrugged. "Sometimes every night, but sometimes they don't come back for a long time. I was seven last time I saw one."

"That's what?" Michael asked. "Six months ago?"

"Yes," Wendy said. "Is it always at night?" Jane nodded, and Wendy turned to Michael. "It's a start. It's not a guaranteed way to Neverland, especially with how long it's been, but it sounds like it's better than any other idea you've had. You and Vanessa could each take a guest room, and Jane could come get you if any fairies show up."

Jane nodded vigorously. "You could spend the night and tell me more stories about the time you went to Neverland."

Michael hesitated. "I don't know. There are things trying to stop me. I wouldn't want to put you in any more danger than I already have."

"Do you really think that if this danger has to do with Peter that we could stay out of it?"

"Maybe not," Michael said, "but that's no reason to go blindly jumping into it."

"Just stay one night, while you try to think of something else," Wendy said. "If it doesn't work out, you can look for some other way in the morning."

"It's as good a plan as any, Michael," Vanessa said. "And you know how much I hate the idea of wasting time."

Michael thought about it for a second before nodding. Though he hadn't spent much time in this house in many years, it still felt like home. He did need a place to rest, and this would work as well as any other. One night wouldn't make a difference.

Probably.

"All right. One night. But if the fairies don't come, we're leaving first thing in the morning."

* * *

CHAPTER 12

They stayed up far later than Michael had intended, but he couldn't say that bothered him. Vanessa lingered but didn't say a word. Jane was curious about every single detail. Even though she had been to Neverland more times than he and had seen things he had never imagined, she hung on every one of Michael's words. Michael, for his part, enjoyed the conversation with his niece. The simple joy with which she saw his adventures almost made him long for his days with the Knights, when such adventures had been common. He began to wonder if Vanessa had been right when she said people didn't change that much. He glanced up at her, and she smiled. He gave her a level look before returning his attention to Jane as she told him of her own adventures.

"It was covered in flowers the first time Peter took me there," Jane said. "It's how I always imagined a fairy-tale land would be, except for the Underworld. That part was scary."

"It wasn't like that for us," Michael said, "but then I never imagined flowers or a scary Underworld, and Neverland shapes itself to what you imagine. What was the Underworld like?"

"Another time," Wendy said.

Jane's eyes went wide. "But Mother—"

"It's nearly midnight, dear, and it's long past your bedtime."

Jane sniffled and headed up the stairs. When Wendy got up to go with her, she stopped. Her eyes wandered from Wendy to Michael and back again.

"I was wondering if Uncle Michael could put me to bed."

"Uncle Michael has other—"

"It's fine," Michael said. "I would enjoy it."

Wendy narrowed her eyes, but nodded and settled back onto the couch. She and Vanessa exchanged uneasy looks as Michael followed his niece upstairs. Jane nestled into her blankets easily, but as Michael was about to turn off the light, she spoke up.

"Can you tell me a bedtime story?"

Michael laughed. "Jane, what do you think we've been doing for the past couple of hours?"

She got a pouty face, and it took everything Michael had not to laugh harder. She could be absolutely adorable, and she appeared to be learning how to use that. He turned off the lights and started toward the stairs.

"You could come with us." Vanessa's voice drifted up the stairs. "They say you knew Pan better than anyone. We could use your help."

"No, I made my decision a long time ago."

"But you could do so much."

"I'm already doing a lot. I'm raising Jane."

Michael came down the stairs and the two went silent. Vanessa looked a little guilty, though Wendy didn't seemed bothered at all. He smiled and pretended he hadn't heard them.

"She really is a wonderful girl," Michael said.

Wendy nodded. "She has more than a little of her father in her." She sighed. "And Peter has certainly had his influence there. Do you really think fairies will come?"

Michael shrugged. "I have no idea. They're not exactly the most predictable creatures."

"What if they don't?"

"Then I'll find some other way," Michael said, surprised at his own certainty. "The Knights are looking for Smee. He won't be able to hide from them for long."

"He'll need a drink, if nothing else," Vanessa said.

"What about . . ." Wendy let the words hang.

He let out a breath. "I know what you said about crossing over that way. You might even be right. I don't think anyone but Peter knows for sure, but I'm not trying to be a hero, no matter what you say. Plus, I don't have very many options. If Smee provides a way, I have to take it." He hesitated. "Vanessa is right, you know. You could come with us. You and Jane both. We could have one more adventure in Neverland."

Vanessa opened her mouth to argue. Michael could practically hear her objections. She would be happy to have Wendy come, but Jane was another matter. She stopped at a look from Michael, however. He realized at that moment how much he wanted Wendy to come. Somehow, it would all be okay if she did. She was tempted. He could see the longing on her face. She had just refused Vanessa, but he knew it would be different coming from someone who had actually been to Neverland with her. After a few seconds, however, she sighed and shook her head.

"No, I don't think I could. Unlike the others, I remember what it was like to be a child, but I don't think I have it in me to be one again."

He raised an eyebrow. "And I do?"

"Michael, you weren't just reminiscing about old times. It's the whole reason you joined the Knights in the first place. You wanted to relive them. You wanted to have more adventures.

You said you left because you decided that was only for children, but I saw your eyes. Eyes that looked eerily like my own in the mirror after I had learned Will had died. Something happened, didn't it?"

Michael stared at her for a few seconds. "Was I that obvious?"

"Obvious to one who knows you. I think you need to do this to get past whatever it was."

He looked over to Vanessa. She mouthed, *Dmitri,* and his shoulders tensed. He looked to Wendy and dipped his head. "Fair point."

"As for Jane, certainly not. I have a feeling Neverland isn't safe with Peter imprisoned."

Michael nodded. "You're probably right. I keep wondering what I'll find when I finally do make it there. Even now, I can't help but picture it like it was when we were there." He grinned at her. "I can imagine what trouble John and Tootles and the others would get into without their mother."

Wendy let out a laugh. "What about you? What trouble would you get in?"

"That's the odd thing. I can't picture myself as a child, not even there. You were right about that. I don't remember what it means to be a child anymore." He sighed. "I should get some sleep. I'll have a long couple of days ahead of me if the fairies do come tonight."

Wendy's smile faded. "Promise me you'll say goodbye before you leave, regardless of whether or not the fairies come."

"Don't worry. I promise."

In spite of how anxious he was to get to Neverland, once he got to the guest room, Michael fell asleep almost instantly. He dreamed of that time, now two decades past, when he'd last visited that wondrous land. He'd been only four, but he'd battled pirates and natives in a place that seemed built according to his imagination. He'd seen wonders most would never even believe.

HE WOKE TO THE SUN SHINING THROUGH THE WINDOW. IT had risen at least an hour before, and he sat up in bed, contemplating his dreams. He'd had no concept of how much danger he'd actually been in back then. The pirates had wanted to kill him in a time when he'd been far too young to really understand what that meant. If he had, he never would have . . .

He paused in midthought and realized he was lying to himself. Maybe his four-year-old self hadn't been aware of all the perils he was in, but even if he had been, that would never have stopped him, any more than it would have any of the other Lost Boys. But time had made his adventurous spirit wane until it was little more than a withered husk—time and what had happened to Dmitri. He had thought himself perfectly content as a train engineer—and what kid wouldn't want to grow up to play with real trains?—but it was actually quite a boring job. A *safe* one. There's no adventure when your path is laid out before you, prescribed by the tracks you *have* to follow.

So he was surprised how much his short time with Jane had reawakened that old flicker of wonder. That desire for action. It wasn't quite what it had been when he had been a child, but it was certainly more than he had felt in years.

He rolled out of bed, wincing slightly. Magic salve or no, he was out of shape and his muscles were sore from exertion they hadn't felt in quite a while. He stretched for a few seconds to loosen them. That done, he went downstairs to find Wendy serving Jane pancakes. The little girl smiled when she saw him.

She was still in her nightdress: blue, much like the one Wendy had worn when they'd first met Peter. Jane's, however, seemed to have an odd sparkle to it when he looked at it in the right light. Wendy saw him and smiled as she set a plate for him beside Jane. After setting one for herself, she sat across from them. They ate in silence for several minutes before Wendy spoke up.

"Did you sleep well?" she asked.

"Better than I'd hoped." He glanced at Jane. "No fairies?"

The little girl shook her head. "They didn't come."

"Is Vanessa up yet?" Michael asked. "She doesn't normally sleep late."

Wendy nodded. "Some men came to see her a little while ago. She's outside."

Michael sighed as he put the last of his breakfast into his mouth. The buttery taste warmed him, but he knew the time for comfort was over. "I'll go see what that's about. We should go, anyway. We'll need to find some other way to get to Neverland."

"Do you have to go so soon?" Wendy asked

"You don't know how serious this is. I don't dare wait."

"I do understand, Michael—perhaps I'm one of the only people who do. It's just . . . don't let it be as long before you visit again."

Michael ruffled Jane's hair. She squealed for a second, and he couldn't help but laugh. "I won't. As soon as this whole thing is handled, I'll come back and spend some time with you both."

They walked him outside. Vanessa was waiting by a car wearing a wide smile. Jane threw her arms around him. "Bye-bye, Uncle Michael. I love you, even more than Nibs."

Michael laughed and held the girl tight for several seconds. He didn't know how she had made him feel like a child again. But it was like a weight had been lifted from him, like he was no longer anchored by his recent past and responsibilities.

Wendy gasped, and he looked in her direction but didn't see her until he looked down. Jane cried out in sheer joy. Wendy's jaw had dropped, and she and Vanessa stared at him with wide-eyed amazement.

"Michael," Vanessa said calmly. "You're flying."

"But how?" he asked as he floated gently to the ground and set Jane down. He noticed the sparkle had faded from her nightdress. Wendy followed his gaze, and dawning realization appeared on her face.

"It's the dress she wore last time Peter took her to Neverland. No matter how many times I washed it, I couldn't get the sparkle out. But then I never wanted to go back, and Jane would only go with Peter. You, on the other hand, you need to go. That must have made the difference."

"I think it's as much because you *believe* you need to go," Vanessa said.

Look for the one who took your place. That was what the salmon had told him. Jane had taken his place as Peter's companion in Neverland. She had provided him with a way back. Michael rose into the air, remembering for the first time in decades the sheer joy of flight. He looked down at Jane and Wendy, silently asking them again to come, but Wendy shook her head. They would wait for him, but they would not go with him. He sighed and looked toward the eastern horizon.

"Michael," Vanessa said, "maybe you don't want to be so visibly flying over a London street."

He looked about, and realized just how high he was—and just how light out it was getting. *I've been out of the Knights for too long to be making such a green mistake.* He made his way down.

"Michael, you can't just go to Neverland. Not without a guide," Wendy said.

Michael inclined his head. "I have one," he said as he landed.

He scanned the shadows, looking for one that didn't quite fit. Now that he was actively searching for it, he found it surprisingly difficult. He raised his voice. "It's all right. You can come out now."

"Michael, who are you talking to?" Vanessa asked.

He didn't answer. His sister and niece gave him questioning looks, and he felt his face heat up, hoping that he hadn't been hallucinating as he'd originally thought. He kept scanning the immediate area, searching shadows cast by trees as well as those on the sides of buildings, but he saw nothing.

"I'm sorry about before. I didn't mean to ignore you," he said to the empty street. Still, none of the shadows did anything out of the ordinary. Michael let out a long sigh as he remembered the dream vision he'd had of Peter. He thought he finally understood what it had meant. "I wasn't ready to see you until now, but Peter needs help. That's why he sent you to me. I can't get to him without you."

"Michael, we have another way to get there. They found Smee. They have him at the docks."

"What?"

Before Vanessa could respond, a gust of wind blew, but when it stopped, the branches were still shaking. There, among the shadows, was one that looked like it belonged to a boy. The shadow stepped forward, apparently not caring that its owner was nowhere to be seen. Michael smiled. He wasn't crazy. Vanessa took it with her usual aplomb, but both Jane and Wendy cried out in sheer delight at seeing the shadow of Peter Pan.

The shadow seemed to look at Michael before rising up into the air. Michael followed, stopping just long enough to wave goodbye to Wendy and Jane. The shadow flew around them several times before rising and zipping toward the eastern horizon.

Michael glanced at Vanessa. He knew he should go with her and hear what the pirate had to say. It was the responsible thing to do, but as he hovered in the air, that didn't seem to matter. He grinned.

"Meet me there."

"Michael!"

Without waiting to be chastised, he tore through the air after the shadow, away from the natural world and toward a place that was as much a dream as anything else. Neverland.

* * *

CHAPTER 13

Michael and the shadow flew for a long time. He wasn't sure how long, but the sun drifted across the sky several times. Sometimes it was day, and sometimes it was night, but whenever he tried to keep track, his mind wandered. It could've been days, weeks, or even months. He never got hungry, though, and he wondered if the peculiar magic of Neverland was taking hold.

The shadow led him over clouds and through storms, into burning heat and bitter cold. The land moved beneath them in a blur. From ocean to land, from desert to mountains. Once, he even saw ice floating in the water. By the time the legendary isle came into view, its single peak standing sentinel over lush forests and swampland, Michael's clothes were wet, and he was shivering. His breath steamed, and ice chips had formed on his sleeve. Still, he made no effort to dry himself off. Instead, he willed himself to go lower.

This wasn't like last time, when he'd had plenty of fairy dust. No, this time his fuel for flying had been a gift from his niece, gathered from her clothes. It had barely been enough to make it to Neverland, and he had used all its power. As soon as he tried to go lower, he lost all control and plummeted toward the ground. He focused his mind on thoughts of Jane and

Wendy, but either the happy thought wasn't strong enough or it just didn't matter—he was out of magic. The ground rushed up to meet him. At the last moment, the image of Jane laughing popped into his mind. He went up a few inches, enough to redirect his fall into the bay.

Then, the power failed altogether.

There was a loud splash as the water engulfed him, driving the air out of him. He was swallowed by the dark sea, and he scrambled to the surface, his lungs burning, until at last he surfaced. Gasping, he turned to float on his back. Every part of his body ached from the impact, and he doubted he would've survived if he hadn't managed to get that one final lift. Weary from days of no sleep, it was all he could do to stay afloat. The water was calm, though, and it didn't take too much effort to make it to shore. Still, when he finally crawled onto the sand, he just lay on his back for several seconds and let the waves wash over him. He didn't move again until several armed men gathered around him. He blinked and stared at them.

The leader had skin so tanned that it almost looked like bronze. Markings had been painted on their faces, and each was armed with stone-tipped spears and bows and arrows. Every man among them had the lean muscles that would lend themselves to endurance rather than brute strength. They wore vests made of soft leather, and a few wore necklaces of animal teeth. Michael tried to stand up, but as soon as he was in a sitting position, a spear point pressed against the back of his neck, and he froze.

"Well, what do we have here?" the lead warrior asked. He stood at least seven feet tall and had a scar running down the left side of his face that barely missed his eye. "It looks like an invader, come to scout our lands. We should stop him and ensure that he gets no farther."

He uttered several harsh syllables to one of the others. The man he had spoken to inclined his head and ran into the Neverwood, the forest that started about fifty feet from the shore of the bay. Hesitantly, Michael started to rise. This time, the natives didn't stop him. At least they didn't until he tried to take a step. Then, he had half a dozen spears on him, ready to draw his lifeblood.

"Hello," Michael said. His eyes were wide, and he didn't move so much as an inch. He could feel blood running down his neck from the spot where one of the spears had pierced his skin. "It's good to see you again." The men scowled at him. Michael cleared his throat. "It's me—Michael. Remember?"

One of the men grunted and pressed his spear into Michael's back. He said nothing, but the pressure on the weapon told Michael exactly what his captor wanted. He started walking. The ones in front of him didn't move their weapons, so he moved slowly to avoid being skewered.

"Your people once took me prisoner because you thought we had captured Tiger Lily, but it had been the pirates. We helped rescue her. We were heroes. Don't you remember?"

The spear at his back pressed a little harder, and Michael was forced to keep moving. They entered the Neverwood, and he couldn't help but worry that he'd trip over some raised root and end up impaling himself on a spear. Strangely, that was only the second-biggest worry, the first being: Why didn't they remember him?

He thought about that as he observed his surroundings. It was far hotter here than in the woods outside of Gloucester. Humidity hung thick in the air, and it wasn't long before his salty clothes had dried, only to be drenched in sweat. Birds and insects went quiet as they passed, and more than once, nearby bushes vibrated as small animals darted away from the armed party. In spite of the tropical climate, however, a few times they ran into patches of cold. They were no more than a few feet across, but the plants in those places seemed faded, almost washed out. Once, he brushed a pale bush, and it turned to dust at his touch. His captors either didn't notice it or pretended not to.

After nearly a quarter hour of walking, they came to a clearing containing a large cluster of tents. The natives stared at him as he passed, and he kept hoping he would find someone he knew, but there were far fewer people here than he remembered, and every face he did see belonged to a stranger.

"Let me speak to the chief," Michael said. "He'll know who I am."

Of course, Michael wasn't the least bit sure of that. He was barely more than a toddler the last time he had been here, and there was little chance the chief would associate the boy from twenty years ago with the man he suddenly found in their lands. Not waiting to see if that gambit worked, he looked around.

"Shadow, are you there? Show them. Let them know I'm no enemy."

Michael felt the pressure of the spear at his back increase. He waited, but Peter's shadow, if it was still there, didn't show itself, and the natives forced him through the camp until they reached a clearing at the center. Half a dozen wooden cages sat around a large fire pit. Only one of them was occupied, but before Michael could get a glimpse of its inhabitant, the natives shoved him into one of the empty cages. He crashed into the wooden bars on the other side so hard that he bit his lip, and he winced at both the pain and the coppery taste of blood. He turned around just in time to see his captor turning a heavy iron key. There was a loud click, and the man walked away.

Michael went to the door and pushed hard against it, but it didn't budge. He sighed and looked to the prisoner in the other cage. The man wore a blue coat. Or, rather, what was once a blue coat—it was so filthy and tattered Michael was surprised it still hung on the man's body. His hair went down to his shoulders and was matted with dirt. He was slumped in a corner.

"Hello?"

The man didn't look up as Michael spoke. Michael sighed, turned away, and called to his captors.

"You have to let me out! Don't you remember me? Michael Darling. I came with Peter, and my brother and sister. John and Wendy."

"Wendy?"

The other prisoner's voice was tired—barely a rasp—and as Michael turned to meet his gaze, he realized the worn face matched his voice. He looked up at Michael, who in turn got a better look at the man's clothing. It sent chills down Michael's back. They were faded and torn, but the buttons, though tarnished, were brass, and the color of the wool was unquestionably the blue of an officer in His Majesty's Royal Navy. He looked up to meet the man's eyes, though he already knew what he would see.

A ghost.

They had all thought him dead for nearly seven years. Wendy still wept for him, and Jane had never even met him.

"Will?"

CHAPTER 14

* * *

Will's jaw dropped at the sound of his name, and Michael could see emotions warring across his face. His lip quivered, and he was breathing heavily. For a second, he seemed unable to believe what he was seeing. He blinked, and his voice wavered as he spoke.

"Michael? Is that you?"

"Yes! William, what are you doing here? When we heard that your ship had gone down with all hands . . ." He shook his head. "We thought you were dead."

"I might as well be," he said bitterly. "I don't know what I'm doing here—I don't even know where 'here' is. All I remember was the ocean being so cold." He shivered then, as if the chill still coursed through him. "I thought I would drown, but the next thing I knew, I woke up here, on the shore. These people captured me. They said that for daring to come here, I would never be allowed to leave. They've held me here since then."

"*Seven years?*" Michael said. "You've been here this whole time? Did Peter know?"

Almost instantly, Michael realized his mistake. As far as he knew, Wendy had never told her husband about Peter or their adventures in Neverland, but Will's brow scrunched. "There is a boy named Peter. He comes sometimes, though I can't tell if he's friend or enemy to those here. It seems to change by the day, sometimes by the hour."

Unfortunately, that sounded about right. "It's a little complicated," Michael said. "Still, Peter should've helped get you out." He sighed as he looked around. Some of the natives had crept in close at the sound of Peter's name, though none came close enough to touch through the bars. Though they had a language of their own, they knew English, too, and so could understand everything he and Will were saying. Of course, he didn't have anything to hide, so he went on. "He probably would've helped if he'd known who you were." He thought for a second. "And if he didn't get jealous. But surely, when he brought Jane—"

He stopped short. Jane had never met her father, and though Wendy had pictures of Will, the man standing before Michael looked little like the pictures of the well-kempt sailor that hung on the wall. Certainly, a little girl—even one as precocious as Jane—would not have been able to make the connection.

"Jane? A little girl, right? I remember her coming with Peter once or twice. She would speak to me sometimes." He gave Michael a weak smile. "She's nice."

"She's your daughter." Michael's voice was barely above a whisper. His mind was reeling.

"My . . ." Will took a deep breath. "My *daughter*?" Tears filled his eyes. "I always thought she reminded me of Wendy, but I never suspected . . . Michael, what's going on? Where are we?"

"It's hard to explain," Michael said. "Wendy never told you about meeting Peter when we were children, did she?"

"Peter?" he asked, scanning the sky as if expecting him to arrive. "The same Peter that I've seen?"

"Yes."

"You mean she knows him? But how could you have met him back then? He couldn't be more than twelve."

Michael sighed. "Like I said, it's complicated. Right now, we just have to figure out a way to get out of here." He scanned the natives, looking for a familiar face, but he still saw none. He spoke to the gathered group, hoping one of them would remember him. "I know we fought sometimes, but we were allies just as many times. We helped you fight against the pirates."

"Wendy fought pirates?" Will asked.

"It's complicated," he said . . . again. It was going to get frustrating if the only discussion he had in this cage was with Will, explaining every little thing. However, the natives didn't seem interested in talking with him, so he let out a deep breath. *Seven years, and all he's seen is this cage. And now you're in one, too, so maybe a little less with the high-and-mighty, Michael?* "Are you okay? This is a lot to take in."

Will blinked several times before giving Michael a half chuckle. "You could say that. I'm a bit confused, but that's not terribly surprising, is it?"

Michael laughed. "Actually, you're taking this a lot better than I would've expected."

The mirth faded from Will's face. "I've had seven years to get used to this place." He let out a long breath. "Where exactly are we? Somewhere in the Atlantic? Does the navy know where we are?"

Michael shook his head. "The navy couldn't get here if they had all the ships in the world. As to where, I don't think definitions like that can be applied to Neverland."

"Neverland." Will drew out the word and made a face, as if he had tasted the word and found it unpalatable. "Is that what it's called? It's an odd place, and I can't help but feel that it dislikes me. Isn't that strange?"

"Not as strange as you might think," Michael said. "Neverland was never a place for grown-ups. I think even the pirates were only here to be something for the children to fight. That was probably enough for Neverland."

"You're talking about this place like it's alive."

"Not alive. Not exactly, anyway, but I do think it's aware."

Will stared at Michael, then muttered, "Maybe you're as mad as I feel."

"Maybe you're right. But after seven years of a fever dream, why would you suddenly think of *me* as the narrator of your madness?"

"Because you were always a bit of an uptight jerk?"

Michael gave a loud bark of laughter. "You were marrying my sister, Will. It's a brother's job to be a jerk."

Will snorted, but didn't seem angry. "Touché." He looked around. "So you're saying we're on an island with a mind of its own."

"Something like that."

Will said nothing. Michael glanced at his brother-in-law, and thought of something then. "Tiger Lily."

Will glanced at the flowers growing around the clearing. "I don't see any."

"What?"

"You were talking about flowers."

Michael refrained from yelling at the poor man. "No— Princess Tiger Lily. Is she here? Maybe if I can talk to her, I can convince her to let us out."

"Is that her name?" Will asked. "There is a girl who comes to glare at me every once in a while. I don't think she'll help, though. Every time she looks at me, I get the feeling that she hates me."

"Why?"

"I have no idea. Maybe she and the island have been talking."

"It's still our best hope."

"What is?"

"Tiger Lily!" he called out. "Tiger Lily, it's Michael Darling! I helped rescue you when the pirates took you prisoner. I was Peter Pan's friend."

Some of the nearby natives went silent at that. A few moved a little closer. One that Michael thought looked a little familiar squinted at him. Michael called out again, but got no better results the second time than the first. The third time he tried, one of the natives came over and pointed his spear at Michael. Will whimpered and retreated into a corner of his cage. This obviously wasn't the first time he'd been threatened, and the threat had to be real enough for Will to be afraid of it. Michael sighed and nodded to the native.

"I understand. I'll stop calling for Tiger Lily, but can you at least tell her I'm here?"

"What makes you think that I do not already know?"

The native holding the spear looked over his shoulder and gasped. He scrambled out of the way, bowing deeply as the girl, no more than thirteen, walked past him. Her lean muscles told Michael that she was every bit as much a warrior as the men around her.

She stopped in front of Michael's cage and stared at him. "You called for me. Did it not occur to you that if I was going to answer, I would have done so when my people first took you?"

"Hmmm." Michael shrugged. "I guess I just thought that we used to be friends and that you would help me. Your people took me prisoner just for coming where I used to be welcome."

The native girl frowned. "I was friends with a *boy*. The man who has trespassed on our lands is unknown to me."

Michael stepped up to the bars. Preserved by Neverland's magic, the princess of Neverland's native people looked only a little older than Peter himself, and Michael towered over her. Despite her name, however, Tiger Lily was no delicate flower.

This was a girl who had once snuck onto the *Jolly Roger* armed with only a knife, intent on taking out as many pirates as she could. This was someone who, when captured by those same pirates, had faced her death with a silent dignity that was the equal to that of any Knight Michael had ever known. She was not a person to be intimidated by size. Though her hand rested lightly on her bone knife, the look on her face said she regarded him with utter contempt.

This might take some work.

"I am still the same person I was when the pirates left you to drown in the lagoon. I helped you then."

"That was a long time ago," Tiger Lily said.

"And time ends our friendship? I am still the same person you knew, Tiger Lily," Michael said.

She threw back her head and laughed. "Are you? You're older, for one thing," she said, her eyes narrowing, "and that doesn't happen to a friend of Neverland."

"I was a friend of yours, too, and of your tribe."

"What use do we have for a traitor as a friend?"

Michael raised an eyebrow. "Traitor? What are you talking about? I never betrayed you or your people."

Her voice became flat, and the grip on her knife tightened. "You betrayed Peter and Neverland. You grew up. How could the boy I once knew do that? How could you still expect me to trust him?"

"But—"

"You *left*, Michael. And now that you're back, you're one of *them*. There is no place for someone like you in Neverland."

Michael sighed. "Tiger Lily, there is more to life than Neverland."

"Maybe for you," she said. She turned and started walking away.

"Peter!" Michael cried out. "I know he is in trouble."

She paused. For nearly a minute, she just stood there, neither turning to look at them nor moving. Finally, she spun, her face showing an expression that mixed rage with concern. "Can you help him?"

"I'm not sure," Michael said. "That's why I came back." He spread his arms to encompass the cage. "I can't do anything from in here. Hate me for growing up if you want to, but at least let me go do what I came here to do."

She stared at him for a long time. For a second he thought she would agree, but then there was a commotion at the tree line. They all looked to see a member of the tribe coming out of the forest. Someone behind him had an arm around his neck in a tight, viselike grip. It took Michael only a second to recognize Vanessa. Instantly, half a dozen arrows were leveled at her, though she seemed not to care.

"Now that I have your attention," she said in a perfectly calm voice, "let him go."

"You seem to have overlooked the fact that you are outnumbered and surrounded," Tiger Lily said. "Perhaps that's not the attention you expected, but there it is."

"And perhaps you consider me an idiot—I assure you I'm not. You didn't think I came alone, did you? I've captured half a dozen of your people. If I don't come back, my friend will deal with them."

"You expect me to believe that?"

"I expect a leader to care about their people."

Vanessa tensed her arm, and her prisoner blanched and spoke in that language that Michael had known once but that had long since faded. Tiger Lily scowled and made a chopping motion with her hand. One of the warriors stepped forward with a spear raised. Michael backed up, but the weapon slammed into the lock, knocking it free.

"Go," Tiger Lily said.

Michael took a step forward and turned to Will. "Him too."

"You're not in a position to make demands."

"You don't have a reason to keep him. Let me take him with me, and we'll both go far away from here."

She clenched her jaw and shook her head. "No. A former friend of Peter's I can believe will be an ally of Neverland—and if he's not, I only have to track down one person to kill. But him? No, I don't think so."

Hope drained from Will's face. Michael remembered Jane. She had never known her father, but she could, and he would not let that chance slip away. One look at Tiger Lily, however, told him that she had been pushed as far as she would go in terms of reason.

He would have to try something else. "He is Wendy's husband."

A series of emotions danced across her face, passing too quickly for Michael to guess at them. Tiger Lily's jaw dropped. "Wendy? The one that Peter . . ."

She took in a deep breath, and Michael could practically see the thoughts running through her mind. Wendy and the native princess had never particularly liked each other. In fact, at times they were almost openly hostile, but that was because they had both been vying for Peter's affection. A perpetual child, and an immature one at that, Peter had had no idea of the conflict happening right before his eyes. Though Wendy hadn't been here in decades, Peter had remembered her—and that was truly remarkable, given that most thoughts in his mind lasted only a few minutes. The fact she'd made such an impact on Peter must have driven Tiger Lily crazy. And although she would have no desire to do Wendy any favors, if Wendy was married . . .

Michael knew it was ridiculous, but he played into that insecurity. "She misses him very much, and she always said that she would never love another as long as he lived. Of course, she's thought he's been dead for years now. She might decide to love again."

"I know what you're trying to do," Tiger Lily said.

"I'm not doing anything. Peter has always been fickle, but there's been one constant for him for almost twenty years. If that constant was suddenly an *option* . . ."

"Take him," she said, her voice on the verge of fury . . . and hope.

The warrior opened his cage, and Michael extended his hand. Will looked at it, as if he couldn't believe it was real. Tears welled in his eyes, and his weather-worn hand closed around Michael's. The cages had been relatively large—big enough to move around in—but the lack of true activity for seven years had made Will weak. He was unsteady as he walked, but with freedom so close at hand, he didn't waver as they made their way to Vanessa. When they neared, she shoved her prisoner forward. She opened her mouth to speak, but Michael gave her a slight shake of his head.

She nodded and started leading them away, but they had gone only a few steps when another warrior, bruised and battered, stepped out of the woods, leading a bound Smee in front of him. The pirate's words were tumbling over each other.

"—you can't trust them, but you can trust old Smee. Take care of them for me, and I'll leave you alone. That way everyone is happy."

This won't end well, Michael thought.

Vanessa must have thought the same thing, because she'd quietly drawn her knife once more.

In fact, everything was quiet. Even the birds stopped singing. Then, as one, every bow was raised. Most were pointed at

Smee, who seemed to just now realize he had wandered into the village. But Michael, Vanessa, and Will all had their share of arrows pointed at them, too. The color drained from Smee's face, and he sputtered so much that Michael had no idea what he was trying to say.

"That," Tiger Lily said through clenched teeth, "is one of the pirates that bound me and left me to die. Why did you bring him here?"

"We didn't bring—"

At the same time, Smee had lifted his hands toward her. "Now, young lady, let's not be hasty. That was a long time ago, and no one was hurt."

"I release you and then discover *this*? Take them all!"

Vanessa stepped up next to Michael, holding up the long knife ready. Michael had no weapon—not that his having one would have made much of a difference. They were outnumbered badly.

"Michael, what do we do?" she asked quietly.

"I take it your friend was Smee?"

"Bad idea, it seems."

"It was working until his inevitable betrayal."

"I figured he'd betray us a little later."

"I can't say I blame you."

"Appreciate that."

Just then, a small white bird flitted down from the sky, landing on Michael's shoulder. It hopped over closer to his head and idly pecked at his clothes for a few seconds before turning to Tiger Lily and cawing. Underneath the call, Michael thought he heard two words.

"Trust him."

He gaped at the bird. "You can talk?"

The bird cocked its head and stared at Michael. "You can understand?"

Dumbly, Michael nodded. Then he realized Tiger Lily was gaping at them both. He didn't have time to figure this out.

"You can speak to the Never Bird?" the princess asked in a voice barely above a whisper.

"Can't you?" Michael asked.

"No one can. She is a sacred animal, the first living creature to be made in this land." The awe in her voice was colored by disgust that Michael was able to talk to the bird.

"Then you should listen to him," the Never Bird said. "Let him go. Trust him."

"She can't understand you," Michael said.

"She doesn't know my words, but she grasps my meaning." The bird turned to Tiger Lily and chirped loudly. "Trust him."

Tiger Lily took a step back, as if she really could understand what the bird meant. She nodded once and, for a second time, motioned for the others to lower their weapons.

"But princess—" one of the guards said.

"Let them go or disobey both me *and* the Never Bird. I wouldn't want to be you if that happened."

The man winced, though whatever was meant by the threat was lost on Michael. All of the warriors lowered their weapons.

"Let's go," Vanessa said, "before they change their mind."

"Yes, good idea," Smee said, already turning to leave.

"No," Tiger Lily said with fierce authority.

"But the Never Bird—"

"Not him. I will not allow him to freely roam Neverland. Not even for the Never Bird."

Michael nodded. "I don't really have a problem with that."

"*What?*" Smee said, waving at Vanessa. "But—but I brought you here!"

"You tried to betray us," Michael said. "And you tried to have us killed at the pub."

"That . . . that was nothing personal."

Michael shook his head and turned away as Tiger Lily's people took hold of Smee. He and Vanessa helped Will support himself. The old pirate's howling echoed after them as they staggered out of the village, the Never Bird riding silently on Michael's shoulder. Michael could almost feel the stares of the tribesmen as they disappeared into the woods.

* * *

CHAPTER 15

As soon as they got out of sight, Michael started to lean Will against an old oak tree. Part of it had rotted away, a thing Michael had never seen in Neverland. Vanessa, not understanding the significance of the tree, urged them on. Michael needed the rest, too, but he also knew Vanessa was right. They walked for another half an hour before stopping. This time they had no choice, as Will stumbled and couldn't get back up. They helped the weakened man slump against a rock, and Michael sat on a stump. Tiger Lily's people were probably still watching, but he thought they should be safe as long as they kept heading away from the village.

"Who is this?" Vanessa asked, looking Will up and down.

Michael used a large leaf to form a makeshift bowl and got water for Will out of a nearby stream. The other man drank gratefully.

"This is Will, Wendy's husband."

"Wendy's . . . The one who died in the Great War?"

"Apparently not," Michael said, not really willing—or able—to explain everything to Vanessa right now. He turned to the bird that remained perched on his left shoulder. "Why did you help us?"

"Because you looked like you needed it."

Michael glared at her. "Will has been a prisoner for seven years. He's needed help for a long time, but you only came for me."

"I didn't know that."

"How could you not know?"

"I'm a bird, Michael. Where I fly is not set, and I tend to avoid most people—especially the ones with bows and arrows."

That made a certain sense. But something nagged at Michael. "And yet you knew to come for me?"

"Your companion requested my aid."

"Vanessa?"

"No, not that companion."

Before he could ask what the Never Bird meant, Vanessa asked, "The dragon's blood?"

"I think so. I heard the birds first when I was waiting for the salmon. I think the potion doesn't just allow you to speak with animals. It actually allows you to learn their language."

"I didn't know that."

"Me either. Speaking of things I don't know, how did you find us?"

She started to answer when the bird cooed. Vanessa began staring into the distance. Michael looked, too. There was movement, but no sound, as Peter's shadow flowed out of the darkness.

That settled, Vanessa continued. "Smee helped me guide a boat here, but then the current caught us and it smashed against the rocks." She grimaced. "I lost my pistol while we swam to the shore, but Shade was waiting for me once we got to land."

Michael cocked his head. "Shade?"

The shadow darted around Vanessa and jumped up and down, obviously approving of the name. She grinned.

"A bit less awkward than simply calling him 'Peter's shadow,' wouldn't you say? Anyway, it didn't take me long to figure that I should be hiding from the people in the woods." She thought for a second, then said, "Do you have any idea why it was so easy? I'm good at avoiding being seen, but not that good."

Michael shrugged. "I'm not sure."

"Because they're not really people," the bird cooed. "Some beings, like fairies, came to Neverland from your world. Others, like myself and Tiger Lily's people, were created by Neverland, by Peter. They were given skill enough to challenge children. They came upon you unaware, but your friend—her talents overmatched theirs."

Michael nodded, though he translated when he saw Vanessa's confusion. Then he addressed the Never Bird again. "'Never Bird' is a little clumsy. Can I call you Nev?"

"I'm not sure. I've never had a nickname . . ."

"How many people have you ever talked to?"

The bird blinked at him. "Good point." The bird thought about it for a moment, then did a little shake of her feathers, clearly pleased. "Nev . . . I like it. Thank you."

For some reason, the gratitude of this tiny bird filled Michael with a delicious feeling of happiness, as if the approval of the sacred animal was some sort of blessing. Eyes shining now, he said, "You're welcome. Can I ask you a question?"

"Of course."

"When I was captured, you just came because"—he glanced at the shadow—"because Shade asked you to?"

"Of course. Many of the creatures of Neverland would come for the shadow of Peter Pan, if it was important."

"But didn't Peter like to play practical jokes on you?"

The bird's head bobbed. "He's a flighty god, but I'm a bird, so flighty doesn't bother me. And like so many of the creatures here, I still remember who created us, even if he does not."

"He really created you?"

She spread her wings, and the woods erupted with the sounds of insects and birds. Leaves and branches rustled, and

Michael thought he saw yellow eyes staring at him from the shadows. Will looked ready to bolt, and Vanessa tensed. Even Michael scrambled to his feet, though when Nev stayed perched on his shoulder, serene, he relaxed a bit. After a few seconds, the noise ceased. The quiet that followed was almost empty, as if the noise had been a strain on the land. Michael looked at the Never Bird.

"As Tiger Lily told you, I was the very first thing he made when he created this place. Many have great respect for me, but we are all his creations."

"Amazing."

"Indeed."

"And you're connected to the land, right? And Peter Pan? Do you know where he is?"

"I am connected. But not in that way. The only thing I know for certain is that he is in Neverland somewhere."

"That's not much help."

"It narrows it down from your giant world, does it not?"

He couldn't argue with that, but he still had so much to ask when Will cried out, "Michael, can you stop talking to that bird and explain to me what's going on?" The bedraggled man was frantic. He kept looking into the shadows as if expecting some creature to jump out at him.

"I— It's complicated," he said lamely.

"You keep saying that! I *know* it's complicated! But it doesn't help that you're talking to a bird and not to us."

"You're right. Vanessa, we need to get him home."

"We need to get us all home at some point. Unfortunately, I told you: our ship is destroyed."

"Right." Michael thought about it for a second, then snapped his fingers. "We need to get you some fairy dust. We can probably even get a fairy to guide you home."

Will gaped at that. "A *fairy*? Are you serious?"

Even after seven years, it seemed Will had never truly understood the magic of where he was. *Or maybe he never got to see anything other than the view from his cage.* Michael shuddered at the thought. He also grimaced at the idea that Will was too firmly rooted in his adult reality. He could only hope that a grown man who had never been to this island as a child could actually learn to fly.

"There are no fairies," the Never Bird said.

"What do you mean?" Michael asked, caught up short.

"Well . . ." Will bit his lower lip. "It's just that fairies aren't real, so one of them can't lead me home."

Michael shook his head. "I wasn't talking to you."

"The fairies are gone," the bird said. "A few weeks ago, they all just disappeared. Even Tinker Bell is nowhere to be found."

"No fairies . . ."

"What?" Vanessa asked.

"Nev just said the fairies have disappeared."

"Then . . . no fairy dust." She chewed her bottom lip, only for it to fall from between her teeth. "Then that means—"

"—we don't have a way home."

Will stared at both of them . . . and quietly started crying. Vanessa went to put an arm around the sailor, while Michael stood frozen in place. Finally, he said, "Nev—do *you* know a way home for us?"

The bird chirped. "I have no existence outside of this island. I have no idea how to leave it."

Michael turned to Shade. "What about you? You've gone to our world. Could you take us back?"

Shade shook his head, and mimed sprinkling dust from his fingers.

"Do you at least know where Peter is? Or the fairies?"

The shadow sagged and shook his head.

"His memory isn't any better than Peter's," Nev said. "I saw him flying away from the island weeks ago, no doubt to get help. If he hasn't joined with Peter in all that time, it's a wonder he remembers anything at all."

The shadow puffed up its chest, looking indignant, but Michael suspected that Nev was right. It had been such a long time . . .

For me, too, he realized. His own memories were still pretty fuzzy, and yet there was something right on the edge that was gnawing at him.

And then he remembered.

"Maybe there's another way."

"What's that?" Vanessa asked, looking up from Will.

"We can go to the underground house. There could be some fairy dust in Tink's old room. I think I remember the way, but I've never gone on foot."

"I can guide you there," the bird said.

"Great—thank you." Michael walked over to Will, putting his hand on the man's shoulder. "Will?"

Will looked up, his dirty face streaked with tears.

"I know this isn't easy—I know it's been impossibly hard. I can't imagine what you've been going through these last seven years. And I know we're talking about things that don't make sense. But I *am* going to get you back home to Wendy and Jane—I promise you."

"How?"

"I'm not sure," he said with a rueful laugh. "But I've got an idea of where we can go next that could help us."

"It's a next step, at least," Vanessa chimed in, even though she didn't know Michael's plan. It didn't surprise him—as a Knight, they were trained to always move forward, always work toward a goal. Sitting here like this must have chafed her to no end. At least now they had a course of action, and she was supporting her partner to enact it. "We follow Michael, and then we can always regroup."

"I—"

"You're a sailor, right?" she said.

"Yes."

"Then act like one. This is an order—get up and march!"

"But . . . sailors don't really march."

She looked at Will, incredulous, but then he gave a weak laugh. She was even more incredulous at first, but then she laughed, too, helping him up. "You're going to be okay, Will. Go wash up a bit, and then we'll get moving."

Will shuffled over to the stream, and Michael mouthed *Thank you* to Vanessa. She gave him a mock salute in return, and went over to the stream for a drink before they set off.

With Nev's guidance, they made their way to his old hiding place. The last time he was in Neverland, they'd traveled almost entirely through the air, and he hadn't fully appreciated how rough the terrain was. No paths had been blazed, and while they did run across an occasional animal trail going in the right direction, those rarely went more than a dozen feet or so. The rest of the time, they did their best to force their way through the thick plants, though they could only move at what seemed like a snail's pace.

While they walked, Vanessa scouted and Michael did his best to tell Will of his and Wendy's adventures in Neverland. Will didn't believe most of it, but that wasn't particularly surprising. As Michael had surmised, Will might have lived here since his supposed death, but he hadn't truly experienced Neverland. And even with what he'd seen so far, it probably wasn't enough to shake him out of the reality that grounded his sanity. Still, they had nothing better to occupy their time, so Michael kept talking.

He was just explaining about how they had each had their own tree that they used to enter their home beneath the hill, when the hill itself came into view. Michael stopped and stared while Will collapsed to the ground, Vanessa leaned against a tree, and Shade flew around her.

Michael couldn't believe he was back. Though he'd been only four at the time, he still had vivid memories of sliding up and down the inside of his tree. It didn't take him long to spot it. As he approached his own tree, a lump formed in his throat. This had been the base for so many adventures. But it had also been a home, a place of safety and family. And now he was back.

He ran his hand along the bark. The hole he had once entered so easily then seemed so small now.

"You really lived down there?" Vanessa asked.

Michael nodded. "It was in the report I submitted when I joined the Knights."

"I know. I just didn't expect it to be so . . ." She waved her hand at the tree as Nev landed on his shoulder.

"So . . . ?" Michael prompted.

"So real."

"Even after all the things you've experienced as a Knight?"

"It's strange, but those things always still happened in *our* world. This—this is something completely different."

That was something he could understand.

"Are you going to go in?" she asked.

Michael stared into the hole. "I don't think I'm going to fit."

"Why don't we just make the hole bigger?" Will asked.

"No!" Michael cried out without thinking. Will and Vanessa stared at him, but after a moment, he relaxed. It was foolishness, of course. The reaction had been pure instinct. Though Peter had ingrained it into them that they were to fit the tree, not the other way around, that had been a rule meant to keep adults from chasing children. There was no reason not to widen the hole now, but then an idea struck him.

There was no reason to do it, either.

He explained that they didn't need to ruin his tree. "We all had our own tree, you see, and Peter's rule was that we stay the same size so that we would always fit."

"But you were children," Vanessa said. "Children are growing all the time."

"Not here. But that's not the point."

"Oh?"

"The point is that Slightly was a little too fond of sweets. He got too big and carved his tree to fit himself instead of slimming down. He was almost as big as a grown-up at that point, and when Hook found his tree, he almost made it into the house because of it."

Will stared at him for a few seconds before shaking his head and letting out a long breath. "Your brother Slightly had a tree? And a pirate almost went through it?"

Absently, Michael nodded. "We told you he was adopted. Where did you think he came from?"

"From an adoption agency like every other adopted child," Will said. He sighed. "Okay—which was Slightly's tree?"

Michael looked from one to another. Not all trees in the woods led to the underground house, of course, and in the intervening decades the forest had grown up around their old home, creating a tangle of vegetation. Michael shook his head. "I don't remember," he said and started to wander around the trees.

But Shade leaped up and down, waving his hands wildly. Before Michael could ask what he was doing, he had dashed to a nearby tree and started darting in and out of a hole in the trunk.

"That's Slightly's?" Michael asked, and the shadow nodded.

"That's surprising," the Never Bird chirped. "I'm pretty sure Peter forgot about the Lost Boys a few days after they left..How is it that Shade remembers?" The shadow stamped his foot at the bird, who flew up to a branch in Slightly's tree. "Be calm, Shade. I meant no offense. I just didn't expect to find so capable a companion in you."

The shadow thought for a second. Finally, having decided that the bird had given him a compliment and not an insult, he nodded and extended his hand toward Nev, as if to shake. The Never Bird cooed at it and then the shadow—obviously realizing that Nev couldn't shake his hand—smacked his head with his palm before flying around the tree.

Will stared at the scene with wide-eyed shock. He looked to Michael and took a deep breath before speaking. "A sentient shadow arguing with a magical bird. Every time I think I've seen everything . . ."

"Just keep an open mind, is all. This place will continue to surprise you, but if you can try to accept it, it can prove to be wonderful." Then he paused and eyed Nev. "How are you talking with Shade? I get that Tiger Lily could get a sense of what you meant, but Peter could never understand you. Shouldn't his shadow be the same?"

"Though he is a god," Nev said, "Peter thinks of himself as a boy, and boys aren't supposed to understand birds. He didn't understand me because he chose not to. That limitation would appear not to apply to his shadow."

"I guess that makes sense," Michael said, not entirely certain that it actually did.

He had more pressing issues now, though, and stepped closer to examine Slightly's trunk. It was part of an ancient tree, the kind that had existed for centuries. It was wide enough that he couldn't have closed his arms around it. At eye level was a hole that, initially, seemed to be rotted, but when he touched it he felt only hard wood. The trunk almost looked like it had grown around the passage. He stuck his head in and peered down but saw only darkness.

"I think it goes all the way down, and it looks wide enough for me to fit." He took his head out and turned, first to Vanessa and then to Will. "Are you coming?"

Vanessa looked as if she dared him to try to stop her, but Will looked as if Michael was mad.

"Into the tree?"

Michael nodded. "Yes."

"You're saying that this leads to some sort of underground house?"

Michael nodded again.

"Where you, Wendy, and John, along with your adopted brothers, lived when you were children while you fought against pirates."

Michael let out a long breath. "Will, until we find a way to get you back home, you're going to have to accept this. Once you get back, you can forget any of this ever happened."

"How could anyone forget this place?"

Michael thought about his brothers, both natural and adopted, and for a moment he envied them. "You'd be surprised. The mind adapts. You might be able to convince yourself this was all a hallucination after you were lost at sea." He shrugged. "For what it's worth, I think you should come with us. I always thought there was a part of Wendy that she left in Neverland. It might help if you see where she spent most of her time here."

Will looked the tree up and down. He actually seemed afraid of it, but after several seconds he nodded. Michael made his way to the hole and was about lower himself in when he felt a hand on his shoulder.

"I should go first," Vanessa said.

"Why?"

"For one thing, I'm smaller than you," she said, pointing at Michael's stomach, which wasn't quite as flat as it had been when he was a Knight. She continued, "For another, I'm more agile than you. For a third, if there's trouble down there, I'm in much better shape to fight than you. For a fourth, I'm a better fighter than—"

"I'm going first," he said. "This is *my* home." He tried to ignore the voice that told him his pride was wounded on multiple levels.

"Don't get stuck," Vanessa said, backing away. "Or killed."

Frowning, Michael crossed his arms over his chest in an effort to make himself thinner. He took a deep breath, then exhaled and squeezed into the hole headfirst. It was a tight fit. Though Slightly had been a big child, he'd still been a child, and it was all Michael could do to inch forward. He grunted as he forced his way lower. More than once, he got stuck and had to twist and wiggle to get through. Abruptly, the opening widened, and he fell the last couple of feet. The door at the base of the tree had long since rotted away, and Michael tumbled into the house. Will came through the door a second later, dropping into the single-room home and crashing into Michael. They both went down in a tangle of limbs. In the confined space, the fact that Will hadn't bathed since the last time it rained became nauseatingly obvious. Vanessa, who had somehow managed to come down gracefully, now stood over them, wearing a wide smile.

"Ah, chivalry. Our gallant naval officer wouldn't deign to let me go before him, either. I'm so glad I have such capable men to lead the charge." She held out her hands to both men. "Shall we?"

They took in the room. A bed took up most of the chamber. Michael stared at it for several seconds as memories washed over him. It was so much smaller than he would've thought.

Once, seven children had slept in it at the same time, and the idea that it might be too small had never even entered their minds. Now, though, it hardly seemed big enough for half that many. None of the three had thought to bring a light—even Vanessa, for all her snark—but years of being untended had allowed rot to form several small holes in the ceiling, through which the light now shone. Scattered pieces of clothing and other odds and ends covered the dirt floor, but there was no sign anyone had lived here for a long time.

"This is nothing like what I expected." Vanessa touched a portion of wall, and it crumbled beneath her fingers.

"It wasn't always like this." Michael walked to the other side of the room, moving around the large mushrooms that had once served as stools. A small curtain had been drawn closed, hiding a cubby that was no larger than a bird cage. Michael started to pull it aside, but it turned to dust as he touched it, revealing a room occupied by a tiny couch, a dresser, and a bed, all of which had been overturned. The two-inch mirror lay broken on the ground.

Will peered inside before turning to Michael. "A dollhouse?"

"A fairy's home."

He ran his fingers along the ground and pulled back when he felt a sharp sting. A tiny shard of mirror glass had become embedded in his finger. It took him a few seconds to extract it with his fingernails, but there was no sparkle of fairy dust. He shook his head at Will.

"I was hoping we'd be able to get you home after this. I have no idea where to go from here."

Will, who was walking around the small room and running his fingers along every surface, turned to him and nodded. Then he knelt and pushed against a large mushroom with a red cap and white spots, his mouth half open in a look of wonder.

"Let's go back to the surface," Vanessa said. "Maybe your bird will know something."

"She's not my bird," Michael said absently, but she was right.

Michael started heading for the way up but paused. He walked over to the bed and knelt to look under it. He pulled back as a small claw lashed forward, grazing the tip of his nose. He fell backward. A small creature, no more than a foot tall and with mottled gray-and-black skin, darted out from under the bed. It was vaguely humanoid, though its arms were longer than its legs and ended in sharp claws. It had ears about the size of Michael's palm. It leaped at him, but Vanessa slammed her fist into it in midair. It flew across the room and smashed into a wall. Relative to its size, the blow should have knocked the creature out. Instead, it just rose and grumbled something before scrambling up one of the smaller trees.

Will stared at the hole the creature had climbed up through. His face had gone several shades paler. "What was that?"

"Gremlin, I'd say," Vanessa said. "They're the mortal enemies of the fairies, but they're rare. I haven't seen one since training."

"What was it doing here?" Michael asked.

"Scavenging, most likely," Vanessa said. "It looked like it was carrying some pieces of junk."

Michael nodded, suddenly feeling a little uneasy. He hadn't lived here in a long time, but it had been home once. It should have been safe. Of course, that was childishly naïve, but wasn't Neverland supposed to be about such beliefs? Ignoring the ramifications of that for a moment, he hesitantly knelt and looked under the bed again. This time, he couldn't help but smile. Children were always leaving things under their beds, and the Lost Boys had been no different. He reached forward and pulled out three curved swords. They were small, sized for children. Each had a few spots of rust, which caused Michael to stare. He had never seen rust in Neverland. In spite of that, however, the swords were sharp and had been used in combat often. He handed one to Vanessa and another to Will.

"What am I supposed to do with this?" Will asked.

"Keep it with you," Michael said.

He showed Will how to tie the sword to his belt with a bit of vine. Its weight felt familiar on his waist, reminding him both of his time in Neverland and of the years he had spent with the Knights. He'd never been as good with a blade as a master like Vanessa, who looked natural in spite of the undersized weapon, but he'd been good enough—at least, until he hadn't been. He didn't allow himself to dwell on that too much as he led Will and Vanessa back to the surface.

Moving back up the tree was an ordeal, especially with the swords at their waists, and it took nearly an hour for the three of them to reach the surface—most of that time taken up by Will and Michael. Nev, who had spent part of the time they were inside gathering fruit and nuts, reported she hadn't seen the gremlin. They sat down in the shadow of a nearby tree and ate what she had gathered.

"Is this the sort of thing you ate before?" Will asked.

"Sometimes," Michael said. "Other times, the food was make-believe, and we just had to pretend we were having dinner."

"Didn't you get hungry?"

"Well, yes," Michael laughed. "We never starved, though. Thinking back, I don't know why."

"Peter pretended the food was real, too," Nev said. "Neverland is *his*. If he pretends something here, it stops being entirely make-believe."

Michael nodded, but Will looked confused, and Michael remembered that the other man couldn't understand the Never Bird. After several seconds, Will worked up the nerve to speak.

"Does it—"

"She," Michael corrected.

Will grumbled and nodded. "Does she have any idea what to do next? Maybe we could find other fairies." He let out a laugh that sounded strained. "I can't believe I just said that."

Michael smiled but shook his head. "Most fairy nests are on the tops of trees. I don't know that I feel up to climbing every tree on the island until we find them."

"It wouldn't do you any good," Nev said. "As I said, the fairies are gone. Even the few villages they have are empty."

"The gremlins," Vanessa said after Michael had translated. "They hate fairies. Maybe they did something."

"It's as good an idea as any." He glanced at Nev. "From what Jane told me, they live in the Underworld, right?"

The bird cooed. "That is where they generally make their home, yes."

"All right." Michael met Will's gaze, and the other man nodded, but before he could say anything, Michael went on: "First, though, there's a stream nearby, and you need to take a bath."

"I washed up back at the last stream."

"Not enough," Vanessa said.

CHAPTER 16

* * *

There are three ways that I know of to get into the Underworld," Nev said as Will was bathing. "The easiest, provided you can fly, is through a cave at the top of the Never Mountain."

Michael glanced toward the peak, the top of which could be seen from any point on the island. Moving through the forest had been difficult enough. Even if they had possessed the proper equipment, climbing that mountain would be all but impossible. He translated for Vanessa before shaking his head. "Unfortunately, only you and Shade can fly."

Nev looked to the east in the direction of the bay, though a wall of trees obscured her sight. "There is also the water way. That path starts in the Coral Caves and leads to an underground sea."

"Which would require us to breathe underwater," Michael said.

"Perhaps you could locate a tribe of nixies to help you there," Nev suggested.

Nixies, or water fairies, gave off dust that allowed one to breathe water. Unfortunately, most of them lived underwater in the first place, and it was impossible to track one down without drowning. Once again, Michael shook his head. They might as well wish to fly as hope to find a nixie.

"Besides, we would still have to deal with the mermaids," he said.

Nev conceded the point, adding, "And I have heard of things inside the Coral Caves that are just as dangerous."

Once Michael translated, Vanessa looked from the mountain to the forest in the direction of the bay. She shivered as Will rejoined them. He looked like a new man, though his clothes were little more than rags. He had even used the sword to cut off the more ragged parts of his beard. He sat on a stump while they talked.

"What's the third way?" Michael asked.

The bird sighed, a thing Michael hadn't realized birds could do. "The third way is the witch's way. You know that all people, not just children, cease to age once they are in Neverland?"

"Yes. Hook was over two hundred years old when he died, and Will and I are probably the same age now."

"What?" Will asked.

"Never mind."

The bird looked from one to the other before bobbing her head. "Before even Hook landed on these shores, there was Mora, the first mortal to ever set foot in Neverland. She was old even then and skilled in the arts of dark magic. The centuries have only sharpened her abilities, and she has a malicious side to her. She built her house in the Dark Swamp, at the entrance to a cave that leads to the Underworld. None can pass that way without getting permission from her, and she extracts a price for every passing."

A chill ran down Michael's back. "What kind of price?"

"What kind of thing would a witch want?" the bird asked. "Personally, I would rather climb the mountain or find a nixie.

Even the best of your kind can be cruel, and Mora was never one of the best."

"We don't have time for either of those, though. Don't you feel it? Neverland is getting darker. Who knows what will happen if we don't free Peter soon?"

"The Dark Swamp it is, then," the bird said.

"Unfortunately, yes." And he explained the plan to the rest of the group.

Shade seemed to fade slightly. Vanessa would have seemed calm to someone who didn't know her well. She was on edge, and Will looked like he was going to be sick. He gripped the sword at his side so tightly that his knuckles turned white.

Michael nodded at the bird. "Lead the way."

"IS THE PLACE WE'RE GOING TO REALLY CALLED THE DARK Swamp?" Will asked after they had been walking for most of the day.

"Yes," Michael said as he cut away a piece of shrubbery. "Why?"

"It's just that it seems like something out of a story."

"It is," Vanessa said.

"I don't understand."

Michael turned to Vanessa, but she motioned for him to continue. He glanced up, though the forest's thick canopy prevented him from seeing the sky. "There are fairy villages in the trees above us. There are mermaids in the lagoon. Last time I was here, there were pirates. We're following a talking bird and a living shadow. Neverland *is* the stuff of stories. Peter may have created it, but it was shaped by the imagination of children all over the world, especially those who came here. It's the Dark Swamp because children believe such a place exists."

Will mulled that over as they continued their journey.

Vanessa moved in close to Michael. "You explained that well."

"It's part of me. And it was part of all of us at some point in our lives."

"Exactly. You'd be surprised how easy it is for people to forget that, even Knights. Do you understand how valuable that knowledge—that perspective—is, and not just for our mission now?"

Wary, Michael said, "What's your point?"

"My point is that you belong with us. We need—"

"Leave it alone, Vanessa."

"But—"

"I said leave it alone."

"I will . . . for now."

He glared, but she pretended not to notice, and they walked on in silence.

The border between the Neverwood and the Dark Swamp wasn't clearly defined. The ground gradually became more and more soggy, and the air took on the scent of rot. Michael's boots stuck in the mud more than once, and flies and biting insects buzzed around. Even Shade seemed bothered by the suffocating heat, and if Michael hadn't known better, he would've sworn the shadow was sweating. Ghostly lights flickered blue in the distance. Will stared at them and took an involuntary step toward one, but Michael put a hand on his shoulder and jerked him back. Will blinked several times and squinted at the lights before looking at Michael.

Vanessa had gone pale. "Are those what I think they are?"

Michael nodded. "Will-o'-the-wisps." He glanced at Will. "Fairies of the dead. Most types of fairies are harmless enough, but wisps will lead you into the dark and pull your soul from your body."

Will gaped at him. "You can't be serious. What child came up with that?"

"I wouldn't even want to guess. Keep your attention forward. Focus on our goal. Remember Wendy. That should help. Just don't stare too long at any light."

They started slogging through the swamp again. Taking his own advice, Michael didn't allow his eyes to linger on a single light for more than a second, but still the wisps called to him. He found he *wanted* to be drawn into them. They offered a peace that he had been seeking for a long time, an end to pain and confusion . . .

Involuntarily, his eyes settled on one of the lights, and before he knew what he was doing, he had taken a step forward. Vanessa grabbed his wrist, and Shade flew between him and the wisps. Somehow, looking at the fairies through the shadow lessened their power.

"Not so easy to look away, is it?" Will asked, not unkindly. "Maybe you should think of Wendy, too."

"Sorry," he said.

Will inclined his head in acknowledgment.

"And thank you," Michael said to Vanessa and Shade.

"We'll get through this," Vanessa said, and he knew she wasn't just talking about the swamp, or even their mission to find Peter. And even though he didn't quite believe her, he knew it was exactly what he needed to hear. They pressed on.

As the sun neared the western horizon, they picked up the pace. Even in the best of times, Neverland wasn't safe at night, and the swamp was one of the most dangerous areas there was in the *day*. The full moon had just started to rise when a light appeared in the distance, and Michael immediately looked away. But it wasn't exactly like wisps, and he forced himself to look back. It was orange instead of blue and lacked the pulsing quality of the death fairies. It didn't have that peculiar draw to it, either. Oddly, because of that lack of draw they headed *toward* it, though they had to wade into knee-deep water. Once they got closer, Michael saw that the light was coming from the window of a cottage that seemed to be made of mud and loose sticks. As they neared, Nev cried out, "There is something in the water."

Ripples in the water flowed past them, and a faint ticking sounded over the croaks and chirps of the swamp animals. Michael's blood went cold. "Run!"

Will gripped his sword. "But—"

"That won't do any good. Run!"

He grabbed Will's arm and pulled him toward the cottage. Vanessa, who had been looking around, fell in half a step behind him. The ticking grew louder, and the nearby animals went silent, so he could clearly hear the crocodile tearing through the swamp. He turned to see a rush of water that obscured most of the creature, though he caught a glimpse of wicked teeth. Ahead of them, a small woman, no more than four feet tall, hobbled out of the cottage. In the darkness, he couldn't make out any features, but he had a sense that she was glaring. Suddenly, the water went completely silent—no ticking at all. A wave washed over Michael, Will, and Vanessa, bathing them in the stench of the swamp, but the creature that caused it was nowhere to be seen. Fear welled up inside of Michael. Who was this woman that even the most fearsome creature in all of Neverland turned away from her?

The three of them pulled themselves out of the swamp, rancid water dripping from their clothes. Only the woman's pointed nose was visible from under her hood, but he could still feel her eyes on him, and the weight of her gaze was such that he couldn't move until she turned away. As soon as her eyes fell on Will, he froze as well. Vanessa's hand went to her weapon, but when she touched the hilt, there was a hissing sound, and she drew back. Michael caught the slightest hint of burning flesh.

The witch smiled. "What do we have here?"

Her voice sounded like dead leaves being crushed underfoot and made Michael wonder if he wouldn't be better off going into the water and facing the crocodile. He looked at the woman and tried to be brave, though his voice quavered as he spoke.

"I am—"

"Don't," Vanessa said. "Never give a witch your name. Even if she already knows it, giving her your name of your own free will can give her power over you."

Chagrined, Michael said, "Right. I should have remembered that." He looked at the witch. "We're looking for Mora. If you're her, I suspect you already know who we are. If you're not, we have nothing to talk about. Are you her?"

The woman pulled back her hood, revealing a wrinkled face and long gray hair. Her pale blue eyes flickered to Vanessa, and there was a faint hint of annoyance in her features before she nodded. Vanessa, for her part, stared back at the witch without blinking.

"Yes, I am Mora. It has been a long time since I've had visitors."

"We're not here to visit. We want to cross into the Underworld."

"Right to business, I see. Very well. Such things do not come cheap, not even to one with allies such as yours."

"Do not play games with us," Nev said. "What is your price?"

"Are you sure you wouldn't like some tea?" the witch asked, apparently perfectly able to understand the bird.

"Just let us pass," Michael said.

"A shame. If you had indulged me in some of the courtesies, I might have allowed you a cheaper passage."

"Why don't we just walk by her?" Will suggested. "It doesn't look like she can stop us, and we could probably find this cave if we really looked."

Mora scowled, and the sound of buzzing insects faded as an ominous thunder sounded overhead. "Please, by all means, walk by me. But before you do, consider this: I stopped the crocodile. Why do you think I can't stop the likes of you three?"

She cackled then, seeing how no one made a move to pass her. "As I thought. Hmmm . . . What could you possibly have of value to me? Perhaps I should demand a servant, one indentured to me for a hundred years. After all, the land would keep them young. Why not the husband of your sister, Wendy? He has already been absent from your world for years. Surely none would miss him if he were not to return. Surely you can't have much affection for him. Why would you care if he came back or not? You need not even tell your sister, Michael. You could leave him out when you told this story." She gave him a grin that showed yellow teeth. The smell of her breath almost made him gag. "If you survive, that is."

Will went pale, but Michael shook his head. "No."

"No, you won't survive? I'd give you a one-in-ten chance. Ah, no, you mean you won't give me this man. I see. Are you certain, though? What if I demand nothing else? What if, barring that, I will not allow you to pass?"

"No."

"Very well." Mora lifted a bony finger at Vanessa. "Her, then. She dragged you into a life you had left behind. You must resent her greatly."

The truth was, she wasn't so wrong in her assessment of him. He did resent Vanessa dragging him into this, and he wasn't sure he cared more about Will than he did about saving Peter.

Yet being partially right wasn't the same as knowing his heart. He resented Vanessa, but he also thanked her for reminding him what it meant to adventure. And he didn't care all that much about Will, but he loved Wendy and Jane, and the thought of their happiness more than outweighed his feelings toward their husband and father.

Heart resolved, he stood up a bit straighter.

"Pick something else."

"Are you certain? What if I demand nothing else?" she said once more. "What if, barring that, I will not allow you to pass?"

"Then we'll find another way. We'll go through the mountain or the Coral Caves. Regardless, I'm not leaving Will or Vanessa." His eyes roved over the rest of his companions. "Or anyone else, for that matter, so don't even bother asking."

"Not like it'd be up to you to leave me in the first place," Vanessa muttered. "You try to do that, and I'd offer *you* to the witch."

There was that, too.

The witch cackled again. "No, I suppose not. I wonder what else I can ask. Perhaps you have a suggestion."

"Beware, Michael," Nev said. "You are dealing with the oldest living human in existence, and her cunning is greater than any who have ever walked the earth—in Neverland *and* your own world."

"Don't you know, dear bird, that it is not polite to speak of a lady's age. Perhaps I should demand your ability to fly."

It might have been Michael's imagination, but he thought he heard a faint animal cry from within the cottage, as if a creature had been hurt and was whimpering for relief. He was about to respond when Nev waved a wing at him, and he got the distinct impression that she was telling him that she would handle this.

Nev looked right at her. "Do your worst. If that is what you want, I offer it freely."

She shook her head. "No, I think not. You are too ready to part with it, but then your nest isn't in a tree, is it? It floats in the Never Bay, and you need the ability to swim more than to fly. No, don't offer it. I do not want it. But perhaps your eggs. They take a hundred years to hatch, do they not? How many are left?"

"No," Michael said.

She scowled. "There is much you hold back, for one who is so desperate. I know what it is you seek to do. Are you certain it is not worth a higher price than you are willing to pay?"

"Tell me your price," Michael said. "I'm not going to give anyone to you, but other than that, tell me."

"I want merely a simple thing, then," she said after a moment's thought. "A drop of blood."

Chills ran down Michael's spine. "Blood?"

He wasn't a spellcaster, but he knew the principles. Vanessa had warned him not to give Mora his name, and blood would be an even more potent channel.

"You must think I'm an idiot. Blood would grant you the ability to work all kinds of spells on me."

"True, but it is what I demand."

"What kind of spells?" Will asked.

She turned her grin on Will, who took a step back until his feet were in the water. "Spells to harm. Spells to enthrall and to summon." She ran her fingers through matted gray hair. "You need not worry over much. The power in a single drop would soon be expended if I worked more than a single spell with it."

"One spell is usually more than enough," Vanessa said.

"Come now—I ask for very little."

"Yes, but that's what makes us so cautious: *Why* would you ask for so little?" Michael asked.

"Now, that is my business, is it not? I could tell you, but such knowledge is only for my apprentice. Do you wish to learn, Michael Darling? My price for that would be far higher than for the passage." She breathed deeply and seemed to look inside of him. "Ah yes, I believe you could learn, if you had the desire.

It is easier for those you call the veiled. Would you become my apprentice? Learn of my power, so that it can one day be yours? The power to heal and kill, protect and destroy? To command. To control. To never be afraid again."

It was tempting. The kind of power she'd displayed with the crocodile—it was impressive. She had frozen the three of them with a stare—he could imagine what other spells she had at her disposal. How much good he could do with such power.

And yet, she didn't hide the awful nature of her magic, either. *Kill. Destroy. Command. Control . . .*

Michael shivered and shook his head. "No, that's okay."

"What a shame. But that brings us back to your blood. One drop, please. A fair trade: one drop now, instead of all your blood spilled on the ground should you try to get past me against my will. That's nothing. And you need not worry. Even my magic cannot so easily cross the boundary between worlds, certainly not with a single drop of blood to power it. I am quite satisfied in this world. I have no desire to return to yours. Once you leave Neverland, you will be beyond my reach."

Michael glanced at Nev. "Is that true?"

The bird's head bobbed. "Even Peter couldn't reach beyond Neverland without great effort."

"So I have no choice."

"You always have a choice," both Nev and Mora said at the same time.

Michael let out a long breath. It felt like the words were being dragged out of him. "Fine. A drop of blood."

"From each of you," the witch said.

Michael hesitated. "Wait—each? That wasn't part of the deal."

"What deal? We just started talking. One drop from each who wishes to pass. How is that unreasonable? What—would you expect a single drop to account for all five of you?" Mora spat. "Such hubris."

"We need to discuss—"

"I will agree to this," the bird said firmly.

"But you won't be leaving when this is done," Michael said.

She ruffled her feathers. "Do you think I did not know that I would be risking my life when I chose to join you? I am old, but hardly powerful. There is little Mora could do with my blood that she could not also do without it."

Before Michael could say anything else, Mora's left hand emerged from her sleeve, holding five small glass vials. In her right, she held a long thin needle. "Yes," she said. "So very little I can do with the blood."

Michael's throat went dry, knowing this was a mistake, but not knowing if there was any better option. He extended a hand. In spite of her age, Mora moved too fast to be seen, pricking Michael's index finger before he had a chance to change his mind. The next thing he knew, one of her vials held a single drop of blood, somehow suspended in the center and looking like a ruby bead. She looked to Will and held up the needle.

Will hesitated. "She's really a witch?"

Michael nodded. "It looks like it."

"And you want me to give her some of my blood?"

"If I thought there was a better way . . ."

Will waved him off. "This whole thing is insane. I just wanted to understand exactly how insane before I went along with it." He extended his hand. "Go ahead."

Once again, Mora's hand moved like a blur. Will drew back, but Mora was already putting away the vial. A quick prick to Nev took a drop of her blood. Vanessa glared at her as she took her blood, and then Mora looked at the shadow.

"You can't be serious," Michael said.

"I said from everyone, unless the shadow does not wish to pass."

"But Shade is a shadow. He doesn't have blood."

"And I am a witch. Extend your hand, Shadow of Pan."

Michael's eyes wandered from the Never Bird to the shadow.

The bird fluttered down from a tree branch to Michael's shoulder. "I am not sure about this. You and Will and Vanessa shall leave Neverland and place yourself beyond Mora's power. I offer her nothing more than the wisdom of a bird who knows far less than she, but Shade—"

"—is the shadow of a god," Michael finished, "and one who lives in Neverland."

"And yet it is not the blood of the god himself," Mora said. Michael couldn't tell if her calmness hid eagerness, or if she was simply a toll collector and was waiting for her prize.

Nev was much more suspicious. "Then why . . ." She narrowed her eyes, thinking over what the witch could want with Shade's blood, but saying nothing.

Michael glanced at the shadow. "What do you say?"

The shadow rubbed his chin before nodding vigorously. He extended his hand. This time, Mora moved slowly. She gripped the air, though her hand was nowhere near the shadow. Her own shadow, however, gripped Peter's, and the shadow of the needle pricked him. Though the vial in Mora's hand remained empty, its shadow showed a single drop floating within.

"That's a little eerie," Will said.

"Tell me about it," Michael said. Turning to the witch, he said, "You'll let us into the Underworld now?"

"Of course. Please, come in."

Her door creaked as it opened of its own accord, but Vanessa motioned for the others to stay back as her hand fell to the hilt of her sword. "That *definitely* wasn't part of the deal."

"The entrance is inside my home." Mora's smirk showed

her yellow teeth to their awful imperfection. "Of course, I will not require you to enter, but I will not return what you have paid."

"We may as well go in," Nev said. "I doubt she intends us any harm. If she did, she could have done so already, blood or no."

The witch gave a wicked grin and turned around, the least inviting invitation Michael had ever received. Nevertheless, he followed Vanessa and Shade to the door, where they all peered in.

The interior of the cottage was dark, and even the light of the moon didn't pierce it as she disappeared into the darkness. Shade neared and reached inside, though he drew back almost instantly. He looked at Michael and made an exaggerated shivering motion. Mora laughed from inside.

"You did not think my home would be without protections, did you?" her voice asked from the darkness. "They will not harm you. You have my promise."

Michael looked at Vanessa, who stared into the darkness.

"Going into a witch's lair can be almost as dangerous as giving her your name," she said.

Michael nodded. "You're right. We might turn into pigs."

Her face reddened. "That happened one time!"

He grinned and looked at Will, who said, "I don't know why you're looking to me for advice. I have no idea what's going on."

Michael looked back to Vanessa, who pursed her lips and nodded once.

"All right," he said. "Let's go."

Still, a chill ran down Michael's back as he entered. The darkness felt almost tangible, and he kept expecting something to grab at him. He was about to turn around when a purple light came into existence just above Mora's hand. It didn't seem to illuminate as much as it should—even the witch's face remained shrouded in shadows, and other than vague outlines, the light revealed no details of her home. But it was better than nothing, at least initially. After a moment, though, Michael started to wish for darkness once more. Nev's weight on his shoulder, slight as it was, gave him a measure of assurance, however, and he pushed forward. Eventually—time seemed to have no meaning in this darkness—Mora stopped and waved a hand. A piece of the dirt floor collapsed, revealing the natural rock walls of a cave that descended into the earth.

"Here you go."

"What good does this do us? We can't see down there," Michael said.

Abruptly, light flamed into being a foot over Mora's hand, revealing the torch she gripped in her fingers. It illuminated the cave entrance, though it did even less to light up the cottage than the purple light had. Mora held it toward Michael. But when he reached for it, she held it back.

"What is your name?"

"You can't really expect me—"

"Tell me or walk in darkness."

Michael clenched his teeth. He should have thought of that before following her in here. Without some light, they'd be blind. He could probably make something out of materials in the swamp, but Mora wasn't likely to let them back in without paying something else—everything was a transaction for her. She had them trapped.

"I am William Harden."

Mora smiled and handed the torch to Will, who had stepped forward. Michael was going to stop him, but Will shrugged the hand off his arm. "I might as well do something useful."

"The danger—"

"—is one of *my* choosing. If this gets me closer to Wendy and my daughter, I'll take the risk. No matter what."

"That's very brave," Vanessa said, her tone cutting off any further protests from Michael.

"Yes," Mora said with a dark chuckle. "So very brave, William Harden." She tongued the word, seemingly chewing it with those yellow teeth. "On you go."

Will started toward the opening.

"I will close the way after you pass," Mora said after a beat.

"But how will we get out?" Michael asked, turning on her sharply.

She cackled and tried to meet his eyes, but Michael looked away. "You did not buy the right to exit through my home, though if you wish we may bargain again . . . There are so many names I can still take from you.

"So much blood."

"No, that's fine," Michael said, speaking almost before she was done.

She snorted and stepped out of the way. "So brave," she mocked, motioning for them to go on. "Half a league onward."

Michael's blood felt like it turned to ice. He eyed his companions, though he could barely see them in the torchlight. They each nodded in turn, though Vanessa was visibly shaken. And, one by one, they descended into darkness.

* * *

CHAPTER 17

Their footsteps seemed to echo forever as they walked through the passageway. The air held a perpetual chill, and the light of Will's torch seemed all too small when compared to the oppressive darkness around them. Michael stayed close to Will, and more than once he actually stepped on the other man's heels. Vanessa walked more confidently, but even she stayed close. When he looked at her, he could see the question on her face, though neither gave voice to it. Shade faded in and out of visibility as he passed through places beyond the reach of the flickering flame, which barely served to illuminate the walls three feet on either side of them. Nev stayed perched on Michael's shoulder, remaining oddly silent.

"She knew about Dmitri," Michael said.

"It's a famous poem," Vanessa said. "She might have heard it before."

"What are you two talking about?" Will asked.

"What she said at the end," Vanessa said. "'Half a league onward.' It's from a poem. 'Charge of the Light Brigade.' We had a partner who used to quote that whenever we were about to do something particularly dangerous."

"Used to?"

"He died," Michael said.

"I'm sorry."

"You didn't cause his death," Michael said a bit too bitterly.

"Neither did you," Vanessa said. "It wasn't your fault."

"Whose was it, then?"

"Offhand, I'd say it was the mahr who killed him."

Michael hissed at the stab of pain her seemingly casual words caused him, but he didn't answer. He looked at her sharply and she returned the look, not at all perturbed by his reaction. He walked on, self-reproach on constant loop.

If only, if only, if only . . .

Though he had no way to keep track of time, he was sure at least two hours had passed before they crossed into a wide cavern, coming out of an opening halfway up a wall that went up farther than he could see. Glowing crystals had been set into the walls at irregular intervals, illuminating the area in a soft blue light that barely served to reveal shadowy outlines. Still, it was a welcome relief after the witch's house and the cursed tunnel. That was short-lived, though. The path they had been walking on narrowed again until it was only a few feet across as it wound down the side of the wall, which was pockmarked with cave openings. Gradually Michael's eyes adjusted to the darkness.

Will, who apparently had better night vision than him, spoke as soon as they reached the bottom. "Is that a city?"

Vanessa let out a sharp gasp and stepped forward, squinting as she stared into the darkness. She took the lead, though she had no more idea where they were going than he did. It was several more seconds before Michael could see what Will was talking about. At first, he thought it was just an odd formation of rocks, but he soon realized that the rocks had been shaped. The top of some had been squared off, forming squat little houses with flat roofs. Most were no more than four feet tall, and he caught the occasional glimpse of movement between the buildings. Vanessa wore a wide grin, which he could understand. The number of people who had seen true cities of mystical creatures could be counted on his fingers.

As Michael's eyes continued to adjust, he realized that the movement he'd seen was caused by creatures. Some of them carried small crystals, dimmer versions of the ones that illuminated the cavern, but they were still bright enough to reveal mottled gray skin. The beings were all gremlins, scurrying in and out of the buildings in a way that reminded Michael of ants.

"What do we do now?" Michael asked.

"This is *your* mission," Will said.

"Right. Well, I'm open to suggestions."

"We could sneak closer and see if we can formulate a plan, then?" Vanessa said.

"I think the idea of us sneaking down is going to be pretty tough—we're twice the size of those buildings, let alone the gremlins."

"So we go in with force," she said.

"I concur," Nev said. "We charge in and demand they tell us what they were doing in the underground house."

"Just like that?" Michael asked.

"You're not going to convince them with diplomacy," the bird said. "Gremlins only respect strength."

He wasn't so sure. Unfortunately, he could see no other choice. Vanessa gave the bird a wink of mutual agreement after Michael translated their conversation, and they moved forward. The gremlins, it seemed, hadn't noticed them, even though they made no effort to hide their approach. So maybe they could have snuck up on the city, but Nev had been right: gremlins respected strength over stealth, and creeping up might have been the more hostile act in the creatures' eyes.

The five companions were near the edge of the tiny city when one of the creatures appeared in front of them, seemingly materializing out of nowhere. He wore armor that looked to be made of beetle shells, though Michael had never seen an insect large enough to provide parts that big. Like the gremlin's skin, the armor had a mottled pattern that allowed its bearer to fade into the rock and be almost invisible. He carried a stone sword that had been polished until it had an almost reflective sheen. Vanessa raised her own sword as the creature walked up to them. The gremlin took in the sight of the taller woman and lowered his weapon, but didn't sheath it.

"Greetings, friend of fairies." His voice sounded like stone grinding against stone. "The gremlin queen awaits your coming."

Michael and Vanessa exchanged glances. "We were expected?" she asked.

The gremlin brought his fist to his chest, causing his beetle armor to rattle. "Once she learned that you interrupted our scavenging, she suspected that it was only a matter of time before you came here."

"What does she want?"

The gremlin stiffened. "She does not trust her plans to the likes of me."

"What if we don't want to go?"

The gremlin growled something in a language Michael didn't understand. The next thing he knew, half a dozen gremlins, hidden all around them, answered. One even rose up from the ground in the middle of their group. Will and Michael drew their weapons, joining Vanessa. Shade lifted his fists, as if he could actually help fight off a foe. With only six enemies, and all of them much smaller than the humans, they had a reasonably good chance of fighting their way free, especially if they struck first. The lead gremlin, apparently reading something in Michael's face, growled. After a few tense seconds, he uttered a harsh word, and the surrounding creatures sheathed their weapons.

"We do not have the strength to force you. Come if you wish or remain if you wish. Either way, you have nothing to fear from us."

He turned and started walking away, only to be joined by his companions. For several long moments, Michael could only stare.

"That was unexpected."

"That doesn't fit with what I know about gremlins," Vanessa agreed.

"It's stranger than you know," Nev said. "What little knowledge I have of Neverland's Underworld says that the gremlins are a mighty nation. They never simply request that you come to them, and they are more than strong enough to at least try to force the issue. For them to admit that they're too weak . . . I don't think they captured the fairies. There is something else going on."

"So you think we should go?"

"I think we're trapped underground, and our only lead just evaporated. At this point, we don't have much to lose."

Michael looked to Will and started translating what Nev had said but Will raised a hand.

"I think I got enough from hearing your side. Let me ask: What would we do if we don't follow them?"

Michael thought for a second before he realized he had nothing. "Let's go."

They started after the gremlins. The creatures had just turned a corner, and Michael, Vanessa, and Will had to rush to avoid losing them. As they fell into step behind the gremlins, their diminutive postures stiffened. They obviously didn't like the situation, and Michael had the feeling that they wanted nothing more than to turn their stone weapons against the lot of them, size be damned.

It took them only a few minutes to reach the city, and when

they did, most of the gremlins who had ambushed them scattered, leaving only the leader to guide them. It hadn't been apparent from a distance, but up close now, it was clear the buildings were in ruins. Many had crumbled, and rock dust covered everything. Once, Michael's foot brushed a building, and it collapsed into dust, drawing angry mutters from gremlins that he hadn't noticed were there. He suppressed a shiver. There could be a hundred watching and he wouldn't know.

"Is that a statue?" Will asked.

Michael looked to where he was pointing. A gremlin stood perfectly still, though it was grasping its chest. It didn't even seem to be breathing. He scanned the area until his eyes settled on a pair of the creatures standing near the still one. They glared at him and Will, their faces twisted by hatred. They barely moved, but it was more than the other was doing.

"No, not really," Vanessa said, her voice barely above a whisper. "Gremlins turn to stone when they die."

Michael had heard of that, too, though he had never seen it. Their guide turned to glare at her with murder in his eyes. Vanessa met his gaze without blinking until the gremlin spun on his heels and continued toward the center of the city. Now that Michael knew what to look for, he spotted other statues scattered about, each having their hands over a wound or frozen while they were crying out in pain. He glanced at Nev, who was still perched on his shoulder. Her eyes roamed around, and he had the impression that she was even more surprised than he was.

The castle in the center of the city was as run-down as the rest of the buildings. Half of it was simply gone. The edges that remained were too smooth to have been broken off in battle. It was as if it had been cut by some impossibly sharp sword. Holes dotted the remaining structure, and it looked like it would collapse at any moment.

"What did this?" he asked, half to himself.

"Ghosts," a gravelly voice said. "Gremlin stone is alive, and the touch of the restless dead kills everything."

It took Michael a second to find the figure that was speaking. She blended with her surroundings even more perfectly than the rest. Her robe seemed to be made of rock that moved like fabric. Even her eyes more resembled gems than anything that had ever graced a human face. Abruptly, her skin darkened until she was clearly visible, which she was obviously doing by choice. Vanessa took in a sharp breath.

"Do you see that pattern of her skin?" Vanessa said in a voice just loud enough for him to hear. "That's the queen."

The gremlin's ears twitched. As if summoned by Vanessa's words, another gremlin appeared just behind the monarch carrying a pole with a jagged skull flag.

"I am Queen Tolphan, as much as one can be the queen of a shattered people. No doubt you came here to find out what our role was in the events on the surface. Well, the answer is simple: nothing. We sent a raid up to Pan's house because we thought he had sent the ghosts after us. Imagine our surprise when we learned that they were gone, the house empty, and him devoid of any of his possessions."

"We caught one of yours looting Peter's house."

The queen's laugh sounded like rocks crumbling. "Yes, you did. Pan and his friends are still our enemies. We found his home unoccupied. Of course, we would try to take what we could, and we didn't question it when we found the structure unoccupied. It was none of our doing, though."

"Then who did?"

"In that, I am as ignorant as you, but I suspect all our problems have the same cause."

Michael pursed his lips, but didn't say anything.

The queen laughed once more. "Very well. You do not wish

to say anything lest you tell me something I do not already know. I will start. Peter Pan is missing, very likely captured, though he remains in Neverland. That would be the crux of it, if I do not miss my guess."

"How do you know?" Vanessa asked.

"Do you think a god could go missing with no one noticing?" Tolphan shook her head. "Many of us are aware, though most aren't willing to admit it."

"Do you know what happened to him?" Michael said.

"I know he is not in the Underworld."

"The world under Neverland encompasses more area than everything on the surface," Nev said. "You cannot know that for certain."

"This is my domain even more than the skies are yours. If he were here, I would know. I suspect if you find who sent the ghosts, you will also find who holds Pan."

"If the ghosts exist," Vanessa muttered.

"You doubt her?" Will asked.

"You don't?"

"After everything so far—I guess not."

Nev didn't seem to hear much of what the two whispered about. Instead, she asked Michael, "Why is the queen helping us?"

"Good question. Why are you helping us?" Michael translated.

"Because we are on the same side."

"Since when?"

"Since the penalty for failure became the destruction of Neverland. I want that no more than you."

Nev flapped once but didn't rise. Michael glanced at her before answering. "An alliance of convenience, then?"

"I would not go so far as to call it an alliance," the queen said. "Unlike you, Never Bird, Pan did not create us. We came here because this land suited us, but we can leave and return to the mortal world, if we should choose. It would not be an easy thing, but we could do it."

Vanessa's hand fell to her hilt. "Michael . . ."

He nodded. Gremlins still existed in the real world, but they were scattered and nowhere near as organized as they were here. On occasion, one caused malfunctions in a plane or similar device. They could be dangerous under the right circumstances, and if such a large colony were to relocate, there would be chaos. Michael took a deep breath.

"Relax, Knights," the queen said. "I only say that so you know that we have a choice to make. And we *choose* to stay here. But only if that's still viable."

"So you need our help. And in return, you stay in Neverland."

"Exactly."

"What are you proposing, then? How can you help us?"

"The Still Lake," the queen said after a second. "If there are answers anywhere, it is there."

"What is the Still Lake?"

"A dark reflection of the Never Bay, where the dead gather," the queen said. "There are dangers there that even I would fear to face."

"And that's where you're sending us?" Will asked.

"I am."

"Why don't you go yourself? Doesn't seem like you're helping us out too much by sending us to do the dangerous work."

"We have dangerous work of our own. We need to defend our city."

Michael eyed the ruined castle. "From the ghosts."

"Yes, though ultimately the ghosts are but a minor threat, and enough things down here have access to wisp dust to be able to hurt them."

"It didn't do too good last time, did it?" Vanessa asked.

"We were attacked with no warning," the queen snapped. "This time, we'll be prepared."

"While we go to the Still Lake and save *your* land," Michael said.

"Exactly."

"This isn't exactly how an alliance works."

"As I said, it's not really an alliance. Or rather, it's what we gremlins see as one. Anyway," the queen said in a dismissive tone, "it's the best I can offer. Either that, or you can envision your own world full of my people.

"And, you can see if you're able to leave our city alive."

A stillness hung with those words. Looking around, Michael saw just how large an audience Tolphan had gathered. They weren't all armed, but they vastly outnumbered Michael and his friends now.

"What is it about the Still Lake that has got you so scared?" Vanessa said. "Especially if the ghosts don't bother you."

"What I fear is the thing that is *controlling* the ghosts, getting them to work together. They have never done that before, and you can see the results."

Michael gave her a slow nod, even as he looked at Vanessa with indecision in his eyes. Her normally confident demeanor was shaken, too. He turned back to the queen. "I don't suppose you have any wisp dust you'd be willing to part with?" he asked. "I mean, since we're on the same side."

"What we have is needed for the defense of our city."

Michael sighed. "That's what I thought. How exactly do we get to the Still Lake?"

CHAPTER 18

＊　＊　＊

Wait—why are we doing this?"

Michael stopped and turned to Will as they made their way from the center of the city. His brother-in-law had stopped, a look of confusion and anger on his face.

"What do you mean?" Michael asked.

"Why are we helping the gremlins? They gave us nothing. If anything, we're doing their dirty work. So what do we get out of this?"

"Hopefully, the next clue to where Peter—"

"Another clue? Another *clue*?" he said, cutting Vanessa off. "Every place we've gone has been worse than the last. I didn't give my blood and name to a witch for another clue! I want answers! I want to get out of here!"

Vanessa was shocked at the outburst. Michael, however, thought he understood.

"Will," he said, putting his hand on Will's arm. "I know this isn't easy."

Will snorted with derisive laughter.

"Okay—that's an understatement. This is incredibly difficult. Impossible-seeming, even. But that's the way it is."

Will looked up, anger flashing in his eyes. Before he could say something, Michael continued.

"It's the way it is *here*. In Neverland. This place is mad because it's made up of the whims of children, including its god. It's magic and chaos and nightmares and monsters. But it's also wonder. It's also whimsy. It feels like a fantasy because it's fantastical. And in that fantasy, we need to follow different rules. Back home, you'd be on your ship. You'd have a routine, and you'd have regulations you'd need to follow, right?"

Will didn't answer.

"Will—right?"

Finally, Will nodded.

"Yet those rules—the ones on your ship—they are a lot different from how you'd act in London. How you'd act around Wendy. Each place has its own rules. And in this one, going on quests is a rule."

"Quest?"

"Yes—what did you think this was other than a quest?"

"Like . . . like Odysseus?"

"Yes! Like him and Hercules."

"Like Arthur," Vanessa put in.

"Exactly," Michael said. "The original Knights didn't just find the Grail, did they?"

"In a lot of the tales, they never found the Grail," Will muttered.

Michael realized the logic trap he had led himself into, and looked for help. Once more, Vanessa stepped in.

"But what child do you know who—in their play—doesn't find the treasure? Save the princess? Defeat the monster?"

"We're not children!" Will shouted.

"We are here," Michael said quietly. "Because if we're not, then we're the monsters."

Will stared at the two of them for a moment, then muttered a quiet curse to himself before once more heading toward the lake.

Michael made to follow, but Vanessa held him back.

"Give him some space," she said.

"Right." He took a deep breath. "Did you mean that? About how children's stories end?"

"Of course."

"So you believe we're going to win?"

"Oh, I wouldn't go that far," she said, starting after Will now. "You clearly haven't read a lot of the original Grimm brothers or Hans Christian Andersen."

The thing was, he *had*. And he knew all too well what happened to a lot of their characters. He had *seen* it, and far too many times.

Swallowing, Michael followed, wondering if Neverland without Peter would lead to much, *much* darker conclusions to this particular tale.

THE WAY TO THE STILL LAKE WASN'T PARTICULARLY DIF-ficult. It lay almost directly beneath the gremlin city, and apparently most caves in the area that sloped downward eventually ended there. The queen pointed them toward the closest such passage. They left the city without further incident, though Michael could feel the weight of all the gremlins' gazes, and he was sure that he missed many more than he saw. They were walking rather quickly by the time they passed the last building. It didn't take them long to find the passage Tolphan had spoken of, though they were an hour out of the city before Vanessa took her hand off her weapon.

"Why did you ask the queen for wisp dust?" Will asked as they started down, finally speaking to them again.

Michael pried a glowing crystal about the size of his closed fist out of the wall before motioning for Will to put out his torch. "No sense in wasting that if we don't need to."

"You didn't answer my question."

"I asked her for it because the dust from different types of fairies have different effects. Wisps are the fairies of death, and their dust lets you exist partially in the spirit world, which lets you hurt ghosts and other spiritual beings."

Will glanced upward. "There were plenty in that swamp. Why didn't we just gather some up there before we came underground?"

"It wasn't necessary."

"What do you mean?"

"Wisps and ghosts are drawn to each other," Vanessa said. "If there are that many ghosts here, then there are wisps nearby. There were probably a few ghosts in the swamp, too."

She held a glowing crystal she had pried out of the wall in front of her. Its soft blue light wasn't as bright as the torch, but it didn't flicker as much, either, and the steadier light proved to be better illumination.

Will started to speak, but before he could get so much as a word, a flash of ghostly light flickered to life around a bend in a passage, though it vanished before Michael could get a good look at it. His breath caught in his throat, and he paused. The light didn't appear again, though. Will held his sword hilt in a white-knuckled grip.

"Like I said," Vanessa said, "wisps."

"What do we do?" Will asked.

"A smart person would turn away and look for another passage," Michael said. "If only we had the time to behave smartly. We keep going." He hesitated before turning to Vanessa. "If I fall under the wisps' spell and you can't bring me out of it, leave me. Maybe Nev or Shade can lead you out of here. Get Will home."

Vanessa raised an eyebrow. "How exactly do you propose we do that? If the gremlins are right and Peter isn't here, we're not likely to find any pixies, either. We have no way out of Neverland, even if Shade can lead us from the Underworld."

"More than that," Nev said, "if any one of us falls into the thrall of the wisps, it could only be because the others have already fallen."

"Try," Michael said, not bothering to translate what Nev had said. "Wendy's suffered enough. She deserves to get her husband back, at least."

The Never Bird's head bobbed. "I will try, of course, but I cannot see such a plan succeeding. I believe it would be better if you were to stay alive."

Shade appeared in front of them just long enough to nod before disappearing again. Michael couldn't help but laugh.

"Don't worry. I have no intention of dying." He smiled broadly, but after a second, the joy just seemed to drain out of him. He glanced at Will. "Just be ready in case it happens."

They turned a corner, and the tunnel widened to a small chamber that was twenty feet across. The walls glittered in the crystals' light. A vein of quartz ran along one wall, catching the light and shimmering along its length. The refracted light created an odd sort of beauty, and Michael stared at it for several seconds. Beauty or no, a chill washed over him, though he couldn't say why. He didn't remember moving, but he found himself only a few inches from the wall, reaching out to touch the quartz. Then, without warning, a small ball of pale blue light appeared from a cavity in the wall. Michael could just make out the vaguely human figure inside. A series of quick notes sounded from the fairy, and Michael felt his mind fogging. A hand seized his wrist. He blinked and turned to see Vanessa. She pulled him away, and he felt the call of the fairies lessening. Behind her, however, stood Will, his attention held by the glowing light of the will-o'-the-wisp.

"Don't," Michael said as he pulled away from her.

"It's so beautiful." Will's voice seemed far away.

Another wisp appeared next to it, followed by a third. Michael grabbed Will's shoulder and forced him to turn around. Will tried to return his gaze to the fairies, but Michael punched him in the face. He shook his hand against the pain. Will blinked several times and brought his fingers to his mouth. They came away bloody, but he had obviously come back to himself.

"Don't look at them," Michael said, aware of his own hypocrisy, having just been pulled to the fairies himself.

Will took a deep breath and nodded, though he was shaking.

"We offer only peace, Michael." The ghostly voice made him want to listen, and it was all he could do not to fall into their trap. "Surely, you have had enough struggles. Who deserves peace if not you?"

"Yes," a different voice said. "Lay down your burdens and come to us."

"We can bring an end to suffering."

They were all around him now, with more appearing by the second. Each voice offered a fresh temptation, and each new fairy made it harder to avert his sight. It didn't make sense for him to fight so hard. Surely it wouldn't be so bad to give in, just for a second. He had just started to listen when a screech sounded over their haunting call. Nev dove from the cavern ceiling and snatched one of the fairies out of the air. She held the creature to the ground with her beak closed around its neck.

"Leave them be," she cawed, still able to speak in spite of the fairy she held.

"You would dare strike at us?" three of the fairies spoke in unison, giving their voice an odd resonance.

"Do not pretend innocence," the bird said. She squeezed the neck of the one in her beak. "You attacked us first."

"Only to give you peace. We wanted to help."

"I don't need your kind of help," Michael said, the spell of the fairies having been broken. Then something dawned on him. "No, actually, I do."

"What are you doing?" Vanessa asked.

"Getting us out of here."

With that, he tugged at the fairy in Nev's beak. The bird resisted, but after looking in his eyes for a second, she let it go. The fairy's glow was bright, and he could make out just enough to tell that it was male, not that that made a difference. While its companions screamed in protest, he held the wisp over his head and shook it, showering himself in its dust. He did the same to Will, who sneezed. Vanessa shivered, and Nev accepted the dust with an incline of her head. Shade, being incorporeal already, didn't need any. Then Michael released the fairy. It fluttered above him, uttering curses in the quick speech of fairies.

"What was that?" Will asked.

"Wisp dust. Their song works by tempting us with what lies beyond, but their dust allows us to exist partially in the spirit world. The temptation doesn't work as well when we're close to it, so we should be safe from them now."

"You will pay dearly for this insult," the one he had shaken said.

"Take it up with Peter," Michael said.

The fairies recoiled from the words as if physically struck, and instantly Michael regretted releasing the one he'd held. He tried to grab another one, but they darted just beyond reach. Vanessa moved quicker than he did, and while she succeeded in touching one, it slipped out of her grasp. He looked at Nev, who ruffled her feathers, but as soon as she took to the air, the fairies darted away.

"They know something," Michael said.

"It looks like it," Vanessa said. "You don't think we should go after them, do you?"

The tone in her voice caught Michael off guard. "You don't think it's a good idea?"

"You know how dangerous they are. Do you really want to chase them after what we just did to them?"

"It's never wise to take dust from a fairy against their will," Nev said. "Tinker Bell never forgave you after Peter did that to her, and that caused you more than one problem, as I recall."

"Peter didn't take dust from her. He already had it in his hands."

"But it *came* from her, and look what happened because of that. She nearly killed Wendy."

Michael shook his head. "Tink never liked any girl that Peter looked at for more than two seconds. Besides, I doubt that they can get people to shoot arrows at me like Tink did for Wendy."

"What?" Will asked. "Who shot arrows at Wendy?"

"The Lost Boys," Michael said absently. "Only Tootles hit her, though, but she was wearing an acorn button on a chain around her neck. The arrow hit it instead."

Will's eyes had gone wide, and he practically shouted, "Your brother *shot* Wendy with an arrow?"

"He wasn't our brother then. And it all worked out in the end." He smiled. "Neverland is a strange place. Maybe when you get back, you and Wendy can exchange stories about your adventures." He turned to the bird. "Nev, do you think we should keep heading to the Still Lake?"

The bird inclined her head. "If there are really ghosts there, it's still our best idea."

Michael touched his sword. "I'll be able to hurt them if they're hostile, right? I didn't need to actually sprinkle the sword."

"A weapon treated with the dust would work, but the hand

that wields the weapon matters far more. You're partially in the spirit world now, so you can hurt them, regardless of what you use."

"Good," Michael said, and let the others know. Vanessa gave her sword a practiced swing, while Will looked at his own, bemused. "Trust me, Will."

Will swallowed. "I'm trying."

"I know you are. Everyone ready?"

Nods and ayes all around.

"Let's go."

CHAPTER 19

* * *

Michael cried out as a ghost flowed out of the rock wall right in front of him. Vanessa moved like a snake. Her blade passed through it. It screamed and collapsed into mist. It took several seconds for Michael to calm down. He had lost count of how many such encounters they'd had. It had been a constant battle since they'd gotten the wisp dust. It was as if Neverland knew that they could now fight this kind of foe and sent them as a challenge.

That's probably exactly what's happening.

Finally, they reached a small cavern that seemed more defensible than the rest of the area. Michael was about to suggest that they rest for the night, or whatever passed for night down here, but Vanessa raised her finger to her mouth. When he was about to say something, she put her finger over his lips.

"There's something up ahead," she whispered.

Without waiting for anyone to respond, she drew her sword and stepped forward. Michael and Will exchanged glances before following. Vanessa seemed to glide across the stone, her footsteps making no more sound than a breeze. Will was clumsy by comparison, and Michael wasn't much better. They rounded the corner, and the cave opened up into a wide chamber.

It was larger than the cavern housing the gremlin city. The

roof of the chamber was lost to darkness, as was the far wall, though an occasional glowing crystal, presumably set in the wall on the other side of the lake, told him that this body of water was enormous. True to its name, the waters were completely still, looking almost like glass. Vanessa had moved right up to its shore and was scanning the water. Faint lights danced about, both on the shore and beneath the surface of the water. They lacked the allure that had tempted Michael earlier, and now that he could look on them, he noticed that many of them trailed a faint light that didn't quite match with the glow of the fairies themselves.

"I was at Berry Pomeroy Castle when the Knights tried to banish the spirits there," Vanessa said, not taking her eyes from the light. "They sent us running, in spite of our wisp dust, and there was an entire squad of us and not even half of the ghosts here." She took a deep breath. "This is insanity, you know."

Michael nodded. "We're not going to fight with them, but we need to talk to one if we're going to find out who sent them after the gremlins."

"Have a care," Nev said. "They may not be interested in talking."

"I'm aware." Michael ran a finger along his hilt but didn't draw his sword. "Let's not threaten them unless we need to."

Nev bobbed her head, and they stepped closer to the shore. Michael listened closely. They had almost reached the water before he realized what he was listening for. The ticking of the crocodile. He paused for a moment. The only sound was the song of the wisps, and he realized how strange it was that he considered that the lesser danger. He suppressed a shiver and stopped at the edge of the water. He would have to wade in to get close enough.

"What are you waiting for?" Nev asked.

"I guess I'm just a little worried that they might be offended. This lake seems almost holy."

The bird's eyes wandered over the waters. The spirits of the dead floated in the distance, their light reflected on the surface of the lake. "Rather the opposite, I'd say."

Will stalked up to the water and brushed his fingers against the surface before anyone could stop him. Far more ripples than his light touch could account for spread from his fingers. Though the cavern hadn't been particularly loud before, now it went deathly quiet as every being, ghost and wisp alike, turned their gazes to the small group. Will looked like he wished he could disappear.

"Maybe that wasn't the best idea," Will said.

Michael raised an eyebrow. "Are you serious?"

"How was I supposed to know what would happen? All you do is talk to the bird."

"Just . . . just don't touch anything," Michael said through gritted teeth.

But it was too late for that—they'd been noticed. Fairies darted toward them from all corners of the cavern, and the dust allowed Michael to see through their light. Their skin was pale blue or green, and their eyes were sunken. Their hair was wispy to the point of being almost transparent. A few had sharp teeth that looked capable of tearing flesh. They fluttered around Vanessa, Will, and Michael with a grace far beyond human capabilities.

"What do you want?"

It was like every wisp had spoken at once. The air was filled with the sound of their voices, and in spite of the protection offered by the wisp dust, their call made him feel like he had ice water running through his veins. He didn't even realize when he fell to his knees. He clenched his teeth. Standing felt like it took only slightly less effort than lifting a mountain, but he managed.

"Why are you attacking the gremlins?"

As one, the fairies hissed. The spirits let out a collective wail that infused the air with a cold energy. The surface of the lake roiled and waves washed up on the shore as ghosts came at them from all directions. One of the spirits, a pirate with a wicked-looking cutlass, flew at Michael and slashed. Ghostly weapons should not have been able to cut his flesh, but in order to protect him and allow him to strike the ghosts, the wisp dust had brought him partially into the spiritual world. The sword tore through his shirt and left a line of frozen blood on his chest. It didn't hurt at all. The only thing he could feel was his heart slowing. His movements became sluggish, and a chill spread from the wound to the rest of his body.

Vanessa was a blur of motion and deadly grace as she mowed through the spirits. Each one her sword sliced through howled and seemed to melt, its form flowing along the ground until it was swallowed by the lake, but there were too many. Dozens of others swirled around them. Shade did what he could to slow them, and Nev was a white streak, flashing through the air and piercing spirits at an impossible speed, but there were just too many. To make matters worse, the wisps darted in and out, singing a haunting dirge. While the wisp dust granted them a high degree of protection, it wasn't total immunity, and more than once, Michael found himself pausing to listen. It never lasted more than a moment, but here, a moment could be deadly.

Before long, Michael and Will stood back to back with Michael struggling to hold his weapon up in shivering arms. Nev perched on his shoulder, frozen blood splattered on her feathers. Vanessa fought on, turning away all but a few of the attacks, but those few were adding up. She was slowing down.

Shade circled them, his form seeming even more intangible than normal.

"I don't suppose you have any ideas," Will said.

Michael clenched his teeth, and tried to suppress the guilt. None of them would be here if not for him. Vanessa would still be in the real world. Will might be trapped in a cage, but at least he would be alive. No, he couldn't let this happen to his companions. Not again.

"I'll throw myself at them, and try to open a path. The two of you run. Get to the surface if you can. Find a way home."

Vanessa cut down three ghosts with a single swing. She glared at him with a look that told him exactly what she thought of that idea. She never had been one to run from a fight.

Will's teeth were chattering. "I don't suppose you have any *good* ideas."

"I don't have anyone back home. You do. You have a wife and daughter who have been waiting too long. Go back to them."

For what felt like an eternity, Will didn't respond. When he finally spoke, the words were quiet. They shouldn't have been audible over the spirits wailing, but Michael had no trouble hearing.

"No. We'll get out of this together."

Michael tensed his muscles, but before he could argue, a chilling laugh sounded from above. Michael looked up and froze, unable or unwilling to believe what he was seeing. His body refused to respond. The spirit descending on them was no ordinary ghost, for none of the others had inspired this kind of fear. Though death had washed away the colors, Michael could imagine the deep red of his greatcoat and his midnight-black hair, which hung over his shoulders, reaching halfway down his chest. The eyes, which had been blue in life, now shone dull gray, glowing with a cold light. The spirit wore an evil grin as he floated down. Almost involuntarily, Michael's eyes wandered down his right arm, and he let out a small gasp of surprise. It had been so much a part of this man's self-image that even in death his right hand was missing. When he'd been alive, he'd been almost universally feared, and the grave had only enhanced his aura of terror. It took all the strength Michael could muster not to scramble back as the ghost of James Hook landed in front of him.

CHAPTER 20

* * *

For a moment, everyone froze. Some of the ghosts, the ones resembling pirates, scurried back. Most actually looked afraid. Hook gave Michael an elaborate bow, and he couldn't tell if it was mocking or not. But as the captain rose, he swung his hooked hand, slicing through three of the spirits and reducing them to incandescent puddles. Michael's confusion grew. In the next instant, Hook's sword took the head of another while his hook disemboweled two more. He flowed from one ghost to the next, death given form. Even when the spirits tried to retaliate, their weapons never seemed to touch him. Both Will and Michael were awed at the sheer savagery of the battle. All at once, the spirits broke, fleeing in all directions. Hook let out a bone-chilling laugh and darted after the large group.

"Traitors!" he called out. "Living or dead, you'll not survive betraying me!"

They all vanished into a cave, leaving the rest of them to look after him. It was Vanessa who eventually broke the silence.

"Is that who I think it was?"

"Hook," Michael said, staring off into the distance.

For a second, she just stared. "Michael, I've met more legends in the past couple of days than in all my time with the

Knights. But I never imagined meeting a pirate like Hook, much less his ghost."

"*James* Hook?" Will asked. "I heard men in the navy talk about him, but I always thought he was a children's story."

"Remember where you are, Will—everything here is a children's story." Michael sighed. "But the truth is Hook is more than a story. Read up on your history when you get a chance. He was Blackbeard's bo'sun, and the only man Long John Silver ever feared." Will opened his mouth to respond, but Michael shook his head. "He was real, too. The world is not as simple as a lot of people believe."

"You fought him before?"

Michael shook his head. "Peter fought him. No one else ever stood a chance." He let out a long breath and forced back the fear that welled inside of him. "I never really thought of that. Has there ever been a man so terrible that it took a god to oppose him?"

"He died?"

Michael waved in the direction the ghost of Hook had disappeared. "Obviously. It just doesn't seem to have inconvenienced him." He looked at Shade. "Can you follow him?"

Shade jumped and backed up several steps, shaking his head vigorously. Then he flew back and hid behind a rock. He poked his head out and looked at Michael before shaking his head. Michael stared at him before glancing at Nev.

"That's surprising. Peter was never afraid of Hook, even when he should have been," Michael said.

"Peter never faced him with anything less than his full strength. Hook now has all the power of a ghost added to the cruelty he had as a man. He's somehow stronger now than ever, and he might even be able to destroy Shade. That would be a tragedy almost as bad as the destruction of Peter himself."

"What about you?" Michael asked. "Can you follow him?"

"Why does anyone need to go after him at all?"

"He helped us. That's reason enough, but also, is there anyone else you think is more likely to have kidnapped Peter? Is there anyone else who could?"

The bird fluttered to a nearby rock ledge, illuminated by a glowing crystal in the wall. In the blue light, she had an eerie cast to her.

"Michael, this is *Hook*. Even in life, no pirate, and few men, were more feared."

"Exactly."

Both Shade and Nev stared after the pirate. The bird squawked and spread her wings, but Shade shivered for a second before standing up straight and puffing out his chest. He launched himself into the air, darting in the direction Hook had gone. Will stared after him for a second before shaking his head. His gaze fell back on the water.

"I think we should get away from the shore. Those things might come back."

Michael looked over the water. Ripples washed over the shore, and in the distance, a vaguely human figure appeared out of the lake only to vanish a second later.

"What's that?"

Nev took off, gliding over the water for a few seconds before returning to Michael's shoulder.

"Mermaid."

"There are mermaids here?" Will asked.

"There's everything here," Michael said. "Or near enough. I wouldn't advise getting too close—they're not the nicest of creatures. How did it get here?"

"I told you," Nev said, "one way to get here is through the Coral Caves."

"Then that's a way out?"

"We are no more capable of breathing water than we were

when we first came here. On top of that, if the mermaids are aware of us, it'll be all but impossible to make it through the caves without a fight."

Michael chewed his bottom lip. "Still, that may be our best option." Once again, the lake looked like glass, but he could see movement in the distance beneath the surface. From so far away, he couldn't tell if it was one being or many, but he guessed that it didn't really matter. "What was the mermaid doing?"

"She was watching us," Nev said. "I got the feeling she would've wrung my neck if she'd been able to reach."

"Really?" Michael asked. "I know they didn't like us, but they've never bothered you, have they?"

"No, and it worries me. Will is right, though," Nev said. "We should get away from here. Shade should be able to find us as long as we don't go too far."

Michael nodded, and they retreated back to the entrance of the cavern, never taking their eyes off the water. It wasn't long before humanlike torsos poked out of the water and stared at them. Will gaped openly, though Michael advised him to ignore them until Shade came back.

While they waited, Will peppered Michael with questions, everything from what kind of fairies lived in Neverland to where they had gotten their clothes. Some things he accepted without question, but others seemed utterly unbelievable to him. For example, he had no trouble believing that they had been able to fly or that a fairy had lived in the underground house with them, but that the fearsome Hook had been afraid of a crocodile, he found ridiculous beyond belief. Then, there were some stories that just made no sense at all to anyone who hadn't spent time in Neverland.

"You have to understand," Michael said as he talked of a particularly odd battle they'd had with Tiger Lily's tribe, "Peter sometimes decided to switch sides on a whim."

"He betrayed you?"

"No, it was nothing like that. He would just decide he was part of the tribe, and we would follow his example."

Vanessa shook her head. "How very like boys."

Michael lifted an eyebrow, but Will was the one who spoke. "So the battle ended?"

"No, the tribesmen decided they were Lost Boys at that point, so we'd keep fighting."

"But that doesn't make sense."

"So like boys," Vanessa repeated.

Before Michael could respond, Shade drifted out from behind him. Michael jumped as Shade flew in a lazy circle around his head. Then, he pointed down a nearby passage.

"You found him?"

Shade nodded once and darted down the corridor, moving at a steady pace. When he saw that Michael and the others weren't following, he flew back and made like he was grabbing on to Michael's shadow and tugging it along. Michael thought he felt a slight pulling sensation.

"We're coming," Michael said. He lifted his glowing crystal so the shadow was more clearly outlined. "Show us the way."

Shade began drifting down the passages, moving quickly but not so much as to get out of sight. They didn't encounter any other creatures, but they didn't feel comforted. Indeed, the lack instilled the caverns with an eerie emptiness. Wails, be they from spirits or some other source, echoed through the caverns. Wind howled, bringing with it a bone-chilling cold—though how wind got down here, Michael had no idea. Gradually, the cold gave way to an oppressive heat, and through it all the wails only grew louder.

They turned a corner and found themselves on a ledge overlooking a wide chamber illuminated by a fiery glow. The floor sloped down, giving the impression that they were looking into a crater. Michael's eyes wandered down, and when he saw what lay in the center of the valley, his jaw dropped. Even Vanessa seemed awed.

"Well," she said, "I've always wanted to storm a castle."

Pools of magma made the castle's obsidian walls glimmer. Soaring towers rose over a collection of buildings around it, each large enough to be a palace in its own right. A thick wall of black stone surrounded the complex, and aside from ghostly lights flickering in the windows, nothing moved.

Vanessa took a deep breath. "Hook is in there?"

Shade nodded.

"And Peter?"

Shade turned from the castle back to Vanessa and shrugged.

Michael sighed. "It's better than nothing. How do we get in?"

Shade pointed down a winding path that passed over a river of molten rock and led to the front gate, an obstruction seemingly made of black iron.

"That's a little obvious, isn't it?" Vanessa asked.

Shade spread his arms, as if to ask if she had a better idea.

She sighed. "I see your point."

"Shade, keep yourself between them and us, if you will," Nev said.

Shade nodded, but Michael raised an eyebrow. "Why?"

"Just because we're going to the front gate doesn't mean we should broadcast our approach," Nev said as she preened her feathers. "White feathers aren't exactly the best camouflage down here. Added to that, the path passes right over a river of magma. Its glow will make approaching unseen extremely difficult."

"He's not that big—will he cover us all?"

Instead of answering, Shade turned from Michael to Nev to Vanessa to Will. Michael had the odd impression that he was smiling as he spread out before them, forming a wide blanket. Vanessa lifted an eyebrow at that.

"I didn't know he could do that," Vanessa said.

"Neither did I," Michael said.

Shade drifted over them, shrouding the way forward in shadow, which made it difficult to see more than a few feet ahead of them. They were halfway down the path when a light in one of the windows flickered, and they all froze.

"I think I saw someone," Vanessa said. "We may have been spotted."

Panic crept up Michael's spine, and he suppressed the urge to shiver. "It doesn't matter."

"How can it not matter?"

"Because even if we were spotted, it wouldn't change anything. We would still have to go forward."

"Michael, I don't know," Will said.

"No, he's right," Vanessa said. "Let's keep going."

They started up again, and the smell of sulfur grew steadily stronger. When they were less than twenty feet from the iron gate, it swung open on silent hinges. At that, Will and Michael jerked back, but Vanessa didn't even flinch. Clearly spotted, Shade shrank back to normal size. This had the feel of a trap, but it didn't make sense. If Hook had wanted to hurt them, he could've done so earlier. And they didn't really have much of a choice, not if they wanted to question Hook.

Vanessa stepped through the gate, with Michael and Will right behind her. The obsidian practically shimmered in the light of his crystal, revealing a courtyard that was completely empty, save a few small buildings. Michael couldn't help but wonder if the battlements were manned by ghosts who were even now invisibly watching them. He didn't see any sign of wisps, so they were probably safe. Probably.

Like the gate to the courtyard, the castle door swung open as they neared. The corridors of the castle were empty, and nothing hung from the walls. Even their footsteps sounded muted. In spite of the intricately carved stone, the whole thing seemed lifeless. After a few minutes, the hall split into three identical passages. Michael turned to his companions.

"I don't suppose any of you have an idea where to go?"

They all shook their heads. Michael thought for a second, but since he had no idea whatsoever, one way was as good as another. He picked a path at random, repeating the process when he came to another fork a few seconds later.

"Aren't you worried that we'll get lost?" Vanessa asked when Michael took the third fork.

"Not really," Michael said as he turned a corner.

"Why not?"

Michael shrugged. "It's Hook, and we're in his castle. Even when he was alive, it took a god to stand against him. The dust lets us touch him, but honestly, if he appeared in front of us now, we wouldn't stand a chance. Even if we did know exactly where to find Peter, we have no way of getting back to the surface. Next to all that, I can't really get worked up over getting lost."

Will glared at him. "You didn't have to make our situation seem completely hopeless."

"It's not," Vanessa said. "I've faced ghosts before, and Michael has stood against more spirits than you can imagine, and he's always come out on top."

Michael looked away from them. "Not always, and even when I did, people still died."

"Michael, that doesn't mean it's going to happen again."

He stared off into the distance. "I hope not."

CHAPTER 21

*   *   *

Michael was about to lead Will and Vanessa down another fork when Shade stepped in front of him and pointed down a different passage. Michael raised an eyebrow but followed as Shade drifted down the hall just ahead of them. The corridor went on for about twenty feet before turning sharply to the right, then going another hundred before stopping at a door. Shade landed in front of it and pointed. Though made from the same obsidian as the rest of the building, the stone had been carved in such a way as to resemble wooden planks. Michael pushed it open to see a stairway heading down.

"A dungeon?" Will asked.

Michael and Vanessa exchanged glances before Michael spoke. "Going down into the basement of a dark spooky castle. You realize this is a trap, right?"

Vanessa rolled her eyes. "That's been obvious since we came into the castle."

"You mean you knew?"

She rolled her eyes again. "Of course I knew. But the thing about traps is that if you know they're there, you can turn things around." Abruptly, she swung her sword in a wide arc, bringing it to rest against Shade's neck. Everyone froze, but Vanessa kept her eyes locked on Shade. "You didn't do a very good job," she said. "You were very calm when you showed us the way here, never moving so fast as to get out of sight. The real Shade is constantly jumping around, and I'm pretty sure he can't change his form like you did. That's a power of ghosts, so why don't you show me who you really are? What happened to the real Shade?"

The thing masquerading as Shade shook its head, but after a second, its shoulders sagged and its body rippled. Its form shifted, but it didn't grow into the shape of Hook, like Michael had begun to suspect. Rather, it shrank into a feminine form, with dragonfly wings emerging from her back. The shadow took on the pale coloring of a ghost. For a moment, Michael worried that he was looking at the ghost of Tinker Bell, but the features were wrong. The nose was a little smaller, and the hair was worn long instead of tied up in a bun. But there was no doubt it was a fairy, or at least it had been once. Vanessa lowered her weapon.

"Who are you?" Michael asked.

The fairy spoke quickly. Michael had learned the rudiments of the fairy tongue the last time he was in Neverland, but that was two decades past, and it took him a while to make out the words. "Rosebud?"

The fairy nodded.

"What are you doing? Why were you pretending to be Shade? Where is he? Did Hook send you?"

She spoke too quickly for him to make out, but before he could ask her to slow down, she drifted down the stairs. Her ghostly light remained visible in the dark, though only barely. Michael turned to Nev, but the bird shook her head. "I had a hard enough time learning your language. That of the fairies is beyond me."

Vanessa shrugged. "If you needed someone to speak Gremalkin, I could help you, but I never learned Fairy."

"Why would you learn the language of demon cats?"

Vanessa motioned to the ghostly light. "Do you really want to discuss this now?"

Michael thought for a second. "I think it was something about being afraid we wouldn't believe her. She wants us to follow her. She knows where Shade is."

"Well, it is a strange ghost fairy that was disguised as our now-missing companion and was leading us God-knows-where," Will said. "I'm not sure we *should* believe her now. She could be trying to hurt us."

"Fairies aren't like that," Michael said. "At least most fairies aren't. It's not like she's a wisp. Rosebud is a pixie, or at least she was. They're good." Nev let out a series of calls that sounded annoyingly like a laugh. Michael glared at her but sighed after a second. "I mean they're not always good. Tink did try to kill Wendy once."

"*What?*"

Michael waved off his surprise. "She was jealous. Peter set her straight, though. Anyway, that was a spur-of-the-moment thing. This fairy has been guiding us for half an hour. Do you have any idea how hard it is for a fairy to focus on one thing for that long? Whatever she's doing, it's not just some whim."

Vanessa shook her head and mumbled something about the veiled, but Will gave him a level look.

"So you're saying fairies can do evil things, but we should trust this one because if it was going to do something evil it would have done it already?"

"Not evil," Michael explained. "They're more petty than any-thing else, but they have a hard time holding on to one thought for a long time. If Rosebud managed to concentrate for that long, I'd guess she has a good reason. We should go with her."

"So just like that, you trust her?" Vanessa asked.

"She's a pixie."

"I know you were friends with one, but that doesn't make the entire race trustworthy."

Michael smiled. "She's a pixie," he said again.

He followed the ghost down the stairs, but Vanessa called after him, "That's it? That's all the reason you have? Has it occurred to you that she could very well be working for Hook? This could still be a trap."

Michael didn't stop as he responded, "A pixie would never work for him, so unless you have a better idea, you may as well come with me."

After only a few seconds, Michael heard the sound of footsteps coming down the stairs behind him.

The dungeon consisted of a long hall lined with barred rooms. The rancid smell of stagnant water hung thick in the air. No sooner had Michael wondered where it came from than he stepped in a puddle and groaned. He did his best to shake his foot dry as he examined the cells.

The room was darker than it should have been, and the shadows didn't yield to the light of his crystal as much as they should have. Though the individual cells were only six or seven feet across, his light could barely illuminate one at a time. Most were unoccupied, but as he neared the end of the hall, a shadow with no apparent source lay on the ground in one of the cells.

"Shade!"

The shadow sat up and stretched, as if he were waking up. He turned to them, and if he'd had eyes, Michael guessed they would've gone wide. Shade jumped up and down and ran to the bars, gripping them. He seemed to be trying to squeeze through the bars. Michael cocked an eyebrow and ran his fingers along one of the bars. He brought it up to his eyes.

"Wisp dust. It must keep him trapped."

Nev gripped his shoulder to anchor herself and flapped her wings. The wind of the motion sent a puff of glittering dust out from the bars. In the next instant, Shade had squeezed out of his cell. He flew around Will and Michael several times before landing. He pointed toward the back of the prison.

"Is there someone else here?"

Shade nodded.

"Show me."

Shade flew toward one of the last cells and pointed. Michael heard a shuffling movement inside. He lifted his crystal, but rather than finding Peter, there were seven children sprawled all over each other. When Michael's light fell over the one nearest the door, the child stirred and looked at Michael, blinking several times while his eyes adjusted. He was pale, like a ghost, but more solid. He wore glasses and a top hat, and though he stared at Michael with a blank expression, Michael knew him. They had grown up together. John worked in an office these days, having fallen so far from Neverland that when his children asked him for a story, he couldn't think of one. He hadn't looked like the figure now before Michael in a very long time. Shocked, Michael turned to Nev. The bird bobbed her head.

"It appears to be your brother."

"How?" Michael asked. "This was him twenty years ago."

"No one leaves Neverland," Nev said. "Not completely. Especially not children. As they grow, they leave the memory of this place behind. They remember being a child, but think of Neverland as something they imagined, if they think of it at all. Neverland, still bound to them, creates that child—for a little while, at least. They're not entirely real. That's why the house was still abandoned. There's not even enough substance to keep Peter interested, though they are as much his creation as anything else."

Michael pursed his lips. "It almost sounds like how fairies are made, except that instead of the first laugh, you're saying these were created by the last thoughts of childhood."

"It is similar, in a way. You might even say he *is* a fairy, along with the others."

He had almost forgotten about the others in his shock in seeing John. He didn't need to see their faces to know who they were. Though they didn't rise, he could make out the plump shape of Slightly, and there was Nibs, laying against a wall. The twins leaned against each other, snoring. Tootles and Curly were there, too. Michael's six adopted brothers slept in the cell, seeming not to have aged a day since they left Neverland with him, John, and Wendy.

"The Lost Boys," he said under his breath.

* * *

CHAPTER 22

L ost," Nev said, "but not forgotten, at least not in this
place. Neverland remembers."

Michael scanned the children, still hardly able to
believe what he was seeing. Vanessa stared into the cell, her
mouth moving though she didn't speak. After a few seconds,
she looked at him.

"That's your brother, isn't it? And the Lost Boys?" she asked.
"So . . . what about you?"

"What about me?"

Vanessa pointed. "Why isn't there a double of you?"

Michael did a double take before glancing at Nev. "Well?"

"I am not sure exactly how it works. Like Wendy, you never
forgot this place, and as you said, you never longed to be a child.
Perhaps that didn't leave enough for Neverland to work with."
Nev shuddered on his shoulder. "I am actually glad of that. I
would hate to see the reflection of one who remembered Neverland and still turned against his childhood."

"Is this really the best time to be discussing this?" Will
asked. "I assume you want to get these children out."

Michael nodded and stared into the cell. "John." He drew
out the name, only half expecting the boy to actually respond,

but the young John looked up. Michael took a deep breath. "How did you get here?"

John blinked at him. "We were captured by Hook. How else would we get down here?"

"That's not what I mean." Michael let out a long breath. "Oh, never mind. Step back."

He drew his weapon. The rest of the children, who had remained on the ground, scrambled to their feet and backed against the far wall. Michael gripped his sword in both hands and swung. The lock, apparently made from the same obsidian as the building itself, shattered at his blow, sending shards of black glass in both directions. Michael closed his eyes but felt only a gentle stinging. When he looked again, the door was swinging open, and the children spilled out. John stopped in front of Michael and stared up at him.

"You look familiar."

A lump formed in Michael's throat. He nodded, though it took him several seconds to find the words. "Yes, we met a long time ago. My name is Michael."

John rubbed his chin. "Michael. I think I've heard that name, but I can't remember where."

It made sense. Peter frequently couldn't hold a memory for more than a few minutes, and many who stayed a long time in his realm developed the same memory loss. Even Michael had been affected the last time he was here. By the end, he hadn't remembered anything of his life before, and like the Lost Boys, he had believed that Wendy really was his mother. Now, Neverland had erased him from his brother's memories.

"You should come with me," Michael said. "It won't be long before Hook finds out you're free."

All seven boys looked around, as if afraid. Slightly pointed at Rosebud, his lower lip quivering in fear. Before he could do anything, Nibs batted away his raised arm and glared into the other boy's eyes, as if daring him to be afraid of such a small ghost. Slightly looked pale, but he nodded. Michael considered for a second before handing his sword over to John.

"What are you—" Will started.

"Trust me," Michael said. "They're a lot better at using those things than we are."

"They're children," Will said.

"They are the embodiment of youthful adventure in a land created for ones such as they," Nev said. "They were trained by its maker for just such a task as this."

After Michael translated, Will stared at his blade for a few seconds before sighing. He handed it over to Nibs. Once armed, their backs stiffened and worry vanished from their faces, as if they were ready to conquer the Underworld all on their own.

"I think I'll just keep mine," Vanessa said.

All the boys stopped and stared at her. Most had their mouths open in shock.

"Is that . . ." Curly began.

"I think that's a lady," Slightly said.

"A lady."

The word echoed through the boys, as if they had never seen a lady before. Then again, given what Nev had told him, it was entirely possible that they hadn't.

"Miss Lady," John said, taking off his hat, "it's just that we don't have a mother. You, being a lady—"

"No," Vanessa said.

"What?" John stammered.

"I said no. We have too much to do without me having to worry about that. Trust me, kid—I'm *not* 'mommy' material." She eyed Michael. "When I read your report, I half thought you were joking—but they really want me to be their mother, don't they?"

Michael nodded. The Lost Boys looked devastated. "We can

talk about this later. For now, we need to get out of here as quickly as we can," Michael said. "Can any of you fly?"

The children exchanged glances with one another. Nibs examined a wall quietly while Tootles never lifted his head. "What is it?" Michael asked.

"It's just," the reflection of John said, "we haven't been flying in a long time. I don't remember how."

Michael nodded. "I see."

The real Lost Boys had also forgotten how to fly, though granted, that had been only after living in the real world for several weeks. John puffed out his chest, looking mildly offended.

"I'm quite sure that I only need someone to show me, and I can manage," John said.

Michael sighed. "I'm afraid I've forgotten, too."

"Well, of course you don't know," Slightly said. "You're all grown-up, and everyone knows that grown-ups can't fly. Did you know that, Tootles?"

"Of course I did," Tootles said. "Did you know that, Nibs?"

"Yes, that's exactly it," Michael said, interrupting them before they went through the whole group, as they tended to do. One of the twins stamped his foot, seemingly upset that Michael had denied him the chance to say he, too, knew that Michael couldn't fly. Michael turned to the fairy. "I take it this is what you wanted to lead us to."

The fairy bobbed up and down.

Vanessa spoke before Michael could. "Why?"

"What?" Michael asked.

"Why is she helping us? Did she see us on the shores of the Still Lake and decide to lead us to Hook's castle on a whim?"

Rosebud uttered a series of rapid syllables. She had to repeat herself twice before Michael had gotten enough of it to translate.

"She's Peter's friend, too. It wasn't too hard to see we had come to help. She knew we needed allies, so she brought us here. Is Hook in the castle now?"

Rosebud shook her head.

"Can you lead us to him?"

She shot back a couple of feet with an incredulous look on her face. After a second, though, she nodded and flew up the stairs. She hovered at the top, an eerie blue light hanging in the darkness.

Michael glanced at his companions. "I guess we should follow."

* * *

CHAPTER 23

As soon as Michael had reached the top of the stairs, the ghost fairy pointed and chattered something too fast for him to understand. Her gestures were clear enough, though. Michael motioned for her to lead the way. She flew back to him and darted around his head a few times before heading down the hall. Nev landed on his shoulder as he followed.

"Is this wise?"

"She seems to know where she's going," Michael said.

"I don't like this blind trust you put in her," Vanessa said. "Just because she's a pixie doesn't mean she can be trusted. Tinker Bell certainly had a malicious streak to her, according to your report."

"It's not the same thing," Michael said. "We can trust her. I know it."

He sounded more confident than he felt. Pixies had migrated to Neverland from other worlds—Peter hadn't created them, but they were almost slavishly loyal to him. Most of the time. Still, it was their only hope, and Neverland was a place for such hopes. But as he thought back to the crumbling landscape and rusted weapons, he found himself hoping there was enough of Neverland left for that to still be true.

Vanessa gave him a hard look as if she'd heard his unspoken words, but didn't respond. They moved through the passages as quickly as they could. The Lost Boys kept silent in a way that only those accustomed to adventure could manage. The shadows seemed darker in the halls, and if Michael stopped and stared at them for a second, he swore he could almost see ghostly eyes looking back at him. It didn't take them long to find the castle gates and rush out of the building. They practically ran up the slope to the passage that would lead out of the cavern. It was only after they had left the massive chamber holding the castle that anyone spoke.

"What happened to you?" Michael asked.

"We came down here to see if we could find Peter," John said. "Only we didn't really know where to look. Hook has a whole army of ghosts, and they captured us one by one."

"Then Peter's not in the castle?" Michael asked.

"I have no idea," John said. "Maybe we should have stayed and looked."

"I am just as happy that we do not have to face Hook in his own home," Nev said. "We stand a much better chance out here, though I still wouldn't say it's a good one."

"Can you really talk to the bird?" Nibs asked.

"He can," Vanessa said, "and he's entirely too smug about it."

"Even Peter couldn't do that." Nibs glanced at Shade before turning to Vanessa. "Who are you? Do we call you Mother?"

"I'm *not* your mother," Vanessa said. "Just call me Vanessa."

"No," Nibs said. "I'm certain it wouldn't be proper."

"This is Will," Michael said, trying to cut off the argument. "He's Wendy's husband."

"Wendy." John drew out the name. "Yes, I know that name, too, but I don't see how I could know her. If she's your wife, she must be grown-up, and I'm quite sure I don't know anybody that's grown-up."

"Peter knows Wendy." A thought struck Michael. "What about Jane? Do you know her?"

John's eyes widened and excited murmurs rippled through the rest of the Lost Boys. "Yes, I do. She was my mother once, I believe, during spring cleaning." He pursed his lips and looked at Vanessa. "I suppose if Jane is our mother, you can't be."

Vanessa let out a breath. "That's what I've been trying to tell you."

"What does he mean?" Will said. "He thinks Jane is his mother?"

"It's part of the mythos here. After we came home the first time, Peter wanted Wendy to come back with him to be his mother. She agreed, but only for spring cleaning. When she grew up and had Jane, apparently my niece took Wendy's place."

"That makes no sense."

Fearing he'd have to explain that, too, he said to the Lost Boys, "He's Jane's father."

"Oh, I've never had a father before," Nibs said. "What about you, Slightly?"

"We can get to that later," Michael said, again interrupting the question before the others started repeating it. "Right now, we have to find Hook. Rosebud, you said you could lead us to him."

The fairy thought for a second before spouting a series of syllables too quickly for Michael to understand. He thought she said something about "up," but other than that he had no idea. The Lost Boys, apparently, had no such problem.

"But we can't fly," Slightly said. "We need fairy dust."

An idea struck Michael, though apparently everyone else had the same thought because they all turned to Rosebud. She looked from one to another before she gasped and started bobbing up and down in the air.

Michael smiled. "So it's possible? You can give us fairy dust?"

She nodded, but then she paused and thought for a second before shrugging. She moved to fly over Michael, but Nev flew in front of her. "Not you three—at least not yet."

"What do you mean?" Michael asked.

"Rosebud is dead, and I've never even heard of a fairy leaving a ghost. You're already partially in another world because of the wisp dust, as are Vanessa and Will. I would not want to try out a ghost fairy's dust on you. The results could be unpredictable."

Michael thought for a second. "You may have a point."

Shade nodded, but Will spoke up. "A point about what?"

Michael translated, and Vanessa nodded. "Mixing dusts can have unpleasant effects."

The Lost Boys all looked at one another for several seconds before John stepped forward.

"Use your dust on me. I don't have any of the other kind."

Michael started to object, but Rosebud was already flying over John's head, showering him with shimmering dust. He closed his eyes for a second, and when he opened them again, light flashed from his pupils, and he collapsed. Michael moved to catch him, but Will was faster, moving behind John and laying him down gently. He shook him, but the boy didn't move. Will went pale.

"He's not breathing."

This wasn't John. It was just something that looked a little like John. Michael kept telling himself that, but seeing the unmoving body made the words catch in his throat. He took several deep breaths before trying again, but the words refused to come.

"It worked!" a voice said from above.

They all looked up to see John, with the pale translucence of a ghost, flying around them. For several seconds, no one moved or spoke, struck silent by the boy's arrival. In a way, his faded form reminded Michael of Neverland itself. John, finally grasping that something was wrong, set down in front of Michael. Shade came up next to him and poked him in the chest. To everyone's surprise, John reacted as if he'd been physically touched.

"How did you do that?" His eyes landed on his unmoving body, and if he'd been able to grow paler, Michael was sure he would've done so. "What . . ." He took a deep breath—though Michael thought that might have been only an illusion, since ghosts, so far as he knew, didn't breathe. "Am I dead?"

Michael's heart pounded in his chest. The color had drained from Vanessa's face but was slowly returning. She looked from body to ghost and back again. His throat was dry when he spoke. "I don't know. Why don't you try getting back in?"

John nodded. "Yes, that's probably a good idea."

He walked up to his body, for a moment unsure as to how he should proceed. Finally, he lifted into the air ten feet and turned and dove in. They all just stared for what felt like an eternity. Michael kept telling himself that this wasn't truly his brother, but that felt like an empty excuse. Relief washed over him as John open his eyes. He rose slowly, as if waking from a long sleep. He looked himself up and down and smiled.

"Well, that wasn't so bad. I think I should like to try it again." John took in the area around them and cleared his throat. His face took on a slight greenish cast. "That is, I would if I didn't have to leave my body in a place like this."

"Well, it's a shame," a gravelly voice said from seemingly nowhere, "that you won't be leaving anytime soon."

The two Lost Boys with swords drew their weapons, falling into a fighting stance with a speed that any Knight could envy. The rest of them moved with catlike grace. Vanessa held her own sword. Her movements were more polished than the boys', more formal. Under normal circumstances Michael would have bet that her years of training would be more effective than the undisciplined Lost Boys. But in Neverland, he took nothing for granted.

They weren't fighting each other, though. As he tried to find the source of that gravelly voice, Michael caught movement out of the corner of his eye. He spun to face it. It took several seconds for him to make it out. The gremlin's skin was glossy black, but was even now fading to visibility. Two dozen others appeared, each bearing a stone-tipped spear. The leader, which Michael recognized as the same one that had taken them to the gremlin city, pressed his weapon to Michael's throat. He motioned down the passage toward the castle.

"Now that you've led us to a new outpost we can claim, why don't we discuss what else you can do for the gremlin people."

* * *

CHAPTER 24

Michael felt the trickle of blood running down his neck. He tried to step back, but the gremlin pressed the cold stone point of the spear forward as he moved. The creature scowled, and Michael froze.

"What are you doing?" he asked. "Your queen agreed to help us."

The gremlin sneered. "She helped for the good of our people, not for yours."

"Rescuing Peter helps everyone."

"What good is the survival of Neverland to a shattered people?"

"You'll still have a place to live, for one thing."

"A broken city is not a home. The black palace, on the other hand . . ."

"You want Hook's castle?" Michael asked. He tried to back up, but the gremlin stayed with him. "Fine, we'll leave. You don't need to do this."

"For Peter!" Nibs cried out, his sword moving so fast that it was barely a blur.

"No!" Michael said, but the blade had already sliced through the spear shaft like it was made of paper. One of the twins leaped forward and seized a spear from one of the creatures, swinging the weapon so the butt slammed against the side of another gremlin head. The gremlin fell limply to the ground and the other twin swept up its fallen weapon. By then, all the children had managed to pick up a spear, and several of the gremlins were down.

One of the gremlins threw a net on Shade. Michael expected it to pass through the shadow, but it brought him to the ground. Another creature jabbed at him with a spear, and Shade threw his head back. Though he didn't make a sound, a chill ran through Michael's body, and he could see the effect ripple through the Lost Boys. Even Vanessa shivered.

"Put down your weapons!" the lead gremlin said.

Everyone looked at Michael. For all his training, he had frozen during the fight. He refused to be responsible for the death of anyone else, especially children. He gave his companions a single nod, hoping he was doing the right thing.

"So you like to fight," the gremlin said. "Good. We'll need that when you help defend us from Hook when he comes to reclaim his home."

"We're not defending you from anyone."

All the gremlins, even those who were barely conscious on the ground, erupted in laughter. The Lost Boys gave the gremlins uneasy looks as the leader strode toward them. He then walked around them in a slow circle, chanting in a language Michael didn't recognize. His voice took on an odd cadence, and Michael felt a tingling against his skin. It had to be powerful magic for it to be so apparent to him. His thoughts became sluggish, and though a part of him screamed to resist, the gremlin's chant lulled him into listlessness. Dimly, he was aware that other gremlins were dancing around him, chanting in the same strange language. He recognized them as enemies, and with that recognition came the almost blinding desire to attack. He clenched his fist so hard his nails bit into his hand, but then, the song changed rhythms, growing faster and deeper. His heart raced, and he threw his head back and screamed. The world went red.

The next thing he knew, Michael and the Lost Boys were waking up outside of Hook's palace, on the other side of the path through the molten rock. John and Nibs had their weapons beside them, but the others had been given swords of their own. Where gremlins had gotten human weapons, though, Michael had no idea—just as he didn't have any idea why they'd been left with weapons in the first place. That was, until he saw that the swords all glittered with wisp dust, which made sense if the gremlins really intended for them to hurt Hook's forces. To his surprise, small clusters of gremlins stood nearby with weapons bare.

He was in the process of making sure everyone was all right when Nibs cried out and pointed. Dozens of caves led into the cavern housing the palace, and all of them glowed with a faint blue light. A heartbeat later, an army of ghosts poured into the cavern.

Though Michael had been too young to fight in the Great War, he had studied enough military doctrine to know that this wasn't truly an army, at least not in the traditional sense. There were no battle lines, no discipline. Rather, the ghosts were just a chaotic mass of spirits. Even the pirates fought in groups of only three or four, or even one or two, darting in to attack with neither reason nor strategy. If they had fought as one cohesive unit, Michael and the Lost Boys would've been overcome in a matter of seconds. Instead, they managed to hold their own, fighting back to back, with Nev and Shade covering them from above.

Michael fought mechanically at first, performing the maneuvers he'd learned when he'd been one of the Knights, but he hadn't practiced those in nearly three years, and small hesitations cost him. More than once, the cold blade of a spirit danced across his flesh. His arms grew numb as the icy power of the ethereal blades coursed through him. His limbs felt heavy, and he began to slow. One pirate stabbed at his chest. His sword came up and deflected it in a maneuver that had nothing to do with the precise motions of a trained swordsmen. Rather, it was something taught to a boy of four by a god who never grew up.

The ghost's sword flew from its hand and vanished before it hit the ground. Michael's blade sliced through its stomach, and the pirate cried out before fading out of existence. Emboldened, Michael darted forward, cutting through the spirits like a scythe through wheat, fighting with utter abandon in a way that would've made his old sword masters wince. Vanessa fought in a more traditional manner and was holding her own, though only barely. Small packs of gremlins battled in disorganized groups. Will had backed up to a large rock, holding his sword in shaky hands and striking whenever a ghost got into range, which wasn't often. The ghosts apparently didn't see him as much of a threat and focused their attention elsewhere. The Lost Boys did best of all, having never forgotten what it meant to fight in Neverland as friends of Peter Pan.

Nibs fell, but before the ghosts could move in for a killing blow, the twins were there, darting back and forth in a way that would make cats seem clumsy. John cut a hole through the crowd of ghosts until he stood over his companion. His sword moved so fast that Michael saw little more than a blur, and though the battle wasn't going as well where the gremlins engaged the ghosts directly, there was one thing Michael could not deny. They were winning. Or at least they were until a chilling laugh filled the air.

Michael looked around, batting aside the ghostly weapons with his own blade, but he saw no source for the laugh. Suddenly, the spirits backed up, forming a wide circle around him. Before Michael could figure out where the laugh came from, an apparition rose from the ground directly in front of him. Though he tried not to be afraid, he couldn't suppress the cold shiver that ran down his spine. Hook drew his sword, a curved blade half as long as the pirate captain was tall. He wore a wicked grin as his weapon tore through the air toward Michael's neck.

Michael didn't have time to think. He wasn't sure it would do any good. Instead, he just fell backward. The blade cut through the air where he had been. Michael slammed into the ground but rolled to his feet almost immediately. His own blade snapped forward, piercing the leg of the ghostly pirate. Hook didn't even notice the wound as he grinned at Michael. A couple of quick slashes sent Michael's sword flying. The pirate laughed as he sent a killing thrust toward Michael's heart.

From off to one side, John threw himself at Hook. Empowered by wisp dust as he was, he slammed into the ghost. He wasn't big enough to do much more than knock Hook a bit off balance, but it was enough. Michael spun out of the way, and Hook's sword sliced into the side of his stomach. Cold pain lanced through Michael's body, but he didn't stop. He swept his sword off the ground and lunged, but Hook batted his weapon aside. They exchanged a dozen blows in half as many seconds, but Hook was clearly the more skilled, and his ghostly weapon often made it past Michael's defenses and sliced into his flesh.

John tried to help, but Hook just as easily held back two as one. Then, Nibs joined, and Curly, and Slightly, and the twins. Michael had been so caught up in fighting Hook that he hadn't noticed that the rest of the ghosts had fled. Now Hook stood surrounded by the Lost Boys. Slightly stabbed his left leg while Nibs cut into his right. Each of the twins seized an arm, and John and Curly dragged the pirate to the ground. His sword vanished as they piled on top of him, and just like that the battle was over.

Michael looked down at the captive pirate. He was struggling against the boys holding him, but he stopped when he saw Michael looking at him. Hook's face twisted in anger, but he didn't seem nearly so terrifying now. Michael took a step forward and staggered. His legs were numb from having taken blows from the ghostly weapon, but gradually feeling returned to him, and he was able to stand up straight.

"Where's Peter?" Michael tried to put menace in his voice.

To his surprise, Hook laughed.

"Where?" Hook asked. "Oh, you're very good. Is that how you got the gremlins to help? By telling them I took Pan?"

"We're helping the gremlins, not the other way around. But that's beside the point. If you didn't take Peter, then who?" Michael asked. Hook blinked. He stared into Michael's eyes for several seconds. Finally, he nodded and gave Michael another one of his chilling grins.

"It was you. *You* kidnapped Pan."

* * *

CHAPTER 25

H im?" Vanessa asked. "That doesn't make any sense. He didn't take Peter. He hasn't been to Neverland in decades."

Hook looked around at all the people. He wore that same grin, in spite of his situation. He looked back at Michael, who found himself taking an involuntary step back when he met the pirate's gaze.

"You're trying to hide this from them. Why?" Before Michael could answer, Hook squinted and wrinkled his nose. "Ah, of course. When I saw you, I assumed you had absorbed him. But it wasn't you, was it? You're the real one."

Michael had no idea what he was talking about. *Absorb? The* real *one?*

Hook started to rise, but instantly, half a dozen swords were pressed against his neck. Gremlins poured out of the castle, though Michael had no idea when they had gotten there. They leveled spears at both the Lost Boys and Hook. The Lost Boys took their weapons off the captive and turned to face the gremlins. It was the very chaos Peter Pan loved in Neverland, and it meant a confusing mess for Michael, darting his eyes everywhere to figure out his next move. Hook, however, ignored everyone else and kept his attention focused on Michael.

"Very well. If you don't know yet, I suspect you soon will."

"Know what?" Vanessa asked.

"Michael, please tell your wench to keep her mouth shut when men are talking."

"*Wench*?" Vanessa stepped forward, knuckles white around the grip of her weapon.

"Vanessa," Michael said, gently touching her sword arm. "Can you handle the Lost Boys? Make sure they don't start another war with the gremlins."

"He called me—"

"I know." He turned to face Hook. "But he's just a pirate—and a dead one at that. Who cares what he calls us?"

Hook laughed at that, but Vanessa was stone and fury. Finally, she said, "Okay. For the sake of the mission, I'll play this game." She turned to start hissing orders at the Lost Boys.

"Very spirited," Hook said. "Does she really know how to use that sword?"

"I don't think you'd want to find out. Might wound your pride to be beaten by a mere girl."

Hook laughed once more. "Ah, Michael, you amuse me."

"And you're starting to bore me," he said with a bravado he didn't feel.

"So direct. Fine: a score of days ago, Pan and I were fighting. It was one of our longer bouts, and we had been going for almost six hours. Then, you came." He motioned to the Lost Boys. "I knew about those, but it was the first time I had encountered a reflection of you."

"I don't have a reflection here. I can't."

"That's what I thought, too. So prim and proper, there's nothing of the child in you in spite of the fact that you remember this place. And yet, there you were. Except you weren't. The reflection wasn't like any of these boys." He then flicked his hand toward Shade. "It was more like that thing than anything that looks human. It had red eyes, but I could still make out a hint of your face."

The hairs on the back of Michael's neck stood on end. He turned to Nev and shivered. The bird, seeming to read his mind, bobbed her head. "I never knew, but it makes sense that the spirit of the forgotten would take form here."

"Wraith," Michael said. "You mean Peter was taken by my wraith."

Hook nodded. "A wraith who wants nothing more than to achieve a semblance of life. He's been here for three years, though he hasn't been strong enough to be any sort of a threat. I assumed that's why he captured Pan. Draining the life force of a god would be more than enough to make him solid. When I saw you being attacked by that rebellious squad of ghosts, I assumed that's what had happened."

"So you helped us?"

He gave a grin that made Michael's mouth go dry. "If you had beaten Pan, I wasn't about to try to stand against you. I could do with you owing me a favor, though."

Michael's blood felt like it had turned to ice. He tried to speak, but it took him several seconds to work moisture back into it.

"How? He's a god, and you're a powerful ghost." Michael shivered. "How could a wraith capture Peter right out from under you?"

"We had been fighting almost an entire day. We were both exhausted, and the wraith did not come alone. A veritable legion of ghosts and creatures of the water came with him. Before either of us could react, they had taken him. Seeing him do what I had failed to do after so many years, some of my crew decided he would be a better leader. After I took care of the mutinous dogs, I returned to the castle. Imagine my surprise when my home was invaded, and it turned out to be you."

"I don't understand," Will said. "This thing is some kind of evil version of you?"

"Not exactly." Vanessa didn't take her eyes off the gremlins as she spoke. "We don't entirely understand how wraiths are created, and there are a lot of other things it could be. But if it's here, it's probably . . ."

Her voice drifted off, but Michael finished her thought. The wraith had been in Neverland for three years. Three years ago, when the dream spirit had killed Dmitri, and Michael had turned his back on the Knights and everything they stood for. "My childhood."

"Which you rejected," Hook said, "and it was from that distain that it was formed."

Michael suppressed a shiver as he broke out into a cold sweat. He stared at Hook and tried to tell himself the pirate was lying, but he couldn't. Hook was telling the truth. Vanessa motioned for him and Will to move away from Hook. The gremlins allowed them to pass, but Vanessa didn't speak until they were out of earshot.

"Wraiths don't have corporeal bodies, but with the wisp dust, we should still be able to hurt it. They tend to get stronger the older they are, but if this one has only been active a few weeks, it should still be weak enough for us to deal with, provided we can get past its followers." She let out a breath. "I didn't even know wraiths could have followers."

"Neither did I," Michael said. "That still doesn't tell us where it is."

He glanced at the Lost Boys. Rosebud fluttered around their heads while they teased Hook by sneaking behind him and making a ticking sound. Though he was long dead, it seemed the pirate retained the fear of the crocodile. The gremlins had somehow used their magic to put a binding circle around him. Hook wouldn't be able to cross, but anything physical could pass over it without breaking the spell. Michael neither knew nor cared what they intended to do with him.

"Should you really be letting them do that?" Will asked. "They're only children."

"They're not children," Michael said. "Not really. Still, you're probably right. We should at least see what else he can tell us."

Hook was darting back and forth in his invisible cage when they returned. He flew to the edge closest to Michael and landed.

"You must tell them to stop this. I was the terror of the seven seas. Blackbeard's bo'sun. I was the only man Long John Silver ever feared!"

"You were the most evil man I ever knew," Michael said.

"Exactly!"

"Then why should I help you?"

"Because I helped you. I offered to spare you when I captured you," Hook said. "You must remember that."

"I remember you wanted us to become pirates."

"You wanted that as well."

Michael sniffed. "It was a childhood fancy."

"And you were a child."

Michael glared at him. "You expect me to take that as some kind of justification? You deserve all of this."

John and the Lost Boys were all staring at Hook, grinning now. The only sound was the ticking boys' teasing, echoing through the cavern. Hook looked in the direction of the sound for several seconds before turning back to Michael.

"I also saved you from the ghosts at the Still Lake!"

"No, you just said it yourself—you were getting revenge on your mutinous crew."

"Still—it saved you!"

"I don't know if unintended consequences count as heroism," Will said.

Michael huffed in agreement and moved to walk away.

"I can tell you where your wraith is."

Michael paused. "It's a start."

"Just get them to stop." Hook was on his knees.

Michael rolled his eyes. "Oh, for heaven's sake. You're dead. It's not like the crocodile could do anything to you, even if it was here."

"And you could make the wraith weaker if you only stop remembering your past," Hook said after glancing into a nearby cave. "Why don't you try that? Because it's not so easy to just stop something like that, is it? What we've done lives inside us. *Is* us."

It bothered him how right Hook sounded. "Maybe. Tell me where to find Peter."

"Let me out!"

Hook was shaking. He slashed at the gremlins' barrier with both sword and hook. His efforts had no effect, but that didn't stop him from trying all the harder. After several long seconds, Michael spoke up.

"Stop the sound, boys."

The grins faded from the faces of the Lost Boys as they all exchanged glances.

"I'm not doing it," Curly said. "Are you, Nibs?"

"I'm not. Are you, Slightly?"

"No, how about you, Tootles?"

Michael stopped listening as he scanned the group. They were all there. All six Lost Boys as well as John were silent, but the sound was still coming from one of the nearby caves. In fact, it seemed to be getting closer.

"Shade, is that what I think it is?"

Shade leaped into the air and flew into the cave. Rosebud asked if she should follow, but Michael shook his head. Will started to ask what it was, but Michael held his hand up to silence him. After a few seconds, Shade zipped back out. He landed in front of Michael and bent over, holding his stomach as if he were breathing heavily. Finally, he nodded. Michael drew his sword and held it ready. The Lost Boys looked confused, but they all followed suit.

"What is it?" Vanessa asked.

Before Michael had a chance to answer, the crocodile burst out of a nearby cave. The thin scaled arm hanging limply from its jaws told them that it had just torn through whoever the gremlins had on patrol. The limb seemed comically small in those teeth. Its beady eyes focused on Hook, who cried out and leaped to the topmost boundary of his mystical cage.

"Save me," he said. "I can't help you if that thing eats me."

"We can't help anyone if it eats *us*," Will said.

Michael sighed and rushed forward, his sword leaving a silvery blur behind it as it sliced through the air. He hit the monstrous reptile so hard that his sword should've cut through its hide easily, but the blade just bounced off. The crocodile swished its tail, knocking Michael off his feet and sending his sword flying. Then it snapped at Hook, its teeth closing around the edge of his coat. To Michael's surprise, the fabric tore free, evaporating as it came free of the ghost.

"It's been treated with wisp dust," Michael said under his breath. He got up and looked for his weapon but couldn't find it. "Help him!" he cried out to the Lost Boys. The seven children stared at him like he was mad. Finally, John took a hesitant step forward.

"That's a good lad," Hook said as he pointed to a series of runes drawn in the dust at the edge of the circle. "Can you open that?"

"Open what?" John asked.

"The circle," Hook said.

John stared back at Michael, but though he understood the

basic theory behind rune magic, he'd never heard of something like this.

"Try scuffing it with your shoe," Vanessa said as she slashed ineffectually at the crocodile.

John nodded and carefully stepped around the crocodile as it tried to snap up Hook. Suddenly, the creature whirled to face the child. The movement was so abrupt that John hadn't even had a chance to avoid the crocodile's tail when it knocked his feet out from under him. The beast opened its wide mouth to bite into John—but before it could manage, two squalling children zoomed into the cage and jumped on the reptile. Their swords moved in a blur. Either they hit a thinner section of its hide or their swords were somehow sharper than Michael's because they sliced into the crocodile, sending out sprays of blood. The twins yowled in delight as the creature yowled in pain.

Vanessa moved in close and delivered a powerful blow just behind its head. Her sword bit into the creature, too. A smaller animal would've been killed, but this crocodile was as large as any that had ever walked the earth. Nearly twenty feet long, its hide was thick, and though Vanessa's blow had gotten through it, it hadn't gone very far in. The animal spun and lunged at her. She fell back, but there was no way she would avoid the creature's next strike. Hook's weapon came down on its tail, the only part of its body that yet remained in the circle. His ghostly blade had none of the trouble that Michael's physical one had, and the animal's tail went limp. It spun, spurting blood from many of its wounds. One twin was thrown off, but the other continued to pepper it with his sword. The animal let out a rumbling roar and snapped at the pirate ghost, its jaws closing around the stump of the arm that held the hook.

The pirate ghost threw back his head and screamed. The sound was so chilling that all the warmth seemed to leach out of the cavern, and Michael was surprised when a nearby puddle didn't freeze. Even the crocodile pulled back. Hook, his face twisted in rage, lunged at the creature. He slammed against the gremlin's circle. A green wall of energy sprang into existence, bending outward. John rushed forward, bringing his shoe over the mark in the cage. All at once, the whole thing shattered, and Hook leaped forward and drove his sword into the animal's skull. A ghostly light flashed from within the animal's eyes, then it went still. For a moment, Hook gave the corpse of his old enemy a wide smile, but that faded as his eyes wandered down to the stump where his hook had once been. Michael didn't understand how the spirit could still be dismembered, but the crocodile, it seemed, had done Hook very real harm that had transcended even death.

Hook looked up at Michael. "Your wraith sent him."

"How? And how do you know?"

Hook snorted. "If I knew how to command the beast, do you think I would have spent decades of my life and death afraid of it? Why do you think I haunt this place instead of the lagoon where I spent over a century? I told you, he had control over creatures of water. He commanded that animal to hunt me." He looked right into Michael's eyes, and for a moment, Michael thought his blood would freeze in his veins. "I only seized the Lost Boys in an attempt to draw Pan out. I thought if he knew they were in trouble, he would use his power to break free."

"You *want* him free?"

"Of course I do, boy. In life, I was a man, an extraordinary one, but now?" He motioned down to himself. "Only the living can fly out of Neverland. With a ship, I could, perhaps, make it to your world, but otherwise I'm stuck here. I could no more exist without him than Neverland itself could. If I must be forever his enemy to avoid meeting my maker, then that is what I will do."

"Then tell me where he is."

Hook pursed his lips and nodded. "I will do so—on one condition."

Michael stiffened. "What is it?"

He held up his ragged stump. Something very like blood was dripping out, though it faded once it had gone more than a few inches from the arm. "Grant the wraith no mercy. When you find him, destroy him."

A wave of cold washed over Michael at the request. Still, he only hesitated a second before nodding. "I'll do it."

* * *

CHAPTER 26

He's in the Coral Caves," Hook said. "The mermaids, the nixies, and even a few elementals that have wandered in from other parts of the world are his to command."

Michael pursed his lips and looked to his companions. The twins were still poking at the dead crocodile. The rest of the Lost Boys were staring at Michael.

"I guess that's something. Now, does anyone have any idea how we get back to the surface?"

"Well now," Hook said, "I can help you with that as well."

"How?"

Hook grinned and waved his stump at the gremlin city. "Do you think the workings of the Underworld are unknown to pirates?"

"He makes a valid point," Nev said from Michael's shoulder. "When men choose to be dark, they take that darkness into themselves. It is not impossible that they would be drawn to this place, maybe even to a path unknown to those of light."

"Where's the exit?"

Hook's grin widened. "Oh no. It's not that easy." He looked around. Even now, gremlins who had scattered at the arrival of the crocodile were poking their heads out of various windows in the castle walls. Some threw the dead animal uneasy glances, but many kept their attention locked on Hook. He sneered at one in particular, and the hapless creature scurried back into the courtyard. "The moment you leave here, they will destroy me."

"After what you've done, you deserve it," Michael said.

Hook chuckled. "I deserve far worse than that, but that doesn't mean I won't do everything in my power to avoid what I deserve. If you want my help, you're going to have to get me out of here."

"So you can stab us in the back the first chance you get?"

"You can trust—"

"*Trust* you?" Michael said. "Are you kidding me?"

The pirate let out a bark of laughter. "No, I would never suggest that you trust me. I don't think you're half so foolish. You can, however, trust that I want you to win. That's what's in my best interests."

A commotion was coming from the castle. Michael glanced in that direction. A large procession of gremlins, all garbed in their beetle armor and carrying stone swords, marched in their direction. The jagged skull banner of the gremlin queen flew over them, and Michael's skin tingled with the sense of her power. He hadn't even realized she had come to the palace. Rosebud hid behind him, obviously hoping to avoid the notice of the gremlins.

"The gremlins will capture you if you try to leave," Michael said. "If we're going to go, we have to do it now. I just wish we could distract them somehow."

The Lost Boys looked shocked at the idea of letting Hook go, but their surprise lasted only a second before they huddled together and started speaking softly. Nibs poked his head up only once to see how close the queen was. He smiled at Michael before ducking back into his discussion. Abruptly, the group burst apart, each child dashing in a different direction.

Nibs ran toward the queen's procession. They had just gotten past the magma, and the gremlins all drew their weapons, but Nibs jumped, landing on a rock wall and running several steps before gravity caught up with him. The maneuver took him past the guards, and just as he was coming down, he reached out and grabbed the queen's banner, tearing it from the pole that held it. Squealing with delight, he turned and ran right along the edge of the molten rock. For several seconds, the gremlins just stared at each other. Then there was an eruption of screams before the guards took off after the boys.

At first, Michael couldn't help but watch. Then, Hook waved his stump in front of Michael's face, drawing him out of his daze.

"Right. Let's go."

They followed the pirate into one of the nearby caves.

"When the conflict with Pan and his followers became too much, we needed a place to hide and lick our wounds, and the Coral Caves weren't always available to us," Hook said as he floated down the passage. "Smee found this cave. We didn't go deeply into it, just enough to be sure nothing else was using it. Just before you came to Neverland the first time, we were hiding out after a particularly nasty defeat. One of the crew, Starkey, came deeper into the cavern than ever before. It didn't take us long after that to find where it led to."

They reached a four-way fork and stopped for a few minutes until the Lost Boys caught up with them, laughing as if they'd come from a celebration. When Michael asked how they had gotten away, John just laughed harder. Michael rolled his eyes and turned to Hook. A stream trickled out of the middle of one of the passages, filling the air with a moldy smell. Hook floated down that one.

Of course he picks the one that stinks.

They walked for nearly an hour without incident. It took Michael a long time to realize why that bothered him. Neverland was a place of adventure. It shouldn't be possible to walk here for an hour and have nothing happen. It went against everything that Peter represented.

But then, Neverland is dying.

Shade constantly darted in and out of the darkness. Eventually, he came back and leaped up and down in front of Michael, pointing and waving his arms wildly.

"He knows the way out now," Hook said. "So, if it's all the same to you, I'll take my leave of you."

"You're not coming with us?" Michael asked, though almost immediately, he wanted to call back the words.

"I've gotten in enough trouble opposing that wraith of yours, and for all your confidence, I'm not entirely sure you can win, and I've no intention of being destroyed while you try.

"More to the point, you can't stop me."

Before Michael could reply, Hook floated upward and passed right through the roof of the cavern. Both Michael and Will stared at the spot for several seconds before Michael turned his attention back to Shade. "Lead the way."

It didn't take long for Michael to catch a whiff of fresh air, a relief from the stench of the cave's stream. They walked faster, though they had to keep to the side of the cave as the stream had widened until it took up most of the ground. It kept widening, and by the time they saw light from outside, they were ankle deep in water. They were swimming when they finally made it out into the open air of Neverland.

Michael had never been so happy to see the sun.

CHAPTER 27

* * *

Lush trees rose up all around Michael and the others, and
he breathed deeply of the fresh air, a welcome relief after
being underground so long. The current flowing into the
cave wasn't very strong, and the sound of the water lapping
onto the shore was almost soothing. They were somewhere in
the Neverwood. The stream was no doubt one of the many that
broke off from Neverland's main river.

Michael glanced at Nev and Rosebud. "Why don't you go find
out exactly where we are?"

The bird bobbed her head and took off, with Rosebud trailing behind her.

While they waited, Vanessa started a fire, and they gathered around it to dry off. The surface of Neverland was never
really cold, and it was no great inconvenience to sit there and
wait for Nev, especially once they got the fire going. The Lost
Boys spread out to see if they could find food, and Shade floated
around the area, alert for trouble. Nev and Rosebud came back
just as the Lost Boys returned with an armful of fruit.

"We are, perhaps, an hour's walk from the lagoon," Nev
said. "Have you thought of what you're going to do when we get
there?"

"Get down to the Coral Caves." Michael hesitated. "Somehow."

"If you could do that so simply, we would not have needed Hook's help to leave the Underworld."

"Do you have any better ideas?"

"How much do you trust Hook?"

"Not at all," Michael said.

"Then, perhaps we should appeal to the mermaids. I cannot see them truly helping any who would want to harm Peter, no matter what Hook said."

"They didn't exactly like us last time."

"No," Nev said, "but they liked Peter. It is not impossible that they could be convinced to help."

Michael shrugged. "It's worth a try."

They decided to eat before setting off. Like the rest of Neverland, the fruit was something formed out of a child's imagination instead of the result of the seeds of the natural world. Some pieces looked like a cross between bananas and oranges, while others seemed to be nothing more than an assortment of shapes. A thing that looked like a seven-pointed star tasted like an apple. It was all sweet, of course, but it all had the exact same flavor, which was disturbing in and of itself. He couldn't remember two of the *same* fruit ever tasting the same here. Neverland didn't have much time.

There hadn't really been time for their clothes to dry completely, but they didn't want to wait any longer than necessary. Their trek through the forest was slow going, and their wet clothes made it even more uncomfortable. The woods seemed wilder than the last time Michael had been there, more than even the lack of flight could account for. The sunlight never completely pierced the canopy, leaving them in a perpetual twilight. Every shadow felt like it hid some dangerous beast, and given the nature of Neverland, it was entirely possible that they did. No wild animal leaped out to attack, though, and they continued their journey in relative silence.

The thick foliage caused the trek to take three hours rather than the one Nev had originally estimated. Finally, just as the sun was dipping beneath the western horizon, they came out of the tree line and beheld the lagoon, shining with the golden light of sunset. Dusk had painted the sky orange, and the surface of the lagoon was so smooth it almost seemed like glass. Only the occasional splash of a fish leaping into the air disturbed the illusion. The warm wind of early spring gusted across his face, carrying the scent of a myriad of flowers. All in all, it seemed far too peaceful a place to house a foe strong enough to have nearly thrown the whole world out of balance.

He wasn't sure how long he stared at the lagoon before Will stepped up next to him.

"A stunning view," the other man said. "It's hard to believe it's not a dream. Do mermaids really live there?"

"Yes. Not sure it will matter, though—they never liked anyone but Peter. I hope we can at least get them to talk to us."

Will grinned. "I'll be happy if I can only see one."

"Didn't you see them at the Still Lake?"

"I saw something, but I wasn't able to get a good look."

Michael gave him a half smile. "I'm sure Wendy will be thrilled to hear that."

Will coughed and looked away, and Michael laughed.

It didn't take them long to make their way to the shore. Though he didn't really expect it to work, Michael called out for the mermaids, but there was only stillness. Even the fish jumping from the water seemed to have calmed. Michael sighed. Will gave him a confused look, but Michael didn't explain. He stepped into the water. When his foot broke the surface of the lagoon, a ripple spread out over the water.

"What are you doing?" Vanessa asked.

"Trying to save Peter," he said, not looking back at her.

As the ripple he created passed over the middle of the lagoon, something about the size of a human head poked out of the water.

The mermaid had black hair, almost like it was made of woven shadow. Her pale skin gleamed in the light of the setting sun, and even at that distance, Michael could tell that her eyes were a deep shade of sea green. As she glided through the water toward them, barely disturbing the surface, Michael found his heart speeding up. Sweat broke out on his brow, and he realized he couldn't look away. She was gorgeous. He hadn't noticed it last time he was in Neverland, but of course, he had been a boy of four then.

"Be careful," Vanessa said. "You wouldn't be the first man led to a watery grave by a siren's song."

Will gave her a sidelong glance and nodded. He obviously thought the warning was meant for him, as he'd taken an involuntary step forward. Michael was glad for the distraction, as he felt his own face redden. The mermaid stopped when she was about twenty feet in front of him.

"You're not supposed to be here," she said in a voice that was almost a song and that made him want to listen. "Only children are supposed to be here, unless you're a pirate." Her eyes widened. "Are you?" Before they could answer, she shook her head. "No, I can see that you're not." She glared at Vanessa. "*You* certainly don't belong here, but that still leaves the question of why the other two are here."

"Peter." Michael's throat was dry, and he took a few seconds to moisten it before speaking again. "We're looking for Peter."

Anger flitted across her features, and she hissed at Vanessa before addressing Michael. "Peter Pan belongs to no surface dweller, least of all to you, who grew up long ago." Her eyes hardened and she turned to Vanessa, who was both alert and amused at the mermaid's anger toward her. "And you will not take him away from us."

"What's that supposed to mean?" Will asked Vanessa.

"I think she's worried that I'll steal Peter's heart, like Wendy and Tinker Bell and Tiger Lily."

"Wendy stole his heart?" he asked, voice strained.

"*He* would say so," Michael hissed. "Now be quiet."

But the mermaid had already turned to swim away, and Michael blinked several times to clear his thoughts before he could call after her. "We're not here to capture him or"—he gestured at Vanessa—"steal him. We're here to *save* him."

"As if I'd want to steal a twelve-year-old boy," Vanessa muttered. "I've got enough problems with the grown-up boys around me."

Michael gave her a dark look, but she responded in kind, and he didn't have a leg to stand on in this argument. He turned his attention to the mermaid, only to find she had already disappeared beneath the surface. He moved deeper into the water, knowing it was futile, when she came back up a little so that only her eyes showed. In spite of that, Michael had no trouble understanding her words. "You've come to set him free."

"Yes," Michael said.

Another head, this one with sky-blue eyes and deep brown hair, rose from the water near the first. A third appeared just out of Michael's reach. Others popped up, each with a different shade in their eyes and hair, but one thing was the same.

They all looked at him with anger.

"Maybe you shouldn't have said that," Will said.

The sailor was standing on the shore, but one of the mermaids glared at him and started to sing. It sounded vaguely like the song of the wisps, but this song, it seemed, had lost none of its potency. Though it wasn't directed at him, Michael found himself lulled into listlessness. He tried to resist it, but he could as easily have resisted a storm as that voice.

In a moment, all he knew was the song.

He wasn't sure how long he listened, but when the song finally cut off, Will stood right next to him, and they had both
waded in until they were waist deep. Vanessa was on the shore,
angrily calling out to them. Will blinked. He looked around and
paled. Michael gasped as the water near them rippled. Half a
dozen mermaid heads rose out of the water once more. Before
Michael could act, one of them grabbed his leg. Though she
seemed small, she pulled with a strength that would've been
more suited to a gorilla than any human. He cried out as she
dragged him into the water. Will's screams cut off as he, too, was
submerged. Michael kicked and tried to pull free, but he might
as well have been fighting a statue. Quickly, his lungs burned
with the need to take a breath, and he knew he wouldn't be able
to survive much longer. He looked around, but his struggling
had filled the water with a hazy murk. Will was a blur at the
edge of his vision, though the other man had already stopped
moving. The world started going dark.

A shadow passed before him, moving too fast for him to tell
what it was, but the grip around his leg loosened. He jerked his
leg up, and suddenly he was free. He made a frantic struggle
and barely managed to grab on to Will before he swam to the
surface.

The air had never felt so sweet as it did when he took that
first breath. He fought to get air and water from his eyes and
keep Will afloat, even as he kept on the lookout for the mermaids. But they never came. In fact, the surface remained
smooth, aside from the ripples he himself made as he paddled
to keep them afloat. As soon as Michael's head cleared from the
lack of oxygen, he headed for the shore, pulling the unconscious
Will along with him. He kept expecting a mermaid to reach up
and pull him back down, but no opposition came.

They reached the edge of the lagoon. Vanessa waded in and
helped Michael drag Will to the shore. Will wasn't breathing,

and his skin felt clammy. She rolled Will onto his stomach as Michael collapsed on the ground. He watched as she pressed on Will's back. Soon—but seemingly a lifetime later—water started to flow out of Will's mouth and the man started coughing. She kept pushing until he wheezed, "Enough!"

Vanessa got off Will, and looked over to Michael. From her ears she pulled out two wads of cloth—pieces of a ripped-up handkerchief. "You okay?" she asked.

"Just a little embarrassed," he said.

"Don't be," she said. "I would have been out there with you if I hadn't had these." She held up the wads of cloth.

"Clever. Should have thought of that."

"That's what you get for being out of the Knights for so long."

"Yes—I don't encounter deadly creatures day-to-day, so I forget how to defend myself."

"What happened?" Will asked as he struggled to sit up.

"It was a warning," Michael said, helping the other man to his feet. "Don't make the mermaids angry, especially if you're in the water with them, and never go with them if they ask you to follow."

"Couldn't a simple signpost have worked?"

"I don't think they know how to write."

"They have no written language as far as I know," Nev said.

"That's what I figured." To Will, he said, "I thought we were dead for sure. I'm still not sure how I got free."

In just that moment, there was what seemed to be an explosion on the lagoon, causing a wall of water to rush at them. Will raised his hand to ward off the water, but it wasn't necessary. The wave just passed through him as if the water was nothing more than an illusion. Michael looked up just as Shade floated across the surface of the lagoon toward them. He remembered the shadow that had flown in front of him while they were underwater.

"Shade, did you free us?" The shadow jumped up and down and nodded. Michael glanced at Nev, who seemed to shrug, though Michael couldn't say what gave him that impression. "How?"

Shade lifted his fists and made a motion like punching. He landed a blow on Michael's shadow, and Michael felt a slight pressure on his arm. His eyes widened.

"You can touch people by touching their shadows?"

Shade doubled over and made a motion like he was breathing heavily.

Michael nodded. "You can, but it makes you tired."

Shade nodded.

"Can you actually do enough to hurt someone?"

Shade held his thumb and forefinger together so they were nearly touching.

"A little?"

Shade nodded, and Michael looked to Nev. "Did you have any idea he could do that?"

Nev shook her head. "I thought he was entirely insubstantial, though I suppose I shouldn't be surprised at learning what the shadow of a god can do. It does leave us with another problem, however."

Michael nodded. "How do we get to the Coral Caves if the mermaids won't help us? I don't suppose you know where we can find a colony of nixies, do you?"

"The only ones I know of are submerged in the lagoon. Shade?"

Shade thought for a second before shaking his head. Michael translated their conversation, but neither the Lost Boys nor Rosebud had any better ideas.

"There is one thing," Nev said. "Hook spoke of taking refuge in the Coral Caves. Before you and Peter defeated them, I often saw the pirates come from a hidden cove on the other side of the bay. We might be able locate their base."

Again, he translated.

"It's as good an idea as any," Vanessa said. "Lead the way."

* * *

CHAPTER 28

Nev led them on a slow trek around the bay. With the mermaids acting so hostile, no one wanted to risk swimming across, so they moved along the shore. Since most of the human inhabitants of Neverland tended to either fly or travel by ship, there were precious few trails large enough for a human on the island, and pretty much none around this dangerous body of water. With their swords, they cut away the worst of the foliage, but they could do nothing about the rock formations or marshy grounds, and they found themselves traveling in the water as often as on the shore. They had no encounters with any wildlife or magical creatures, and the calmness of it all was unnerving.

"I do not like this," Nev said as they were in the middle of crossing through the lagoon at the mouth of a large river.

"Peter is captured, and Neverland is dying," Michael said. "We have to somehow get to caves that are underwater and guarded by vicious mermaids. And to top it all off, we're following the advice of someone who just might have been the most evil thing to ever walk the shores of Neverland. I don't think *anyone* likes it."

"No," Nev said. "That's not what I mean. Have you ever known the lagoon to be this quiet?"

Michael paused for a moment. Nev was right. There were no animal calls. No birdsong. Even the wind rustling through the leaves felt muted. He looked down. The water in the lagoon was clear, and he should've been able to see schools of fish, but there was nothing.

"It's because of us," Michael said, trying to convince himself as much as anyone else. "Animals avoid humans."

"Do they?" Nev asked.

Michael rolled his eyes. "I'm not talking about you. I mean other animals, ones that aren't intelligent."

"Most of the beasts of Neverland have a similar intellect, but even if they do not, you know very well that they are just as likely to stalk us as ignore us. These aren't natural creatures. They are of the story. I don't believe it would ever occur to them to be afraid of people. They haven't been this quiet since the crocodile hunted along these shores."

For a moment, Michael thought he saw something moving in the trees. The crocodile was dead, though. Then again, Hook was dead, too. He hesitated before turning to Nev. "Can they do that? The beasts, I mean. Can they come back as ghosts?"

Nev inclined her head. "If a thing can lead to adventure, then it has a place here. In the past such things could happen, but the crocodile died only a few hours ago. I am not certain that any new ghosts could come to exist when Peter's power has been curtailed as it has. Hook might be able to raise a ghost, but he would not do that to the crocodile. No, it has to be something else. Perhaps the mermaids have been hunting."

"I assumed it was because of Peter. He's imprisoned, so there's less adventure here."

"Perhaps. I don't know."

Michael looked out over the water. It rippled in the distance, as if a fish had jumped out or a stone had been thrown in, but he saw no other signs of either. He paused. It could be any number of things, but something Hook had said tugged at his memory, something about the wraith having command of creatures of the water.

Vanessa gave voice to the thought before he did: "Could a water elemental drive away the animals?"

Nev followed Michael's gaze. "Yes, if it were hostile."

Michael looked back, but they were closer to the shore ahead of them.

"Run!" he called as he splashed forward.

Will, who had apparently learned from his time here, was running almost before Michael had finished saying the word. The Lost Boys were right on his heels. Vanessa also started to run, but she tripped and fell facedown into the water. Michael stopped to help her up, and by the time she had risen, the others had reached the shore. Vanessa and Michael pushed forward, but the water churned in front of them, and an amorphous blob formed on the surface, growing until it had reached a height of nearly twenty feet. A dozen tentacles emerged from its body, lashing out at random. One of them reached out and tore a tree from the ground of the nearby shore, causing the Lost Boys to scatter. Two eyes, formed of bubbles that churned within the creature, focused their attention on Vanessa and Michael.

One of the tentacles shot toward them. Michael leaped out of the way, but it closed around Venessa's waist. The creature lifted her out of the water. She slashed with her sword, but it had about as much effect as one would expect steel to have against liquid. A mouth formed in the body, revealing two rows of teeth, seeming to be made of solid water, and he was pretty sure they'd have a lot more effect on her flesh than her sword did on the creature. Elementals were forces of nature. They consumed because it was in their nature to do so, but they didn't need teeth to do it. That was a mark of cruelty that, as far as he knew, only one of their number had ever shown, and Michael knew its name.

"Comshemar!"

The creature paused, but Michael had never been skilled in magic, and name magic was extremely complicated. What he had done was little more than a pinprick to the elemental, but such a being was unused to pain of any kind. It roared, a sound like crashing waves and frothing rapids, and threw Vanessa at him. They both went tumbling into the water. *At least he let her go.*

But the triumph was short-lived. As Michael tried to get up, the current itself seemed to grab him and pull him under. Desperately, he made to call out the elemental's name again, but submerged as he was, it was impossible. He fought to get to the surface, but he might as well have been struggling against the ocean itself. Once again, he was about to drown, only this time he would take Vanessa with him. A water elemental would cast no shadow in water, so even Shade with his limited abilities wouldn't be able to help.

Panic painted Vanessa's face, and he was pretty sure it reflected his own. Soon—much too soon, in his estimation— their expressions would shift to the stillness of death, but just then several objects splashed into the water. Michael looked about, and could barely make out the Lost Boys. More than seeing them, though, he could hear them. They were crying out something.

Its name.

They must have heard him call it and realized its importance. Comshemar's grip weakened. Michael tried to get to the surface once again, but the elemental found him once more and forced him down.

Too far down.

His lungs burned, and the pressure made his head feel like it was going to explode. He had mere seconds.

Vanessa floated nearby. Her movements were slowing, but even so, she attacked with her sword. No doubt she knew it wouldn't do any good, but still she fought on. She was dying like a Knight. Like Dmitri.

Like me.

He didn't want to die, didn't want Vanessa to die. He didn't want to leave Will stranded, but he could at least face his fate like a Knight. No. Not like a Knight. Like a friend of Peter Pan. And no friend of Peter would drown like this. Peter wouldn't allow it. *Neverland* would never allow it.

As if in response to the thought, Rosebud appeared in front of him, her ghostly form unaffected by the water. She flew around his head twice before pointing down. Michael's eyes looked to where she was indicating and he would've gasped if he'd been able to. The struggle with the elemental had brought them down quite a ways, and they were closer to the bottom than the surface now. So far, in fact, that they were very near the hull of a sunken ship, upside down on the floor of the lagoon. Though the elemental had been weakened by the constant use of its name, it was still obviously strong enough to keep them from going up.

They just might be able to go down, though.

He gestured wildly to get Vanessa's attention, and pointed at the ship. Vanessa's eyes widened, and she shook her head. He needed to convince her this was the only way, but there wasn't time to argue. He hated abandoning her, but if he didn't move now, it was all over.

Michael started swimming down. There was a hole on the bottom of the hull, and he swam through it. Some kind of glowing algae had grown on the interior, giving him a faint light.

His lungs felt like they would explode, but as he swam around, he found what he was looking for: a pocket of air that had been trapped in one of the corners of the ceiling. Muscles crying out from the strain, he swam to it. The relief when he could finally take a breath brought quiet tears to his eyes. A second later, Vanessa appeared next to him, her face red. She was gasping.

"That was an incredibly foolish thing to do," she said between heavy breaths, but he thought she might have been holding back a laugh.

"You're alive, aren't you?" Michael asked, breathing in the salt-saturated air just as hard. "We can't stay here long. We'll use up the air in a few minutes."

Vanessa nodded, finding her calm much more rapidly than he. "How far down do you think we are?"

Michael shrugged. "Fifty, maybe sixty feet."

"That's a long way down."

Michael nodded. He had heard about problems divers had if they came to the surface too quickly, though he didn't know any of the specifics. For that matter, he wasn't sure such rules applied in Neverland. He wasn't willing to risk it, though. "Long enough to cause problems if we try to go straight to the surface."

"Right."

They trod water, unsure what to do.

"Oh good. There you are," a voice came from above.

Michael cried out, reaching for his sword, but he had apparently lost it in the struggle. He looked up and was shocked when he saw John's face poking through the wood. All color had drained from his body, and even the frames of his glasses were closer to gray than black. It took Michael a second to figure out what had happened.

"You used some of Rosebud's dust."

"Yes," John said. "She said you were down here and that you

had survived, but I didn't know how that could be." He looked around and nodded. "Very clever. How did you know this was down here?"

"We didn't, and it won't last long," Michael said. The air was already smelling a little stale. "Can you go through the ship and find any more air? I'm afraid we'll drown if we go looking for it."

John nodded and disappeared back through the wall without saying another word. They waited in silence for almost a full minute, not wanting to speak and use up more air. As it was, the effort of keeping themselves afloat had them panting. Eventually, John came back.

"Michael, you won't believe it. I didn't believe it myself, but I saw it, and you can't very well deny what you saw, can you?"

Michael suppressed a chuckle, but as he breathed in, he started feeling dizzy. "There are some people that do just that, but before you tell us whatever it is, did you find any more air?"

"Oh yes! There's a room just down the hall that you should be able to breathe in for a long time, but that's not all."

"It's enough for now. Why don't you lead the way to this other room, and we'll talk when we get there?"

John nodded and floated down beneath the surface.

"See you in this special room," Vanessa said.

"Looking forward to it."

They dove down. The glowing algae kept John's form visible, and they had no trouble keeping up with him. Still, it was a longer swim than Michael expected, and he was almost at the end of his air. John turned a corner and Michael could only hope it would lead them to their destination. When the ghost floated up into a room, Michael kicked viciously until he emerged from the water.

John had been right about this place. The room was huge, no doubt built to hold cargo. More important, it held a lot of *air*. Above them, the curved ceiling showed the shape of what would've been the bottom of the ship. Boxes floated all around them, though some had rotted away, spilling their contents. One garment caught his eye. It had been ruined by floating in the salt water for so long, but the greatcoat had once been bright red. Michael had seen only one man wear that kind of coat.

"That belonged to Hook." He turned to John. "You mean that this is the *Jolly Roger*?"

John nodded. "Isn't it great? This is the ship that the pirates used when they were fighting against us."

"It's more than that," Michael said. "This is how we got home last time."

* * *

CHAPTER 29

When we finally beat Hook last time," Michael said, "Peter piloted this ship to get us back to England. This might be our way home."

He had floated near a wall and ran his fingers over it, wincing at the slimy feel of the glowing algae.

"You think we can sail to London in this?" Vanessa asked, obviously skeptical.

Michael thought for a second before letting out a breath and shaking his head. "No, probably not. Even if we could get it to the surface, it's too badly damaged, and even if it wasn't, I wouldn't want to try without someone who knows what he's doing at the helm."

Vanessa cocked her head. "Like Will?"

"Maybe, if we could figure out how to bring it to the surface. I wish I knew how it got here, but we don't really have time to wonder about it. This air won't last forever." He turned to John. "How far are we from the Coral Caves?"

John looked at him as if he were crazy. "Michael, even if you could get into the caves, you still can't breathe there."

"We can if you'll tell us where the air pockets are."

"Don't you think it would be a better idea if we just went to the surface?" Vanessa asked.

Michael shook his head. "I'm guessing the elemental doesn't realize where we went or it would have already come after us. This is Comshemar, and you know as well as I do that it loves playing with its prey. It's almost certainly looking for us. If we try to get to the surface, it'll see us for sure."

"So your idea is to go even deeper?"

Michael waved at the flooded room. "There might be half an hour of air here. We can keep going from cavity to cavity until all the air in the ship runs out or we can try to do something. Unless you have a better idea . . ."

He let it hang. John looked at him for a second before sighing and disappearing through the wall again. Vanessa stared after him.

"Is that really what your brother was like?"

"It's a reflection of him, but it is the John I remembered."

"I read the Knight's report on your family. They always made John seem so serious, like . . ."

Like me, he thought. "He is serious, now. We're all different from who we were as children."

"I'll be serious now, then: Do you really think this is the best idea?"

Michael shrugged. "It's the only one I have."

"That's starting to become a theme of yours," she muttered.

"Starting?"

Vanessa gave him a half grin, then looked up, as if trying to see the surface in spite of the ship that was in the way. "Aren't you worried about sea monsters?"

"There are no sea monsters in the lagoon."

Vanessa snorted. "You mean besides that elemental that tried to eat me? And the mermaids that tried to drown you?"

"Yes, besides those. I suppose some people would consider the mermaids monsters, but I think they're mainly indifferent."

"Michael, this is a land of stories," Vanessa said. "I know

you've been here before and all, but if there's any place that might have sea monsters, it's here."

"I think it's a risk we'll have to take, then."

"Wonderful."

"It's not close," John's voice said an instant before the spirit of the boy appeared. "You might be able to make it, but I still think you'd have a better chance of getting to the surface."

"Is the elemental still out there?"

"There was something churning in the water above me. Will was watching for it. Maybe we could move farther down the shore and distract it away."

"We caught it off guard, but I don't think we'll be so lucky again."

"How do we kill it?"

"We don't," Vanessa said. "Elementals are difficult opponents in the best circumstances, and right now definitely doesn't qualify. It's generally best to just stay out of its way. Without magic of some kind, you probably won't be able to hurt it."

John pursed his lips and tugged at his glasses as he'd always done as a boy. Finally, his shoulders sagged. "It's best to go out of the ship from the deck. There's another air pocket by the entrance, and that'll leave you closer to the caves."

"Fine," Michael said. "Lead the way."

John led them from one air pocket to another. Michael hadn't realized the ship had so many passages, and they never would have been able to find their way without John's help. It wasn't long before the cold had seeped into his body, and he started shivering.

Finally, they reached the bottom of the sunken ship and saw a hole rotted through the floor. If the ship had been right-side up, that would've led to the deck. Instead, it was a path to the open ocean. There was no time to delay. The air pocket they were in was small, and he doubted it would last a minute. He looked at Vanessa.

"Are you ready?"

Vanessa raised an eyebrow. "Do I have a choice?"

Michael gave her a half smile. "You could stay and suffocate."

Vanessa narrowed her eyes. "You know, I like you a lot better when you're not trying to be funny." She looked up at the opening before meeting Michael's eyes. "Let's go."

The ghost of John floated in front of them. Often, he would dart ahead, only to come back when he realized he had left them behind. It felt like they were moving painfully slow. It wasn't long before a worried expression appeared on the ghost's face, and a feeling of dread crept into Michael as he was filled with a certainty that John had misjudged the distance. They wouldn't make it to the caves in time.

The water was clear, and Michael could see the reef-covered rock rising up before them. An opening near the base of the structure grew closer as they approached, but it was too far away. His lungs burned, and the weight of the water pressed down on him. His vision was growing dark. He tried to swim faster, but that just made him even more desperate for air. Next to him, Vanessa went limp.

Michael stopped in the water. He looked from Vanessa to the cave. It was close. Maybe close enough to make it, but he couldn't just leave her. He reached forward and seized her collar. He pulled with all his might, but carrying the extra weight made his movements even slower. The very act of swimming leached the strength from his limbs. So close. It was right in front of them.

With a last rush of strength, Michael crossed into the cave. John appeared strangely clear in his darkening vision. He pointed up, and Michael could practically feel his hope die. The surface rippled in some unseen light, but it was impossibly high. He kicked as hard as he could, but Vanessa felt like she weighed a thousand pounds. Michael's lungs were on fire. He pushed one more time, but it wasn't enough. The surface was closer, but it might as well have been leagues away. He felt Vanessa slipping from his grasp. He tried to hold on, but his strength had left him.

Not again. Please, not again . . .

A ball of light fluttered in front of him. For a second, Michael thought it was Rosebud, but the glow was different, deep blue like the ocean instead of her ghostly pale blue. It swam in front of his eyes, and he could feel the movement of water along his face. He should have known what this was, but his thoughts were sluggish. He just wanted to breathe. He opened his mouth, expecting the cool, suffocating liquid to fill his mouth, but instead he inhaled fresh, clean air. He almost choked on that and blinked, unsure as to what had happened. What he did know was that he was still in the water, dragging the unconscious Vanessa behind him. She was all that mattered. The surface was so close, and with renewed strength he swam up and pulled himself onto the shore.

*   *   *

CHAPTER 30

Michael blinked several times, trying to understand what had happened. The smell of salt water hung heavy in the air. His back ached, and he tried to get up. He rose only a few inches before he started coughing and expelling water from his mouth. Vanessa lay next to him. Michael put a hand on her chest. Her heartbeat was weak, but it was definitely there. Water dribbled from her nose and mouth, but there had to be more. He put her on her stomach, like she had done with Will, and expelled the remaining water from her lungs. She gave a weak cough but didn't awaken.

A wave of terror washed over Michael, and for a moment he could only stare. He could practically see the color draining from her, taking her life with it. A fat droplet of water dripped off his nose and splashed against her forehead. She twitched, and the movement brought him out of his trance.

"John?" he called out. "John, are you there? Rosebud?"

Neither of the spirits answered his calls. Michael looked around, hoping to see Shade, but the shadow was nowhere to be seen, either. He struggled to his feet. The ground was slippery with algae, and he fell a few times before he managed to stand. The water lapped up onto the stones from a nearby hole in the ground. A passage trailed off from the chamber, disappearing into the darkness.

"Hello?"

The blue light from before flitted in front of him, and Michael blinked several times before he could focus on the creature. It wasn't Rosebud. Green iridescent scales covered a lithe, feminine body. It looked more like she had the fins of a fish than the dragonfly wings that most fairies possessed. She hovered in front of his eyes, moving her arms and legs slightly, as if she were maintaining her position in water. She chattered rapidly, but her accent was unusual, and she had to repeat herself several times before he understood.

"You're a nixie?"

The fairy darted around his head several times before stopping in front of him again. "I thought . . ." He paused, unsure of how to continue. "I thought all the nixies followed that other me."

She shook her head and stamped her foot in the air, and Michael almost chuckled. The scowl she gave at his response, however, sent him into fits of laughter, and it took him a few seconds to compose himself.

"Not you, then?" Again, the nixie shook her head. "You saved us, didn't you? You used your dust to give us the ability to breathe underwater."

Her expression softened, and she nodded.

"Why?"

She darted around the cavern, chattering rapidly. Michael's eyes went wide and he looked around. "This is a fairy home?"

The fairy nodded.

"I've heard about old magic protections, but I had no idea it would keep out spirits entirely. That's why John and Rosebud couldn't come in here."

She nodded once more. Michael walked over to the hole. He shivered at the thought of how close he had come to drowning. How close *Vanessa* had come. He peered down. Just beneath the surface of the water, John stared up at him. He seemed to let out a breath of relief and waved. Michael smiled and returned the gesture.

"Can you hear me?"

The spirit pursed his lips and nodded slowly. He tried to talk, but Michael shook his head.

"It's no good. I can't hear anything. It looks like it only works one way."

John nodded. He lifted his hand to the surface of the water, but it was like he was pressing against a window. He banged his fists on the barrier, but the water didn't so much as ripple. After a few seconds, he pressed his face against it, which looked so ridiculous that Michael laughed. John scowled and pointed at Vanessa, who would be barely visible from the hole. Michael nodded.

"She's alive and breathing, and she should hopefully wake up soon. How about you? I didn't get a chance to ask in the ship: Are you and the others all right? The elemental didn't hurt anyone, did it?"

John shook his head.

"Good." Michael glanced down the passage. "I think this passage leads to a network of caves. Once Vanessa wakes up, we'll go down it. We have nixie dust, so I don't think we'll encounter any obstacles we can't get around. Maybe we can find a way to the other me's headquarters. Take Will with you, but watch out for him. He's still new to all this. If we're lucky, we might be able to meet up in the Coral Caves."

John nodded, but he looked concerned.

"Don't worry. We'll be fine. This cavern is some sort of nixie sanctuary. That's why you can't come in. There's powerful magic here, and I think my new friend is protecting us."

The spirit didn't look certain, but he nodded again and floated through a nearby wall. The nixie, who had been looking down at the ghost from Michael's shoulder, started chattering as she bobbed up and down in the air. Once again, she had to repeat herself before Michael understood.

"How can I help you? If it's that your people have turned against you, I don't know what I'll be able to do, not if they're also working against Peter."

The nixie shook her head.

"That's not it?"

The nixie paused and then chattered.

"Wouldn't the power of the fairy home protect them?"

The nixie chittered.

"Why did they leave? Who's controlling them?"

She floated to just above the watery hole, then flew in a rapid circle. Her body skimmed the edge of the water, and slowly a bulge formed within her circle. Tentacles no more than an inch long extended from it. They lashed about for a few seconds before the figure collapsed into water again.

"How could the water elemental do that? It's a creature of brute strength. It doesn't use magic, and it certainly shouldn't be able to control fairies, no matter their type."

She spoke a few words. He gave her a sad smile.

"I guess you weren't really strong enough to stop it from coming in here and taking your friends out of the sanctuary. I guess you got lucky it didn't find your hiding place."

Again, the fairy nodded, and Michael's heart skipped a beat.

"Was this a trap, then?" After a second, however, he shook his head. "That doesn't make sense, though. It didn't need to lead us here. If it had come at us when we were in the ship, there would've been nothing we could do." He looked at the nixie. The little creature was obviously terrified that what happened to her people would happen to her as well, and not only to her. The hairs on the back of Michael's neck stood on end. "It doesn't want to kill us. It wants to capture us."

The fairy bobbed up and down before flying around his head several times. He held out a hand, and she landed on his palm.

"What's your name?"

She chattered.

"Merran?"

The fairy nodded before flying over to Vanessa. She fluttered over her face, spilling fairy dust on her. Vanessa groaned, and Michael rushed to her side. She opened her eyes. She seemed to have trouble focusing, and she squinted for several seconds.

"Michael?" She looked around. Her eyes focused briefly on Merran before she looked to Michael. "What happened?"

Michael scanned the area, his eyes briefly stopping on the pool where Merran had created a miniature elemental. It might have been his imagination, but he thought the water rippled a little too much. He could picture a larger version of the creature coming out and attacking them.

"You must have still had water in your lungs. I'll explain later. We're in trouble. Come on. We have to move quickly."

Vanessa blinked and struggled to her feet, though she had even more difficulty standing than Michael had. She had to lean on Michael's shoulder, and she stared at Merran.

"That's . . ."

"A nixie."

"Lucky us."

"Maybe not." He explained to Vanessa what Merran had told him. When he was done, he turned to the nixie. "Can you leave this place without being controlled?"

She chattered.

"Can you guide us? The one we're looking for is in these caves. Hopefully, you won't have to be away from your protections long enough to be taken."

She spoke several quick words.

"We'll help you. I promise. I think I know who's controlling the water elemental, and it's probably the same one controlling your people." As the fairy hovered in front of his face, he added, "You already know who it is, don't you? You know who kidnapped Peter."

She stared down the passage for several seconds before turning to Michael and nodding. Then she darted into the darkness until only her light was visible.

"We follow?" Vanessa asked.

"We follow."

It was slow going. Algae covered much of the floor, and they couldn't move at any pace faster than a moderate walk without slipping. The sound of the ocean echoing through the caverns made speech difficult. Every time they passed a fork, Michael couldn't help but look down the other passages and expect the water elemental to attack from the shadows, but no such attack came.

After a quarter hour, the passage opened up into a large chamber. Tiny buildings lay scattered about. It looked almost like the gremlin village, though it seemed somehow neater. Both cities had buildings that were falling apart, but these had been arranged in rows. Like the walls, the buildings were white. At first, Michael thought they were made of marble, but it didn't make sense for nixies to live in something like that. He bent down and took one of the crumbled remains between two fingers. It felt gritty and collapsed to dust in his fingers. He brought his fingers to his mouth and touched one against his tongue.

"Salt?" he asked. "You build your buildings out of salt?"

Venessa stepped up next to him. "Nixies that live near the

ocean do. Salt water. With her people gone, the magic holding the buildings together is fading away. Her city is dying."

Merran looked away. Michael walked over to her, making sure to avoid stepping on any of the buildings. He knelt by her, and she looked up and hugged his shin, though she was so tiny that her arms barely made it a fraction of the way around. He smiled and lowered his hand for her to get on. He raised her to his shoulder. It might have been his imagination, but he thought he heard a soft weeping coming from her direction.

"Don't worry," he said. "We'll find a way to help your people."

He couldn't see her face, but the sobbing stopped. Something light pressed against his cheek, and he wondered if she had kissed him.

They moved through the empty city without saying a word. The bone-white buildings gave Michael the impression that he was moving through the skeleton of some great beast. As they reached the edge of the city, and the passage on the other side, Michael stepped into a puddle with the consistency of mud. He looked down, but rather than ordinary dirt mixed with water, it seemed to be more salt.

"Does that happen often?" Michael asked.

Merran looked down at his salt-covered shoe for a few seconds before shaking her head and saying something about how ordinary water didn't dissolve their buildings. Michael sighed. "I was afraid of that. Vanessa, we'd better get ready."

"Ready for what?"

Rumbling echoed from the passage in front of them. A vague outline, not quite illuminated by the glowing algae, flowed into the passage and began lumbering down toward them, its watery tentacles flailing.

Michael barely had time to remember that he had lost his sword—or that his sword had been ineffective in the first place—before the water elemental surged forward, seizing

Vanessa with one tentacle and waving her around as if she were a toy. She had somehow managed to hold on to her sword through their swim, but now she lost her grip and it clattered to the ground. She cried out as Michael swept it up and swung it at the arm holding her, even though he knew it was futile. Surprisingly, the sword met resistance, slowing for a second before passing through the tentacle.

Suddenly, a sapphire light appeared near the monster, flying through the air so quickly that, at times, it seemed to be in two places at once.

"Merran!" Michael cried out.

The nixie hesitated for only a second before shooting forward. She darted in and out of combat, often passing within a few inches of the tentacle holding Vanessa. For a second, that appendage move sluggishly. Abruptly, it collapsed into inanimate water, and Vanessa fell to the ground. The elemental roared in pain. Michael felt a surge of hope that the nixie's power would be enough to defeat this creature, but that optimism vanished as the water on the floor flowed into the elemental. One of its tentacles slammed into the fairy, sending her flying through the air. She crashed into a building, smashing through the wall and out the other side. Michael ran to her and picked her up, but she didn't move. His hands glittered in the sapphire dust that flowed off of the nixie. There was so much there that it completely covered his palms. She opened her eyes and managed a weak smile. He put her down gently.

"Thanks," he said. "Rest now. We'll handle this."

Vanessa had already picked herself up. She was staying away from the elemental, though she managed to keep its attention. Michael rushed forward and slashed at it with his sword. The elemental turned and gave him a hungry look, then wrapped its tentacle around Michael and jerked him off his feet before he could land a blow. He cried out and struggled against it, but it did no good. It squeezed, and his bones creaked. Vanessa ran at it and hit the tentacle with a rock the size of her head. Once again, her improvised weapon slowed as it met resistance, but if it had an effect, it was a minor one. The elemental opened its mouth. Michael cried out as it shoved him in.

Almost involuntarily, Michael took in a breath, but rather than a rush of water, there was crisp, clean air. There was a quivering across his skin as the elemental tried to crush him, but just as the nixie dust granted Michael immunity to the pressure of the ocean's depths, it also protected him from the elemental's power. With renewed vigor, he attacked with his sword. With so much dust on his hand, the nixie magic coursed through him, and his blade sliced through the elemental with ease, opening a hole in its middle. The water parted as the creature roared.

Michael spilled onto the ground. The impact drove the air from his lungs, and his sword skidded across the cavern floor. He scrambled toward it, but the elemental seized him once more and lifted him into the air. Rather than trying to squeeze him, though, it slammed him against the stone ground. There was a snapping sound and agony shot up his arm. Tears blurred his vision.

"Michael!"

He looked up to see the sword flying through the air. He caught it in his good arm, though the effort sent a surge of pain through him. Gritting his teeth, he sliced anyway. But he was fighting at an awkward angle, and he was injured, so his attack was weak. Still, the weapon cut through the tentacle, and Michael once again fell to the ground. He bit his tongue to avoid crying out as he got to his feet. He should have run away, injured as he was, but instead he limped toward the elemental. It tried to grab him, but Michael managed to get his sword in front of him. The elemental cut itself on the blade and withdrew, roaring.

Summoning every ounce of strength he had, Michael thrust the sword into the elemental's central mass. It had gone in only a few inches when the elemental's tentacle slammed down on the weapon, snapping the blade in two. One of the tendrils wrapped itself around the broken sword and pulled it out. Before Michael could do anything, it flung the blade down at him. He threw himself to the side, and the sword plunged into the ground where he'd been standing. He didn't even have a chance to get up before the elemental seized him again.

Michael looked around, hoping Vanessa would be able to help, but the creature had grabbed her as well and shoved her into its mouth. Unlike Michael, however, she didn't have the benefit of extra nixie dust. Inside the elemental, she grabbed her throat, obviously unable to breathe.

In desperation, Michael bit the tentacle holding him. His teeth closed on something solid, and he ripped a chunk off of the tentacle. It loosened, and he slipped out of its grasp. He fell, slicing his broken arm on the sword blade that was still embedded in the earth—luckily the pain already there numbed him to the new wound, although a distant part of his mind told him that wasn't a good thing. The elemental tried to grab him with another tendril, but he grabbed the blade with his good hand. He didn't know where he got the strength, but he forced the sword out and held it up just as the tentacle came down hard on him. Instead of pulverizing Michael, the creature impaled its appendage on his blade. Michael rushed forward, tearing the weapon free, and swung it. It ripped into the elemental, but he didn't stop this time. He moved his sword in a wide arc. The elemental actually steamed as he cut pieces free. He struck again and again, until finally, the elemental collapsed into water.

Then the pain was too much, and Michael fell into unconsciousness.

* * *

CHAPTER 31

M ichael," Vanessa's voice said from the darkness. "Michael, are you all right?"

"What?"

His eyes opened slowly. Vanessa stood over him, looking worried. Michael tried to sit up, but the pain in his arm almost brought him to tears, and for a second, he thought he would throw up.

"Take your time."

"We don't have time," he sighed. "Help me up."

Vanessa frowned but helped him into a sitting position, and he looked down at himself. She had managed to bind up his wound and had made a sling for Michael's arm out of his coat. It was better than nothing, though only barely.

"You should rest."

"I should. I'm just not sure I can." He held out his good hand.

"You're an idiot," Vanessa said, but there was respect in her voice as she helped him to his feet.

He looked around. Much of the nixie city had dissolved when the water of the elemental had washed over the salt buildings. Merran flew around his head, though her movement was erratic. She fluttered in front of his face, having trouble staying aloft. He extended a hand and she landed on it. He started to speak but was overcome by a fit of coughing. He tasted blood on his breath and tried to force a smile.

"We beat it. Thank you. I never could've done it without you."

She smiled and hopped from one finger to another. Vanessa cleared her throat. She looked him up and down, seeming reluctant to speak.

"You too," he told her.

"That's not— Michael, if you're up to it, we have to keep going."

Michael winced and looked down at his arm. He tried to move it, but the pain made tears well in his eyes. He nodded. "We need to get to the surface."

"What about Peter? What about taking on your wraith?"

Michael tapped his injured arm. Even that light of a touch sent a jolt of pain through him. He shook his head. Dried blood had crusted on his sleeve. The next words were practically dragged out of him.

"There's no way I can go on like this." He hesitated. "You're the Knight. You'll have to be the one to save him."

Vanessa missed a step. She stared at him.

"Michael . . ."

"I left a long time ago." He waved a hand at the surrounded area. "This was never a place for someone like me. I grew up."

"I've never been here at all! How am I any better suited for this?"

"Because this is a place of adventure, and that spirit is in your blood."

"Michael—"

He stepped up closer to her. "Do you think I could fight a wraith like this? He would tear me apart."

She took a step back and bit her lip. Then she straightened, a determined look on her face. "Fine. I'll take the lead, but I'm not going to let you just give up." She looked at Merran. "Can you lead us out?"

The nixie glanced down at Michael's arm before looking at Vanessa and then back to him. Rather than fly away, though, she pointed down the passage the elemental had appeared in.

"Go," Michael said. "I'm right behind you."

The ground was coated in the glowing algae, and more than once Michael forgot about his injury and moved to steady himself when he slipped, only to be prevented by his sling. He tried not to worry about what he would do if they faced another fight. The way Vanessa constantly looked back to check on him and his injured arm said she was thinking the same thing. She had wrapped the bottom of the broken blade in a cloth as a make-shift hilt and held it ready. Fortunately, she had come out of the fight with nothing more serious than a few scrapes and bruises.

Merran had injured a wing and rode on Michael's shoulder at first, but she recovered before a few minutes had passed. She still didn't fly ahead, though. Instead, she hovered before them, as if she intended to protect Michael. It would have been funny, but he hadn't done a very good job of protecting himself. She couldn't be much worse.

With Merran pointing the way, the nixie led them down a series of corridors before coming to one that, initially, seemed to be a dead end. Before Michael could ask, she fluttered to the ground near the end of the passage and entered what Michael had assumed was another puddle, but as she sank deeper, he realized the path continued underwater. Submerged, her wings functioned like fins, and she glided through the water far more gracefully than she had maneuvered through the air. She went down about five feet and waited.

Vanessa had been sprinkled with nixie dust when Merran had first found them, but that had only been a little, and their battle with the elemental had shown it wasn't enough. His hand still glittered, though, and he reached out to Vanessa, only to remember how protective fairies were about their dust. He looked to Merran. The fairy nodded, apparently guessing his intent, and Michael sprinkled the Knight.

"Thanks," Vanessa said, and he realized she was addressing Merran.

Michael walked up to the edge of the passage. He took a deep breath and stepped in, allowing himself to fall. His arm was all but useless, and he controlled himself with just his legs. He had to force himself to take a breath, but once he did the air came easily. Apparently, the dust also did something to his eyes, too, because the water didn't distort his vision at all. Even the cold of the water barely touched him. He descended several feet and waited. Above, Vanessa hesitated, but when Michael waved at her, she closed her eyes and took a step, splashing into the water. By the time she'd reached Michael's level, she had opened her eyes and was breathing.

"That's certainly strange," she said. "I've never used nixie dust before. Somehow, I expected our voices to sound more . . . watery."

He almost laughed, but Merran started talking. He was surprised how easy he could understand her now—the oddness of her accent was gone. Michael realized that her voice was always meant to be heard underwater.

"I think I can lead you around the traps. Your double may have taken control of my people, but he does not have the benefit of my experiences, and I have existed for nearly as long as the Coral Caves themselves have. Even among my people, few know all the secrets I do. I will take you where you need to go."

Unlike what she had done in the air, Merran darted ahead, disappearing through forks and branches only to come out again as Michael approached. With all her back-and-forth, she had to be traveling at least ten times the distance that he and Vanessa were. She took them through more twists and turns than Michael could count. Some areas weren't illuminated by the algae, and in those places Merran stayed close only to depart again once they could see more clearly. Finally, Michael heard voices distorted by the water. Merran ascended, and Michael caught a glimpse of firelight shimmering through the surface of the water. He glanced at the nixie, who beckoned, and they all swam up.

As soon as he broke the surface, he found himself surrounded by sword blades. The threat only lasted a second before young voices cried out in surprise.

"Michael!" John said. "How did you get here? What happened to you?"

Michael grunted as he pulled himself out of the hole and into the cavern. He cried out in pain as John grabbed his injured arm in an effort to help him up. The boy pulled his hand back and looked worried. "What is it?"

"My arm is broken." He looked around as Will helped Vanessa out of the hole. The six Lost Boys, along with Nev and Shade, were seated around a fire. Michael wondered where they had gotten the wood, but before he could ask, he noticed that the smiles they normally wore were gone. "What happened?"

John scowled, and even in the dim light of the torch, Michael could see John's face redden. "We got lost. We were trying to find our way out when you found us."

Vanessa gave them a reassuring smile. "We have a guide now."

"Thank you, Mother," Tootles said.

"I'm. Not. Your. *Mother.*"

Michael couldn't help grinning at the exchange as he held out his hand. Merran darted to it and came to rest on his palm. The Lost Boys stared at her in shock. Even Rosebud seemed taken aback. The nixie chattered excitedly and pointed down a passage. John shook his head.

"That's the way we just came."

Vanessa raised an eyebrow. "Didn't you say you're lost?"

John nodded. "Well, yes."

"Then I don't know why you're complaining. Is that the way to the wraith or to the surface?"

Merran bounced up and down in the air before coming to rest lightly on Michael's injured arm. She spoke slowly and wouldn't meet his gaze. He shook his head.

"I already said—I can't go on like this."

She spoke again. This time, her words were more rapid. Rosebud flew around her before voicing her agreement.

"They're right," John said. "I can feel it. Neverland doesn't have much time."

There was a round of nods from the Lost Boys. Nev landed on his shoulder but didn't say anything. Even Shade seemed more transparent than normal.

Michael took a deep breath and nodded. "But what can I do?"

"You can believe," Nev said, although it was little more than a whisper. "Just . . . hurry."

It was hard for Michael to ignore the urgency in Nev's voice. Even harder to ignore the lack of adventure and creatures around. The air felt heavier, and the rainbow had disappeared. Everything seemed empty—both around him, and inside him.

"All right. Let's go."

Vanessa took Will's sword, and they started after Merran. They all looked determined, and Michael couldn't have asked for better companions.

He just hoped he wouldn't lead them all into failure.

＊　＊　＊

CHAPTER 32

They moved slowly, constantly alert for traps. More than once, their path took them through underwater tunnels, so the nixie had to sprinkle her dust on Nev and the Lost Boys. The longer they traveled, the more Michael's arm hurt. He could see Vanessa checking on him out of the corner of her eye, but she said nothing.

She knows there's nothing to say.

They swam for nearly an hour. This time it wasn't just the unnerving quiet that got to Michael. The stone wall seemed somehow less substantial than it should have been. Once, he brushed against a rock, and his hand sank in, coming away with a substance that he told himself was mud but that he feared was the substance of the rock itself falling apart beneath his touch. Finally, they swam out of a narrow passage near the bottom of a wide cavern that was almost completely submerged. A myriad of caves dotted the wall they had come out of, though each was shrouded in darkness. Dozens of feet up, firelight glimmered above the surface, and he could just make out shadows moving around. Michael raised an eyebrow to Merran.

"Yes, he is there," she said.

"I'll get out of the water and take out the wraith," Vanessa said. "The rest of you, watch and make sure none of his other followers get in the way. If you get a chance to free Peter while he's distracted, do it. Michael, you come with me."

"What? Vanessa, I can't help you like this."

"Peter is expecting you, but he has no idea who I am. I'm not sure it's a good idea to go without you."

"He probably doesn't even remember he sent me a message. He forgets things like that almost instantly."

"Isn't this why you came in the first place?"

Michael paused. "I didn't think I'd have a broken sword arm and barely be able to walk."

"Stop feeling sorry for yourself, and be ready to help get Peter," she said. "If the ghost of Hook was telling the truth, the wraith caught them by surprise when it captured him, but Peter is still a god. I can't believe any wraith would be a match for him if he's ready for it. As soon as Peter is free, we win. I'm counting on you."

And that was what he was afraid of. He had dived into action so many times without that fear, but one false step had ruined his spirit. He thought he'd been gaining his confidence back while in Neverland, but that had been shattered like the bone in his arm. He had been holding it before him like a shield ever since, but Vanessa had just batted it away.

The truth was, he did feel sorry for himself. He hated the pain, not just in his arm, but in his heart. It was easy for Vanessa to be so cavalier—she had never lost anyone under her command. She—

No, that wasn't right. It *wasn't* easy for her. He had seen that time and again during this mission. She was carefree at some times, stoic at others, but even though she sought adventure, it didn't mean she wasn't scared. What it meant was that she was trained—and trained well—and that she never had the chance to rely on the same experience Michael had in Neverland. She had worked hard to get to this point—even harder due to her gender—and that was from where she was drawing strength.

All she was asking was for him to look for an opportunity to free Peter. She was going to take on a wraith—*his* wraith—until he could do it.

I . . . I can do it.

A look of determination was all Vanessa needed, and as the Lost Boys muttered their assent, she motioned for everyone to follow. Michael kicked as hard as he could, propelling himself to the surface. This was the first time he had actually tried to swim fast since he'd received the nixie dust, and he was surprised at how quickly he moved through the water. It was wonderful, and it buoyed his spirits. The Lost Boys cried out in exhilaration, and they must have felt the same way.

They hadn't even gotten halfway up, however, before the waters were alive with mermaids. They poured out of the passageways and surrounded the attacking party. In spite of their nixie-dust-powered swim, Michael and the Lost Boys were no match for creatures who had spent their entire lives in the water.

The next thing Michael knew, a net entangled him along with Will and Vanessa. The strands obviously had some magic to them because both Merran and Rosebud were captured as well. The Lost Boys and Nev were similarly held in another net. Even Shade had been caught. It took four nets to hold them all, and the mermaids hauled them to the surface with long ropes that held the nets closed.

Once they neared the surface, their captors threw their ropes at a great stone pillar that rose from the shore. Michael could barely see a person pick up the ends of the ropes and move around the pillar before tossing them back into the water. The mermaids took the ropes and swam down, dragging their prisoners up onto the shore. Michael resisted the urge to cry out as the treatment sent pains shooting up his arm. They broke the surface, and his heart fell.

The area was remarkably well appointed for a cave. Rugs, which Michael recognized as belonging to Tiger Lily's tribe, covered much of the floor. Elegantly carved chairs, no doubt looted from pirate hoards, surrounded a gilded table. There were other items, too, ones that had been shoved into dark shadows. Broken weapons and faded animal pelts littered the ground. A lump that might once have been a wooden carving but that now resembled a piece of melted wax was sitting in the middle of a pile of dust, and Michael wondered what it had been. Everywhere he saw signs of Neverland's decay.

Wooden shelves had been built into the walls, and on each one sat an iron cage. Some held only a single fairy prisoner, while nearly a dozen had been crammed into others. In one, he saw the green dress and dragonfly wings that could only belong to Tinker Bell.

Near the end of the cavern, entangled by heavy iron chains, lay the being who had in ancient times been the god of youth and one of the few ancient powers still active in Michael's world. He was known by the name of Maponos to many, but to Michael he would always be Peter Pan.

He looked young, no more than twelve. His green tunic and hat were neat in spite of his situation. His eyes, every bit as green as his clothes, focused on Michael, and a wide grin split his face in the cockiness that had always been characteristic of Peter. Michael half expected him to slip out of his chains, but whatever magic had been built into them held him fast. He had obviously been weakened by his ordeal and seemed almost insubstantial. That didn't stop him from laughing at the thing who stood next to him.

It looked almost exactly like Michael, the same height, the

same nose that seemed just a little too big. Unlike Michael, it wore a business suit, as if it had the position Michael had always craved. The one other difference was that all color had been drained from its body and clothing. It didn't quite look like a ghost, but it wasn't far from one, either. It looked at the trapped Lost Boys with contempt, and Michael was reminded of his own views of wayward children. Then, the wraith turned its attention to him.

Though he tried not to show any reaction, Michael couldn't stop the shiver that ran down his spine. It was like someone was walking on his grave. This was far more solid, far more real, than the wraith that had assaulted them in the catacombs of the Knights. It smiled.

"You actually came. I have to admit, I'm a little surprised. I expected you to be more cautious." Its eyes wandered down to the sling. "I certainly thought you'd have more prudence than that. And attacking from underwater, even with the help of a nixie—did you really expect that to work?"

"Why are you doing this?" Michael asked, ignoring the wraith's questions.

It looked down at Michael, and for just a second, its eyes were utterly black, and dark smoke rose out of each one. It blinked and they were back to normal—or as normal as a spirit's eyes could be. "Do you know what it means to be a wraith? Constant hunger, and a need to *be*, to *exist*." It brought its hand over Peter's face. The child god shivered as a tendril of black smoke streamed from his mouth only to be breathed in by the wraith. "The power I get from Peter is almost enough to make me solid. Almost, but not entirely."

It took several quiet steps across the cavern until it was standing right over Michael. It knelt down, and much as it had done before Peter, it moved its hand in front of Michael's face.

The universe felt like it had turned to ice. Nothing mattered aside from the utter cold that washed over him.

"I came from you, and you have what I need to be solid. To be real."

Michael was shaking. "Let Peter go."

The wraith shook its head. It had a fuller color than a moment before. "Now why would I do that?"

Michael tried to get up, but he was too weak. He could practically feel the strength flowing out of him and into his wraith. He was fading. The wraith sneered.

"There it is." It gave a smile that looked all too human. "You had the one thing I lacked."

Michael looked up at the creature. He tried to ask what it was, but he didn't even have the strength to speak. It was all he could do to breathe. The wraith wiggled its fingers in front of Michael, and he saw the faintest glitter of fairy dust.

"Happiness," the wraith answered the question in Michael's thoughts. "Creatures with a dim mind, like the crocodile, can cross into your world almost at a whim, but something like me? I'm different. I'm—special. And that means I require flight."

It touched Michael's face again, sending another wave of cold through him. Michael reached toward the nets holding the Lost Boys, but it was too far. They were struggling to get free, but the nets held. The wraith laughed.

"Don't expect any help from them. They're not even real." Its eyes landed on Will before moving to Vanessa. "They first came here as adults. They are closer to pirates than Lost Boys, and no pirate can affect the course of Neverland."

On hearing those words, Vanessa looked like she was going to be sick. The Lost Boys seemed to deflate, as if the life had drained out of them.

"You're wrong. They *are* real," Peter said as he struggled

against his chains, causing them to rattle against the stone ground. "They're as real as I am."

The wraith sneered. "As if that means anything."

Peter met his eyes. "They are as real as you. But unlike them, you can't even leave Neverland."

"I couldn't before." It placed a finger on Michael's forehead. Michael tried to cry out, but his voice was gone. "But now I have him. I didn't thank you for that, did I? For sending your shadow to bring him here."

For the first time, Michael saw Peter struck silent. The whole cavern was fading into darkness. The only light came from the Lost Boys' nets. The glow of one of the fairies shone brightly, visible even in Michael's fading sight.

What is that . . . ?

"Once I take it all from him, I will *be* him. Everything that was his will be mine."

Michael couldn't see shapes anymore. The wraith appeared as little more than a blob of darkness. A band of dark energy connected them, and as the wraith breathed in, the life drained out of Michael through that band.

"Everything," the wraith was saying. "His life. His family. All mine."

John, the real John. Would he even notice if this thing replaced Michael? The Lost Boys—the grown-up ones—would hardly do any better. They had left their childhoods behind even more than Michael himself had. They wouldn't be able to imagine anything like this. Wendy and Jane might notice that something was wrong, but no one else would. He would be truly lost, forgotten by all.

This was the end.

Abruptly, the light coming from the other net shone like the sun, bright enough that he could actually see it. The wraith cried out and drew back. Then, she was there. A brilliant woman made of shining energy with glowing wings floated in front of him. She wielded a sword made of fire. She rushed the wraith and impaled him, and the creature cried out in sheer agony. Power reversed itself, flowing into Michael instead of away from him. The dark energy snapped, and Michael realized much of his strength had been restored. He blinked, and his vision returned.

The wraith looked faint, though it was still solid. It took several deep breaths before looking around to figure out what had happened. It didn't take long to notice the small fairy between itself and Michael.

Rosebud stood there, her inch-long ghostly blade bare. She hadn't grown. Neither had the wraith shrunk. Yet somehow, she had been able to wound it. The wraith glared at her. Michael was stunned into silence. All fairies had magic. In a way, they *were* magic, but alone they could do relatively little. It was too difficult for them to use their power outside of themselves. No fairy, particularly not a dead one, should have been able to hurt a creature as powerful as a wraith. He couldn't even imagine how she had reversed the flow of energy.

Rosebud looked over her shoulder and laughed. It was so strange coming from her that it took Michael a second to recognize it. He realized he hadn't ever heard her laugh, but now that she did, he knew it. He couldn't tell where he had heard it, but he knew he had. It tickled a memory so old that by every rational standard, he should have forgotten long ago. Then it hit him.

"You're *my* fairy."

It wasn't a question, but Rosebud nodded anyway. Fairies weren't born like normal creatures. When a child laughed for the first time, that laugh became a fairy. He hadn't realized that they maintained a link to the person that birthed them, but he could feel it so clearly now. Rosebud had been born when Michael himself had first laughed, decades before, and she was still a part of him. His power was hers, and since the wraith had come from him, its power was hers, too. Slowly, the realization dawned on the creature.

"Well, that was unexpected." It held its hands before its eyes and blinked several times. "I hadn't ever seen the ghost of a fairy do anything, but this . . ." It shook its head. "It doesn't matter. I've taken enough." Slowly, it rose into the air. The wraith picked up Peter's chain in one hand and a rope that Michael hadn't noticed in the other. It wound through all the fairy cages, and as the wraith rose higher, it dragged them all into the air as well. It looked up. There was a hole in the ceiling, and Michael saw a faint light that could've only been the sun. The wraith didn't even pause to look at them; it just floated into the hole.

"No!" Michael cried out, but it was no use. His double, the wraith made from his own memories, was gone. No doubt it had taken the fairies to make sure they couldn't follow it back to London, where it intended to replace him.

Shade came out of nowhere, flying up the hole, and didn't respond when Michael called after him. Slightly had been in the same net as Rosebud and Shade, and apparently whatever they had done to break free had weakened the bindings because the Lost Boy was able to break out after a few minutes of trying. Michael barely noticed. He just kept looking upward in utter shock. Slightly freed the rest of them, not that it did any good. The wraith was gone, as was Peter and every fairy that could help them get to the real world.

Neverland was doomed.

CHAPTER 33

* * *

Michael wasn't sure how long he stood there. Dimly, he was aware that the Lost Boys had joined him, though no one said anything. Finally, a small voice coming from the water broke the silence.

"Peter?"

The sound jolted Michael out of his shock. He scanned the surface of the water. The light from the wraith's fire didn't allow him to see much, but he could just make out the vague outline of a woman's torso rising up from the water. He took a step in that direction. Will grabbed his arm, but Michael looked him in the eye and shook his head. Will's hand fell away, and Michael approached the water. He knelt by the shore, and the mermaid swam closer, her face seeming to lack the hostility the others had shown him. She scanned the area before looking to Michael.

"What happened to Peter?"

"He took him away." Michael looked up to the hole again. "To our world."

The mermaid shook her head, and Michael could make out others swimming just below the surface. "No, he can't! He was supposed to keep Peter here forever."

That made Michael stand up straight. "What?"

"He promised," she said, apparently seeing nothing wrong with what she was admitting. "We would shelter him, and teach him the magic to command the creatures of the water. In return, he would keep Peter down here with us, forever." Suddenly, her face twisted in anger, and her words echoed through the cavern. "This is your fault. If you hadn't come here, we wouldn't have failed, and Peter would still be here."

She grabbed his arm and tried to pull him under, but either her grip was weak or some lingering effect of the nixie dust made him able to resist, because her hand slipped off, unable to get a grip. She screamed and dove beneath the surface, though the water still churned with activity. Nev, apparently having worked her way free of the net, landed on his shoulder.

"I knew they were infatuated with him, but I didn't suspect they would go so far."

"There's nothing we can do about that." Michael sighed and looked back at the hole. A sense of hopelessness washed over him. "Is there anything we can do about anything?"

"We should at least get back to the surface. Your wraith may have left traps, and there are too many creatures in these caves that do not like you."

Michael stood a while longer until he felt Nev shuffle on his shoulder, and then started gathering the others. John and the Lost Boys seemed to be in a state of shock, which he could empathize with. Slightly, who had gotten the others out of their nets, just sat on the ground, staring blankly forward. In the end, Michael had to lead them by the arm. He grabbed John's with his good hand. Will took Nibs and Slightly, and Vanessa led Curly and Tootles. The twins, seeing their companions walking, followed in listless silence. Rosebud rested on Michael's other shoulder. Merran hovered in front of them, seeming confused.

Nev was the only one who could lead them back up, so they followed her.

"What's wrong with them?" Vanessa asked as they wandered through the passages.

"They're part of Neverland," Michael said. "The one who created the realm is hurt, and possibly dying. Worse than that, he was taken. It wouldn't surprise me if all of Neverland was suffering."

"I fear that you're right," Nev said. "I can feel it myself: a desire to just give up. More than that, though, listen."

Michael stopped moving forward and motioned for Will and Vanessa to do the same. The twins kept walking, not stopping until Will grabbed them by the shoulder. The two boys blinked and looked back sheepishly, but neither said anything. A warm wind carried fresh air, which was a nice break from the constant smell of salt water. Their small group stood there in silence for nearly a minute before Michael heard what Nev was talking about. There was a faint rumbling in the air. Will realized what it was a split second before Michael did.

"Is that thunder?" He smiled. "That's a relief. We must be almost to the surface to be able to hear that."

"You don't understand," Nev said as she hopped from rock to rock. She turned to Michael. "In all the time you were in Neverland, did it ever rain, even so much as a drop?"

Michael thought about that for a second before shaking his head. His heart fell as Nev explained.

"That's because there hasn't been a storm here, not ever. Since this realm was created, it has never rained here. It's been maintained by Peter's power. The land must be suffering terribly for this to happen."

"Suffering," Michael said. "Because of me."

"Because of your wraith," Vanessa said.

"But it came from me."

Thunder crashed so loud he felt it in his bones, drowning out whatever Vanessa had said, but it didn't matter. The Lost Boys looked pale, and some of the color had drained from the cave walls. They were fading. Neverland was dying, and it was all his fault.

* * *

CHAPTER 34

As they walked, the smell of fresh air and rain grew steadily stronger. It wasn't long before they reached the entrance and looked upon the dying land. The storm clouds were so thick overhead that it almost seemed to be night. Thunder shook the very air, and only the occasional flash of lightning allowed them to see. It looked like the area had been hit by a hurricane. Trees had been uprooted and tossed around like they were toys. The winds had torn large rocks out of the ground and hurled them at whatever plant life was still standing. Michael cried out as he tried to dodge a boulder hurtling toward him, but it faded an instant before it hit. He and the others stared at the spot where it had been, then retreated several yards into the cave. He wondered when the rest of the island would fade, too.

"We can't go out into that," he said.

Vanessa stared into the storm. "I'm pretty sure we have to."

"Then what?" Michael asked. "What do we do once we go out into this storm? Didn't you see the stone? Neverland is fading, and there's nothing we can do."

"We'll think of something."

Michael wanted to argue, but just then a tree as wide as he was tall fell in front of the cave mouth, crashing so hard that rock dust fell from the ceiling. They all scrambled back. He knew he should say something but he just couldn't find the words, and the only sound was the storm rustling the leaves of the tree blocking the entrance. The rain seemed to have an almost hypnotic quality to it, and he found himself lulled into a sort of listlessness.

Michael wasn't sure if it had been minutes or hours before the rain softened. It didn't stop entirely, but it became nothing more than a light shower. Vanessa was the first one to get up, then Will. They helped the others up, Michael included, and led them out.

The land had been torn to shreds. Gashes had been ripped in the ground. Massive holes where trees had once stood dotted the landscape. Most of those holes were filled with muddy water. He could just make out the Never Bay, littered with fallen trees. Even the rain seemed more like tears than natural weather. Neverland was in ruins. Nev took to the air to see how much damage had been done while the rest walked through the woods, but Michael already knew the answer.

"Michael," Will said, "what do we do?"

Michael didn't know the answer to that. The sky rumbled again, and he found himself wondering if Neverland would be destroyed by weather or if it would just fade away. *If we'll be destroyed, or just fade away.*

"Smee!" Vanessa said.

Michael blinked. "What?"

"Smee, if he's alive anyway. He guided me here. He can take us back to London. We just need a boat." She waved at the lagoon. "And I know where we can find one."

"The *Jolly Roger*?" Michael asked. "That's been underwater for decades. It had holes in it, and the wood looked like it was rotting."

"We'll fix it. Otherwise, it seemed pretty intact to me." She nodded at the Lost Boys. "And this land does seem to preserve things."

"That's people," Michael said. "Not ships."

"They are closer to ideas than people," Nev said as she landed on his shoulder. "In that way, they are the same as the ship."

"You think it'll work then?"

"The ship, possibly. As for Smee . . ." The Never Bird let out a sound that might have been a sigh. "I got high enough to see the tribal lands. The storm utterly destroyed Tiger Lily's village. Smee did not survive."

"Smee is dead?" Tootles said once Michael had translated.

The rest of the Lost Boys also seemed to be awakened by the news. A cloud of sadness hovered over them. Smee had been an enemy, but he had been a kindly one. He hadn't been hated, not exactly, not as much as the other pirates had been, and now that he was gone, they mourned.

Because they didn't know just how dastardly the man had become.

Vanessa, missing the significance of Smee's passing, muttered under her breath. She turned to Michael. "Maybe we don't need him. Neverland won't let anyone come who doesn't know the way. But what about leaving?"

"What do you mean?"

"I mean is there anything to stop us from raising the ship ourselves and leaving? The island won't keep us against our will, will it?"

Michael shrugged. "I have no idea. Peter was at the helm last time, and that changes things. I'm not sure it would be safe."

"Do you have a better idea?" she said with a tight grin.

Michael smiled at having his own words thrown back in his face. "We might as well. We need to get back to London if we can."

"The mermaids," Will said. "They can help us."

Michael shook his head. "The mermaids hate us. They blame us for my wraith taking Peter."

"And he won't come back unless someone goes after him," Vanessa said.

"Right," Will said. "And what I'm saying is they have to know that, and they certainly can't do it themselves. They *need* us."

Michael stared out over the lagoon. He let out a long sigh. "I guess it's worth a try."

* * *

CHAPTER 35

Rain continued to drizzle down on them. The wind was still strong, but it no longer hurled boulders. The ground where the trees had been torn out seemed softer. That might have been the rain, or it just might have been the land struggling to recover from the shock of losing its god. The group went out to the shore of the bay. Droplets created odd shapes on the surface of the water, and if Michael focused on them, he could almost see a pattern. It was probably his imagination. But then again, this was Neverland, so maybe not.

He thought about the Lost Boys standing with him now. When he had been here the first time, they had often played in the bay, but Peter had been here then. Without him, the bay was a frightening place, and even in the best of times, the mermaids had never been friendly. Will was right, though—they were out of options.

Merran assured him that her dust still held its potency, so—with no worries he might drown if they tried to pull him under—he stepped out into the water.

"Hello? Are you there?"

The sound of the rain splashing into the lagoon swallowed his voice, and for a moment it seemed like no one would answer. Then, the pattern created by the drops, which had spanned several yards, shrank until it was the size of a human head. Deep blue eyes appeared, and a moment later, a mermaid rose halfway out of the water. Her hair was pitch-black with what almost looked like a faint green tint. Her face was the tan of someone who had spent hours in the sun, and her eyes were so filled with anger that Michael half expected the lagoon to start boiling around her. She drifted through the water, whatever ripples she made hidden by the rain.

"You," she hissed. "How *dare* you return to this lagoon after what you have done? I should drag you into the depths and leave you there until the nixie dust wears off."

Michael took a sharp breath; Merran hadn't mentioned how *long* her dust would be potent.

"Oh yes. We know about that."

Rosebud darted between Michael and the mermaid. For a second, the mermaid backed up, but tied as she was to her creator, the fairy's power apparently worked only on Michael and the wraith that had come from him. The mermaid sneered, and the water around Michael churned. He was only waist high in the lagoon, and he told himself that it would be extremely difficult for mermaids to get around him without him noticing. A shadow passed on his right side, and he shivered.

Difficult, but not impossible.

"Your anger is misdirected. This is *your* fault," he said, trying to sound sure of himself. "That other mermaid already told us. *You* taught the wraith how to control the elemental and the nixies, didn't you? *You* let Peter get captured."

The mermaid practically spluttered. "We just helped him bring Peter to the water. Peter always enjoyed that."

"But it's one thing to bring him to the water. It's another to keep him there so he could be with you forever," Vanessa said from behind with more than a little contempt in her voice. She had come into the water, too, and was a few feet behind him.

The mermaid hissed, and the water around them churned more. "He *wanted* to be with us. No matter how many times he went to your world, human, he always returned to us. But we were sad when he left, so, yes, we wanted to keep him here. Where he is *happy*."

"But now he's gone, and he won't return this time." Michael spoke quietly. "The wraith took him prisoner. And he'll keep feeding off Peter until there's nothing left. Is that what you want?"

"No!"

The voice came from behind him, but when Michael looked, he saw only the rippling water. Vanessa, who had drawn quickly, lowered her sword but stayed alert. Michael turned back to the mermaid he'd been speaking to.

"We don't want him stuck in my world any more than you do. You're right—he belongs here. We can bring him back, but not without help."

The mermaid rose higher out of the water so that her fish tail just began to show. "What help would you ask of us?"

"The *Jolly Roger*," Michael said. "The ship that's on the floor of the bay. We need you to bring it to the surface."

The water around Michael bubbled in agitation. "The pirate ship! That is no tool for an ally of Peter."

"Peter used it, after he captured it from the pirates. You know that."

"Leave them alone, Michael," Vanessa said. "They're just spoiled little girls. They know what they did, and they know that if Peter ever came back, he would never forgive them. He probably hates them. They don't really want him to return."

She sounded bored. He looked at her sharply, and her face remained impassive, even as he heard the mermaid suck her teeth in anger and dive beneath the water.

Then, Vanessa winked.

He had to work hard to keep from laughing.

There was a splash behind Michael. He turned to see a yellow-haired mermaid practically leap from the water, her green fish tail glimmering in the sun. Her face was red with anger. "That is not true! We all want Peter back! He'll come back as soon he can."

The black-haired mermaid rose up next to the blond. "Get back beneath the surface, Aria."

Aria turned to the leader and glared. "We won't let that wraith keep him away, no matter what you say, Gianna. Tell them!"

"Tell them what? We don't need him. Peter will escape, and he'll come back without *their* help."

"No he won't," Vanessa said. "Not unless someone goes after him. You can do it if you want, but unless that wraith is hiding him in the English Channel, there won't be a lot you can do about it."

"We can't cross over," Gianna said as Aria passed beneath the waves. "We are too much a part of this world. Peter created us, just like your bird."

"Then you know how much you need our help," Michael said as Nev landed on his shoulder. "I promise you, if it's in our power, we will free Peter and send him back."

"Or die trying?" Gianna asked.

He paused. Because that was always the question, wasn't it? Yet, now, he was pretty sure he had the answer.

"If we can't free him, it will be because my life has ended. If there's an opportunity for me to give my life for Peter's, I will." Michael held out his pinky finger.

"Michael, no!" Vanessa shouted, but he cut her off with a curt shake of his head.

The mermaid looked at him suspiciously. But, slowly, she came close to Michael, reached out her own pinky, and wrapped her finger around his.

"Done."

And she dove beneath the lagoon.

"What did you do?" Will asked.

"I made a promise."

"A promise *here*," Vanessa said. "I know what that means—"

"What does it mean?" Will demanded.

"He pinky-swore," Slightly said, in awe.

"Pinky-swore," Tootles echoed.

"Pinky-swore," said Nibs and Curly and the twins.

"So what?" Will said, confused.

"It means it can't be broken," Vanessa said quietly.

"I don't—"

"Remember when you made a promise as a child, Will?" Michael asked. "It was a matter of life or death, wasn't it?" He gestured around. "Well, this is the land for children. And a promise in Neverland means something."

As if to punctuate his point, in the distance, a large shadow approached the shore. Six mermaid heads poked up out of the water, each pulling a rope over her shoulder. A few seconds later, a broken mast rose up over the surface. Michael watched as the *Jolly Roger,* flipped so it was right-side up, emerged from the lagoon. The leader swam before them, shouting in the musical language of the mermaids.

Gianna came before them once more. "Take your ship and go.

"And remember your promise."

CHAPTER 36

* * *

The *Jolly Roger* was in terrible shape. The hole Michael and Vanessa had entered through was six feet long and almost as wide. Years underwater had rotted the wood at the edges of the hole. The mast was little more than a stump, and several planks on the deck looked to have been pried off. Barnacles covered much of the surface, both inside and out. The rudder had rotted or been broken off, and the wheel practically fell apart under Michael's touch.

"Well, we certainly have our work cut out for us," Vanessa said.

"This was your idea," Michael said.

"I'm very much aware."

"Don't worry about that," John said. "We'll get it fixed in no time."

Will raised an eyebrow at that. "Do you know anything about fixing ships?"

John shrugged. "It's made of wood. Wood floats."

Before Will could respond, the twins, along with Tootles and Curly, came out of the nearby woods, carrying a thick tree trunk that had been trimmed of all branches. "We found a mast!"

"Where on earth did you get that?" Will asked.

One of the twins looked over his shoulder at the forest, and then back at Will. He raised both eyebrows as if to say that Will had just asked the dumbest question in the world.

Michael watched them in awe as they went at it. It shouldn't have worked. The boys were neither carpenters nor shipwrights, and raising a mast wasn't exactly an easy task. In short order, however, they cut the trunk to the proper length with their swords, which should have dulled but didn't, and attached the mast, which stayed up in spite of not being properly grounded. It wasn't long before ropes had been strung and a sail, made from who knew what, had been raised.

Will's eyes were wide, and he sputtered for several seconds before he could find his words. "Where did they get all that?"

Michael shrugged. "I haven't the slightest idea. I think the ropes might be vines, though."

"You can't use vines for ropes. That only works in stories."

"How many times do we have to tell you, Will?" Vanessa asked.

"Until it starts making sense."

She chuckled as she walked away to check on the Lost Boys' progress. Once the mast was done, they started repairing the hull with planks cut from other trees. Will stepped forward and threw his hands up in frustration.

"That won't work either! Wood needs to season before it can be used on a ship. You can't just—"

"Actually, I think they can," Vanessa said.

"I was fine with that before," Will said, "but then, you weren't asking me to sail on a story."

"Wait until they're finished," Michael said. "They may surprise you."

The three of them watched in silence as, gradually, planks were nailed over the hole in the ship. The boys sang as they worked, tossing tools to one another. The melody triggered half-remembered adventures Michael had had when he'd been no older than they.

By all rights, their patches should have been a poor fit. The boys never measured anything, but by some miracle, each plank fit perfectly. They hadn't finished by the time the sun dipped beneath the western horizon, so one of the Lost Boys, Michael didn't see which, built fires along the shore. In the distance, Michael thought he saw mermaids poking their heads out of the water, but in the fading light, it was impossible to be sure. In the end, Michael lay down on the sand. As tired as he was, he could imagine it to be a bed. He fell asleep to the sound of hammers banging against nails and the gentle patter of raindrops falling onto the water.

He woke to the sun shining on his face. He opened his eyes and gasped. The storm clouds were gone, but that wasn't what shocked him. The full sails of the *Jolly Roger* caught the wind as it blew through Neverland. The ship was perfect. The hull was completely smooth, showing no sign that less than a day ago it had been underwater. The sail was a white so pure that it almost looked like new-fallen snow. All the barnacles had been scraped off, and the name of the ship had been painted on in gold letters. The *Jolly Roger* looked so new that it could've come out of a shipyard that very day. The Lost Boys were all in the crow's nest, which was far bigger than it needed to be. One by one, they climbed to the top of the mast and crowed, a thing Peter had always enjoyed doing. Michael got up and brushed the sand off his clothes.

His arm felt better, and he could move it without pain. An injury like that should've taken months to heal, but in this land of children and adventure, it made sense that such a thing would heal quickly. He had always suspected that would be the case, but he'd had no way to test it. After flexing his arm for a few seconds, he headed toward the ship. As he neared, he noticed Will and Vanessa walking the deck. Vanessa saw him approaching and waved him to the other side, where Michael found a rope ladder. He climbed.

"It's amazing," Will said. "The ship is completely sound. There are even cabins for each of us. The beds are only hammocks hung from the ceiling, but it's still one of the most impressive things I've ever seen."

"Did they sleep at all?" Michael asked, his eyes wandering up the crow's nest.

"I don't think so," Vanessa said. "I fell asleep a few hours after you and Will bedded down, and they were still going strong. They were just finishing up when I woke, but it doesn't look like they really needed it."

"Are we ready to go?"

Just then, lightning split the sky, rattling the planks beneath them. For a moment, Michael feared the whole ship would fall apart under their feet, but the Lost Boys' work held. The sea churned, rocking the ship. Vanessa gripped the ropes and came close enough for him to hear.

"Is this Neverland's doing?"

"I think so, yes," Nev said, coming to land on the railing. "Because it doesn't want us to leave, or because it's on the verge of being destroyed. I have no idea which."

Michael translated.

"Do we wait it out?" Will shouted.

Michael glanced at the Lost Boys. Even though they had been hearty when putting the ship back together, they seemed somehow less than they had been when they'd been freed from Hook's castle. Michael half expected the storm to blow them away, but they all held on tight. He closed his eyes against the rain and shook his head. "We don't dare! We have to go, and we have to go now!"

He would have sworn John had been too far to hear, but the boy swung down from the rigging and landed by the wheel. He spun it, turning the ship into the direction of the storm, sailing right into its teeth.

"I must remain," Nev said. "I lack the ability to cross between worlds."

"I'll miss you," Michael said.

"And I you, Michael. Save him," the bird said as she headed toward the shore, "or there won't be anything to miss—not even a memory of me."

And Nev flew off.

CHAPTER 37

* * *

The storm tossed the ship like it was a toy. Michael was almost thrown off the deck, but Will grabbed him while holding on to one of the ropes. The rain fell so thickly he couldn't see more than a few inches in front of him.

Keeping a grip on the rope, he made his way to the wheel only to find it spinning uncontrollably. He looked around, but John was nowhere to be seen. He threw himself at the wheel. He'd thought his arm was fully healed, but grabbing the wood-spoked wheel told him he'd been mistaken. Pain shot through him as he struggled to bring the ship under control. A wave washed over the deck, and before Michael knew it, he had been slammed against the rail.

Suddenly, Rosebud fluttered before him, the wind and rain passing through her incorporeal body without so much as moving her clothes. She spoke, her voice coming through as if it were a clear day.

"I'm fine!" Michael shouted. "Where is John?"

She said something about him being caught in the rigging. The other Lost Boys were still fine, too, but that wouldn't last for long. Unless he did something, the *Jolly Roger* would sink again, and it would take all of them with it. He tried to get up, but another wave washed him off his feet. Suddenly, he was dangling in the air. Vanessa held his good arm and struggled to pull him back onto the ship. The twins leaped from above and landed right behind her. He started to rise. Together, they pulled him onto the deck just as another wave came close to washing them all overboard.

"This is hopeless without a real crew," Vanessa cried out. "We have to go back!"

"Will, you're a sailor, aren't you?"

"On a steam ship! Michael, the storm is too bad," Will said. "We'll be smashed on the rocks."

They were going to die. Him, Will, Vanessa: their lives would end here. He wondered what would happen to their bodies when Neverland disappeared. What would happen to the people back in London? The wraith would take his place, and no one, except maybe Wendy, would know the difference.

And Jane.

Jane would know the difference. She had been to Neverland. Even more than he or Wendy, she knew what kinds of things were possible. The wraith would never fool Jane, and once she saw through its disguise, what would it do to prevent being exposed?

No. He couldn't allow it.

A wave as big as a mountain carried the ship into the sky. The wave peeled away, and for a second they seemed to hover in the air. The *Jolly Roger* pitched forward. Like a knife, it stabbed into the water, going almost completely under. If not for their recent exposure to the nixie dust, they would have probably drowned or been carried away by the current, but they were able to hold on. The ship still had air in the lower decks, and that made it shoot toward the surface. They emerged from the water with a deafening *pop*.

Vanessa was right. They needed a real crew, one that knew both the ship and the waters around Neverland. There was only one thing to do, only one person who could help them . . . though "person" was perhaps the wrong word.

Of course, Michael doubted even he would be able to hear them—the storm was too loud; it would swallow his words. But Michael had been able to hear Rosebud. If one ghost could speak to him, perhaps another could hear him.

"Hook!"

Instantly, the pirate captain was at the wheel. He turned it, but the current carried them sideways. The ship tilted, on the edge of falling over.

Hook glared at Michael. "I can't help you."

"If we die, Neverland dies. You know what that means. It'll end you, too."

"It's not that I don't *want* to help you, boy. But I can't do this alone, and you lot are worthless. I need my crew."

"Well, where are they?"

He turned the ship into a wave, and they sliced through it. "Ghosts are different. We are more of this world than yours. We cannot board unless you give us permission. You need to call for us."

"Michael, no," Vanessa said. "Think of who they are."

He knew exactly who they were. And he knew he couldn't trust them. But the image of his niece flashed into his mind. The pain in his arm suddenly seemed less, and the sense of hopelessness that had been weighing him down vanished. He had to get back, no matter what that meant.

"Come aboard!"

And they were there. Dozens of ghosts manned the rigging. Some rowed spectral oars, which shouldn't have had any effect, but their course steadied. The ghost of Smee walked up and down the deck, calling out orders. Michael gaped at him, but the stout man didn't notice. Michael got to his feet and was surprised to find that even the wind died down a little.

"How are you doing this?"

"I traded much to learn how to cross between worlds," Hook said. "I will not surrender that secret easily."

"Traded?" Michael asked. "To who?"

Hook spun the wheel but didn't look at him. "Who do you think?"

Michael hesitated only for a moment. "Mora?"

The pirate bowed his head. "Of course."

"What did you trade?"

Hook snorted as he examined a compass that hadn't existed a second ago before shouting an order and spinning the wheel. The ship turned, and they headed away from the shores of Neverland and back toward London and the real world.

A magically repaired ship, full of ghosts and the remnants of the Lost Boys, leaving a make-believe land to fight a wraith.

"All in a day's work for the Knights," Vanessa said.

God, I hope so.

* * *

CHAPTER 38

As soon as the shore of Neverland vanished, the storm died, and a thick bank of fog rolled in. At first, Michael thought it was natural, but it remained long after a normal fog would've been burned away by the sun. It was so thick that water droplets formed on his face, and he couldn't even see the ocean.

The ghosts crewed the ship in silence, and even the attitude of the Lost Boys was subdued. Often, the only sound he heard was the ship cutting through the water. To Michael's surprise, Merran stayed on the ship the entire time. When he suggested she might want to go into the water, she shivered and shook her head, though she didn't explain further. With the fog obscuring the sun, it was impossible to tell how much time passed. It was days at least, though that was to be expected.

As the days drifted by, the close quarters started to get to everyone. The Lost Boys began acting with a great deal of bluster around the crew. The ghosts, for their part, sneered at the children. The hostility in the air seemed almost as thick as the fog. More than once, weapons were drawn. To Michael's surprise, it was Hook who most often stopped a fight. With one glare, he could turn the ghosts' anger to fear, and they would go scampering away. The spirits obviously resented him, but they were just as obviously afraid, and many times, Michael caught them grumbling after the dead pirate captain had passed out of earshot. Smee did his best to calm them down, but he didn't seem to be succeeding very well.

One day, as Michael stood near the forward rail, searching the fog for any sign of land, Will came up next to him, speaking in a voice barely above a whisper.

"I think they're going to mutiny." He looked over his shoulder as he spoke. No one seemed to be close enough to overhear, but with ghosts that didn't necessarily mean anything.

"I don't think so," Michael said. "They're terrified of him."

"When he's around. Mutinies usually form when the captain is away."

Michael shook his head. "He was like this when he was alive, too. He led them for nearly two centuries. If they didn't rebel against him then, I doubt they'll do so now."

"Then what has you so worried?"

Michael blinked at him. "What do you mean?"

Will narrowed his eyes. "You didn't sleep again last night, did you?"

Michael looked out into the fog. The ship had remained in the same uniform gray since they'd departed. "There's not really a night right now, is there?"

"You know what I mean. You're evading the question."

Michael pursed his lips and looked at Hook, who was cheerfully manning the wheel. As if sensing his attention, the pirate met his gaze. The cold gray eyes sent a shiver down Michael's spine, and he turned away. He moved closer to Will and spoke in a quiet voice. "I know we couldn't get back to London without them, but the fact is they couldn't get there without us, either. I just worry about what we're about to unleash on the world."

"So we keep our eyes open," Will said.

"It's why I'm not sleeping."

AFTER WHAT HAD TO HAVE BEEN AT LEAST A WEEK AT SEA, Tootles called that he had spotted a light in the fog. Michael stood next to the boy and stared out into the gray murk, but it seemed even darker than usual. He squinted. There *might* have been figures there. He thought he saw movement, but it might have easily been wind stirring the fog.

"The water's calmer," Will said. "I don't think we're at sea anymore." He let out a breath. "With all this fog, we could be in the middle of the Thames, and we wouldn't know it."

Michael nodded, but didn't say anything. He just stared out, hoping to find some sign of land. There was a flicker of light, and his breath caught in his throat.

"It's thinning," one of the twins said. "There, that's definitely something."

Michael stared in the direction the child was indicating. He jumped as a horn sounded through the fog. His eyes went wide as he realized what it meant. Everyone was looking over the side now, and suddenly, it was there, coming out of the fog like some great lumbering giant. A ship, twice as long as the *Jolly Roger* and made of steel, glided past. The ghosts made gestures to ward off evil, a thing Michael found ironic to the point of being laughable.

"What sorcery makes metal float?" one of them asked.

It took Michael a second to understand. These men had been preserved by Neverland's magic. When they had left the world, ships had been made of wood, like the *Jolly Roger*. They had probably never even imagined one made of metal. He didn't think he had the time or words to explain.

Also, they were pirate ghosts, and he didn't mind them being a little afraid at the moment.

Through the mist, Michael could barely make out the bridge they passed under, and his heart raced.

"There," John called out. "The tower!"

As if dispelled by his words, the fog parted, revealing the imposing figure of the Tower of London, turned red by the last rays of the setting sun. Relief washed over Michael. Vanessa grinned, and Will laughed. Michael glanced at him and was surprised to see tears streaming down his face.

"I've been living in a dream for the past seven years. I never thought I'd see an English shore again."

"You're home, Will. We'll have you to your wife and daughter within the hour."

Will kept his eyes locked on the shore. "What will I say to them, I wonder?"

Michael slapped him on the back. "You can tell them that you're glad to be home."

"Alas," Hook said as he drew his curved sword, "I regret that I cannot allow that. You see, now that we're fully crossed over, we no longer need you, and you've been too much of a nuisance to just allow you to run free."

Three other pirates rushed toward them, drawing their weapons as they glided through the air. One placed his sword against Michael's throat, and he could practically feel his blood freezing. Will had the point of a blade pressed against the bottom of his jaw. Only his eyes moved, and he glanced at Michael.

Michael let out a long breath, though he tried his best not to move. "You didn't really expect this to surprise us, did you?"

"What—"

Slightly fell out of the sky and drove his blade into the back of the pirate that had captured Michael. The ghost's jaw dropped. He turned around, his ethereal body passing through the sword as if it weren't there, but as his back came into view, Michael saw the pale blue motes of light leaking from the wound. Slightly's blade was still enhanced by wisp dust, and it was empowered to hurt the dead. These were the same blades the gremlins had given them to fight Hook before. The pirate seemed to fade. Then, his form solidified. He cried out, and his body exploded into a shower of blue lights.

"Now that's a surprise," Will said.

"Not now, Will," Michael said, throwing off his captor as the other Lost Boys cried out from above as they swung from the rigging. The ghosts exchanged glances before flying in different directions. One passed right through Michael, and his hand went to his chest as his breath was stolen from him. The sensation faded after a second, and he saw two of the ghosts fleeing into London. Other spirits scattered. Some were taken by the Lost Boys' blades, but most made it off the ship. Finally, only Hook was left, surrounded by the Lost Boys, with Rosebud and Merran floating above him. The pirate didn't seem the least bit disturbed. In fact, he laughed.

"I'm impressed, boy. You planned to betray me from the very beginning, didn't you? That was almost pirate of you."

"You can't betray a betrayal, Hook. I just took some precautions." Michael lifted his sword. "The time for James Hook to live in this world was two hundred years ago. I won't unleash your evil on the world today."

Hook's eyes wandered from one Lost Boy to another and then to Will and Vanessa before finally settling on Michael. The half smile never left his lips. He spoke in a loud booming voice that chilled Michael to the bone.

"Pan couldn't stop me, boy, not even at the height of his power. Do you really think *you* can stand against me?"

Michael realized he had taken a step back and steadied himself. It was an effort to speak without his voice cracking. "You're the one who's surrounded."

Hook smirked. "So it would seem."

Then, he sank through the floor. Before any of the Lost Boys could react, Hook shot out of the deck, his sword swinging in a wide arc. The Lost Boys tried to get out of the way, but they weren't fast enough. The spectral blade passed through John, Tootles, and one of the twins. The boys' faces took on an expression of pure shock as color drained out of them. They cried out, and then, they were just gone. For a moment, Michael was struck silent. Tears welled in his eyes.

"John! No!"

His eyes scanned the sky for Hook, but the pirate was already gone. Grief welled up inside of him. He tried to force it down. He told himself that hadn't really been his brother— John was grown and had a family now. He had an ordinary life. He had forgotten Neverland so completely that he didn't even know a single story to tell his own children. This boy had not been John. The others had not been his adopted brothers. Michael shook his head. They were what his brothers had been before they had forgotten what it meant to have an adventure, before they had lost what was most valuable.

But they were his companions nevertheless. They had helped him, and even saved him on numerous occasions. And he missed them terribly. He tried and failed to keep his voice steady. "We have to find him before he does any more damage."

Rosebud fluttered in front of his face and chattered rapidly. Michael bit his lower lip and nodded. "You're right. We have to find Peter. He might be able to find Hook, and he's the only one who'd be able to stop him. Even if he can't, powerful spirits have been loose in London before. The city can survive. Peter is the mission."

"Still," Vanessa said, "I should warn the Knights."

Michael nodded and armed himself with the sword of a fallen Lost Boy. "I'll go after the wraith."

"Where can we find him?" the other twin said, obviously having trouble keeping his composure.

Michael scanned the city. The wraith had come from him. It might try to find a sanctuary, but it would be one that Michael himself knew. His own home was a possibility, but that didn't feel right—it was just a place he lived; it had no special meaning to him. A wraith was made from things that were forgotten, and Michael had worked for years to forget Neverland and all that was associated with the legendary island. It had driven a wedge between him and his family, most of whom were an unavoidable reminder of his time there. He took in a sharp breath. Nowhere had that division been more pronounced than between him and his sister, the only one of his siblings who still remembered the imaginary land.

"Wendy," he said under his breath. "It's gone after Wendy."

CHAPTER 39

* * *

They approached the house quietly. The night was dark, far darker than a night should be. Above, the full moon shone, though its light was muted. It had been full when he had left, and Michael wondered how long he had been gone. Vanessa had gone to warn the Knights of the invasion of the ghosts. That left him and Will with only four Lost Boys and two fairies to help him stop a wraith.

He wasn't sure he liked those odds.

The light in Wendy's house was on even though it was nearing eleven o'clock. The street was empty, and the heat of summer filled the air. Will looked ready to charge in, but Michael put a hand on his shoulder and shook his head.

"Let's not act too hastily. Rosebud, why don't you fly up to the window and see if he's in there? Merran, look around. Make sure we're not surprised."

The fairies nodded and flew away. Will watched them go. He was breathing heavily, and he held his sword with a white-knuckled grip. He took a step forward again, but Michael stopped him.

"Calm down," Michael said. "It won't make any difference if we delay a few minutes, but if we just rush in, we could stumble into a trap."

"I know, but . . ." Will took a deep breath. "It's Wendy."

Michael pursed his lips. A part of him wanted to charge in next to Will, but just then, Rosebud and Merran came back and bobbed up and down in the air. The remaining Lost Boys raised their weapons and looked at Michael. They didn't remember Wendy, but they did know Jane, and they loved her every bit as much as the original Lost Boys had loved Wendy. They were prepared to do whatever it took.

"Can you climb up to the second-story window and wait there for my signal?" Michael asked. "It might help us if we can get a drop on it."

The Lost Boys nodded and scrambled up the side of a nearby building, making it look effortless. As they ran across the roofs toward Wendy's house, moving far more quietly than he would've believed possible, Michael couldn't help but wonder how much the laws of the physical world mattered to them, even here. He and Will walked toward the house with the fairies trailing behind them. They reached the door and stopped. Will's expression showed a mixture of excitement and fear. He glanced at Michael.

"What do we do now?"

"Rosebud, were they in the front room?"

The ghost fairy flew around his head once before she started chattering as she mimed bringing food to her mouth.

"They were at the dinner table?"

Rosebud bobbed up and down.

Michael frowned at Will. "It's a bit late to be eating, wouldn't you say?"

Will nodded and turned the doorknob slowly in a shaky hand. The door swung inward, apparently having been left unlocked. They crept into the house. At the end of the long hall, they could see a portion of the dining table. Jane was seated there, dressed in pajamas and wearing a worried expression.

Faint hints of conversation drifted down the hall. Michael and Will walked as quietly as they could. As they neared, Jane glanced in their direction. Her eyes went wide, but Michael put a finger to his mouth. Her lips parted slightly before she nodded. The conversation in the dining room had stopped.

"Jane, dear," Wendy's voice said. "What is it?"

"Nothing," Jane said a little too quickly. "It's nothing." She made an exaggerated yawn. "I'm just sleepy. May I please be excused?"

"Michael," Wendy dragged out the name, as if she didn't believe it was really him. "Why don't you let me take Jane to her room? She should have been in bed hours ago."

"But I love my niece," Michael's voice said. "I haven't seen her in so long."

Jane looked a little pale at the response. Will took a step forward, his sword shaking with his anger. Even his whisper was loud enough that Michael feared it would be overheard. "He's threatening my family."

"They're my family, too. Let's not do anything that will put them at greater risk." Will tensed but didn't move into the dining room, and Michael spoke to the shadows. "Rosebud, do you think you can distract him?"

She bobbed up and down.

"Good. Do that. Will, run in and get between him and the ladies. Peter isn't in there, is he?"

Rosebud flew from left to right to indicate no.

"Go."

The fairy ghost rushed into the dining room. Wendy screamed, but it was more out of surprise than fear. There was the sound of dishes crashing to the floor, and Will and Michael rushed in with swords bared.

All three were standing around the dining room table. Food had been spilled on the ground when they had stood, but no one was paying attention to that. The wraith looked even more solid than before, though his eyes were empty pits of pure blackness. Rosebud swirled around his head, darting in and punching him in the head with ineffectual blows. Wendy backed up and took Jane in her arms. For her part, the little girl actually seemed excited. Of course, she had been to Neverland, where this sort of thing was common. She didn't understand that in this place, she was no longer under the protection of a god.

Wendy looked at him, and relief washed over her features. "Michael." When she saw his companion, her voice came out as a squeak. "Will."

She blinked, and a single tear ran down her cheek, but she clenched her jaw with a resolve that Michael had seen only among the Knights as they prepared to go into battle. She had been to Neverland, too, and she understood. There would be time to sort all this out once the danger was dealt with.

The wraith reached out and plucked Rosebud out of the air. It threw the fairy against the wall so hard a crack formed, though how such a thing could happen from an insubstantial fairy, Michael had no idea.

It glared at Michael. "So you managed to get out of Neverland. I can't say I'm entirely surprised."

"I couldn't care less about your level of surprise. Where is Peter?"

It sneered. "What makes you think I would tell you?"

"He's in the guest room," Jane cried out.

"Jane, no! Don't tell him anything."

It was startling to hear the wraith say that, and with such conviction. The wraith seemed genuinely confused that Jane would say anything to Michael. It was as if the creature truly believed itself to be real.

"Jane, go upstairs," Michael said. "Some of the Lost Boys are at your window. Stay with them. They'll keep you safe."

"But—"

"Go, Jane," Wendy said.

"No," the wraith said, "it's not safe for her out there."

"As if you cared about her safety," Michael said. "Jane, up-stairs. Now."

The little girl looked from the wraith to Michael, and then back again before nodding and scurrying up to her room. The wraith moved to stop her, but both Will and Michael raised their swords. The wraith, caught without a weapon, paused and glared at them.

"You're going to get her killed."

"Never!"

"You will if you let her leave. You did this, didn't you?"

"This?" Michael asked.

"You filled the streets of London with the ghosts of the pirates."

Michael hesitated and took a step back, though Will stood his ground.

"I knew it. You brought Hook here, too, didn't you? You, who helped defeat him in the first place, brought him to London. How could you be such a traitor?"

Michael clenched his teeth. "You kidnapped the god of youth and drained him of his power. You would rob every child, from now until the end of time, of their very childhood. You captured Peter and tried to kill him. You're in no position to accuse me of being a traitor."

The wraith cried out in animal rage and leaped at Michael. Both men tried to stab it, but it was moving too fast. It crashed into Michael, and the two went down in a tangle of limbs, Michael's sword skidding across the ground. What followed was not combat. Michael had been trained by the Knights. He had never been the most skilled fighter, but he was still good, and the past few days had brought back a lot of his skill. His wraith, however, knew everything he knew. And Michael's arm was still not completely healed.

Yet none of that mattered. No, there was too much emotion on both sides for either one to focus. He could feel the creature try to drain him, but Rosebud had recovered and floated about them, her power countering its.

So it was just . . . ugly. A brawl. It was only as it continued, crashing among the furniture, that Michael realized that—even with the fairy's magic supporting him—the wraith was stronger. It wasn't injured, and it had sucked the life from a *god*. If this went on much longer, there was no way Michael would prevail. But he wasn't sure how he could get any separation, so he kept punching.

It was, at least, cathartic.

Nothing quite like punching oneself to realize just how much self-loathing you have.

Insights or no, Michael felt his strength draining away, but before his foe could gain the upper hand, Will pulled them apart. He held his sword to the wraith's neck while Michael recovered his own weapon.

"Destroy him," Michael said between heavy breaths. "It's the only way we're going to restore Peter."

Will tensed his muscles but hesitated. In that second, the wraith grabbed Will's weapon by the blade, cutting its hand on the edge. Inky smoke spilled from its wound as it tore the weapon out of Will's hand. It grabbed the sword's hilt, but before it could make another move, Wendy drove a carving knife into its side. The wraith coughed up black smoke before looking at Wendy. It took the knife out, and the wound closed, though it was obviously weakened.

"Wendy, why?"

Wendy's anger dwarfed anything Will had shown when he'd learned that his family was in danger.

"Why? Because you lied to us. Because you attacked my brother and my husband. But mostly? You threatened my daughter."

Faced suddenly with not one foe, but three, the wraith lifted into the air. Before any of them could react, it flew over Michael's head and out the front door. Michael ran after it, but land-bound as he was, he couldn't hope to keep up, and the wraith disappeared into the skies of London.

✳   ✳   ✳

CHAPTER 40

"What's wrong with him?" Wendy asked.

Peter lay on the bed in the guest room. His skin was so pasty white he hardly seemed alive at all. He was shaking. Though his eyes were open, he didn't seem to see them. Michael put a hand on Peter's forehead. His skin was clammy, and he felt far too cold. There was a lightness to him, and Michael felt as if his hand would pass through Peter's head at any second.

"He's dying. The wraith has drained him of all his power. There's almost nothing left."

"But . . ." Wendy's voice quivered. "This is Peter."

Will drew her in close and held her for several seconds. The two hadn't been more than a few inches apart since the wraith had fled. Will and Michael still hadn't explained to Wendy what exactly had happened to her husband. For now, she was content that he was here.

"Jane," Michael said.

"What about her?"

"Bring her here."

"What? No. Michael, she's only a child. I can't bring her down here to watch her friend die."

"Wendy, this isn't just Peter. This is Maponos, the god of

youth. They once called him the divine child. I can't think of anything that's more likely to save him than the touch of a child, especially one who has spent so much time with him."

"Michael—"

"He needs to believe, Wendy. A god needs to know that others believe in him, so he can believe in himself."

"That makes no sense."

"Really, Wendy? You've *been* to Neverland."

Shade, who had apparently attached himself to Peter when the wraith had taken him, was already nodding, a particularly odd gesture given that Peter himself didn't move. But Wendy still looked unsure. Seemingly unconsciously, she ran her fingers along Will's arm. She met her husband's eyes, and her lips quivered.

"Oh, you haven't even met our daughter yet."

Will cleared his throat, and it took him several seconds to find his words. "Actually, I have. I just didn't know who she was." To Wendy's questioning expression, he added, "I was a prisoner of Tiger Lily's people for a long time. Jane came to see me a couple of times."

"How?" She glanced at Peter. "No, never mind. We'll have time for all that later. I'll go get Jane."

Will didn't need to say anything more. He just went with her.

Michael stared down at Peter. He tried talking to him, reminding him of all the adventures they had shared. On occasion, Peter seemed to actually see him, but it never lasted more than a few seconds. When he mentioned the final battle on the *Jolly Roger,* Peter took in a sharp breath but otherwise didn't respond.

They walked into the room a few minutes later, with Jane holding her mother's hand on her left and her father's on her right. The Lost Boys were right behind them. Jane seemed almost too amazed to speak, but when she saw Peter, she pulled away from her parents to stand next to the head of the bed, the Lost Boys watching with awed silence.

"Oh, Peter, what did you do to yourself?"

As soon as her fingers brushed against his cheek, Peter started to laugh softly. Color returned to the youthful god's cheeks, and he sat up, blinking. He looked at Jane and smiled. Then, he hopped off the bed and turned to Michael.

"Good, my plan worked," he said as he dusted off his hands.

The Lost Boys cheered at that, but Michael waved them to silence.

"Your *plan*?"

Peter nodded. "My plan to get free of the wraith. It worked perfectly."

Will just stared at him. "Your plan was to be drained by a wraith to the point of almost dying only to be saved because we drove him away after he brought you to London? We wouldn't have even been here if we hadn't formed a temporary alliance with the ghosts."

Peter nodded again. "Exactly. That was my plan."

"You can't be serious."

Wendy let out a musical laugh. "Leave it alone, love. You'll never convince him that it wasn't his plan all along."

Abruptly, Peter's eyes widened as he examined Will's face. "I know you. You were one of Tiger Lily's prisoners. How did you get free?"

"Peter, I wanted to talk to you about that," Wendy said sternly. "Why didn't you tell me about him?"

Peter shrugged. "Lots of things happen in Neverland that I don't tell you about."

Wendy sighed. "I suppose that's true enough, but didn't it occur to you to tell Jane that Will was her father?"

"That's silly, Wendy. Fathers have to do things. He couldn't be her father if he was trapped in a cage."

"He wouldn't have been in a cage if you'd have let him out."

"I didn't think that was a good idea. All the grown-ups from your world that are in Neverland are evil. Since he's a grown-up, he was obviously evil."

Wendy started to say something else but sighed. She gave Michael a knowing look. Though Peter was a god, in some ways that made him even more limited than they were. He could never change or grow, and it was virtually impossible for him to learn. The Lost Boys clamored around him but went silent as Michael stepped forward.

"There are still other things we have to take care of," Michael said, understanding this conversation was going nowhere. "Somehow, I doubt that Jane's touch restored you fully."

Peter shrugged. "Maybe I'm not completely better, but I'm good enough."

"We have to find the wraith, and there are still all those ghosts to consider. Are you good enough for that?"

"You talked about those before. What ghosts?"

"The same ghosts that were a part of your plan," Will said, not quite under his breath.

"The pirates," Michael said. "Their ghosts are loose in London. Hook is with them."

A grin split Peter's face. "Good! I haven't had a good fight with Hook in a long time. Let's go."

He ran out of the room, the Lost Boys trailing after him. After a few seconds, he poked his head back in and looked at Michael. "Are you coming?"

Michael turned to Wendy, whose face showed a mixture of laughter and concern. It apparently hadn't even occurred to Peter that he had grown up. He sighed. "I guess I should."

"Michael," Will said as he stepped closer to Wendy, "I can't—"

Michael raised a hand, stopping the other man. "And I'm

not asking you. You've been gone long enough, and this isn't your fight. Stay with your family."

After several seconds, Will nodded. He pulled away from Wendy and clasped Michael's arm. "Be careful."

"I will," Michael said before turning to Peter. "All right. I'm ready. What do we do now?"

Peter rose into the air and looked expectantly at Michael, who shook his head. "I can't fly. I don't have any fairy dust."

"Oh, well that's easy to fix. I know where the wraith left the fairies. Come with me. We'll have you in the air in no time."

* * *

CHAPTER 41

Peter flew about ten feet above the ground as he led Michael through the streets of the city. Some of the Lost Boys ran alongside Michael while others leaped from rooftop to rooftop. After a few minutes, Peter became bored and turned on his back. He moved his arms as if he was doing a backstroke through the air. Merran stayed close to Peter, mimicking his swimming motions. More than once, he apparently forgot that Michael and the others couldn't fly because he took off into the air and didn't come back again until Michael shouted at him for several minutes. Once, he even had to send Rosebud after him. It was a long time before Michael realized that Peter was leading them to the train yard.

It had been the most ordinary part of Michael's life before he had been caught up in this adventure. It had been his sanctuary. In a way, it made sense that his wraith should choose to hide fairies in a place that was almost the opposite of what they represented. Michael hadn't bothered to find out what day it was, but regardless of the day, at this hour, the place should be abandoned. Idly, he wondered if he still had a job. Time didn't work the same way in Neverland. According to Wendy, it was June now, and he'd left in April, so he probably didn't. That should bother him more than it did, but somehow, it just didn't seem terribly important.

Peter led them to a hole in the fence, though he couldn't tell them how he'd known it was there. Michael sighed and ducked through it while most of the Lost Boys simply climbed over it. The empty yard was eerie. The trains rested on their tracks like great beasts in a deep slumber, and Michael couldn't shake the feeling that they would awaken any second. In the back corner of the yard, where an old car sat awaiting repair, Michael thought he saw a flicker of light. Peter landed in front of it and walked in like he owned the place, the Lost Boys following at his heels. Michael eyed his surroundings but concluded that it was a useless gesture. There were so many hiding places that an enemy could be within five feet and he wouldn't know. He steeled himself and went in after Peter.

The inside of the car was lit by fairies of every color imaginable. Cages lined every surface, and one could hardly take a step without coming down on a fairy cage. Peter and the Lost Boys were already opening them and letting the prisoners out. Merran cried in joy and flew in circles with several other nixies. Even Rosebud joined a group of pixies.

"Tink!" Michael cried out as his eyes landed on a fairy in a green dress. She saw him and fled to the back corner of her cage, but Michael bent down and stared in. "Look at my eyes, Tink. I'm not the one who trapped you. That was a wraith."

She did as he asked and she seemed to calm down a little, but she uttered something in the rapid-fire speech of the fairies.

"I know I'm a grown-up, but you can trust me."

The fairy spoke some more, and Michael could only shrug. "How about I get you out of this thing, and then you can decide."

She looked at him warily, but he tried to focus on getting her out. The lock on the cage door wasn't strong, and all it took was a sharp twisting of his wrist to break it off. The door swung open and he stepped back, giving her space. Tinker Bell took several careful steps forward until she was peering out of the cage. She gave Michael another wary look, but when she saw Peter, she cried out in surprise and flew to his shoulder.

"Oh good, Tink," Peter said, not even acknowledging that she had been captured. "Michael and the others need some fairy dust."

The fairy glared at Michael before turning back to Peter. She stamped her foot in the air and shook her head.

"Peter, I don't think we really need to—"

"You need fairy dust to fly."

Michael waved at the room. All the fairies they had freed had flown away, but they had left a trail of dust in their wake. As more had flown out, they had stirred the air, preventing the dust from settling to the ground. Michael was already covered in the stuff. The Lost Boys were already in the air. He thought of Jane and Wendy and the feeling he'd had when he'd returned her husband to her. The next thing he knew, he was a foot off the ground. A chuckle bubbled up inside of him. Peter smiled.

"Oh, I guess you're right, Tink, we didn't need your help after all. You can go home."

Tink's argument came so fast that Michael couldn't understand what she was saying. Peter didn't seem bothered by it, though.

"I guess you can come if you want," Peter said. "Michael, you don't mind, do you?"

It was just like old times. He bowed to Tinker Bell, and her surly expression softened a bit. "Tink, I would be happy to have you along."

The Lost Boys cheered at that. Before Michael could say anything else, Merran, who had flown out with a group of nixies, zipped back into the car. She landed on Peter's shoulder and started chattering. This time, Michael caught a few words.

"Ghosts?" he asked. The fairy turned to him before launching into the air and bobbing up and down. "How many?"

She thought for a second. Then her words tumbled over each other. Michael couldn't believe what he heard and asked her to repeat herself. She looked at him like he was an idiot, but she obliged. Michael ran out of the compartment and looked up, expecting her to have exaggerated.

She hadn't.

The skies were littered with blue spectral lights. There were so many that they obscured the stars and chilled the air. Peter walked up next to him, not seeming concerned in the slightest.

"That's a lot. How many pirates did you say there were?"

"I'm not sure," Michael said without taking his eyes from the spirits above. "Maybe nine got away from the *Jolly Roger*, including Hook and Smee."

Peter pointed to the sky and started moving his finger around. It took Michael a second to realize he was counting. He stopped after a few seconds. "That's more than nine."

"I know that," Michael said with forced patience. "Where are they coming from?"

Peter had lifted his hand and was apparently trying to count the ghosts again, but he gave up after he'd used all his fingers. He gave Michael an odd look and shrugged.

"You know, you really do that a lot."

Peter gave him a half grin and shrugged again. "They probably come from the Underworld. That's where most ghosts come from, at least."

"This world doesn't have an Underworld," Michael said.

"*Everywhere* has an Underworld. It's where the dead things go."

Michael gritted his teeth. "Fine, but these couldn't have just crossed over on their own, could they have?"

"No," Peter said. "They generally need a summoner or something."

"So who summoned them?"

Peter gave him an exasperated look. "I can barely keep up with the people who can summon a ghost in Neverland. I have no idea who could do it here."

"Ghosts filling the city only hours after a half dozen pirates escape? That can't be a coincidence."

Peter thought for a second. "No, you're probably right. Hook never knew any magic when he was alive, but I guess he could've learned some when he was dead."

"Can't he just talk to ghosts?" Curly asked.

Peter's eyes went wide. "You're right! He wouldn't need magic to talk to other ghosts. He could've just gone to a grave-yard and started waking everyone up. Where is the graveyard in this city?"

"Peter, London is one of the oldest cities in the world. There are hundreds of thousands buried around the city, and that's not even counting the old plague pits from the black death. If Hook can really wake all of those, he could have an army bigger than any the world has ever seen!"

Peter brought his thumb to his chin and started rubbing, like he was deep in thought. "That probably wouldn't be a good thing. We should go and stop it."

*   *   *

CHAPTER 42

They were no more than twenty feet off the ground when a group of a dozen ghosts swarmed them—it was as if they had been waiting for him to manifest magic before attacking. They came out of the surrounding compartments, apparently having been set there as guards, and they caught Michael completely unprepared. Three passed through him, one right after another, each draining away his body's heat as well as his joy. Robbed of his happy thoughts, he was halfway down before he realized he'd started falling. He slammed into the ground, the impact driving the breath from his lungs. With an effort, he managed to roll onto his back.

In the air, each of the Lost Boys had engaged one ghost while Peter battled the remaining eight by himself, that boyish smile seeming a sharp contrast to the dire situation. As far as Michael knew, Peter hadn't been treated with wisp dust, but that seemed not to matter—a benefit of being a god, most likely. Steel clanged against ghostly metal and knocked it aside. The ghosts did not fight as a unit. If they had, they might well have overwhelmed Peter, but as it was, he held them back with almost casual ease.

One of the ghosts came at him from behind. Warned by instinct or some godly sense, Peter dropped, and the enemy blade passed right over him. A heartbeat later, Peter rose, slashing upward, and cleaved the spirit in two. It dissolved with a scream. The others, shocked by the ease at which their companion was dispatched, hesitated. It was only for a second, but that was enough. Peter dove among them, cutting four more down before any of them could react. The remaining three retreated a ways before coming at Peter from different directions, but while six might have been able to beat him with that strategy, three were hopelessly outmatched when facing a being who had been flying long before they had been born, let alone died. Peter moved like the wind, effortlessly dodging a blade even as he knocked aside another. The largest of the ghosts, seemingly more skilled than the rest, waited until Peter seemed off balance to swing, but Peter did a flip in the air, avoiding the strike by inches. A quick slice destroyed his foe before he turned his attention to the remaining two. The pair of spirits looked at each other and then fled. Peter laughed, threw back his head, and let out a loud rooster crow. When Michael had heard that as a child, it had seemed a curious thing for Peter to do, one more oddity in a boy that seemed made of them. Now he understood. This was no mere child's cry.

The Lord of Neverland crowed a call to battle.

Three brilliant, ghostly figures rose from the ground and stopped in front of the fleeing ghosts. They spread out and surrounded the escaping spirits. Michael shook his head to clear his mind. In front of him, Tinker Bell was scolding him to go help Peter while Rosebud told her to leave him alone.

"Sorry," he said as he rose into the air.

He flew toward the ghosts with the Lost Boys at his side. They stopped when Michael met one of the newcomer's eyes. The child form of his brother John smiled at him, took off his hat, and bowed. Slightly and the ghostly twin each engaged a spirit. One on one, the ghosts were no match for those who had been trained by Peter himself, and in short order, they had all been dispatched.

"What?" Michael turned to look at Peter, who was lazily flying toward them with Tink and the living Lost Boys zipping around him. "How?"

Peter shrugged. "Hook's not the only one who can call up ghosts. Now we should be able to stand against his army."

Michael's jaw dropped, and it was several seconds before he found his voice. "Are you serious?" He waved his hand at the sky. Even now, ghostly lights drifted to the southwest, so many that they almost looked like stars. "There are hundreds of them out there. What can we do against all of that with us and three ghosts?"

Peter cocked his head. "Three?"

It was only then that Michael realized that several of the blue lights weren't going with the rest. Instead, they were descending to where Michael and the rest floated. Rosebud floated before him, as if she could defend him. Michael drew his weapon, but between fighting the wraith, running to keep up with Peter, and falling to the ground, he was pretty worn-out, and he didn't know how much good he'd do. Still, he gritted his teeth and waited.

The spirit that descended first looked nothing like the ones Michael had seen before. In fact, it seemed almost solid, a man in the full armor of a medieval knight. His face was obscured by a helmet, and he carried a shield in one hand. His armor almost gleamed in the moonlight. He came to a stop in front of Michael and lifted his visor. The eyes didn't have that sunken appearance of other ghosts. They were the eyes of a man who spent more time laughing than anything else. Michael had never seen a ghost seem so alive. He examined the spirits of John and the Lost Boys and realized that they, too, had that peculiar laughing quality, but before he could ask about it, the knight gave a deep bow.

"Peter, it's good to see you again."

"Hi, Gregor. I didn't know you had died."

Gregor let out a hearty laugh. "Peter, you took me to Neverland nearly five hundred years ago. What could I be but dead?"

Michael eyed the knight. "You've been to Neverland?"

Gregor inclined his head. "As a child." He spread his arms to encompass the descending spirits. "We all have. How do you think Peter was able to summon us?"

"He can compel the spirits of anyone who's been there?" Michael thought it would be the darkest sort of magic to force a ghost back into the world of the living.

But Gregor was already shaking his head. "It's not like that, lad. Peter's call extends beyond the grave, and it opens the way, but it is not a command, and only those who choose to heed it are here."

The living Lost Boys were all nodding as if the explanation made perfect sense. Michael looked around, and saw just how many had come, his worry evaporating. Slowly, a smile crept onto his face. "I get the feeling it's not so easy to say no when Peter calls."

Gregor laughed. "Right you are. Now I suspect that you didn't call us to speak of past adventures, Peter. If the spirits filling the skies are any indication, we are here to do battle."

Rather than answer, Peter laughed again, and let out another crow that sounded through the night. The ghosts that had gathered around them—men and women of all nations and professions—cheered. Michael had seen Peter do so many wondrous things, and yet this sight—of an army ready to save not only Neverland, but this world, too . . . it took his words away. Peter looked at him with a knowing smile and laughed, and this time Michael laughed right along with him.

Then Peter flew off to do battle against the ghosts that blanketed the skies of London.

CHAPTER 43

*   *   *

Even with the ghost army Peter had summoned, they were outnumbered many times over, but that didn't mean that Hook held all the advantages. The pirate had called up dead from every age and every walk of life, but even the warriors among them tended to be weak apparitions. He had been able to summon only those who lacked the will to resist his call. On the other hand, no one who went to Neverland left unchanged, and each of Peter's ghosts was a powerful spirit. The enemy could no more stop them than a man could hold back a storm. They ripped through Hook's ghosts without even slowing. To Michael's surprise, many of the enemy spirits didn't even seem to notice as they were done away with.

"There." Michael pointed. "They're heading southwest. That has to be where Hook is."

"It is," Gregor said. "This Hook lacked the power to call me up, but I can still feel it. He's calling all who will come to his position." He glanced at Peter. "I also sense an aspect of you there. It confused me when I first came into the world."

That surprised Michael. "The wraith? It took part of Peter's power, but what would it be doing with Hook? Those two are enemies."

Peter shrugged. "Maybe they're going to destroy each other. Either way, it saves us from having to find them both, so it's probably a good thing that they're together."

Michael started to say something but Gregor chuckled. "You'll never convince him, lad. As far as he's concerned, there's nothing he can't handle."

Michael nodded, remembering Wendy giving almost that exact explanation to Will.

"I have a plan," Peter said, and he took off before anyone could respond. The Lost Boys laughed and went after him.

Michael looked at the knight. "Was he like this five hundred years ago?"

"He's been like this since the beginning of time, so far as I know. Let us follow! Half a league onward!"

Michael almost lost his grip on his happy thought, but he managed to hold on to it.

"What did you say?"

"Half a league onward." He inclined his head. "I didn't know who you were until Peter said your name. Dmitri sends his regards."

"But—you can't know Dmitri."

"He is not a child of Neverland. He couldn't respond to Peter's call, but those of us who were Knights in life are known to each other in death."

"You're not just a knight. You were a *Knight*?"

"Just as you are."

"But I'm not—"

"Dmitri sends a message. 'Fight on, Michael Darling.'"

Then, Gregor flew after Peter. For several seconds, Michael watched him go. Dmitri's message rang in his mind. He might not have been able to save his old friend, but he could at least honor him. He took off after Gregor and the rest, ready to engage Hook's legion of ghosts. Another line from Dmitri's favorite poem ran through his head.

Into the valley of death.

THE GROUND WAS A BLUR BENEATH THEM. AFTER THEY HAD gone a few miles, a sneaking suspicion began creeping up on Michael. Before long, those feelings were confirmed when he saw Hook's ghosts descending like a whirlwind on a tall Victorian manor that seemed out of place in such a rough area of the city. Some slammed against it, releasing a flash of blue light. And in front of their headquarters, a dozen Knights of the Round did battle against spectral foes, fighting to ensure they never crossed the threshold of the house. Vanessa stood at the fore.

Michael set down next to her. She had discarded the Neverland blade in favor of a light sword, which she wielded with the skill of a master fencer. Her eyes widened slightly when Michael landed, but just then a trio of ghosts came at them. It took only a couple of moments to deal with them.

"Michael," Vanessa said as she ducked under a spectral blade. "I take it you found Peter."

"It's a long story," he said as he skewered a man that looked like he'd been a blacksmith in life. "The Knights found a new supply of wisp dust, I take it?"

She ducked under an ax. "No, but there's magic beyond that of Neverland—the Wizard and the Lady put an enchantment on us." The Lost Boys were holding their own, but Gregor was an absolute terror. He dispatched three ghosts with a single swing of his massive sword. "That one is useful," she said, nodding at the Knight. "These other ghosts are yours, then?"

Rosebud darted into the face of a ghost, distracting it long enough for Michael to disembowel it, spilling its blue light before it winked out of existence. "Something like that."

Vanessa twisted to avoid a cudgel wielded by a burly man with a scarred face. "You know the Court has standing orders to shoot any necromancer we find."

Michael gestured to Peter, who was flying above them, engaged against five ghosts while he laughed like the whole thing was a game. "Technically, Peter summoned them, so I haven't done anything wrong. If they want to shoot him, they can try, but I have a feeling this battle will go very different should he decide to change sides."

"Which," she said, disarming him of his cudgel and running her sword through the spirit's scar, "as you mentioned before, he's wont to do."

"Let's just keep from distracting him with shiny things like bullets, okay?"

She grunted agreement as half a dozen ghosts surrounded them. Even slow and unskilled as they were, that many might well be too much for them to handle. But before they even raised their weapons, a spirit that looked like a scribe, with two young girls flanking him, dove out of the sky. Moving almost too quickly to see, they cut down the enemy ghosts, though they had no weapons Michael could see. Vanessa let out a breath of relief.

"Well, I guess if Peter did it, it's fine."

Michael wasn't sure how long the battle lasted. The Knights and Peter's army were easily more skilled than the invading ghosts, but there were just so many of the enemy. He saw more than one Knight fall with cold skin and looks of terror frozen on their faces. He was breathing heavily, and his sword felt heavy in his arm. Peter's ghosts never tired, but on occasion, one of the mindless dead would make it through their defenses. They didn't fall nearly as easily as the ghosts Hook had summoned, but they did fall.

Then, suddenly, the night went still. The only remaining spirits were the ones Peter had summoned. Knights all the way down the street lay unmoving on the ground. The Lady ran up next to Michael. Frozen streaks on her robes showed that she hadn't been idle during the fight. Her hair, golden in spite of her age, practically glowed in the moonlight. She looked from Vanessa to Michael and then to Peter. Her eyes went wide.

"Lord Maponos?"

Peter stiffened. It was the first time Michael had seen him act with anything other than complete disregard. He shook his head. "No, I don't like that name. I haven't used it in a long time. I'm Peter Pan."

The Lady inclined her head. "As you wish, Peter. We owe you a great deal. I don't think we could've held up if not for you."

"No, definitely not."

The noble looked surprised at his frank admittance.

"He's like that," Michael explained. "You'll get used to it."

"Well, yes, of course." She then turned her attention to Michael, eyeing him suspiciously. "What are you doing out here?"

"I saved Peter, like you wanted me to."

"No, that's not what I mean. I have reports of you running into the headquarters to fight against the ones that got inside."

Michael was confused for a moment, then realized what the Lady was saying. "The wraith."

"What about it?" Vanessa asked.

"It's already inside."

"What wraith?" the Lady asked.

"*My* wraith." Michael's blood went cold, and he turned to Vanessa. "Oh god, no."

"What is it?" Vanessa asked.

"The first thing I did when you drew me into this mission was go into the catacombs."

The Lady nodded, though there was a barely perceptible smile on her face. "You caused quite an uproar."

"I think it's doing the same thing," Michael said.

"No," the Lady said. "It could never get through the defenses. They're stronger against spirits than against flesh. They'd destroy a wraith."

Michael closed his eyes, but he felt nothing. There was no sense of dread, no desire to go elsewhere. He shook his head. "The defenses are gone."

"What?" She reached toward the house and murmured something. She took in a sharp breath and tried again before turning to Michael. "You're right. It must have been all those spirits. He sent them against us just so they would overwhelm our magic. Vanessa—gather the Knights who can fight. We can't let him get into the catacombs."

"I'll go," Michael said.

The Lady stiffened. "You are no longer a Knight. You are not allowed in the catacombs."

Michael ignored her and started walking up the stairs. "I'm Knight enough, and unless you're going to spare people to stand in my way, you're not really going to stop me."

Peter landed next to him and kept stride. "Me too." He waved to the Lost Boys. "They can stay here to help you in case more ghosts come."

"But . . ." The Lady seemed flustered. It was one thing for her to stop Michael, a civilian. But how does one say no to a god?

"I'll go with them," Vanessa said. "I'll make sure they don't cause any mischief."

"Mischief?" Peter said in mock outrage. "*Me?*"

Michael laughed, and eventually the Lady could do nothing but join in. "Hurry, then," she said, but Michael could have sworn he heard her say under her breath that it would be just like last time. Michael didn't really care how she justified it to herself, as long as she didn't interfere.

"Wait," she said.

He stopped but didn't turn around. "We don't have time for this."

"You don't have time to argue with me, either. Knight or no, you don't know everything."

Michael turned around.

"The power of the wisp dust on Sir Vanessa was almost expended when she arrived," the Lady explained. "I suspect your supply isn't much better." She waved her hand over Michael, and he felt a surge of warmth. "If you're going to be opposing ghosts and wraiths, this spell will allow you to touch them."

Michael bowed his head. "Thank you."

Then he, Vanessa, and Peter stepped into the house . . . and froze.

The hall looked so ordinary. The dust that had perpetually covered the floor was gone, as was the musty smell. The halls no longer seemed to shift if he stared at them, and when he took a step, there was no sense of dizziness or nausea. It was just an ordinary house. It even looked nice. Off to one side, he could see the stairs leading down, and he walked straight to them.

"I keep expecting a board to creak or to have to brush a cobweb out of my face," Vanessa said as she ran her fingers along a wall that had been covered in peeling paint before. "I knew part of the defenses were illusion, but I never realized how much. It's almost more unnerving to have those missing."

"I know," Michael said. He stopped at a door and peered inside to see a wide chamber. "It took us fifteen minutes to get from the council chamber to the entrance to the catacombs, and they're practically across the hall from each other."

"What do you think the wraith wants?" she asked.

"It could be anything. Is there anything down there we could use? What about the wraith cage?"

Vanessa shook her head. "It was destroyed, remember?"

He thought for a second. "I brought back a genie lamp the last time I was in Iran."

"It was empty. I told you that, too."

"Right . . . with all that's been going on . . ."

"And your advanced age—"

"I'm not that old!"

"You're very old, Michael," Peter said. "But none of that matters."

"Why not?"

"Because you have me!" Peter said and darted toward the stairs.

Michael and Venessa followed. "Is there *anything* else we could use?" Michael asked in a low voice as he neared the door.

"Besides our unreliable little god?" Vanessa replied just as quietly.

"Yeah. He's back to his usual self—and that's a lot more powerful than you would think—but there's so much down there. If the wraith finds Atilla's sword or Neptune's trident, or anything else like that, we're dead."

Vanessa shook her head. "We should be good there. Neptune's trident was transferred to a stronghold in the middle of the Sahara. The Court didn't really think an island kingdom was the best place to keep that. And another Knight took Atilla's sword for a mission, so it's not here, either. Of course, there are still plenty of other things the wraith could use to kill us." She put her hand on his arm, holding him back for a second. "You know, going down there now that he's had time to prepare is a terrible idea. You could hold off an army with the things stored there."

"I told you, I'm not worried," Peter said from over his shoulders, throwing open the door. He whispered something, and the next thing Michael knew, Shade had darted in front of all of them into the dark stairwell.

Peter smiled back at them. "Let's hunt the wraith!"

"He's entirely too excited about this," Vanessa said.

"He's entirely too excited about everything."

The three walked down for a long time, constantly on the lookout for any sign of either Hook or the wraith, but there was nothing aside from the echoes of their own footsteps. The wet smell of weeds and algae drifted up to them. The silence grated on Michael's nerves, and Vanessa seemed ready to jump out of her skin.

"They're both up ahead," Peter said, though even his normally boundless energy seemed muted.

Michael turned to ask how he knew but stopped when he saw that Peter had his shadow again. He tightened his grip on his sword, and he saw Vanessa do the same. They stopped moving and listened. There was a faint clatter ahead, as if someone was moving dishes around. Michael thought he saw a blue glow emanating from around the corner, a sure sign that a ghost was there. He took a deep breath and rushed forward, Vanessa just behind him. Peter just leaped into the air and shot forward.

They rounded the corner and passed through a door into a large chamber. Various items, from common iron cups to jewelry that seemed to shimmer with its own inner light, were scattered along the floor. On the far end, the floor came to an abrupt stop. They heard the underground river at the floor's edge. They expected to be attacked as soon as they entered, but instead they took in the room, not quite understanding what they were seeing.

Hook was standing in front of a pedestal, reading an old book. He even seemed able to turn the page. The wraith sat on the ground amid a myriad of pots, pans, cups, and other dishes. He would pick one up and examine it, only to toss it aside. The two looked up as Michael and his companions entered, but they didn't seem worried.

Michael was dumbfounded, and the question escaped his lips before he even realized he was asking. "What are you doing here?"

Hook snorted without looking up. "What does it look like? We are learning."

Vanessa grabbed Michael's arm. "We can't let him read that. That's the Necronomicon."

"Indeed," Hook said as he turned another page. "From Faust's own library. He was a legend even before I left for Neverland. After all, what else would a man such as me want in a place like this, other than a book that teaches how to deal with spirits? How better to augment what I already know?"

"You've been working together the whole time." Realization dawned on him. "He captured Shade easily, then *let* him escape the first time. And you. You could always command ghosts, couldn't you? He never turned your crew against you. That was just something you told us to lead us to him."

"Very good, boy. I can wake ghosts, and a handful of them aren't difficult to control. I can even drive a large group like they're cattle, should I need to get through magical defenses." He gave Michael an evil grin.

"But why?"

Hook laughed. "To distract the Knights while I looked through this. Do you have any idea how hard it is for a ghost to get a body again? Not just to possess, but a true body to live in?

"You have our thanks, by the way." He waved at the wraith. "Without your essence, he never would have been able to leave Neverland. And without your invitation on the *Jolly Roger*, I would be just as trapped."

Peter scoffed. "You did all this just because you wanted a *book*?" He made it sound like the most distasteful thing in the world. He pointed at the wraith, who hadn't even acknowledged that they were there. "What about him?"

"His business is his own," Hook said as he turned another page. "I didn't think it polite to inquire." He gave them a vicious grin.

Peter, Michael, and Vanessa looked over to where the wraith picked up a gold inlaid plate and examined it. Michael thought it had to do with some Japanese legend, though he couldn't remember which that was. The wraith, however, just shrugged and tossed it aside. He picked up another one. Peter sagged, as if this—even more than reading a book—were the most boring thing in the world. Then, he looked from Vanessa to Michael. He grinned, threw back his head, and crowed before charging at Hook.

The ghost sank into the ground before Peter had reached him. Without warning, Hook leaped back up from the ground, his sword rising in a blur, slashing at Peter's back. Peter turned in the air, and the blade sliced through the front of his tunic, cutting the cloth in spite of the fact that the ghost's sword was ethereal. Peter struck with his own weapon, but Hook moved like a snake, flowing around the blow.

Michael had been trained by some of the best swordsmen in the country and had learned techniques from all over the world, but he had learned to fight in only two dimensions. Hook had had the powers of a ghost for two decades, and Peter had been flying long before any of them were born. They came at each other from above and below, twirling in the air even as they changed altitude. It was all Michael could do to follow the fight.

A hand on his shoulder brought him back to reality. Vanessa pointed at the wraith, who was still looking through the containers.

"We should take care of him while we have the chance."

Michael nodded and tore his eyes away from the airborne combat. They circled the wraith until they could come at him from both sides. Then, they charged. The wraith looked up and casually pushed itself into the air until it hovered several feet above the ground. It carried a sack in which it had apparently stuffed several containers, and the wraith continued to sort through them, now out of reach of their swords.

Or so it thought.

Michael took flight, following his foe into the upper reaches of the catacombs.

CHAPTER 44

✳   ✳   ✳

Michael darted upward and lunged, but the wraith drew its own weapon and knocked Michael's blade aside. The wraith, coursing with Peter's power, didn't even bother to look up from its examination of the items in the sack. Michael tried again, using both his training with the Knights and the skills he had learned from Peter, but the wraith avoided him effortlessly. Finally, a wild swing tore through the wraith's sleeve, and it glared at Michael and turned its full attention on him.

Michael wasn't sure that was a good thing.

They should have been evenly matched. They were made from the same substance, but the wraith had been formed from the pieces that Michael had tried to forget, and what he had tried to forget most was Neverland. Sure, they had brawled in Wendy's dining room, but that was anger and brute force, not skill. With swords, with flying, it was dawning on Michael how different things were this time around. The wraith knew Peter's techniques even better than Michael himself did. It batted his attacks aside with all the effort that a grown man might have used to fend off a toddler, flying around Michael and slashing from behind only to drop and come at him from below a second later.

Michael was completely outclassed. He was slowing down as he bled from the several small cuts the wraith had inflicted. He was breathing heavily, and his sword arm was slow. To make matters worse, being so outmatched filled him with hopelessness and leached away his happiness. He was having trouble staying aloft. The wraith swung its blade, and the weapon bit into his right shoulder. Michael's sword clattered to the ground.

The wraith—the one who looked so much like him, that was so much *of* him—lifted its weapon to strike at Michael when a beam of blinding light sliced through its right sleeve, burning it and causing the wraith to scream and fall to the ground. It hit with a sickening crunch. The light melted a hole in the stone behind where the wraith had been, then it faded, revealing a single silver arrow.

Michael turned to see Vanessa writhing on the ground, her veins glowing with silver light. Beside her was a silver bow. A dozen arrows had spilled on the ground. Michael realized what he was seeing, and dread filled his heart. The bow of the Greek goddess of the hunt had never been intended to be wielded by mortal hands, and its power had doubtlessly overwhelmed Vanessa. She hadn't been able to aim very well, but even a grazing hit had been enough to wound the wraith badly.

He floated down next to his friend, knelt, and put a finger to her neck. Vanessa's pulse was weak, and she was breathing only lightly. Her left hand and part of her arm were covered in burns. Still, she seemed stable, so Michael turned back to the wraith.

It struggled to get to its feet. Its left side had been burned and twitched, seemingly of its own accord. Black smoke drifted from its body, but rather than rising, part of the smoke split off and swirled around Michael. At first, he tried to avoid it, but there was something familiar about the smoke, something that was inviting. He feared a trick, but his gut told him it was okay. So he breathed it in and found himself getting stronger as he accepted himself, the pieces that the wraith had stolen returned to him. More of the smoke drifted up to the battle between Peter and Hook. It was still very much back-and-forth, but as Peter inhaled, he began gaining the upper hand, striking more solidly even as Hook became more desperate. Joy welled up in Michael, and he found himself floating just a touch off the ground. The wraith was beaten. All it would take was one sword strike.

He lifted his weapon and moved to attack just as the wraith took a step forward. Then, the creature stopped in front of a pile of old containers that had spilled from its sack. A smile parted its lips, a particularly unnerving sight, given that half its face was burned. It bent down and picked up a bronze oil lamp.

Michael grinned at the genie's vessel. "That might have helped you, if it weren't empty."

"I *wanted* an empty one."

Its voice no longer sounded human. It sounded like paper tearing. It lifted the lamp and cried out, "Imprusene!"

The lamp glowed green, and Peter screamed. He dropped his sword. Just as Hook was about to skewer him, Peter became translucent, and the blade passed through him. The sound of his scream abruptly stopped, though it was clear from the look on his face that he was still screaming. He turned to emerald smoke, and the power of the lamp drew him in as the wraith laughed.

No sooner had Peter's smoke vanished than the wraith lifted the lamp to its nose and inhaled, rubbing it slightly. As he breathed in the substance of Peter, his skin crackled, healing even as his flesh writhed, infused with the power of a god.

"You've lost!" it screamed, and it wasn't clear if he was talking to Michael, Peter, or both.

Michael hadn't known he could move so fast.

He was across the cavern in an instant, hacking away at the lamp, hoping to destroy it and free Peter, but though he knocked it out of the wraith's hand, the lamp remained intact as it skidded across the ground and over the edge. Beneath, Michael heard a faint splash. Rosebud charged the wraith, but it swatted her out of the air, and she passed right through the ground. The wraith, its body restored, glared at Michael.

"He's almost gone now, and what I have taken from him is more than enough to destroy you and take everything that you are as well."

Hook landed next to him, the book creating a bulge in the pocket of his greatcoat. "And even if it were not, you now have two of us to contend with. How will you defend against us both?"

They didn't wait for an answer.

They charged.

* * *

CHAPTER 45

The pair of opponents quickly disabused Michael of the illusion that he could defend against both of them. He managed to block one blow from the wraith before Hook's sword sliced into his stomach. His blood turned to ice. The wraith's sword came down on him, but he managed to roll out of the way. The sword slammed into the stone floor, and the tip broke off. Michael got to his feet and pushed himself into the air. A few days ago, he would never have been able to keep aloft, but now Dmitri's message rang clear in his mind, and Michael actually found himself becoming excited by the battle. Rather than going up, however, he headed into a passage that would reach the bottom level, desperately hoping that his foes would leave Vanessa to chase after him. He had barely turned a corner when Hook came out of the wall.

His sword passed through Michael's leg, and the feeling of cold made Michael lose control. He cried out as he fell. A ghostly sword came out of the stone ground, catching Hook's blow just before it cut into Michael. A child wearing a top hat and pajamas rose from the ground, adjusting his glasses as he landed in front of the pirate.

"Hello, Michael."

Hook sneered. "I have already killed you once, boy. It will be no great trouble to do so again."

Slightly's ghost came out of the ceiling and took Hook's hat even as the twin threw himself at Hook's feet.

"Run, Michael," John cried. "We'll hold him off."

"But—"

"Don't worry. Just remember us!"

"Always," he whispered, even as Hook stabbed John in the back. The ghost of his brother coughed up motes of blue light before sinking into the ground. Tears welled in Michael's eyes. Slightly and the twin were doing all they could to keep Hook distracted. Feeling like the vilest person in the world, Michael turned away. Sensation had started returning to his legs, and he managed to get to his feet. It was too much this time, though, and he couldn't bring a happy thought to his mind.

He stumbled down toward the chamber at the shore of the underground river. Every time he looked back, the ghostly glow grew stronger. He didn't know for sure that Hook had destroyed the ghosts of the Lost Boys, but he didn't see how it could be otherwise. He lost his footing more than once, constantly expecting Hook or the wraith to fall on him, but they never did.

He practically fell into the chamber, right at the feet of the wraith. It effortlessly pulled the sword from Michael's hand and threw it aside.

"You fool," it said. "Did it not occur to you that it would be faster to just fly down here?"

The wraith still looked like him, a little, but most of its features had taken on the roundness of youth. It had lost a foot of height, and its nose had sharpened, making it look more like Peter than Michael. An *adult* Peter—something that should not exist. And now those familiar eyes that had so often carried a mischievous sparkle now emanated such cruelty as Michael had never imagined. This was a thing that could kill without sorrow or remorse, and now it held the power of a god. Michael doubted it truly needed him, not after draining Peter so completely.

"Mashikoon," Michael said, almost under his breath.

The wraith put his blade on Michael's arm and forced the weapon down through the flesh and into the stone beneath. Pain shot up his arm, but he clenched his teeth to avoid crying out. He couldn't afford to. Not now.

"Mashikoon."

"What are you saying? There's no magic to save you now—"

"Mashikoon."

The water exploded upward. The elemental that had been trapped inside roared as the third utterance of its name set it free. It washed over the shore, seeming like a wave in spite of the fact that it traveled on solid earth. Michael drew on every ounce of strength he could and ripped himself free of the wraith's sword. He threw himself into the elemental, desperately hoping that the nixie dust had not worn off. He braced himself, half expecting to be crushed by the pressure of the creature, but it was like he was swimming just beneath the surface. He pushed himself through and came out the other side.

Apparently, the nixie dust also did something to soothe his pain while he was in the water, because as soon as he exited, it came anew. He swallowed it down and turned to see the elemental writhing as the wraith worked whatever magic it had learned from the mermaids. Michael doubted he had more than a few seconds.

He threw himself back into the water and took in a breath of relief as the pain faded. He dove until he reached the rocky bottom. His eyes darted around, searching for any sign of the lamp, but it was too dark to see more than a few feet in front of him. He ran his fingers along the bottom and cut his hand on a sharp rock. He sucked in a breath at the pain and realized that the nixie dust was wearing off. Suddenly, a pale blue light flooded the area.

"Did you really expect to escape from us here?" Hook said as he floated down to him. "Oh, you gave us a merry chase, I'll give you that. Your dead friends were a surprise, for the few seconds that they lasted. But it's over now."

"Not over." Michael's eyes went wide as another spirit came out of the wall behind Hook. "You know that Peter called up ghosts that have a will of their own."

"A weakness," Hook said. "Such beings are meant only to be controlled."

"They can make their own choices, and they can come after whomever they choose."

Hook rolled his eyes. "I know . . ."

His voice trailed off as he heard the ticking sound. Michael hadn't known a ghost could go pale, but Hook did. He turned around slowly and cried out in rage.

"*What?*"

John, still bleeding from the wound Hook had given him and barely able to hold together at all, floated there, making the same imitation ticks they had used to torment Hook when they'd first captured him. Hook turned back to Michael, his face twisted in rage, just in time to see Michael aiming the sharp rock he had cut himself on right at him.

Michael drove it into the ghost's throat as the Lady's spell coursed through him. Hook screamed. Beams of blue light shot from his eyes. His flesh seemed to melt away until only an emaciated spirit remained.

Terror painted the face of James Hook. "No." His voice was barely above a whisper.

Michael lifted the rock to strike again and finish the pirate captain once and for all, but a white streak came out of nowhere. Michael could just make out Smee's face as the ghostly bo'sun stabbed into his arm. Cold pierced him. He tried to strike back, but Smee hadn't stopped. He had grabbed Hook and dragged his captain into the rocks below.

"No!"

This time it was Michael's turn to cry the word. He had been so close. Another second, and Michael could've ended the threat of Captain Hook once and for all. Even a ghost would need time to recover from that wound, and he was grateful for that, but it would happen. Hook was not defeated. Michael didn't have time to worry about that now, though. His breathing was watery. He kicked his way to the surface just as the dust wore off. An instant later, the water elemental seized him. It didn't pin his hands, but it didn't really need to. Since Michael was no longer protected by the nixie dust, the elemental's grip felt like it would crush his bones.

"You fought off Hook," the wraith said. It stood right in front of the elemental, clearly in control of it. "Impressive. I don't know that I'll be able to command the rest of these ghosts without him, even with this." He kicked at the book on the floor, the one that Hook had apparently dropped before going into the water. "It's not that I really need to at this point. You fought harder than I expected, Michael, and you should be commended for that. So . . . I commend you.

"But it's over now."

The wraith was echoing Hook's words, but this time, Michael was sure this was indeed the end. He closed his eyes, knowing it deep down. He was upset by that knowledge, yet his talk with his old Knight companions, now ghosts, told him that wasn't so bad. He hated having failed, and he hated that someone else would need to find a way to stop the wraith, but he was also pretty sure they would. Because that was how stories went—the good ones, anyway. And if this was his last adventure in this world, well—there would be adventures elsewhere.

He opened his eyes one last time to look at the wraith without fear, a sense of peace washing over him. A flash caught his attention, just to the side, and—as if in a storybook—the lamp was there, floating right in front of Michael. Only half believing it, he reached out and took it.

John's whispered voice sounded in his ear. "Remember us."

Then, he was gone. Michael looked at the lamp, and the wraith laughed.

"Go ahead. Free him. It won't matter—you didn't get to me fast enough to stop me. There's not enough of him left to be worth consuming."

Michael rubbed it, hoping that the wraith was lying. The lamp seemed to burp, and a puff of green smoke, no bigger than a fingernail, flowed out. It floated in front of Michael, and he could see the vaguest outline of Peter's face. Michael's heart fell. A single wisp of smoke was all that was left of the god of Neverland. Though Peter had always been more spirit than flesh, his power had enabled him to take physical form. That power was all but gone now, stolen by the wraith.

The wraith laughed as the elemental held Michael face-to-face with his double. The wraith took in a breath, and a wave of cold washed over him. Soon, this thing would eat him, draining him of what was left of his essence. Then, having consumed both the person whose thoughts spawned it and the god of the realm whose power had created it, it would become a monster unlike anything his world had ever seen.

Michael took in a deep breath, and he thought his lungs would freeze from the cold. But that was okay, because something was dawning on him: This *wasn't* just a monster. This was a spirit. It had taken physical form, sure, but even that wasn't complete, as evidenced by the fact that it bled inky black smoke.

And if it's a spirit . . .

"Peter," he said, almost under his breath. "Can you distract it?"

The puff of smoke bobbed in the air even as its form rippled. It drifted toward the wraith, who looked at it and laughed. Then, the smoke took the shape of a long needle and shot into the wraith's left eye. It screamed, bringing up its hands to protect its face. Peter was only smoke, and he couldn't actually harm the wraith. It was enough, though.

The wraith's concentration wavered, and the elemental dropped Michael. He ran forward and grabbed the book that Hook had dropped, the one that taught the lore of spirits. He didn't have long, only seconds, but he knew what he was looking for.

He found it almost instantly. There had been only one way the wraith could have known how it could capture Peter. He lifted the lamp, uttering the word that would break its bond with its prisoner.

"Huyin."

Then, the second word, the one to trap a new spirit, the one the wraith had used to trap Peter.

"Imprusene."

The wraith's eyes widened. It tried to suck in, to drain Michael's life, but nothing happened. It tried again, reaching toward Michael, but then, its hand turned to smoke and was sucked into the lamp. It looked at the lamp in horror. Then it tried to fly away, but the power of the lamp had it in its grasp, and in a matter of moments, the wraith had been sucked in.

The elemental roared as the power the wraith had used to subdue it shattered. It surged toward Michael, anxious to destroy anything it could see. Michael coughed and tasted blood. It was all he could do to utter a single word, the last one he had learned from the Necronomicon.

"Kalakush."

Power surged in his hand and then fizzled out as the lamp's magic extinguished the being it held. Smoke poured out of its spout, surrounding the puff of smoke that had been Peter. Gradually, it began to grow. As the elemental picked him up and squeezed, the world started going dark. The last thing Michael saw before he lost consciousness was Peter smiling.

* * *

CHAPTER 46

I think you should let me take him," Peter's voice said.

"Peter, you know you can't." That was Wendy. "He's a grown-up."

"He went back to Neverland, Wendy. People who are all the way a grown-up can't just go there."

"Still, I think it's best if he stays here until he's well."

"But they stabbed him with a needle. You can't tell me that's going to help him get better."

A musical laugh filled the air, and it seemed to give Michael the strength to open his eyes. He was in bed. Sunlight streamed through an open window framed by heavy, thick green curtains. Wendy sat at the windowsill, her soft brown hair glowing in the sunlight. Outside, Peter floated, seeming to lean on a wall that wasn't there.

"What?"

Michael's voice was dry and he started coughing. Almost instantly, Wendy was at his side, holding out a glass of water, which he took gratefully. The water felt amazing going down his throat.

"Michael, I'm so glad you're awake." Wendy spoke so fast her words tumbled over each other. "How are you feeling?"

"I'm . . ." Michael blinked and tried to shake off the groggi-ness of sleep. "Confused. Where am I? What happened?"

"You're in our guest room," Wendy said.

"I told her she should let me take you to Neverland. You would get better a lot faster there."

"He needs quiet, Peter, and 'quiet' has never been a word that could be applied to Neverland."

"I know," Peter said. "We could have some adventures while he got better."

Michael blinked. "Got better?"

He tried to sit up but as soon as he put weight on his arm, pain shot up it, and he fell back down. Dimly, he remembered being stabbed in the arm and tearing the sword away, but the pain he felt wasn't nearly as bad as it should have been. In fact, he could move his arm fine, though it should have been severely injured. Wendy, apparently reading his expression, smiled.

"The Knights had a vial of the Elixir of Life. They weren't happy to learn Peter used it on you. It was the only one they had, though they did say you were beyond the healing salve's power."

Michael looked at Peter and let out a breath. "You know, I'm the one who brought that back for them, when I found Saint Germain's laboratory."

Peter shrugged and glanced toward the sky before looking to Michael. "They weren't using it, and it was just going to sit there."

"Saint Germain?" Wendy asked.

"An alchemist from . . . ," Michael started to say. But his head was throbbing, and he lay back on the pillow.

"Shh, it's okay," Wendy said, stroking his hair. "We'll do ex-planations later."

"It's not important," he said. "But the potion—is that why I'm here instead of in a hospital?"

Wendy nodded. "From what Peter tells me, you'd done permanent damage to your arm before he gave it to you. You're lucky the blood loss didn't kill you."

"Oh, leave him alone, dear," Will said from the doorway. He carried Jane in one arm. Michael hardly recognized him now that he had been bathed and groomed. Jane had her arms around his neck and was laying her head against his chest, and Michael didn't think he had ever seen a man look happier. Will inclined his head, first to Michael, who returned the gesture, then to Peter, who seemed not to notice. "He's had a long couple of days."

"Wait—is my arm okay?"

"Yes," Wendy said. "We thought it better if we didn't have to explain that to the doctors."

"This way you don't end up in Bedlam," Will said with a grin.

"Hush, you," Wendy chided. To Michael, "You'll be up and about in no time."

Peter was fidgeting like a child waiting to open presents on Christmas morning. He kept looking toward the sky, but when he noticed that everyone had gone quiet, he grinned at Michael. "Great. So when do we go?"

"Where?" Michael asked.

"To Neverland, of course."

"Peter . . . I think I'll stay here."

"Really? Why?"

"I don't think I can quite explain it to you."

Peter sighed. "Fine, but watch out for Mora."

Will blanched. "Mora?"

Peter shrugged. "She used your name to follow you out of Neverland. She doesn't hate you, though, so you're probably safe."

"But she still has our blood."

Peter nodded. "Yeah, you should be careful about who you share that with next time."

He darted through the window and flew around Will and Jane once before going out of the room the same way he had come in. All three of them watched him go. How very like Peter to casually drop information about a deadly threat like he was talking about the weather. Only Jane made a sound, laughing as her friend flew away.

Wendy looked like she was going to say something, but instead she nodded once. Tears welled in her eyes. She opened her mouth to speak but closed it again. A few seconds later, she tried again. "Thank you for bringing my husband home."

WHILE MICHAEL WAS RECOVERING, HE RECEIVED A LETTER that his old job at the railroad would be waiting for him when he was well enough to take it. He supposed that could've been the intervention of the Knights, but he decided not to ask too many questions. It would be a while yet before he had to make a decision on that.

He was in bed only a week before he was strong enough to go out into the city. He still tired easily, though. Will went with him once. The other man hadn't decided what he would do with his life, now that he was back. He still seemed to be having trouble believing that he was home, and Wendy had told Michael that, sometimes, Will woke screaming. The pair of them wandered through London's streets with no real destination in mind.

"It all seems so small, doesn't it?" Will asked.

"What?"

"London. It just doesn't seem quite so big when you've seen an underground gremlin city and sailed on a ship crewed by ghosts."

Michael gave him a half smile. "Give it time." He spread his arms to encompass the city. "Eventually, this will all seem important again."

"Should it?"

Michael blinked. "What do you mean?"

"I mean I've seen what's out there. I'm not sure that I should be impressed by a human-built city, not even London. There's too much out there to see and do."

Michael stiffened. "You sound like a Knight."

Will pursed his lips and nodded. "Maybe that's not such a bad idea."

Michael shook his head. "Wendy wouldn't stand for it."

"Actually, we've talked about it. With Jane so often going with Peter, neither of us are sure we can avoid facing the things the Knights deal with. If Mora is out there, too . . . I want to protect my daughter."

"Will, I left that life a long time ago."

"Not so long ago that you couldn't go back when you needed to."

"But now that's done. I'm not sure I want to get involved with"—he took a deep breath—"those things anymore."

Will narrowed his eyes. "If you're not sure, then why did we come here?"

Michael blinked and looked up. He hadn't even realized where he had been walking, but they had wandered into one of the rougher neighborhoods. Before them stood a dark, imposing house that filled Michael with a sense of dread. He wanted to keep going, but a part of him froze in place. He stared up at the headquarters of the Knights of the Round for a long time, unsure of what to do.

Finally, almost without realizing it, he took a step forward. The next thing he knew, he was raising his hand to knock on the door. It opened before he touched it. Vanessa, bandaged from her burns but very much alive, stood in the doorway. Michael started to speak, but the words caught in his throat, and he uttered something unintelligible. Vanessa smiled and stepped out of the doorway, bowing her head, first to Michael and then to Will.

"Good," she said. "We need all the help we can get with all the ghosts still loose." She smiled. "Welcome back."

ACKNOWLEDGMENTS

*　*　*

This book would not exist without a lot of people. First, there is my editor, David Pomerico, who believed in this story enough to have an hour-and-a-half phone conversation with me about it, even before he was ready to make an offer on it. He also recommended an agent to me. Thanks to Rhea Lyons, my agent, who thought that I might have stories worth telling. Special thanks go to Kristin Luna, who helped me put the last couple of pieces into place while I was outlining this story, and to Shannon Marsh, one of the best writers I have ever seen, and who beta-read this book and offered valuable feedback throughout the creative process. Keep an eye out for her work. You won't be disappointed. A million thanks go to Kevin Ikenberry; when I was considering quitting writing, he said, "If you quit, I'll kick your ass." Then, there's Doug Vanner, who didn't actually have anything to do with this book and to whom I haven't spoken to in over a decade, but to whom I gave a promise that, in exchange for beta-reading the first book I ever wrote, he would be the sixth person I thanked when I eventually got a book published by a big publisher. I hope you read this one day.

Kevin J. Anderson, Rebecca Moesta, James A. Owen, Brandon Sanderson, David Farland, and Eric Flint have, for more than ten years, run the Superstars Writing Seminar, which is hands down the best writing event I have ever attended. I would not be half the writer I am without all that I learned at that seminar. On that note, the entire Superstars tribe gets a note of thanks. I met several of my closest friends and colleagues there, as well as my editor, my agent (though this was after I became her client), and my wife.

On that note, I would be remiss if I didn't also thank my wife, Melissa, who has been my unfailing support. She made so many sacrifices to give me the time to write and to make the edits that I needed, and she took on all the aspects of the publishing process that I didn't want to handle. Chances are that if you're not my personal friend, and you heard of this book, it was because of her. I love you, Melissa.

ABOUT THE AUTHOR

* * *

Gama Ray Martinez lives near Salt Lake City, Utah, with his wife and kids. He moved there solely because he likes mountains. He collects weapons in case he ever needs to supply a medieval battalion, and he greatly resents when work or other real-life things get in the way of writing. He secretly hopes to one day slay a dragon in single combat and doesn't believe in letting pesky little things like reality stand in the way of dreams. Find him at http://www.gamaraymartinez.com.